BANQUO'S
SON

ALSO BY T.K. ROXBOROGH

T.K. ROXBOROGH

BANQUO'S SON

A Crown of Blood and Honour, Book 1

f THOMAS & MERCER

Published by Thomas & Mercer, Seattle

www.apub.com

Amazon, the Amazon logo, and Thomas & Mercer are trademarks of Amazon.com, Inc., or its affiliates.

ISBN-13: 978-1503945821
ISBN-10: 1503945820

Cover design by Lisa Horton

Printed in the United States of America

Love is not love which alters when it alteration finds,
Or bends with the remover to remove.
Oh, no! it is an ever-fixèd mark
That looks on tempests and is never shaken.

—Sonnet 116, William Shakespeare

Banquo: O, treachery! Fly, good Fleance,
fly, fly, fly! Thou may'st revenge. O slave!

[**BANQUO** *dies.* **FLEANCE** *escapes.* Act III, Sc 3,
Macbeth by William Shakespeare]

Author's Note

Just as William Shakespeare used real history as the basis for the characters in his play, this novel draws on his created history contained within 'The Tragedy of Macbeth'. I have done what Shakespeare often did: take a real story and people from history and asked, 'I wonder what would happen if . . . ?' Though many of these characters did exist and some of the events contained within this story did happen, this is a work of fiction and should, therefore, not be read as an accurate historical account of events at the time. I have tried as much as possible to draw upon the vocabulary that was in use during the Elizabethan era rather than 11th-century Scotland, as I imagined myself sitting at Shakespeare's desk penning this sequel. I have endeavoured to source the origins of words, beliefs, practices and anything else of the time I am writing about because I do want things to be authentic. However, Shakespeare played around with history, as many other authors have, so I make no apology for twisting the facts to fit my narrative. One of my rules in the writing of this series is this: **if it existed before 1614 then it is allowed to be used in my writing.** This is fiction but I have spent endless hours in books devoted to medieval medicine, Scotland, Norway, Normandy, costume, weaponry, crops, food . . . you name it, I've probably researched it! So, if there is a historical error, consider it author's licence. Don't tell me flagstones didn't exist in 11th-century housing – I KNOW! But Shakespeare and I don't care. We just want to tell a story and give you a sense of place and pain and pleasure.

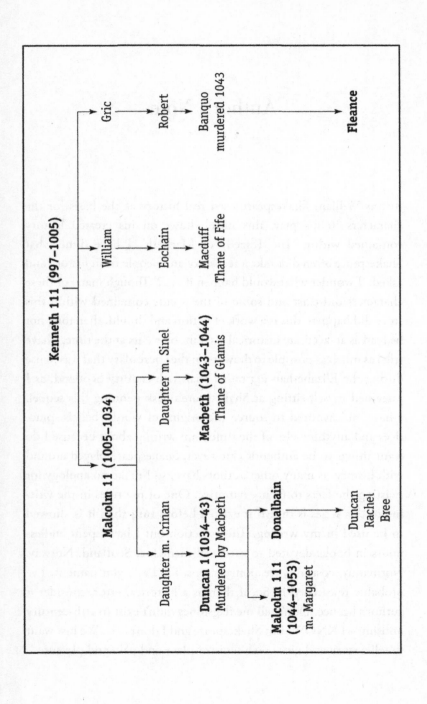

Chapter One
England, July 1053

Fleance held his breath. The stag had sensed him, perhaps, because it lifted its head, drops of water falling from its muzzle. The young man knew, however, that he could not be seen. His dark hair and clothes blended well into the dark browns and greens of the forest, making him almost invisible.

Carefully he lifted the crossbow and aimed for the place above the stag's eye. A bolt there would mean the animal would die immediately and therefore not suffer. It would also mean a better price for its pelt. This stag would be an excellent trophy. The animal was large and its hide, carefully prepared, would fetch a good price at the market. Fleance readied himself. In a moment the stag would be his.

Behind him, a twig snapped.

The stag spun on its heels and bolted into the dense wood. Fleance also spun, his crossbow at the ready, his bright eyes searching for the source of the sound within the forest's shadows.

Another sound; footfalls definitely and the sound of heavy breathing. Whoever it was, was headed his way. He steadied the weapon, waiting for the first sign of movement.

'Flea?'

'Pox,' Fleance cursed, lowering the bow to his feet. 'Damned child.' But his heart was still thrashing. What if she'd not shown herself soon enough? He might have . . .

'Flea?' Keavy called again. 'Where are you hiding?'

Fleance rubbed his forehead, took a deep breath and answered, 'I'm not hiding, bairn. I'm hunting.'

Keavy clambered over a log, puffing, her thick, black braid swinging wildly. Despite his frustration, Fleance couldn't help smiling as she tried straightening her long skirts into order. 'Da will whip you.'

'If I'd brought home our dinner and the skin, Magness'd be writing a song 'bout it before supper,' Fleance said. He picked up his crossbow, annoyed that he had, yet again, lost a precious prize and a means to contribute food and coins for the family.

'Ma says you must come home and fetch the wood. We're having visitors.'

Fleance looked at his adoptive sister. Visitors? This was out of the ordinary. Magness and Miri usually avoided contact with outsiders. 'Who?'

Wee Keavy flashed him her cheeky grin. 'The new family Ma met in the village last month. You know, the ones who travel between here and Scotland. Rosie and her folks. They've been north and are planning to stop in here on their way home – I heard Ma talking with Da about it.'

Fleance's stomach leapt. *Rosie.* He had first laid eyes on her over three weeks ago and had been working hard to distract himself from the strange, empty feeling which sat just under his ribs each time he remembered that meeting. Well, some good would come out of today after all. He'd take a visit from Rosie over a fair price for a pelt any time, even if it did mean a diet of mushrooms and goat's cheese.

'You like Rosie, doncha?' Keavy asked, grinning. 'Ma says she can tell.'

This child was too quick. To distract Keavy from his embarrassment, he changed the subject slightly. 'Their visit will mean a night of arguments.'

'Aye. Ma has already started at him.' Keavy stopped, put her hands on her hips and mimicked her mother. '*I'm telling you, Magness man. 'Tis time to go back tae Scotland.*' She sighed. 'It's going to be a long night.'

Fleance nodded. 'Well, you just keep us all entertained with your music, lass, and that might take their minds off of things.'

'Ma says nothing will keep your mind from Rosie.'

'Why you . . . ?'

But the wee monkey was already skipping away back towards their encampment. Fleance felt his face warm further and his heart race. *Rosie.* If only . . . He shook his head. He mustn't think such thoughts. Still, Fleance followed Keavy, his steps quick like his heartbeat.

Fleance's adoptive parents, Magness and Miri, were travellers and camped in different parts of the countryside in England's north as the mood took them.

The camp where they had set up a number of weeks earlier was one they visited regularly. It was close to a small village but still offered privacy – something Fleance knew Magness valued highly. Tightly organised within a small clearing, the covered wagon and two tents pressed in against one another. In the centre of the small campsite, a large fire pit sat smouldering. It needed feeding immediately and Fleance felt a twang of guilt that he had not set about making the pile of firewood he'd promised Miri earlier in the day.

He shrugged off his cloak and draped it over a tree. Then, he picked up the axe and began chopping the two logs Magness had stacked against the wagon. It wasn't long before a fresh pile of split wood had raised itself behind Fleance, who was thinking once more of Rosie as he worked.

3

It had been less than a month ago – one of the rare times he'd travelled with Miri into the village to trade some of the pelts he'd prepared. On the way, they had stopped at a public house for some ale. Once he'd finished tending to Willow, he'd joined his adoptive mother inside the small, dark building – it was refreshingly cool after the warmth of the summer day.

Fleance had found Miri at a table with two women – one about Miri's age; the other, much younger. All three turned towards him as he approached.

'Ah, there you go, lad. Come and meet Rebecca and her daughter, Rosie. They've not long moved to this part of England,' Miri had said. 'Rebecca's husband, Dougal, is a cooper and is looking to make a living in this part of the world.'

He had sat down on a stool. 'This is Flea,' Miri added.

'Flea,' Rosie had said, bowing her head slightly, her voice low and husky. Fleance noticed her long dark hair was tied into a thick braid that hung nearly to the middle of her back. Stray curls were escaping around her face and her green eyes seemed to hold a secret mischief. Then she smiled and he could not drag his eyes away from her mouth – it was perfect: full, red lips; small, straight teeth. And her skin was as clear and flawless as a young babe's. It was all he could do to refrain from reaching out his hand to touch her face to see if she were real.

'Cat got your tongue?' Miri had laughed. 'Where are your manners?'

Fleance shook himself. 'Sorry, Miri. Greetings . . . Rosie. And to you, Rebecca.'

Rebecca twittered. 'How did you get your lad to speak so well then, Miri?'

'Ah, truth is, he's not my lad,' Miri sighed. 'Spoke like that when we found him ten years ago. He were a bit older than Keavy is now and a right proper boy he was. Magness says he's got royal blood in 'im.'

'Weel,' said Rebecca, 'whatever it is, 'tis a nice wee bit of something. But your name, lad. Seems a strange one to christen a babe.'

Fleance felt his face redden but Miri came to his rescue.

'It suits him well: he's quick and strong and can disappear into the woods like a flea on a dog's back.'

He looked at the girl for her reaction and was relieved to see her smiling warmly at him.

The women had chattered on but Fleance ignored them. The publican brought over his drink but, the whole time he had sat there, he barely touched it. Instead, he kept stealing glances at the beautiful creature who sat across from him.

'Are you planning on roasting a town?'

Fleance swung the axe into the block and turned to face Magness. 'I got lost in my thoughts.'

Magness grinned and began piling the firewood onto the crook of his arm. 'Ah, boy, she's lovely but nae woman is worth losing your mind over.' He turned and walked towards the fire pit.

Fleance wiped his sleeve over his sweating face. 'I'll tell Miri you said that.'

Magness chuckled. 'You do that, boy, and me an' you will spend the nights with the wolves.'

Shaking his head, Fleance also stacked the firewood into the crook of his arm, a lightness in his heart reminding him of how grateful he was for Magness and Miri: a pair of displaced Scots who had found him as a young boy, alone and afraid in the southern parts of Scotland; a couple who had taken him in and treated him as their own.

They were good folk, but Magness kept away from the crowds; he was distrustful of outsiders. Something had happened to them both, he was sure, but they had never told anyone. There was a hardness in Magness's manner when sparring and training which made Fleance wary.

Miri appeared. '*Now* you're doing what you promised. Bless my heart, boy. Being in love has turned you into a milkmaid.' Miri kicked Fleance's foot. 'Ah, Flea, she's worth it, 'n' all.'

'Miri. Leave the boy alone.'

Miri turned to her husband. 'And why would I be doing that? Look how much work I had to do to get you to notice me, you silly lump of soil.'

Fleance smiled. ''Tis all right now, Miri. I just lost sight of time.' He brushed flecks of wood from his shirt. 'Is there anything else you need me to do now?'

'Go wash your face, bairn. 'Tis smeared with the Lord knows not what. Can't have the young lass seeing you this way.' And she pushed him towards the barrel of water.

Even though the water was cold, Fleance's face burned thinking of Rosie.

———

The pig had been cooking some three hours before Rosie's family entered the clearing. 'Magness!' cried Rosie's stout father. 'Get them drinks ready. It's been a long day.'

'Only long, Dougal, my man, 'cos you haven't passed an ale house.'

'Not so. The horse is unwilling, the women are grumpy; and I've had neither a good night's sleep nor a meal in three days.'

Magness laughed. 'Aye, that's good reason enough to break open the barrel.'

Within moments, it seemed to Fleance, there was laughter and happy talk and, among it, stood Rosie.

After the meal, Fleance deliberately sat next to her beside the fire. He was entranced with the smell of lavender and soap which sweetly lingered around her hair and body. Lavender – it was the only thing that could help him sleep. Miri had discovered his difficulty many years before and now, every night, if the season allowed, his pillow was stuffed full of lavender to help allay the twitching he suffered.

Rosie smelt like his comfort. There was no way she could know or understand such things but it was enough for him to move towards her. Occasionally, he had met girls who smelt acrid and foul. Others were not so bad, but none as delightful as she.

He studied her every movement and word, delighting in her gentle teasing and her energy.

'Why does Da think that the nobility are foolish?' Rosie asked when there was a lull in the talk.

'Shush, Rosie. You'll just encourage him,' Rebecca scolded.

Rosie did not give up. 'Da? Is it because you can't abide the tax you have to pay on the barrels?'

'You don't understand.' Dougal positioned himself comfortably against a tree. 'I can barely make a profit what with the money I have to pay for the oak and iron and then give to the Master.' He lifted his tankard to his mouth and drank. 'I've a mind to add to my business and begin making the stuff meself,' he said, waving the cup in the air. 'That way I double my profits but still only pay the same rate on tax.'

Rosie pointed at her father's stomach. 'I think much of your profit would end up there,' she said, grinning.

Dougal patted his belly. 'Aye, a great storehouse – no better place for good ale.' He drank again and then turned to Magness. 'What do you think?' The two men began discussing the various rates of tax on the people they both came across.

Beside Fleance, Rosie sighed. 'So boring,' she whispered. She stood up and went over to their wagon. He watched her go and delighted in seeing the jumping light from the fire highlight the lovely curves of her hips and swelling of her breasts. Inwardly, he shook himself. It was not honourable to think about her in that way all the time.

When she came back, she was carrying a clay pot and sat down beside her mother. Fleance watched as she gently unwound the grey bandages from her mother's hands. He had heard Miri telling Magness of the stiffness and twisting that Rebecca suffered in her hands and how Rosie was called upon to do all the harder tasks for both women. Rosie scooped up some ointment and began to carefully massage it into the knotted fingers and joints of her mother's hands.

By the look on Rebecca's face, it was clear this was painful but she said nothing and her daughter gently rewrapped the bandages, wiping her hands on her apron. Only when her daughter kissed her forehead, did Rebecca speak. 'Thank you, my pet. You're God's gift for any mother.' Rosie smiled and looked over to Fleance. She winked at him and then returned the pot to the wagon.

He barely remembered what he ate or said or did but when Fleance finally crawled into his bed, his mind was filled with only her.

The next morning Rosie and her family left at dawn to travel back to their village.

Fleance had no idea when he would see them again and was surprised at the emptiness their departure left in his world.

A month later, Magness announced that they would all travel south to attend a village carnival. Keavy was excited but Fleance not so. He knew Magness would expect him to compete in the crossbow competition. 'I'd rather keep hunting, Magness,' Fleance said. 'The game is abundant at present and I believe I can earn well with the skins.'

But Magness would have none of it. 'You need the practice against other fellows as skilled as yourself,' the older man told Fleance. 'Besides, the prize money is handsome.'

This should have been enough to tempt him but when Magness turned to Miri and said *Dougal and Rebecca have sent word they will attend,* suddenly the prospect of travelling to a village carnival a day's ride away became more interesting. If Dougal and Rebecca were to attend, so would their daughter.

Over and over he thought about what he might say to Rosie when he next saw her. And then what he would do next; say next; whether he would find the right words or make a fool of himself instead.

The next day, they packed up their camp, loaded the wagons and set off with Fleance driving one and Magness, Miri and Keavy in the other. Willow, Fleance's father's horse, trotted behind. The sun was hot even for this time of the morning so Fleance pulled on his hat to shield his eyes from the glare of the bright day. His stomach was jittery with butterflies so he tried to concentrate on the road ahead.

They stopped for lunch beside a fast-flowing stream and replenished their water skins. Magness unhitched the horses and, after eating well, retired to the shade of an oak tree, promptly falling asleep. Fleance jiggled his legs impatiently – he always became anxious when sitting around doing nothing. The horses did need a rest, but he was keen to get to the village.

Miri was re-plaiting Keavy's hair and the two discussed ribbons and laces while Fleance picked at the bark of the tree where he sat waiting.

Finally, Magness stirred and they were on their way again.

The village was bustling and crowded and noisy when they arrived. Animals, running free or in crates, added to the cacophony of sound that greeted them as they drove the wagons down the busy main road. The actual carnival was set on a large clearing at the north end of the town and many visitors had already set up their caravans and tents. 'We will find a quieter spot,' Magness called back to Fleance.

The whole time they were driving through the village and passing people, Fleance sat up straight and strong, trying to appear taller, grander than he really felt. And, as he did this, he searched for the tall, dark-headed girl who had captured his attention nearly two months ago. But his search was in vain, for she was nowhere to be seen. Fleance slumped back against the seat of the wagon. Perhaps she had not arrived . . . yet.

The two wagons carried on past the main cluster of temporary dwellings and found shelter beside a number of large trees in a spot which pleased Fleance's adoptive father. Magness and Fleance saw to the horses before they began to set up their tents, while Miri and Keavy went to explore. The sun beat down on their backs, so they were soon working bare-chested, sweating as they hauled up the heavy canopy between the two wagons.

The heavy work was a welcome distraction and soon Fleance's mind was focused on the task before him and not on his hopes of seeing Rosie.

Rosie

It was too hot and she should not have worn the tight woollen dress for this day. Ma had suggested the lighter blue dress but the red always made her feel pretty. Children milled around the large, cordoned-off area at the top end of the field, their excited chatter and laughter filling the air. Rosie sighed as she scanned the crowds. There were no girls her age – or boys, for that matter. Those gathered were either older women and men or young ones keen to have a go at the variety of games and competitions the village elders had organised.

Suddenly a voice called her name. 'Rosie!' She looked in the direction of the sound and saw Miri's daughter, Keavy, making her way forward.

'Rosie,' Keavy shouted in excitement. 'You must come!' The little girl flew at Rosie and pulled on her arm.

'What is it?' Rosie laughed as she was dragged along.

'We are to do the three-legged race but Flea won't have a partner.'

Flea? Rosie's heart skipped a beat. She'd only met him twice but each time she had seen something in his eyes that promised so much more. She had not even considered he would attend the carnival. Her parents had spoken of Magness being reclusive and it never occurred to her they would attend something like a carnival. Why hadn't she anticipated this? Still being pulled by the little girl, Rosie tried to tidy her hair with her free hand, pushing flyaway strands back into her braid.

'Keavy, slow down!' she cried as she tried to stop puffing. By now, Keavy was running, pulling Rosie behind her.

'Come on!' Keavy giggled, lifting her skirts above her knees. 'I'll race you. Ready. Set. Go.' And the wee one sprinted off before Rosie had a moment to think.

'That's not fair!' Rosie called after her and jogged along. 'You're faster than me.'

She heard Keavy call before she disappeared into the small wooded area, 'Not as fast as Flea!' And then she was gone.

Flea. Rosie stopped, put her hands on her knees and tried to catch her breath. She remembered the way he looked at her when they first met. Then, the night they had visited Magness's family, he had sat close enough for her to feel the brush of his arm against hers as they laughed and talked around the fire. Her stomach took a sudden flip at the memory, her heart fluttering with excitement. How she'd dreamed of him – his soft blue eyes, his nervous glances at her . . . And now, she was to see him again!

She walked towards the shaded crop of trees, smoothing down her dress and fussing with her hair. With all this running, did she look too wild? Breathe and be calm, she told herself as she walked towards the sounds of people working and laughing which came to her on the warm breeze.

'Whoa, whoa, whoa!' cried a man's voice. 'Look out, lad!' There was a loud tearing sound and a heavy thud as tent and uprights landed in a heap between the wagons.

Rosie walked forward and there he was. 'Oh,' she said, covering her mouth before she was noticed gaping.

Flea stood over the fallen tent. His tunic was tied around his waist and he worked bare-chested. Rosie stared, her mouth dry, her heart pounding. Magness stood there also shirtless but with a deep frown on his face.

'How did that happen?' Flea asked.

Magness kicked the post at his feet and a large piece of wood came away from it. 'Ahhh,' he growled. 'The thing's rotten.'

Just then he looked up and saw Rosie. 'Rosie, lass. Is your father here too?'

'Aye,' she said, trying hard not to look at Flea's naked chest. 'Do you want me to fetch him?'

'But what about the race, Rosie?' Keavy cried.

'Race?' Magness began pulling up the canvas and Flea helped him. 'Concentrate, lad,' he growled again and Rosie was pleased to see that Flea was paying more attention to her presence than the task in front of him.

'Da, there's to be a three-legged race and Rosie hasn't got a partner nor has Flea because they are too big for the other children so they can go together,' Keavy gasped all in one breath.

Both Magness and Flea stopped dragging the tent and stared at Keavy. 'Well,' Magness began. 'I guess I can spare your lad while I talk to Dougal about some wood for the uprights.'

Flea looked straight at Rosie and grinned. 'You'd have me as a partner then, Miss Rosie?' Her stomach leapt.

'There's no one else,' Keavy pleaded. 'Please, Flea. Rosie?'

Rosie took in a deep breath. 'Well,' she said, sounding much braver than she felt. 'I will have you know that I am fiercely competitive, Flea, so I am hoping you are as fast as Keavy boasts you are.'

Flea pulled the tunic from around his waist and put it on. 'Aye, I am known to be good at some things,' he said and she saw the delight in his smile and it warmed her heart.

'Hooray,' Keavy said, now tugging on her adoptive brother's arm. 'It is to start soon. We must go back now or we will all miss out.'

With Keavy between them, Rosie and Flea returned to the main carnival. The wee child's chatter was a welcome distraction. Rosie kept trying to push from her mind thoughts about Flea which threatened to undo her. He was just a man, no more. She should not be so affected by his presence. But, truth be told, she was happy that he walked beside her; that he was so handsome and she knew, the way only a young woman can know, that he was drawn to her also.

The gaggle of children and the colour of their costumes hit Rosie as they approached the starting arena. 'You must tell the judges,' Keavy said. 'I have my partner and we have registered but you must go and say that you are a couple.'

Rosie's heart jolted at the word but she looked up at Flea. 'I will do that. You gather the ties and I will meet you anon.'

With her heart racing, she spoke to the master that there would be an addition to the race. The ruddy-faced man looked at her and then over at Flea and grinned widely. 'Aye. Your father would be pleased then, wee Rosie.'

13

Rosie tried to ignore the assumption but she was pleased others had noticed the potential for a fine match.

Flea, looking slightly out of place, held the ties and was searching for her. She waved at him and smiled and so did he. Rosie breathed out. Be calm, she counselled herself; don't fuss. But, with her heart giddy, the two of them secured the ties around her left and his right leg and stood waiting for the signal.

'If you're too slow,' Flea said, 'I'll lift you and carry you myself.'

She did not know what made her but she thumped him in the arm. 'Or, man, I might have to carry you!'

He roared with laughter and they missed the starting horn so a mêlée of children swarmed ahead and they were left trying to co-ordinate themselves. Rosie could not stop giggling.

'Quiet, Rosie,' Flea laughed. 'You are undoing me. And us.' She tried to bounce along with him, his strong arm around her waist and hers around his, but they were too slow. 'Damn it, woman,' Flea cried, laughing and he picked her up, carried her against his hip and hopped all the way to the finish line.

They had not come last, thankfully, but Flea did not let go of her when they crossed the finish line and they both tumbled to the ground.

Rosie laughed so much she feared she might embarrass herself. They lay there in the hot morning sun, staring at the rich blue of the sky above. She thumped her hand gently onto his chest. 'You made us lose,' she told him, feeling completely at ease.

He grabbed her hand and squeezed it. '*You* made us lose, dear Rosie, for being too unprepared. But I am pleased we were partnered, nevertheless.'

'Me made us lose?' she said sitting up awkwardly. 'I was doing everything right but you are uncoordinated.'

Flea was lying on his back holding her hand, as the noise of the laughing children surrounded them. His eyes were closed and he wore a slight grin. Such thick dark lashes, Rosie thought.

He took a deep breath and opened his eyes. 'You were slower,' he said quietly, 'and I could not lose you, Rosie, so I held back.' Flea rolled over and looked at her a moment, melting her heart.

Then he leant over and gently kissed her.

Rosie knew at that moment she had fallen in love.

Chapter Two

Later that afternoon Magness found Fleance back at the campsite.

'The competition will start soon, Flea,' he said. 'It's a larger reward than I thought.' Fleance thought about the prize. He had become aware a few years earlier that Magness and Miri need not care about earning money – coins (and sometimes even gold) were always available. Where it came from, he had no idea and neither of his adoptive parents spoke of it. They still lived frugally and both he and Magness worked hard on the gathering of pelts to sell at market.

Magness paid the entry fee and Fleance's addition to the entertainment caused somewhat of a stir: the young man was wagered as a skilled marksman. Still, Magness kept a close eye on him.

'You will do well, lad, if you keep your head; you've been trained by the best.'

The crowds stood behind him, and on the left and right, behind a long rope which had been used to secure the shooting range. There were fifteen fellows, so there would be three rounds to start with. Fleance was selected to shoot in the second heat and stood in the middle with two men on either side of him. He removed a bolt from the quiver and loaded his crossbow.

His target stood down the far end of the track and Fleance focused on the yellow circle in the middle of the face. The signal was given and Fleance released the trigger, the butt kicking him back slightly. As the judges checked and marked their shots, they all reloaded and waited again for the signal to shoot their second bolt.

Instinctively, Fleance repeated the action and was rewarded with another excellent result. He was into the next round with three fellows dropped.

The judges waited until the crowd was silent before giving the signal. Fleance thought of nothing else but the feel of his crossbow, the sequence of reloading and firing. Over and over, unaware that he was steadfastly returning to each round.

Finally, four were left and the judges signalled for a respite. Thankfully, Fleance set aside his weapon and took the drink Magness offered him. 'You're doing well, lad. Stay focused and don't change a thing. You're scoring highest almost every time.'

Fleance wiped his mouth and handed back the cup to Magness. Just then, he spied Rosie in a red dress standing beside Miri and his stomach leapt. He had not considered she would be watching.

Inwardly, he shook himself. He must concentrate and remove all other thoughts from his mind but now he was ever conscious of her eyes on him. He raised the crossbow up and in front of him and waited for the signal. Again, he focused on the yellow circle but, before his eyes, this changed into Rosie's soft mouth.

Fleance pulled the trigger and knew immediately the bolt had gone wide. There was a disappointed murmur from the crowd.

Again, second bolt of three. This one hit its mark but Fleance already knew the damage had been done. Final bolt loaded. Signal. Fire. It was not a bad result but, with the skilled men beside him, it would not be enough.

The four waited anxiously for the judges' decision. They finally walked up the concourse, grim-faced and announced their decision. Fleance was not in the final.

He turned to look at Magness but it was Rosie he saw. All feelings of disappointment evaporated. There would be other crossbow competitions but there would only be one of her. He would face Magness's wrath without fear.

⌣

Another long month went by before Dougal and his family paid them another visit. 'I have an extra barrel for you, Magness,' he cried as they rode into the campsite. ''Tis my gift for your hospitality.'

With his heart beating wildly at this unexpected visit, Fleance ran his hand through his hair hoping that he did not look too unkempt, for he and Keavy had spent the afternoon gathering twigs and bracken for the fire.

It was quietly speculated, he knew, between Magness and Dougal that Rosie and Fleance might marry. It had only been a matter of months but everyone knew that the match was a good one.

He'd only kissed her once, after the three-legged race at the carnival, but oh, what a kiss. Her lips were soft and sweet and sent his head spinning.

Fleance hadn't been able to sleep that night. He had lain there reliving that single kiss and the way that she had leant hard into him.

He longed for a repeat; another chance to hold her again in that way. Though the dark corners of his mind warned him: you can't; you mustn't; not yet.

When he was with her, life seemed more colourful and happy. When she left, it was as if she took with her all that splendour. She was so funny, as well, and when they were together at the carnival,

Fleance spent so much time laughing that, when they parted, he smiled for days remembering her wee acts and tales.

Fleance made his way to her side. 'Rosie, you're looking mighty fine.'

Rosie smiled and lifted her hand to his face. 'Ah, Flea. 'Tis nice to see you.'

Fleance put his hand over hers and pulled it away from his face so that he could kiss her wrist. 'I've missed you,' he said quietly.

'And I, you.'

Miri called to them. 'Flea. I forgot to pick some fresh mushrooms. They are in the field below the stream. Would you an' wee Rosie be kind enough to fetch some for supper?'

Fleance grinned. Keavy could have done the errand but Miri was giving them some time alone together. For that he was both ecstatic and terrified.

Rosie grabbed his hand and called to Miri, 'I know where they are but we'll take a light to help us.'

The two of them, hand in hand, Fleance holding the torch and Rosie the basket, walked quickly to the field to fill it with plump, wild mushrooms.

'Keavy's growing up so quickly,' Rosie said.

'Aye. She's clever an' all.'

She sighed. 'I hope to have lots of babes like her.'

Fleance felt his face warm. 'And strapping lads to help with the hunting.'

Rosie squeezed his hand. 'How many children do you want then, Flea?'

He looked down at her and kissed her on the forehead. 'As many as we can.' The moment, though, the answer was out of his mouth, he felt a small panic rise in his throat. Everything he said was true – he wanted lots of babies; lots with Rosie. But he shouldn't be thinking this way.

'Flea?'

'What? Oh, sorry. Away with my thoughts again.'

''Tis just as well you have me to ground you otherwise you'd always be lost to your dreams.'

He tugged on her braid. 'But it's because you're always in them, sweet.'

She laughed out loud. 'You're such a sop, sometimes. If I didn't love you so much, I'd want to pound some better phrases into you.'

That twinge again. Rosie threw the phrase out so easily. *Love.* Fleance knew that it was the power of this feeling and this woman beside him that was adding to the quiet dread which sat in his heart.

'Better hurry,' Rosie said, her voice as light and happy as his soul felt weighted and sorrowful. 'Come on, Flea. The quicker we get these mushrooms, the longer we have on our own.'

In the torchlight, he saw her eyes dance and her beautiful smile widen. Such was the power of her presence, his pain slipped below the surface and, shaking his head to get rid of the last of the ill feeling, Fleance matched her skipping pace towards the field.

On the way back, they stopped by the stream. Fleance secured the torch into the soft soil, took off his cloak and laid it on the ground. 'Here,' he said. 'I need to catch my breath.'

Rosie laughed. 'You're as strong as an ox and as tireless as a mule.' But she sat down beside him. Fleance pushed her onto her back and lay on his side to look at her.

'I'm breathless because of being with you, Rosie.' He stroked the side of her face. 'I've never known anyone so wonderful and so beautiful. You're a princess.'

She rolled onto her side and looked at him. 'No, Flea,' she said softly, 'I've not a jot of royalty in my blood. I'm regular folk through and through.' Then Rosie spoke of the people she'd met on their travels; her descriptions and mimicking causing Fleance to laugh so much that his face ached. Later she reached over to him and ran her fingers through his hair. 'You've lovely locks for a man.'

'What's that supposed to mean?'

'Well, look at Da and Magness – thick, knotted and usually hosting lice. Yours is always clean and soft and so dark at times I see it shimmer blue.'

He stared at her. The stroking motions of her fingers were sending him into a kind of trance. 'Rosie,' he whispered. 'You're very dear to me . . .'

'Shhh,' she said, putting her fingers to his mouth. Then, swiftly she replaced them with her lips. Her hand traced down the side of his neck, over his shoulder.

She pulled his tunic free and moved her hand up. He pulled her close then just as quickly pulled away.

'What is it?' Rosie whispered.

'Mushrooms.'

'Mushrooms?'

'Aye. Miri will be wanting these mushrooms.' Fleance untangled himself from her embrace and sat up. 'We best hurry.' He stood up, and put his hand out to Rosie.

Once she was on her feet, she moved towards him again and gave him a long and sweet kiss.

Then, Rosie, not knowing what he was thinking, but perhaps understanding the way of love, picked up the basket of mushrooms, leaving Fleance to carry the torch, his cloak and his raging passion.

'We're almost dead with hunger,' Miri called when she saw them arrive at the camp.

'Sorry, Miri. We lost sight of the night. But we did find lots of mushrooms.'

'Indeed,' Miri murmured as she took the basket from Rosie, her sharp eyes taking in their dishevelled appearance and the soil marks on their clothing. 'Why don't you take Rosie for a whirl?'

Fleance grabbed Rosie around the waist and dragged her into the light of the fire. Their hands found each other as they swung and danced to the music of Keavy's lute. Too soon, the music stopped and they fell against each other, faces flushed and breathless with laughter.

The next morning, Rosie's family were preparing to set off. Fleance felt a great ache at the thought of her leaving. ''Tis only a month, Flea. We'll be back this way again soon,' she said. But, for him, a month was too long. Rosie looked over at her father who was securing the load on their wagon. 'My birthday is in two weeks,' she whispered. 'You might come and join the celebration. Da would be pleased with that.'

Dougal had climbed up on his wagon. 'A month, then, Magness, before I return this way. Will you and Miri still be here?'

'Aye,' Magness replied. 'We have much to keep us busy in these parts.'

'Flea?' Rosie asked.

'Aye, I will be there,' Fleance said.

Two days before Rosie's birthday, Fleance asked permission from Magness to travel south on Willow to present her with his gift.

'You know I have no legal right to tell you what you can and cannot do, lad,' Magness said, stroking his beard. 'But there are dangers out there you know little of. Men who would feed your mind with fancy stories of loyalties to the wrong side.'

'But I'm well armed and skilled, Magness. And, I will keep to my own company on the journey.'

Magness frowned. 'I can trust you to do that but I know not who will be in Dougal's company. I would ride with you to make sure no harm came to you but I am needed here.'

Fleance felt a pressure below his ribs. He clenched his jaw to maintain control over his rising frustration. 'Magness, I am a man, not a boy. I only ask for your blessing because . . .' He stopped. Why was he asking?

As if understanding something Fleance could put no words to, Magness spoke for him. 'Because you want to know if I find Rosie a good match for you. Am I right?' Fleance nodded, the pressure subsiding as he saw Magness relenting. 'Well, I can deal with you gone a few days but I want to know that you'll be safely back with us soon.'

'Aye,' Fleance said, his heart racing. 'She's eighteen and I am . . .' But what could he say?

Magness rescued him. 'And, lad, she's the one for you and you need to do this – am I right?'

Fleance nodded. 'Do you not think, Magness, she is the most beautiful woman . . . ?'

Magness chuckled. 'Aye, after Miri and Keavy, she's not so bad.' His adoptive father thumped him lightly. 'Go, boy, for I believe there is a long line of suitors for your young lady's heart.'

Fleance mounted Willow, heart racing, a small valuable bundle sitting inside his coat and headed south to Rosie.

He held his mother's necklace in his hand, heart pounding. Would she approve? Would his father have agreed to what he was about to do? *'I gave this to your mother on our wedding day,'* Banquo had told him. *'It was given to me by my mother. She had it made as a celebration of my birth. Now, I give it to you, Fleance, for, one day, you shall give it to another just as worthy.'*

Fleance had wrapped the precious chain and cross in a soft cloth which he had picked from Miri's mending basket. The material was a deep red colour which pleased him. He wanted Rosie to appreciate that his love for her was as solid and strong as the colour of the wrapping.

When Fleance arrived at Rosie's cottage, the light was leaving the day. He tethered Willow and splashed water on his face before presenting himself. Rosie was placing flowers around the table and had not seen him ride in. He put his hands over her eyes and she squealed with fright. Then she turned, her face beaming and threw her arms around his neck. 'I knew you would come,' she said. 'Now I will have the best birthday, ever.' Rosie took his hand and pulled him over to where she would sit.

Dougal, already cheerful from drinking ale, began to organise those gathered to come before a great table which he had placed in front of the stone house. 'Friends,' he cried. 'Come forth for I have some words to say on this occasion.' The gathered crowd laughed and Dougal smiled. 'These are better words than I normally feed you,' he said. More laughter. 'You are doubting my skill as an orator?'

The look on his face and his words were too much for those gathered. They roared with laughter and it took many minutes to bring them back to a sober attitude.

Fleance touched the small package in his pocket. Would it say enough? Would it say too much? Would Rosie shy away from him because he was too plain with his affections?

Dougal had made a wonderful roaring fire and many were gathered around it. 'Go to it. Eat, drink and be merry and give a proud father leeway to make mistakes.'

People smiled. Dougal was right. They were here firstly to enjoy Dougal's hospitality and secondly for Rosie's birthday.

The summer night was not as warm as the fire. Fleance went to find Rosie. She was helping her mother with the food.

'Ah?' he said. 'Can I help you?'

Rosie, her face red and shining with the effort of trying to organise her own party, turned to him. 'Please,' she said. 'Take over the men. They, of all things, need directing.'

Fleance saluted her and she smiled. 'At your command,' he said and left the light to organise the people who had come for the family's celebration.

They ate the cake and enjoyed the feast but he had not yet given Rosie his gift which still sat in his pocket. Fleance breathed deeply.

There would be a time where he could present his birthday gift to Rosie if only they could steal a moment alone.

The night was dark. Stars had not yet made their appearance. It had been an enjoyable gathering, but the whole time Fleance had been looking to give Rosie the necklace. She, laughing, returned from inside where she had been helping her mother. Fleance was standing in the light of Dougal's cottage.

'Flea?' she said, standing still. 'Are you not well?'

His left hand wriggled. Fleance had to give her the right words. 'No,' he said. 'Yes. I'm not sure.'

Rosie laughed out loud. 'I do not know what you mean.'

Fleance was confused. He held out his hands. 'Sorry, I just wanted you to know . . .'

Rosie came towards him, lifting her hands to his shoulders. 'Know that I care for you?' she said.

Was this enough to hand over such a precious gift? Fleance cleared his throat. 'Rosie, the word "care" does nothing to paint the picture of how I feel for you.'

Rosie looked back towards the cottage. 'Flea, what are you saying to me?'

He lifted her hands from his shoulders and held them to his chest. 'Rosie, I have something for you. For your birthday.'

Rosie smiled brilliantly at him. 'But you have been my birthday gift. I need nothing more.'

Fleance put his hand into the pocket. 'A gift which I believe my mother would delight that I give to you.' He pulled out the necklace.

Rosie's looked confused. 'Your mother?'

'Aye. My mother's cross and chain, given to me by my father after she died.'

She pulled him down to sit outside the cottage. 'Tell me,' she said, 'of your mother.'

A sudden painful wave swept up to his throat, surprising him. Now, he was just a boy. Nine years old. How could he explain to her how remarkable his mother's ministrations were? 'I was nine,' he told her, 'when she got ill. It was a surprise for us, and me and Da were not prepared because she had never been ill. I was too young to know the cause except to understand her passing grieved not only me but all who knew her.'

Rosie poured the chain between her fingers. 'It is so beautiful.'

'Aye, and deserving of your wearing,' he said. Still thinking of his mother, he took Rosie's hand. 'She was good,' he said.

'Good?'

'So calm and funny and free. We loved her,' Fleance said.

Rosie nodded. 'The best mother to have then,' she said.

This was the moment Fleance knew he adored Rosie. She took the necklace. 'Put it on please, Flea, for I cannot.'

She bent her neck down and it reflected the flames of the dying fire. Pale and soft and beautiful. He dropped the necklace down around her neck, fastened it and then, before anyone noticed, planted a soft kiss on her bare shoulders.

'I love you, Rosie,' he whispered.

Rosie turned around and looked at him and then smiled.

The weather had turned. Summer had long since become a pleasant memory and it had been a month since Rosie and her family last called upon them, though the two weeks since Fleance had been with her had seemed an eternity. As Rosie's family entered their clearing, Fleance helped to settle the horses and ensure the visitors were well set in their lodging.

Magness and Dougal talked on and on. It was all politics. Fleance was not concerned about the state of England; he had more personal issues. The dreams which he'd suffered ever since his father's death had lately become more regular and nightmarish. He could not shake this powerful feeling that there was something he was supposed to do before he would be free to stay here in England and be with Rosie, building a new life among this comfort and joy. Why did he have to have this black nagging at the back of his mind, his father's last words a haunting command? He would rather not have to think about these things. Fleance desperately wanted to plan and live for the future, not constantly be pulled back into his past.

Rosie came back, sat down and held his hand. She leant into him while the noise of her father and Magness buffeted the night.

'I'm telling you, Dougal. Donalbain's a madman,' growled Magness.

'Well, so long as Malcolm reigns, that's not a bother.' Dougal wiped his stubby fingers with a wash cloth.

'Aye, but Malcolm's not been fruitful where his brother has. Three bairns to none.'

Out of the corner of his eye, Fleance watched Dougal drink deep again before replying. 'I say again: Malcolm's a fine king and been so for long enough. There's no need to fear going back to them dark days of Macbeth.'

Fleance froze. Macbeth? The sound of that name stabbed at his stomach. He stopped stroking Rosie's arm and turned to face the men, listening intently.

'For a wanderer, you've got strange loyalties,' Dougal continued.

Magness spat into the fire. 'An' I got a long memory. Scotland's a hell place for me ever since bloody Macbeth ruled.' He coughed again and then spat. The group was silent, even Keavy who had crawled beside her mother, tucking her arm into Miri's.

Loyalties? Was that it? Why Magness oft threw out a curse towards the royal house of Scotland when he thought he was alone? He had never said anything *directly* to Fleance, but something settled over the family like a dusting of ice every time politics or the past was mentioned. Fleance had learnt not to pry, thankful that Magness seemed to hold by the same attitude.

Dougal coughed. 'But 'tis fine now, Magness, and has been for ten good years. Malcolm's a godly king.'

'That may be but I know the country's still cursed.' Magness's face, even in the light of the fire, reflected deep anger – it was a look Fleance knew very well.

'Magness, man. You're sounding like that fool brother of the king's. Don't tell me you still believe in those silly women's tales.'

Miri roused herself. 'More men would do better to listen to such women's tales.'

Dougal pulled the blanket around his shoulders. 'Ah, well, it's not like we can do anything here. The country has fellows enough to keep it working properly.'

Magness sprang to his feet. 'How can you be saying that? Have you forgotten? Have you forgotten who and what we lost under the tyrant? The wounds are still festering. Don't be fooled into thinking that Malcolm has been able to clean and clear out the rot. Rather he has just kept tight a malignant bandage over a festering gash.'

'An' what are we supposed to do here in England, eh? Nothing! That's all we can do,' Dougal replied angrily.

Magness stood silhouetted against the firelight, a striking sight of a healthy man even though his thick beard was splashed with grey. 'Nay. We can do something. If those of us who have been ousted get together, Dougal, my man, we could ensure Scotland stays strong.'

Dougal also stood and faced Magness, his protruding belly almost touching the other's folded arms. 'This is mad talk. Even for you.' He threw the last of his drink into the fire. 'I'm to bed.' And he stomped off into the darkness to his tent.

Chapter Three

Young Fleance, only eleven, was on his father's horse. They'd ridden all afternoon and were hungry. The sun had already slipped low beyond the hills and they relied on Willow to find his way back to Macbeth's castle in Inverness. His father had been quiet of late and had not talked as freely as was his custom. Fleance knew better than to question it as this often drove Banquo further into himself.

This ride, however, Banquo had been most animated and Fleance had enjoyed the closeness. 'The bags have loosened,' he'd said, pulling up the horse and jumping to the ground. 'Give me some light.' Fleance had held the torch higher. 'No, here. Yes, that's it.' Fleance watched him untie and retie the rope which held together their travelling bags to the saddle of the horse. 'I guess I'll need to teach you how to do this properly, eh boy. Again.' Banquo grinned and Fleance moved back for him to remount the horse. 'Nay, I'll walk for a bit.'

They trod onwards and came out of the trees. A thick cloud moved across the bright moon and Banquo looked up. 'It will be rain tonight . . .'

'Then, let it come down!' A voice roared out of the darkness. Without warning, Fleance saw the light from a sword arc towards his father. Willow reared up in fright and it was all Fleance could do not to be thrown. He heard the sickening thud of metal striking flesh. 'Da?' he screamed.

'Run, Fleance. Run!'

Hesitating for a moment, Fleance saw his father fall to the ground but a dark shadow lurched towards him, grabbing at him. 'Get the boy.'

His father roared. 'Fly, boy. 'Tis treachery. I am finished. Go so that you can revenge!'

With his heart thrashing in his chest, Fleance kicked away the grappling hands and urged the horse into a full gallop. He knew not which direction only save it was away from his father. Fleance clung to the horse's mane, tears blinding his eyes, the words of his father echoing in his head.

'Avenge!'

'Avenge!'

'Flea! Flea! Wake up!'

Fleance tried to push the mist of the dream aside and sat up, the sound of the horse fading. 'Da! Da!'

'Flea. Wake up. It's all right. Shhh! Wake up.'

Fleance turned towards the soft voice, his eyes focusing. 'Da?'

'It's me. Miri.'

Fleance shook his head. 'I'm sorry. Bad dreams.'

'What about?'

'I can't rightly remember,' he lied. 'Just something about my father.'

'Was it something Magness said tonight?'

But Fleance ignored her question. Instead he was reliving the thundering hooves and the scream of his father as the last blow of the sword cut out his life. He wiped a hand over his face. 'Sorry. I didn't mean to wake you.'

There was a spitting and a sudden flare – Miri had struck a flint and lighted a candle. Immediately the visions of the forest, murderers, and the galloping horse evaporated as the soft glow of light washed over them.

'It's been a while, Flea.' Miri tugged Fleance's bedclothes over him. 'What has brought this on, eh?' She sat at the end of his bed. 'Sometimes dreams are sent to us to give us a message. Do you think it might be that your father is trying to remind you of something?'

'I don't know.' He tried to change the subject. 'The night was fine, wasn't it, Miri? And Rosie, more beautiful than ever.'

Miri chuckled. 'Aye, lad. We had fun apart from the silly mules who prattled on 'bout home and the king.' Her eyes appraised him. 'Was that it? Did you remember something about how you came to be all alone on the road with your horse and grown man's get-up?' Miri's voice was soft, quiet. The voice she used every time she tried to get him to tell his story: who he was; where he came from; why he was here. A story of more than just his name and age.

Fleance stared at the flame of the candle. 'I don't know.' But he did know. He remembered everything clearly but he wasn't telling Miri. He wasn't telling anyone that someone had killed his father and tried to kill him. Who knew what danger he was still in? And, what if this danger could also fall upon those here now whom he loved? He wouldn't tell them, either, that he was the son of a nobleman, that his father was cousin to the King of Scotland before his murder – the murder of both of them.

And he wouldn't tell them that for these past months he had been having dreams, seeing visions, imagining things which all had his father reminding him of what he must do. To avenge his murder. But how? That was the thing nagging at Fleance. He didn't know where he was supposed to go and to whom. And he didn't know what he was supposed to do once he got there.

'Thanks, Miri. Go back to sleep. I'll be fine.' She stood up and began to leave. 'But leave the light, if you will.'

Miri nodded and placed the candle inside the lamp. 'Sleep well, lad,' she whispered before making her way outside.

The next morning was cold and damp and Fleance's head felt like it weighed as much as a wagon. He threw off the covers and pulled on his clothes. Hopefully the fire had not been killed by the mist and would be easy to stir into life.

Though it was early, Magness and Dougal were already up, poking the fire and looking as grumpy as they were last night.

However, it was not Scotland that was affecting their moods. It was Fleance. More correctly, Fleance and Rosie.

'Glad to see you up, lad,' Magness said, placing some lighter twigs into the pit. 'Dougal here has some important business with you.'

A jolt went through him. This sounded a serious matter.

Dougal cleared his throat in a rather exaggerated manner. 'Well, m' boy, we all know how fond you are of our Rosie . . .' Fleance blushed. 'An' we know that she's as fond of you.' He let the statements linger in the soggy air.

'What he's asking, lad, is what are your, ah, intentions towards Rosie?' Magness asked.

'My intentions?'

Magness shook his head. 'For a bright wee man, you're awful dense.' His voice softened. 'Do you intend to marry the girl?'

The ground at his feet spun. Did he love Rosie? Yes, more than anything – he thought of her constantly; dreamed of her; wanted her with a hunger that surpassed even thirst after a long hunt. But to marry her?

'I do love her.'

Dougal snorted. 'Yes, we *know* that, boy. What we want to know is do you intend to take her as your wife?'

Intend. Was that the same as desire? Want? Need? What were his intentions? Fleance knew the answer to that: for the last ten years all he had been thinking about was fulfilling his father's dying words – to avenge his murder. Nothing else mattered and yet beyond his wildest hopes he had met someone who offered him another path. But still, honour spoke louder than love. Nothing else could be done before that deed had been settled. The ghost of a dead father spoke more incessantly than the soft voice of a living love.

'One day, yes, Dougal, I would be honoured to have Rosie as my wife.'

Dougal spluttered. 'What? One day? Honoured? What kind of fool talk is that? Do you want to jump the broom or not, lad?'

He did. He did. He wanted to do it right at that moment but he knew that he would not be at peace until he had done what his father had exhorted him to do. The nightmares were becoming more frequent and there could only be one possible way to stop them – go back to Scotland and seek revenge for his father's murder. 'Yes, but . . .'

'But?' Dougal raged. 'What do you mean by this "but"?'

'Flea,' Magness said, placing a gentle hand on his shoulder. 'This is a big thing Dougal is asking of you. Rosie's got many prospects but seems, fool girl, she's got her eyes only for you.'

His eyes ached with the threat of tears and he had to swallow. 'I canna do it right now, Magness,' Fleance whispered.

'Why, lad?' Fleance looked away. 'Flea, there are other folk involved here – and a young lass's heart.'

This was it then. Fleance understood he was being asked to make a choice: between the loyalty to his father and his homeland, and the love and loyalty he felt, not only for Rosie but for Magness and Miri. 'I have a journey to make,' he said, barely audible. 'I can't just yet.'

Dougal roared. 'What? You can't? What foolishness was it then that for these past months you've been leading my Rosie down a path – eh?'

'This is too sudden, Dougal,' Fleance said. 'We've not spoke of it yet.'

'Too sudden, my cock. You've been speaking love songs to my girl all this time and leading her to understand you will be married.' Fleance sat down and pulled his cloak over his shoulders to keep out the damp and cold – and the harsh truth of Dougal's words. 'You're old enough an' all to know which way things lie.'

Fleance raised his head and glared at Rosie's father. 'Life's not always so simple.' He stood up again, his temper rising. How dare this man exert such pressure at this time. He did not understand nor know what it was that Fleance had been plagued with. But getting angry with an angry father was not wise so Fleance attempted to reason with Dougal. 'Listen, do you think I'm a good man?' Dougal nodded but scowled. 'And do you think I'll make a good mate for your Rosie?' This time Dougal frowned but eventually gave Fleance a swift nod. 'Then, Dougal, know that I love your daughter more than anything and I long to be with her every moment. But I have some things I need to do. A promise I made to myself; an honourable one. Would you want me to turn my back on that and live with the shame for the rest of my life?'

The solution came to him. He could go back to Scotland and sort out what it was needed sorting and come back to Rosie – come back to the security and peace and love he'd known for ten years.

Dougal continued to scowl. 'What sort of father do you think I am?' Dougal pushed past Magness and stood in front of Fleance. 'Do you think, lad, I'd let my child forego other chances because there's the possibility you may come back?'

'I will come back,' Fleance said through gritted teeth.

'You may – and when? How long will our girl have to wait for you? Till she's past child bearing and her womb shrivelled up like a prune and no good for no one?' Dougal's tirade had drawn the others out of their tents. Fleance looked over to where Rosie stood, shivering under a blanket, staring at him. She had heard it all.

'I have to . . .' But what could he say without sounding completely mad.

'What?' Dougal spat the question at him, spittle from his mouth flying through the air. 'You either pledge to her now or lose the chance.'

The silence hung as thickly as the mist and Fleance's heart, so full of love and passion just half a day ago, was now so painfully cold with hurt and dread – and fear. He wasn't ready for this yet. Fleance stood and faced Rosie. She stared for a few moments, waiting. She raised her eyebrows at him, expecting him to choose her now. But, when he said nothing, did nothing but let tears fall, she saw the decision he had made.

Stony faced, she turned on her heel and went back into her tent, her mother close behind. Dougal brushed past. 'You're a damned fool,' he muttered, then followed his family.

Magness put his hand on Fleance's shoulder again but he just felt a deadening cold in his belly and chest. Magness gave him a firm squeeze and, with Miri and Keavy, went back to their tent, leaving Fleance alone in the clearing, his head roaring with grief and disbelief.

Chapter Four

The sound of sobbing reached Fleance and it stung his ears like the incessant wails of a babe. And worse, he was the cause of this pain. A terrible thing it was, anyway, to bring grief to another; worse when it was brought to the one he loved. He longed to go to Rosie and comfort her, but he held back. What point would there be in that? Dougal wouldn't let him anyway and he couldn't go back on his decision – what sort of man would he appear to be to everyone?

He couldn't stand it any more so left the camp to go into the forest – at least then he would not hear her crying. But he'd not gone more than a hundred yards, when he heard Dougal shout. 'Rosie! Come back here. Don't!'

'Flea?' Rosie cried. 'Flea – where are you? I need to talk to you.' He could hear her crashing through the trees.

Slowly, Fleance turned and waited for her to find him. Panting, her chest heaving, she found him but stood some distance away, hands on hips, her beautiful face swollen and blotchy from crying.

He stepped towards her.

'Don't,' she said. 'Stay there.' She took a deep breath and wiped angrily at a tear. The sight of her this way made his stomach twist further. 'I have something to say and I'm going to say it. Then I'll be gone so don't bother trying to follow me.' Fleance swallowed thickly, his stomach churning. He watched her take a deep breath as if to steady herself then her voice lowered and in it he heard confusion and pain. 'How dare you do this to me? I gave my heart to you and you never once said anything about leaving this place; leaving me.' Tears had returned and were falling steadily down her face.

'But, Rosie, I—'

She held up her hand. 'No. You can say nothing that will change this. This was cruel, Flea. But I've learnt, it seems, even the sweetest man is still a man. And underneath every man is selfish, self-centred passion and deceit.' She turned her back on him and he could see her shoulders shaking. More than anything, he was desperate to comfort her. Instead, her words had rooted him to where he stood. She began to return to camp.

'No. Wait!' he cried, his voice choking with the pain. 'Rosie. Please. Listen to me. Please.' He reached her and stood so close behind her he could smell that beautiful and familiar scent that belonged only to her. He placed his hand on her shoulder and brought her around to face him. 'I love you, Rosie. This is not what I had planned. Your da—'

'My father is doing right by me,' she snapped, her eyes bright fires.

'Yes,' Fleance nodded quickly. 'Yes, he is but before he died, *my* father asked something of me and I've yet to fulfil his command.'

'What?' Rosie asked.

Fleance was silent. He had held this secret for so long, even his tender love for Rosie was not strong enough to open his mouth. 'Tell me!'

'I can't.' He took a deep breath. 'I may bring danger upon us all.'

Rosie frowned and shook her head. 'This is just foolish talk.'

'No, you don't understand . . .'

'I do,' she cried. 'I see how things are. Flea, I thought you an honourable man. I thought you had strength enough in you to prove that. You are a coward.'

Fleance grabbed her and she struggled. 'That's not true,' he cried. 'Let me go!'

'I won't let you go until you see reason,' Fleance said, desperation making him grip Rosie tighter. 'I love you, Rosie,' he said again. She stood before him, eyes staring past him, stony faced. He touched the side of her cheek but she did not pull away. 'Please understand there are things outside my control that need fixing and I'm the only one who can fix them.'

Rosie looked up at him, eyes brimming with tears. Fleance put his arms around her and she leant into him. He kissed the top of her head but did not stop there as she lifted her face and received his kisses on her eyes, nose, chin, lips. Then, she was kissing him back and her hands went to his face and his hair.

Just then, they heard Dougal's voice through the woods, calling for them. Fleance dragged himself from their embrace. 'Promise you will wait for me,' he said softly. 'When I come back from Scotland we can be together for the rest of our lives. You are the only one I want, Rosie – you have to see that. You have my whole heart but until I do what must be done, you will not have all of me.'

She appeared not to hear. There were no tears, but the look of sheer grief on her face pained him. 'Flea, you can't go,' she whispered. 'We are supposed to be together.' She shook her head in bewilderment. 'I don't understand.'

'There you are,' Dougal came crashing through the undergrowth, puffing loudly. 'Fool girl going off after a fool boy. I've a mind to whip the both of you save we were hoping you'd come to your senses and changed your mind.'

He looked at his daughter and then at Fleance.

Dougal stood there a moment taking in the situation and then suddenly he launched himself at Fleance, punching him powerfully in the face. 'Not content to break her heart once but twice. You're a fiend.'

For a moment, Fleance saw nothing but bright lights as the pain of the assault registered with his mind. He shook his head, trying to clear his vision and lifted his hand to his jaw where Dougal's fist had smashed into him. He tasted blood so touched his lips. Bright red drops lay on his fingertips. He'd bitten his lip.

Fleance looked to Rosie and watched as she pulled herself taller, her chin lifting. 'You have made your choice then, Flea,' she said quietly. 'I may wait but I will not weep and wail while I wait.' Rosie's eyes were full of passion and anger. 'May your heart one day be broken as mine is today.' She walked away from him and past her father without another word.

Her curse hung in the air but Fleance already knew it had hit its mark along with her father's punch.

Later that day, Fleance escaped back into the wood. It was too hard watching Rosie and her family preparing to leave, especially seeing the tension that had arisen between Dougal and Magness. Fleance felt guilty about that as well because he suspected he was the cause.

He had brought his crossbow just in case he spotted game but he wasn't really in the mood for hunting. He kept reliving the two scenes and Rosie's face when she realised he was not going to choose her. Why did it have to end like this? Why couldn't Dougal be reasonable and let him do what he needed to do and then come back?

But, at the back of his mind, he knew Dougal was right. Why should Rosie wait? She was an exquisite creature and could have the pick of anyone. This thought alone gave his heart more pain. Now, more than ever, the idea of Rosie with anyone but him was too terrible to consider.

Just then, a bird let out a frightened squawk and Fleance was brought back to his senses. He looked up into the trees, in the direction of the noise and then watched as a large bird rose off a branch and swooped low between two trees.

There in the shadow stood a man.

Even as Fleance raised his bow, he saw the man wore the fine clothes of the court. He called out, 'My lord, what is your business?' The man said nothing but stared. 'Are you friend or foe?' Still, the man said nothing but lifted his hand. Fleance was horrified to see it was covered in bright red blood. 'You're hurt, man,' Fleance cried and made towards the stranger.

'Flea,' Magness called in the distance.

Fleance turned towards the camp. 'Aye?' he shouted in reply then turned back to the man. He had disappeared. Fleance reached the place where, just seconds before, the man had stood. There was no sign of him anywhere and, looking in the forest all around and listening intently, there were no sounds of a person retreating.

With his heart thrashing and his breath coming rapidly, Fleance turned a slow circle, his eyes searching the dark wood. Nothing. He looked at the ground at his feet. Strangely, even here there was no evidence that someone had stood on this spot.

A cool wind swept down through the clearing and Fleance felt a chill go through him. This was strange. He tucked the crossbow under his arm, his hands shaking. An unknown, bleeding man was walking the woods by their home. Who knew if he was a danger to the family?

'Flea!' It was Magness again.

'Aye, I'm here, Magness,' Fleance called back. Looking once more at his surroundings, he began walking back towards the camp.

In no time, he'd reached Magness. 'Did you see the man?'

Magness frowned. 'I did nae see anyone. Who are you talking about?'

'I saw a man, a nobleman I think, over there,' Fleance said, pointing back the way he'd come. 'And he was hurt.'

'Hurt? How? Was he armed?' Magness stopped and began to carefully study the surrounding trees.

Fleance shook his head. 'Not armed, I don't think, but his hand was a right state.'

'What did he say?'

'Nothing. And then he just, well, vanished.'

Magness stared at him. 'What do you mean, lad, he vanished?'

'He . . . wasn't there. One moment I saw him; the next, he was gone.'

'You're sure you weren't dreaming?'

'I don't know. I . . .' But Fleance couldn't be certain. Was his mind so full of things that it had played a trick on him?

'Come on home. Miri needs our help.' Magness began to walk back and, still uncertain and confused, Fleance followed him. 'But keep that crossbow ready in case we need it.'

They walked in silence, Fleance playing the sight of the man over and over. There was something familiar about him. He hadn't seen his face because the man had stood in the dark shadows. Still, something felt familiar about the clothes and the quiet manner. Or, was it simply as Magness had said – his mind was playing him for a fool. As it stood, his heart was sorely charged what with Rosie's outburst and thoughts of his uncertain future.

Miri and Keavy were lugging bedclothes from the stream, red-faced and unhappy. This added to Fleance's feelings of misery. It must have shown on his face because Magness remarked, 'Won't do no good making yourself more miserable with feelings of guilt, lad. Has been a low day for us all.'

'But, Magness, why couldn't he let me come back? I would have.'

'Och, who's to know the working of a father's heart? If it had been wee Keavy here, perhaps I would have done the same. He doesn't know you like we do.' Magness stopped. 'But, Flea, my boy, why didn't you say? Why didn't you tell our Rosie what was on your mind?'

And that was the thing. Fleance knew he had done wrong – by Rosie, Magness and Miri. But he'd been swept up in the joy of falling in love; the joy of anticipating time with her. Then, the dreams, the nightmares. They intruded upon the comfortable life he'd pulled around himself for the last ten years. Try as he might, he could not pretend that this comfortable world could be his until he had done what was asked of him all those years ago.

He was a man but these emotions threatened to make him behave like a woman. He would not weep. He would take those bedclothes from Miri and Keavy and do what needed to be done, even if it meant doing women's work. 'Here, Miri. Let me.' He grabbed the wet and weighted load from his adoptive mother and hoisted the pile onto his shoulders.

'Ma,' he overheard Keavy ask. 'Why didn't Flea say he'd jump the broom with our Rosie?'

'Shhh, girl. Not now.'

Another stab.

Then, in a flash, the sound of a galloping horse.

'Give me strength,' Magness cried. 'Will we not have the rest of the day in peace?' He turned towards the sound of the approaching horse.

'God bless the king,' said the pale-faced man atop of the horse.

Magness went forward and grabbed the horse's bridle, muttering to the rider. Then, raising his voice, replied, 'Yes. God bless whichever king we choose.'

The young messenger, panting and with a waxy face, stared at them all a moment before he continued. 'I saw the smoke of your fire so came off the main road to give you the news.'

'Who are you?'

'I have come from Scotland. Malcolm is ill. Malcolm has no heir. Donalbain has been named as the inheritor of the crown.'

'Do you need rest and food?' This from Miri.

'Nay. I'm told to take the news to the southern parts of Scotland and the northern parts of England.' He turned his horse around and cantered back into the trees.

'Well, looks like Dougal was right enough,' Miri said.

'No matter,' Magness replied. 'Donalbain's rule, whether it be good or bad, canna reach us here.'

Fleance stared after the rider. It was time for him to go.

Chapter Five

'Have you got everything then? Lavender?' Miri asked as Fleance tightened the girth of the saddle.

'Leave the boy, Miri. If he's old enough to take this journey, he doesn't need a woman clucking over him.' Magness handed Fleance a dirk. 'You'll need this as well as your bow and your father's sword.'

'I can't take your dirk, Magness. I'll do fine enough with the sword. And my crossbow.'

'Don't be fooled, boy. You've got dangers aplenty waiting for you before you even get to the border.' He gave it to Fleance who tucked the sharp dagger into his belt.

'An' that's why he should go by sea,' Miri muttered. 'Sea pirates are fewer than land rats.'

'Don't worry, either of you. I have my wits and Magness has taught me well.'

'Aye, it's true you're handy with them weapons.' Magness sighed, a troubled look clouding his features. 'I just wish you didna have to go.'

Fleance mounted his father's horse and gathered up the reins. 'I'll keep hidden until I get to Glasgow – that's a promise.'

'Well, your first challenge will be finding a safe place to get through the wall and then the second is to avoid the reivers. Don't trust any man – or woman for that matter. They'd like to slit your throat as soon as spy you. Keep your coins well hidden.'

'Thank you, both. For everything. And Keavy,' Fleance called down to his adoptive sister. 'You be good.'

Keavy, like her mother, was quietly weeping. 'Sure, Flea. And look after Willow,' she added, patting the horse's dark neck. 'You bring him home soon.'

Fleance winked at her and then nudged Willow into a trot. As he made his way into the wood, he could feel their eyes boring into his back but he didn't turn around. He hoped and prayed it wouldn't be long before he returned. And, he also hoped it would be soon enough to woo Rosie once more.

'*Rosie*,' he whispered but the name was left behind along with his security and happiness.

He rode north all day, stopping every few hours to give Willow a drink and a rest from his rider. By early evening, he'd found a secluded place to set up camp so that he could sleep. He lit a small fire and roasted the rabbit he'd killed earlier. His arms and thighs ached but it was good to be off the horse and soon the smell of the meal made his stomach rumble.

The flames licked about the meat as fat dripped into the fire with a hiss.

'Smells good,' a man's voice called from outside the light.

Fleance leapt to his feet and pulled out the dirk from his belt. He stood in fighting stance, squinting into the dark.

There was a throaty chuckle. 'Put your blade away, laddie. I'm no' armed.' The owner of the thick Scottish accent stepped into the firelight, his hands empty, spread out before him. Fleance didn't move. 'See,' the man continued. 'I've nothing to worry you. Just me an' my horse.'

'What's your name?' Fleance asked, his heart beating furiously.

'William. Yours?'

Fleance didn't put the dirk down but stood taller, relaxing a bit. 'Flea.'

'You don't look like a flea – I'd say the opposite,' William said, smiling.

'It's the name I'm called by those who know me.'

William stood there a moment, his shaggy head tilted to the side as he regarded Fleance. 'Well, Flea. Here's the thing: I'm mighty hungry and I can see your wee rabbit is going to spoil if you don't take it off them flames. I have a loaf of bread. I'd be pleased to share supper with you.'

Fleance looked down at the rabbit – indeed, it did need to be taken from the fire. But he didn't know who this William was – whether friend or foe.

A few moments later, Fleance conceded. 'I guess we can't just stay like this all evening. Your horse looks like it needs rest as much as you say you need food.'

William chuckled. It was a warm sound and seemed genuine. 'I'll tie the wee beastie up with your great animal, if you don't mind.'

'I'm sure Willow would appreciate different company from me,' Fleance said with less hostility but still as wary. 'After you've settled your horse, would you join me?'

'That's mighty kind,' William said, coming closer and lifting a satchel from his shoulder. 'I found some fruit earlier so maybe that might be a nice way to end the evening.'

Fleance turned his attentions to the rabbit, mindful of the offer of bread and Magness's exhortation not to trust a soul. Still, he was tired and hungry and, though he was bigger than this William, and probably quicker, he was tired from a long day's riding.

In silence they prepared the meal. Swiftly and with skill, Fleance divided up the rabbit while William split the loaf. Fleance was watchful the whole time, his senses keen despite his tiredness. Though his stomach growled in protest, he struggled to finish his dinner.

'You're not hungry, lad?'

'I'm fine.'

'Where are you heading, then?'

'Scotland.'

William studied him. 'Did you hear the king's sickly?'

'Aye,' Fleance replied. He wouldn't be drawn as to how he felt about such news. It was always best to keep much of your thoughts in your skull, Magness had told him over and over.

'I'm on my way to Forres to pay my respects,' William said quietly.

Fleance's head shot up. 'Forres?'

'Aye, the king's castle. 'Tis traditionally been. So, I've got a long road ahead.'

Fleance took in William's cloak and the boots. Though dusty and old, they were clothes worn by a nobleman. He was not sharing a meal with a petty thief or vagabond – unless he was a cut-throat and had stolen the clothes from another. It seemed unlikely because, as Miri often remarked, Fleance was an astute judge of character and the idea of William being a cut-throat didn't fit the slow and gentle nature of the older man who sat across the fire from him.

William wiped his beard with a small cloth. 'That was a very tasty bit of meat.'

'I stuffed it with rosemary and thyme I found along the way,' Fleance said, picking at the bread on his lap. 'Sometimes, a wee rabbit can taste a bit gamey. The herbs mask that.'

'Your mother teach you that, then?'

'No, ah, yes. My adoptive mother.'

William appraised him. 'Are your folks home in Scotland?'

'You ask a lot of questions.'

William laughed. 'An' you do a lot of saying very little.' He pulled his cloak further around him. 'How old are you? Nineteen? Twenty?'

This was a harmless question. 'Twenty-one.'

The old man sighed. 'My boy would've been about your age had he lived. He was killed during the troubles.'

'Sorry to hear that, William. My father was also killed during that time.'

William stared hard at him. 'Aye?'

Fleance had said too much. He put some more wood on the fire. 'Do you have other children?' he asked to take the focus from himself.

'Not any more,' was all the man said, still looking at him curiously.

'I only have my adoptive parents. They won't come back to Scotland because of what happened.'

'So, you're on your own. 'Tis a brave thing, a young man like you, travelling alone.'

'I'm armed and know how to use my weapons,' Fleance said. 'I've been trained by the best.'

William held up his hands. 'No doubt but you've nought to worry about with me. Though, I may have a suit to offer: would you be willing to accompany an old man back to Scotland?' When Fleance hesitated, he continued. 'You seem mighty distrustful for one so young.'

'I have cause for it. There are daggers in men's smiles, my father used to tell me.'

'As I told you: I'm no armed. I've seen enough bloodshed and carnage to last me seven lifetimes – I no longer want to be the cause of another's misery.'

The sight of Rosie's tear-stained face flashed into Fleance's mind and his stomach twisted. 'That's a brave stance to take.'

'Many think it's foolishness. But I'm still alive and it's been nigh on eight years since I put away my sword.' He picked up a small bundle of dry sticks Fleance had gathered and carefully, stick by stick, placed them on the fire. Fleance studied him carefully. There was something about this man which stirred a memory. He was certain he had met him before – whether in the company of Magness or way back when he was a child, he didn't know. Something in William's manner reminded him of someone. He could not be sure that this was a man from his past or his present. He would think on it some more to see if his mind would be able to offer up the answer.

Fleance questioned him, 'Do you not even carry a dirk?'

'No, but I'll tell you, lad, if a man comes against me with his weapon, I will use what I have to hand to keep myself safe.' William shifted his saddle so that it served as a support for his body and then leant back onto it. 'Well, Flea, how 'bout you sleep on my request and let me know in the morning – provided you are happy to share your campsite with me.'

'I will do that and you are welcome.' Fleance pulled his own cloak over his head and lay down to sleep.

Willow was exhausted. Fleance was exhausted. All he wanted to do was creep into a safe place and sleep. How long they had been heading south, he did not know, except the sun had come up and gone down again and it was night.

Fleance was too afraid to stop in case his attackers were still pursuing him but both he and Willow needed water and rest. He roused himself and pulled the horse up. 'Whoa, boy,' he said. Though they'd stopped, he could feel the animal trembling. He couldn't risk making a light but the moon was bright enough for him to make out some ruins and what could possibly be water.

He nudged Willow on and was relieved to see that there was indeed a tiny brook. The horse pricked up his ears and, despite his exhaustion, quickened his pace, the trot jarring Fleance's thighs and backside. Like his mount, he was keen to get there.

A few yards from the ruins, Fleance reined his horse in again, listening carefully for any sign of life. The only sound, thankfully, was the wind in the trees and frogs singing. Fleance jumped down from Willow and immediately fell back, his legs too weak to hold his weight. He sat up, then grabbed the stirrup to haul himself to his feet and then led the horse to the water. While the horse drank, Fleance unbuckled the saddle and, struggling under its weight, walked back to the ruins. The roof of the building had collapsed but one corner was secure. He cast the saddle to the floor and went back to the stream to bring the horse into the old dwelling and out of sight of potential threat.

After he checked Willow was tethered securely (though, in all his time with the family, the horse had never strayed far, so worries about him leaving Fleance behind were unfounded), the young boy had eaten the last of the bread and cheese his father has packed at the beginning of their journey. After that, he fell into an exhausted and fretful sleep.

'Show your face, you coward!'

Fleance woke with a start and reached for his sword – it wasn't there. In the half light, he saw William standing, brandishing his father's weapon. Fear swept through him and he leapt to his feet, drawing his dirk, ready to fight the old man.

'Show your face or I will un-seam you, and your insides will fall out for the wolves to devour!'

It was then that Fleance realised William was not threatening him but rather an unseen foe in the woods. 'What is it, William?' he whispered.

William didn't turn around. 'I've seen a man in the shadows. A Scot, like us. And he didn't look very friendly. Have you got your dirk?'

'Aye.'

A branch snapped behind them. Fleance spun around, his back to the fire.

'I say again. Show your face,' William growled.

From deep within the dark wood, a man called. 'Old man, you and the boy are surrounded. I suggest you put down your weapons.'

'And I suggest to you, you put down *your* weapons,' Fleance cried. 'Or, you'll be mighty sorry.'

A nasty hoot came from his left and then, one by one, three Scots emerged out of the darkness and into the clearing, each brandishing a sword.

Chapter Six

Almost from instinct, Fleance flicked his dirk at the man in front of him. He was surprised to see that the blade went deep into the man's throat before he even had a moment to cry out. As he fell backwards, Fleance lunged forward and grabbed the sword from the dying man who had relinquished his weapon when he clutched at the wound in his neck.

Fleance looked around towards William who was now engaged in a fierce struggle but there was no time to help because the third man was charging towards him, his claymore swinging. Fleance barely had time to get himself into a position where he could defend himself.

He brought the sword up just as his enemy's came crashing down. The power and weight of the sword hitting the one he now held caused a painful jar in his forearms and shoulder but Fleance was strong enough to hold back the pressure bearing down on him. He inhaled and, roaring with all his strength, pushed his assailant's weapon around to his right before spinning away to his left.

The man regained his balance and charged again. It was clear to Fleance that this man was not a skilful fighter but rather someone used to using brute force to win fights. This time Fleance was ready for him so, just before the man reached the spot where he stood, Fleance skipped out of reach. The weight of the claymore, and the lack of a solid target, sent the man off balance. He stumbled and Fleance used this moment to bring his own weapon down on the other's back.

The man fell forward with a heavy thud.

Fleance was shocked at how easily the blade went through the man's body, but worse was the sound of the man's screaming. This was not some rabbit, boar or stag. This was another human being. Magness's words came to him. *Once you've downed your foe, lad, you must finish him off. 'Tis dishonourable to let even an enemy linger in pain.*

Palms sweaty now from the shock of combat, Fleance pulled the weapon from the man's back and swung it again so that it sliced through his neck, silencing him for good. Then he went to the first man and, though feeling ill, removed the dirk from his body.

Breathing hard and shaking, Fleance was roused from his thoughts by the sounds of William and the first intruder.

Their cautious movements showed both men were seasoned fighters. Though obviously much older than his foe, William was strong and light on his feet. Fleance could only stand and watch – this was not his fight now – though he kept a wary eye on the woods in case there were more of them.

'I told you, you'd be in trouble if you messed with me,' William taunted the Scot. 'You have nae idea who you're up against.'

''Tis a weak Scot who needs to boast 'bout his talent,' the man panted but brought his sword in a sideways arc towards William's exposed flank.

William twisted away, using the force from the blow against his sword to push the man off-balance. William lunged forward and smashed the handle into the Scot's face, toppling him onto his back. The man's sword fell out of his hand and William kicked it towards Fleance.

With the tip of Fleance's sword pressed into the throat of the Scot, William bellowed, 'Name an' county.'

'Kelvin of Clan Mitchell, ' he stammered, eyes wide with terror.

'Well, Kelvin, you and your wee friends chose the wrong camp-fire to raid. And, I did warn you.' He stepped away from the prone man and kicked his foot. 'Up!' The man's nose and top lip bled and he tried to wipe away the mess as he scrambled to his feet. 'Flea – get his dirk, there,' he added pointing to the knife which was tied to the man's leg. With the Scot's own sword pointing at him, Fleance nipped in and removed the weapon.

'I should kill you for the trouble you put me and the lad through but 'tis not honourable to attack an unarmed man. Put your hands behind your back. Flea, there's some rope in my satchel. Get it and tie this bugger's hands.'

Fleance did as he was instructed and, with sweat on his palms making him fumble so that he cursed, he bound up Kelvin's wrists. 'Sit down,' William told Kelvin. Fleance pushed him to the ground in front of a tree. 'Bind his ankles as well, lad. We don't want him coming after us again.' When Fleance had finished and stepped back, William continued. 'Now, we're going to break camp and leave you here with the bodies of your companions. If you're lucky, one of your kind will come rescue you before the wolves sniff out the blood.'

Kelvin glared at William and then spat at him, 'You should have killed me too. See if I don't find you and come at you again.'

'I dinna know why you raided us, man. We've got nowt to offer,' William said as he shrugged on his cloak.

'Both of them horses are fine specimens,' Kelvin growled. 'A reiver can get a lot more and go a lot further with four legs under him.'

'I'm pleased, then, that the lad and I have helped curb your wicked ways.' William hoisted his saddle onto his horse and, while strapping up the girth, continued to taunt Kelvin. 'Perhaps 'tis time you considered a change in occupation. You don't seem to be very good at this one.'

William prepared a makeshift torch by wrapping an oiled cloth around a small branch and using the dying embers of the fire to ignite it. He swung up onto his horse and Fleance, who had mirrored William's preparations, did the same. 'Let this be a warning to you, Kelvin of Clan Mitchell. Things are not always what they appear to be. I think your friends there,' he nodded in the direction of the bodies, 'have learnt this the fatal way.'

William nudged his horse on and Fleance followed.

About half an hour later, William pulled up his horse. 'You all right, lad? You're very quiet.'

Fleance had started shaking about fifteen minutes after they had left the scene, and now he was feeling weak and sick.

'Was that your first kill?' William asked quietly.

'Aye,' Fleance replied. 'I've been learning swordsmanship since I was a wee lad but I never imagined myself pitted against real people.' He was finding it difficult to get rid of the scene from his mind. 'There was so much blood,' he added.

'Aye,' William said. 'Man is a messy animal. You were right, though, about your skills. It's been a long while since I've seen such in one so young.'

'Magness, my adoptive father, I have been told, is one of the best with sword and dirk. But I'm better than he is with my crossbow. He says it's because his eyesight is dimmed with age.'

'Ah, well. As to the business behind us: put it from your mind, lad. Thinking too much on it will make your brain sick.' William gathered up his reins. ''Tis almost dawn. We should be near to the wall soon.'

As his horse walked on, the ache in his arm and shoulder reminded Fleance of a particularly gruelling session with Magness.

He would have been about fourteen and it was his first time with the claymore – a heavy, long-bladed sword which was almost as tall as he was. Magness had made him practise swinging in a figure eight, over and over. When he felt he could do no more, Magness demanded he start again. 'A fight with a man lasts an eternity, boy. You need to train your muscles to have a long memory.' Later that evening, Miri had rubbed linseed oil into his burning muscles while Fleance tried to hide the tears which spilled down his face.

The next day, he had to do it all over again. Magness did not relent. That was one of the few moments he almost felt hatred towards the man.

The light began to shift and, with it, the sounds of bird calls. William extinguished the torch and tucked it behind his saddle. As they came out of the forest, Fleance looked at the vast plains which spread out before them. Away in the distance, he could make out some sort of long fortress. It stretched west to east as far as the eye could see.

They headed straight towards it and, as the sun rose, the view became clearer. Though impressive and higher than it first appeared, Fleance could see that there were gaps in places. This must be Hadrian's Wall that his father had spoken of. He remembered many times his father would come into his chamber before bed and tell him stories of warriors, wars, mighty deeds and insane rulers.

'The foolish Roman emperor,' Banquo had told him, 'thought he could contain the marauding Celts out of his conquered England. The people on either side of the wall had to pay taxes to pay for the cost of building the wall as well as the soldiers who manned it.'

'But, if he hadn't built the wall in the first place, the emperor wouldn't need taxes to pay for it,' the young Fleance had said.

Banquo had ruffled the hair on Fleance's head. 'You're a clever wee man.' He'd stood up then. 'Now all that the wall's good for is for folk stealing pieces of it to build houses for their pigs.'

The memory was one of the many Fleance could recall of his father's practical approach to life and his commitment to teach Fleance the best way to live safely. Like the time Willow was bought – a sapling stallion, stroppy and difficult. Banquo told Fleance that, though it an uncommon practice, it was best for his purposes the horse be gelded despite his son's reservations. 'Fleance,' he'd said, 'he's a fine specimen of a horse but a stallion is better with brooding mares than winning battles and riding with the king. This is the reason he was purchased. Mark my words, lad, Willow will be more use to our family as a gelding than a rutting stallion.'

These words were proven true many times over in Fleance's life.

Willow followed William's horse faithfully as it picked its way through a wrecked section of stone. The high, damp walls towered over them on each side, blocking out the sun and causing a chill to flow over them. On either side, rocks and boulders had been scattered by some unknown force and lay embedded in the soil at the foot of the wall.

It was only when they were through the other side that Fleance realised he had been holding his breath. With relief, he let it out and patted Willow's neck.

'You care for your horse, then, Flea?'

'Why do you ask?'

'I see you're mighty tender and kind to him.'

'He was my father's horse,' Fleance replied. 'He and my sword are all I have left of him.'

'You don't see many with his size and colouring,' William said, staring at Willow, a thoughtful look on his face. The old man took a deep breath as if he might be about to say something else. Fleance tightened his grip on the reins and stared ahead. He would give no answer to the invitation to talk about his father's horse.

Instead, they carried on in silence and the worm of worry Fleance had at the back of his mind, now that they were on Scottish soil, came to the fore. He didn't actually know how to get to his home having not mentioned to a soul these past years the place of his birth. He looked ahead at William. Perhaps he could ask directions without giving too much away.

'William,' he called. William turned to face him as he pushed Willow forward so that they rode side by side. 'The place I'm going. I'm afraid I don't exactly remember how to get there. Would you be kind enough to give me directions?'

William grinned. 'You're not afeared I'll chase you down and rob you, then?'

Fleance returned the smile. 'No. The place is Lochaber. Do you know it?'

William was quiet for a bit. 'Aye. I've been there once or twice. 'Tis in the western Highlands, on the way to Inverness. It's a hard ride.'

'I shall travel with you until we must part. Are you fine with that?'

'Sure and there will be folk enough to keep you in the direction. I'm glad of your company for the next few days.'

It took them seven days and nights to reach the outskirts of Glasgow. In that time, Fleance was able to glean almost forgotten stories about the troubles. Though William did not divulge his exact role in the events which lead up to Macbeth's death, it was easy to tell by his demeanour he had been right in the thick of it. What was not clear, however, was William's current feelings about Scotland's tenuous political state now that the king was dying.

William eventually left Fleance alone at a tavern while he continued on towards the castle at Forres. 'I thank you for your company, Flea. I wish you all of God's blessings and good fortunes as you travel.'

Fleance bowed his head as a sign of respect for the man. 'Thank you, William. You have made my journey less wearisome.'

'I hope our paths will cross again, lad. Farewell.'

Fleance watched as the old man and his horse walked off down the road and then he took Willow to the stables for a well-earned rest before the next, and probably hardest, part of his journey.

Rosie
England

The wagon lurched from side to side as Dougal urged the horses through the muddy ruts in the road. The rain had stopped by mid-morning but everything was still damp. Though she was constantly thrown into the side beam of the wagon, Rosie was numb to any pain. She stared without seeing, her eyes stinging and dry from hours of crying. There was a painful lump in her throat which hurt every time she swallowed. Despite her mother's urging, she had not been able to eat since the night of the feast, though a little water gave relief from the tightness of her chest.

How could he do this to her? Why had he never said he had responsibilities elsewhere? Even in the short time they'd spent together, they talked about the present and their future. Never about his past though she had entertained him with re-enactments of her own childhood pranks.

He had told her he loved her. She shook silently and another batch of tears slid down her face. Her stomach ached and the sharp pains in her chest dug in tighter so that the sobs came back.

Her mother reached over and embraced her. 'Shhh, darling girl. Shhh.'

Rosie buried her face into her mother's neck and cried. Dougal flicked the reins angrily but said nothing, for what was there to say to make the situation better?

By midday, they came to a tavern and pulled up outside. Dougal climbed down from the tray. 'We will rest ourselves and the horses.' He pulled out his small bag of coins and went into the building.

'I can't go in there,' Rosie croaked. 'I don't want anyone to see me.'

''Tis all right, love. I will get your father to bring the food out to the wagon. Though perhaps you may like to refresh yourself?'

Rosie considered this. Perhaps a splash of cold water would take the sting out of her eyes. 'Yes, Ma. Perhaps if I wear my hood up . . . ?'

Her mother patted her hand. 'You're a brave lass.' She climbed out of the wagon and Rosie followed. They stood there a moment waiting for Dougal to come back to tend to the horses. It wasn't long before he was out, tucking his purse into his coat.

'You can go in. I'll just take the horses around the back.' He climbed back up onto the wagon and flicked the reins. The horses pulled forward, leaving Rosie and her mother standing in front of the inn.

Rosie pulled the hood of her cloak over her head and followed her mother inside. They made their way to the hearth and the innkeeper brought them over some refreshments. Despite the roaring fire, Rosie was chilled to the bone. 'Will we rest here the night or go on?' she asked.

'I think your father is keen to get home. He has gathered a lot of orders this trip.' Her mother sipped on her ale. 'An' he's keen to plant some vines.'

Rosie looked at her mother. 'He's a cooper, not a farmer.'

'Aye but he has that notion in his head that he can make the barrels *and* fill them.' She smiled. 'I don't know how it will go but he's already spoken to someone who's had his first successful crop.'

Just then, Dougal came through the door, taking off his hat and scratching his head vigorously. He spoke quietly to the innkeeper and then joined them at the table by the hearth. 'The back wheel of the wagon is nae looking well. I'm to be hard pressed finding a wheelwright before the thing breaks. I will have to try to mend it

60

myself.' He looked at his wife. 'Could you stand a night here, lovey, because it will take me some time?'

Rosie understood the meaning behind her father's question. He was asking if *she* would be fine. She turned to her father. 'I am looking forward to my own bed, Da, but I would rather get home one day late than be stranded in the forest fending off wolves and thieves.'

'I will speak with the innkeeper,' Dougal said and returned to the bar. Rosie watched him hand over some coins to the owner before rejoining them. ''Tis settled then. I'll have some supper and get to work on them repairs. He says the room is small but comfortable. I'll sleep in the wagon.'

Rosie carried her belongings through the small door of the lodging and laid them on one of two small beds. In the corner, on a table, sat a large bowl and a jug filled with lavender water. Beside them was a rough but clean cloth. Rosie poured some water into the bowl, dipped the cloth and pressed the cool material to her still burning face. Her eyes stung and the tip of her nose was sore. She stared down at her reflection in the water. Despite the distortion, it was enough show her how distraught she looked. Her face was puffy, especially around the eyes, and her lips were bloodless and cracked where, just yesterday, she had enjoyed Flea's kisses.

She unclipped the brooch which fastened her cloak and removed the girdle around her waist so that the top of her dress opened enough for her to rub the cool flannel around the back of her neck and shoulders. The silver cross Flea had given her on her eighteenth birthday just two months before lay against her throat – another cruel reminder of what she had lost. She touched it and then closed her eyes, trying to hold on to the happiness of that moment when Flea had given it to her.

But it was short-lived. At the thought of Flea, hot tears sprang to her eyes and the pain of loss returned so keenly, her legs gave way beneath her and she dropped to the floor and lay there, sobbing into the coarse mat, praying for darkness to engulf her so that she would not have to face this grief.

Chapter Seven
Towards Lochaber

The damp soaked through everything: his hair, his boots, even his cloak. He could hardly see ten feet in front. The only hope was that Willow still knew the way home.

Home. It had been over ten long years since he had been to his place of birth – that place where his boyhood toys had sat along the casement: the slingshot his father had shown him how to make; the chessboard an aging uncle had gifted as a present; his mother's cradle blanket that she refused to relinquish to anyone else; that place where his clothes and boots had sat ready for the servants to dress him.

Servants. A word like 'home', so unfamiliar to the life he'd been living. Fleance didn't know what he would find when he got to Lochaber castle. Had it been taken over by the renegades who had destroyed so many dwellings, or did it now sit forlorn, nestled in the Scottish hillside?

Man and beast plodded on through the mist and the cold.

Suddenly Willow stopped, his ears flicking left and right. 'What is it, boy?' Fleance asked, peering into the fog. Willow shook his head up and down, snorting, his eyes wide. When Fleance urged him to go forward, the horse took two twitchy steps and then jumped back, almost unseating Fleance.

It was then he heard the noise. Gravelly and nasal; a loud humming more than singing but it was a sound made by a human not a bird or beast. As he looked hard down the road, he began to see a dark, moving shape coming forward. Willow was now pacing and clearly anxious. 'Whoa, boy. Calm down.'

The humming grew louder and what looked like a large, slow-moving beast, now emerged as three beings. 'Greetings,' Fleance called even though a cold shiver went down his spine.

The women, for that was what he now could see they were, stopped walking and were silent. One of them came forward. Fleance put his hand to the hilt of his sword but she looked unarmed. Her face was deeply lined and her hair hung over her face like greasy rope. She wore boots and men's britches which emphasised her rake-thin body. Her coat was matted and filthy and over this was a cloak of sorts made by the pelt of several animals.

'Greetings,' Fleance repeated.

She looked up at him, her eyes red-rimmed and lashes crusted. 'Hail, son of Banquo.'

'What?' Fleance exclaimed, feeling as if all the air had left him. 'How do you know . . . ?' But she put her dark stained finger to her lips and shook her head.

The second woman came forward and grabbed at the reins. Willow squealed but immediately stilled. Fleance's mouth was dry and he felt ill. 'Who are you?' he asked, his voice barely above a whisper.

'Beware the seeds of Duncan,' she sang, childlike and sweet. She stroked Willow's neck. Fleance was mesmerised by the fluid movement of her hands. The nails were very pale, as was the rest of her. He could see thick veins over the surface of her skin. When he was able to pull his eyes away from this sight he saw that she, like the other old woman, was covered in grime. Her hair, though braided, had twigs and grass and some earthy mixture spread throughout. And, like the other, there were hairs sticking out from her chin and above her thin lips. And, even from his position atop Willow, Fleance could smell a rancid stench coming from her.

'What are you doing?' he asked, but now, neither was paying any attention to him. He looked over them to the last woman. She was tall but her hair had been cropped so that just a dark fuzz lay on her skull. Her eyes were large in her gaunt face. 'Answer me,' he called.

She smiled at him and revealed a mouth full of black and rotting teeth. 'Hail to you who will gain the prize amidst bloodshed and sorrow.' She stared at him and grinned. Fleance's stomach heaved. He wanted to ride on.

The first woman turned her back on him saying, 'Hail.'

'Hail,' said the braided one.

'Hail,' echoed the tall one and then together they said, 'Hail to thee and beware.' They took up their strange humming and shuffled on, past Fleance and Willow, disappearing into the gloom.

'Wait,' Fleance cried. 'Come back. Tell me what this means.' But the three odd women moved on as if nothing had happened; as if they had not met him on the heath and named him or warned him or promised strange events. As if they had not passed on to him riddles and confusion.

He turned Willow to follow them but the horse refused to budge. 'Come on, Willow. They're harmless.' The horse did not agree with Fleance and even gave a warning buck. By the time Fleance righted himself, the women had vanished, melting into the air.

Fleance sat staring into the mist then shook himself. He remembered a forgotten warning of his father's about the dangers of trading and trafficking with agents of darkness – for he recognised now that

that was what they were – conjurers, those who have knowledge of the other world. Witches. Black-hearted and deceitful.

Nothing good could be gained by taking notice of such wickedness. Yet, what they said held some truth.

Fleance, always remember this: sometimes, to win us to our harm, the elements of darkness do tell us truths. Win us with honest trifles just to betray us with the worse possible outcome.

The voice of his father came through the fog of his confusion to drown out the fading sounds of the women. It was a warning but also something else. It was a reminder to be careful, to follow through with his appointed mission. Not to stray from the path that his father had set before him.

But as he and Willow plodded on, he turned the words of the witches over and over. They knew who he was – but how? Proof then that they had power. *Beware the seeds of Duncan.* The only Duncan he knew of was the king who had been murdered, it was rumoured, by a relative – he remembered hearing talk of it that terrible night over ten years ago.

His father had come home from battle, sore, weary but jubilant. The king had bestowed great praise and honour on Banquo for his efforts and skill on the battlefield. Though Fleance knew little of what had happened between the Scottish soldiers and the invaders from Norway, his father's usual quiet ways had been peppered with quick laughter and outright joy.

What a delight it had been then, when his father had agreed to his pleading that Fleance accompany him to Macbeth's castle at Inverness where the king was visiting. Proudly, he had sat behind his father who was just three horses back from the king. Twice, King Duncan had addressed him directly: once about whether he had noticed the falcon which was hovering over the fields and the other to enquire if he was tired.

Fleance had basked in the glory of the moment.

In the evening, they had had a late supper with much laughter and food and drink. Fleance had even sung for His Majesty – quite an honour, Banquo later told him.

So, early the next morning, when the alarm bells had sounded around the castle, Fleance could not understand what could have been the problem – the enemy had been soundly defeated. There was no danger. And, though Banquo had ordered him to stay in their room, Fleance had crept down the long passageway to where grown men were howling and women wailing.

He remembered feeling terrified and fleeing back to the sanctuary of the apartment.

When his father eventually came back to the room, his face had been drained of all colour. 'Pack up your things, boy. We're leaving.'

'What has happened?' Fleance had asked.

'The king has been murdered.'

Fleance had been stunned. Never before had he known someone who had died violently. When his mother died, it had been sudden and a shock but from no other's hand, save fate. Her illness lasted a short time but she died in her own bed, Fleance and Banquo by her side. And, she died with a smile on her face.

Yes, when Donnach, their gardener, had toppled over in the cabbages, that was surprising. But he had been very old. King Duncan was strong and healthy and kind. How could someone think of doing such a thing?

He had grabbed his clothes and dressed quickly, stuffing his bedding into a tight roll. Banquo had been stonily silent as he did the same and they left the room, went down the hall and out to the stable to tack up Willow.

Fleance could still hear the sound of the wailing. It was a sound he could not shake for a long while – until it had been replaced by the awful cries of his own father just a few short weeks later.

Willow was tired. The road was uneven and treacherous. Fleance dismounted and man and horse walked on in the cold – a miserable sight. He was lost in his thoughts when a voice called through the fog, 'Ahoy there.' Fleance and Willow stopped dead. 'Where are you heading?'

It was an old shepherd. He held a long shepherd's crook in one hand and, unusual for this time of year, a newborn lamb, yellow and bloody, in the other.

'I'm heading to Lochaber, father.'

The shepherd appraised him. 'You've got a good few days' ride still to go. Why don't you put your feet under our table for a night.' The relief must have shown on Fleance's face for the old man grinned. 'Give that bottom of yours a wee rest.' He continued walking across the moor. 'Follow me if you wish to sample the wife's tasty stew.'

Obediently, Fleance followed the man and was surprised to happen upon a small cottage nestled against the hill. The fog had obscured his vision so it wasn't surprising he'd not seen it on his way up the mountain.

'It's not much to look at but it's comfortable. We were sent here some years back after the troubles. The wife and I worked at a manor but then the master died and the new earl didn't seem to want to keep the old staff. We sometimes miss the fellowship of the folks but this is an all right life for an old couple to live out their days.' The shepherd chattered on which suited Fleance fine – he was too exhausted to offer much towards the conversation.

The old man led Fleance to a stable of sorts – a walled area with a thatch roof but no front wall. Though the ground was bare, it was sheltered from the weather. The shepherd hung up the crook but kept the lamb tucked under his arm. He watching silently as Fleance untacked Willow and rubbed him down.

'I'm most grateful for your hospitality,' Fleance said.

The shepherd snorted. 'I thought you looked well bred an' I was right. Don't worry about thanking us; 'tis our duty to the Lord. After all, you could be a saint or even an angel sent by God to test our obedience.'

Fleance smiled. 'I'm neither, father, but I shall offer my thanks to God then.'

'Aye and over supper would be a right fine time. Come on. The wife will be waiting.' He turned on his heel and headed towards the cottage with Fleance close behind.

The inside of the cottage was warm and light flickered from an open fire and the two candles attached to the wall. A woman was stirring something in a kettle over the fire. By the smell of it, it was the stew the shepherd spoke of.

The old man placed the lamb in a basket beside the fire and touched his wife's arm. 'Agnes,' he said. 'We have company.'

The woman straightened and smiled as she turned. However, at the sight of Fleance, the smile vanished and she let out a piercing scream.

Chapter Eight
Glamis Castle, Scotland

Duncan lifted his little sister from the stairwell and swung her across the dampened floor. 'Here you go, wee one. Rachel will be pleased you dinna get your slippers wet.'

'Ta then, Duncan. Least Father won't have cause to moan.'

Inside his heart, Duncan ached; that the younger of his sisters should be so aware, so young, of their father's temper. 'Nay worry 'bout it, Bree. 'Tis not our fault and 'tis such a small matter.' But they both knew that wasn't true. They both knew that their father, Donalbain, first in line to the throne of Scotland, was an unpredictable, violent, unstable presence in their household.

Giggling now, Bree skipped towards the kitchen where she knew there would be tasty bites before dinner. This was the custom. Duncan had learnt early on that this younger sister needed nourishment little and often despite the protocols of castle dining.

Morag, their cook, was well into preparations for the evening meal. Her face was blood red and shiny with sweat. Still, at the sight of Bree, she grinned. 'Got it right here, bairn. You'll love this.' She nodded towards the side bench. There sat a large plate of cheese and breads and fruit.

Bree rushed over but, mindful of her heritage, mimicked her older sister's slow and polite manner of selecting her food.

'So, Master Duncan, how is it now?'

Duncan smiled. ''Tis all good, Morag.'

'What hearts have you captured this week?'

Duncan laughed this time. 'You ask this every moment I bring wee Bree down here.'

'Och aye, a lad's got to have an outlet. What with your golden locks and your blue eyes, you could catch any filly you set your mind to.'

'Morag, you know that I am in line to the throne. I canna be throwing about my seed.'

Morag roared with laughter. 'You are so blunt there, Duncan.'

'Not blunt, dear one. Just honest.'

Morag tipped the dough onto the table. 'Good. That's the sort o' king Scotland needs.'

Duncan grinned. 'Well, while Uncle Malcolm is still breathing, I'm content to hunt them stag and spear those boars . . .'

Morag threw a ball of dough at him, 'And bed them beauties.'

He shot her a look. 'Not in front of the child, Morag.'

Immediately, Morag's expression changed, reminded, no doubt, by his comment that she was speaking to someone who was destined to be the Scottish king one day. 'Sorry, Sire,' she said, her face reddening further.

Duncan regretted his rebuke. 'My dear Morag. This family is, and will always be, indebted to you. Never feel sorry for anything you say or do.'

Bree spoke up. 'Morag, Rachel's got a new story for me. She started it last night.'

'An' what's this one about?'

'A handsome prince who's lost his way over the moor.'

Duncan grinned, thinking of Bree's older sister. 'Rachel's stories always have a handsome prince in them.'

'I know, Duncan,' Bree said, nibbling on a slice of apple. 'But this one's even more handsome than all the others.' Duncan's and Morag's eyes met and they both smiled. 'This prince is going to get hurt, Rachel said, and a beautiful princess makes him better.'

'You'll be looking forward to bedtime then,' Morag suggested. 'So as you can hear the next part of the tale.'

Bree stopped chewing and by the look on her face, Duncan could tell she wasn't certain whether she should admit to it, especially as she never volunteered to go to bed.

Duncan came to her rescue. 'Are you finished, lass? I have some errands to do before supper.' Bree nodded, jumped off her stool and began to skip out of the kitchen. 'Bree. Aren't you forgetting something?'

Remembering her manners, she stopped and stood facing Morag. 'Thank you, Morag, for a delicious meal.' When Duncan nodded, she scooted out the door.

'Sire, you don't have to make her do that. 'Tis my duty and honour to serve your family.'

'And, because of that, it's important she learns how to maintain that duty and honour,' Duncan smiled. 'Having a thankful heart lightens any weight on the soul. Now, I shall leave you to your tasks otherwise supper will be late and it will be my fault.' What he didn't add but which they both knew would be true, was that his father would take out such tardiness on the kitchen staff.

As Duncan followed his sister up the steps to the main quarters, his thoughts went back again to the state of his family. Uncle Malcolm, loved and respected by most, would not see out the year. Preparations, though not obviously, were being made in both castles, Malcolm's in Forres, and Donalbain's in Glamis: for the death of one king and the crowning of another.

Donalbain's advisors, aware of the people's distrust of him, had warned him of the need to be extra careful; that an assassination attempt could be possible. This news had only served to fuel his father's irrational moods and send him back to the black sisters who had a stranglehold on his father's mind.

Duncan picked up the bronze water jug, poured some water into a goblet and sat on the wide seat under the narrow window. The afternoon sun, when it showed its face, would squeeze itself through the glass, making this position in the castle favoured by Rachel's cat and Donalbain's two hounds.

This afternoon, however, the day was gloomy as if matching the mood of the nation and especially matching the mood of the family. The corner was deserted so Duncan had only himself and his thoughts for company.

As he sipped on his drink, his mind went over the things that needed to be done to ensure peace would be maintained. Since their mother's death, and his father's descent into madness, the parenting of Bree had fallen upon the shoulders of Duncan and Rachel.

Rachel didn't seem to mind. Her stories and songs and the games she made up were a pleasant contrast to the dealings he had with his father – often fuelled by too much wine and not enough sleep.

A rustle of skirts brought Duncan back to the present. It was Rachel coming down from her chamber. Her thick, blonde hair was pinned in a pretty mass on top of her head. A conversation he'd overheard from the servants flicked into his mind: *"Tis a pity the master is so jealous else the girl would hae been married off years before. Such a waste to be lingering in this unhappy place when she could be warming the bed of a prince and producing sons.'*

'Have you seen Zeus?' Rachel asked, as she passed by.

'Not since this morning.' Rachel continued down the stairs. Duncan called after her. 'Rachel, are you well?' His affection for his sister added another stone of concern to the ever-increasing pile.

She turned and smiled. Yes, Duncan thought, she's as beautiful as Mother was. 'I am, Duncan.' She came back up the stairs and sat beside him. She laid a hand on his arm. 'You worry too much.'

'There are things to be done.'

'Yes, but you're not always the one who has to do them.'

Duncan turned to his sister. 'Things are getting worse with him.'

'Then keep out of his way. It's not a surprise that his mind is filled with fear: his brother is dying and he's to be king.'

Duncan picked up her small hand and enclosed it in his larger fist. 'You always seem to understand what goes on in another's heart. The man who chooses you will be blessed indeed.'

Rachel pulled her hand from his and stood up. 'Must go find that dratted cat. He's got some mousing to do.' She went quickly down the stairs leaving her brother alone again, feeling more upset than before. Though Rachel had moved away quickly, he still saw the tears which had sprung to her eyes.

Perhaps things would have been better had they stayed in Ireland. When they had fled there from the false accusations of patricide, they still had their mother. Donalbain, though grieving the murder of his father, was not yet affected by witchcraft and spells and Duncan had been able to live relatively happily under the careful watch of Morag and the other servants.

Coming back to Scotland nine years ago was the beginning of the change. Within a few months, Mother had died giving birth to Bree; Rachel took on the role of lady of the house, even though she was only ten; and Duncan began to feel the weight of the impending kingship even though he had barely turned twelve. They could not go back to their own place in the north because it had been ransacked by either Macbeth's men or the dispossessed and angry men who'd suffered under Macbeth's reign.

Uncle Malcolm gave them Glamis castle as compensation – it was far larger and more impressive than the one they had left. However, Father spent a lot of time away from the castle either raiding the borders of northern England for booty or consorting with those who would tell him what he wanted to hear. The relationship between Donalbain and Malcolm had deteriorated as well, for Uncle Malcolm disapproved of his brother's obsession with the dark arts and had distanced himself from the family not long after they arrived back at the castle.

Outside, the sound of horses galloping through the castle gates roused Duncan from his thoughts. He sighed deeply and stood up. That would be his father come back from Forres, the king's palace. He knew by the way his father rode his horse that the meeting had not gone well. As he walked down the large staircase, he wondered, not for the first time, what he could do to soften the blow of his father's temper.

Chapter Nine

Duncan watched his father pull hard on the horse's mouth and swear at the page who had run forward to help his master. Donalbain dismounted and rearranged his cloak before striding up the wide steps and through the door which now stood open for his entrance. Duncan waited for him in the entrance hall.

'Chambers. Now,' he barked at Duncan. 'Firth,' he shouted to his manservant. 'Drinks! Food! We have work to do.' He strode past Duncan without looking at his son and continued on through the cavernous halls to the battle room. 'Duncan! Keep up.'

All hopes of a quiet evening fled as Duncan followed his agitated father to the heart of the castle – a room he had come to despise. The only good would be that Bree and Rachel would get a reprieve from their father's erratic and violent temper and enjoy the meal Morag had prepared.

'Sit!' Donalbain ordered. He paced the room. 'That damn fool of a brother, even in his dying days, thinks it best to dictate to the next in line how things should run.'

Duncan saw the sweat beading on his father's forehead so poured him a drink. 'Here, Father.'

Donalbain scooped up the chalice without acknowledging his son's thoughtful action. 'He says, fool that he is, he says, I must agree to comply with our dead father's wishes. Our father, who was stupid enough to trust in men who sought to destroy him.' He took a gulp of wine. 'Think about it, Duncan. Your grandfather was twice betrayed because he did not know that men will only do that which pleases and promotes their own cause. The king,' he added, taking another swallow, 'should have been alert to the possibility of treason.'

'Yes, Father,' Duncan replied, the same reply he gave every time Donalbain was in this frame of mind. He'd learnt very early on that trying to placate his father or to offer solutions often invoked more intensive moments of rage and paranoia.

'I am to be king,' Donalbain shouted. 'Why should I be dictated to by my brother who has not proven himself to produce an heir whereas your mother, may God bless her soul, your mother and I have been productive in the furthering of the royal blood?' He drank some more and Duncan's heart pained some. 'It was not *he* who slew that bloody tyrant Macbeth but the faithful Macduff; it was not *he* who rallied against those who would bring Scotland down. Your uncle waited. He fled to our cousins in England to secure support and then used them and our faithful thanes to overthrow the one who murdered your grandfather.

'Do not be deceived, Duncan. Malcolm appears virtuous to the people because of the pain and suffering they endured under the reign of Macbeth. What they don't know is that I will bring prosperity and invention. I have been given word from the prophets that I will acquire knowledge of the world which can thrust Scotland ahead of all the other nations.'

'Father,' Duncan interrupted. 'Uncle Malcolm is dying – the doctors say it is so. What preparations are there for his funeral and your coronation?'

Donalbain ceased pacing and stared at his son. 'You are right. Yes. Malcolm will die and it will be soon. And I will be king. Margaret, his doting wife, wants him buried with the kings at Iona. I think this is a fair and worthy request that Malcolm be buried with our father. She has also asked that she remain at Forres but I have said that is impossible. We shall find some place for the barren wench to reside.'

His father's word stung. Margaret, Uncle Malcolm's wife, was a kindly creature. That she had produced no children who lived past infancy was grievous to all.

'Yes, Father,' was Duncan's pained reply. 'I am sure there is some lovely abode where she can live out her days.'

Donalbain stared at his son. 'Yes. Indeed. You are right.' He stood up. 'As to this notion that I must follow my father's exhortations. It is foolish to have such ideas at this time. I need better counsel.'

That meant another trip to the weird sisters. What were their motives in encouraging his father? What were they wanting for Scotland? Or, for themselves? It seemed that last trip (only five days ago) had spurred their father into further agitation.

Duncan became practical. He stood up and, though Donalbain was tall, Duncan matched him well and was therefore able to look directly into his father's eyes. 'Father, Uncle Malcolm is like to die soon. We must be prepared. The threat to Scotland is not so bad that you need to care at this time. Better that you are seen to mourn the loss of your kin.'

Donalbain stopped drinking and pacing. 'You are your father's son. Good care and advice.' He then put down his chalice and walked out of the chamber, leaving Duncan to worry about the details of the coronation which was destined to happen.

Duncan poured himself some of the wine. Though his father's rage exaggerated his claims, there was truth to them, nonetheless.

Uncle Malcolm had not been an effectual king in later years. Yes, in the beginning, when Malcolm had called all the exiled home, there had been a sense of rejoicing among the grieving. People got to work to restore that which had been destroyed by Macbeth's year-long tyrannical rule. Malcolm had invested the church with gold and men to find widows and orphans and help them rebuild their lives. For the first year, the young Duncan had travelled with the bishop all over the county, meeting people and keeping a record of what had been destroyed or lost and who had come back. At times, they had to travel with soldiers because skirmishes broke out over property.

Duncan had been very pleased to have helped and proudly presented his census to the king after they had completed their survey. Uncle Malcolm had barely glanced at it; he was more interested in asking the bishop how much gold was left, how many worthy fellows there were and whether they could turn their energies to serving the kingdom.

A year after that, on his own, Duncan had visited some of the outlying holdings and was dismayed to see the land overgrown and the cottages empty. When he had seen a shepherd driving a scraggly herd of sheep along the road, he had stopped him.

'Can you tell me where the families have gone who were working this land yonder?'

The shepherd stared up at him and, when he realised who Duncan was, bowed deeply. 'Sire,' he had said. 'They, along with many folk, have gone back to England or to Ireland. Life here has been too hard for them.'

Duncan had been stunned. Where had the promised gold and goods gone? Why had the king not ensured that what he had invested was returning some fruit? It had been the same all around the county and Duncan had returned to his castle disturbed and saddened.

With each following year, and with the death of each babe borne to the king and Queen Margaret, Malcolm had spent more and more time at the monastery. He would be gone for weeks on end, seeking wisdom from God and the priests. In this way, Duncan had thought a few winters ago, the two brothers were very similar—seeking counsel from the spiritual rather than relying on the corporeal life in front of them. Duncan's thoughts turned to the past.

Donalbain and Malcolm began to quarrel. It started when there had been a banquet in honour of the winter solstice. Many thanes and their families travelled long distances to join the king so the palace was filled with the sounds of laughter, music and children playing.

As usual, Father drank too much wine before the feast was served and when Malcolm called upon the priest to give thanks for the meal, Donalbain's snort of derision was heard throughout the great banquet hall.

An anxious hush descended and almost all the guests turned their attentions to the beautifully decorated plates which waited eagerly for the meal, not daring to look at either the king or his brother.

'You have a problem with asking The Almighty to bless the meal of the king?' Malcolm asked, his voice soft but as cold as a blade.

'No problem at all, Your Majesty. But I would have thought that the kind of blessing He has bestowed upon you would not be ones you would wish upon your guests,' Donalbain said before taking another gulp of wine.

The silence was terrifying. What would the king do? Donalbain was his only kin. Though to be so openly rude to the monarch meant a treasonable offence, the thanes knew how tolerant his majesty was to his younger brother.

'Would you welcome a thanksgiving prayer then, brother?'

'As you wish, my lord,' Donalbain said but he made it sound as if the word was as distasteful on his tongue as hemlock.

'We ask, then, for a prayer of blessing for all, except my brother Donalbain . . .' There was a collective intake of breath. 'And a prayer of thanksgiving for all, especially for my brother, Donalbain.'

It was a stinging slap to Donalbain's face and the king's intention, though thinly masked behind a gracious tone and smiling face, was designed to remind everyone present how different the two were.

Once the main meal had been served and consumed, one of the king's advisors appeared behind Donalbain. 'The king says you are to come to his chamber.' When his father didn't move, Duncan put his hand on his arm. The advisor continued, his voice hard. 'Immediately!' Then added, 'Sire.'

For a moment, a look of pure terror swept over Donalbain's face and he turned to Duncan. 'Malcolm will not let me have my aides with me but he will allow you. Duncan, lad, you must accompany your father into the king's throne room.' He took another long drink and then wiped his face and hands with the warm cloths the servants had been bringing around.

Duncan looked over towards his uncle who was talking and laughing with one of the old thanes. Macduff was his name and he was a cousin of Duncan's grandfather, Duncan the First. There was nothing in the king's face to suggest what he was planning to do about his brother's inappropriate outburst. But then Duncan had recalled long ago, not long after the defeat of the Norwegians and rebels, his grandfather discussing the traitor Cawdor. The king had turned to his sons and remarked that he could not believe, after all he had given the thane, he would turn against him. 'He was a gentleman,' King Duncan had said, 'on whom I built an absolute trust.' The sadness in his voice had been clear even to the young Duncan and he had grieved even then for his grandfather's distress.

Later, after the thane had been executed and the news had been brought to the throne room, there was no celebration of the fact. Duncan had watched his grandfather go out onto the balcony and look upon the swinging corpse of one who had been his closest friend. 'I do not know of any way, unless through supernatural means,' the king had mused, 'to understand how the mind works in a man, simply by looking at his face.'

He had turned to the small group gathered in the throne room, some still nursing injuries from the battle. 'Take heed, my friends. Even the best among us can fall to the temptation to challenge God – as Adam and Eve did in the garden of Eden.'

It was not long after that event that his father had come charging back from the celebration feast at Inverness and ordered the household – servants, livestock and family – to pack quickly, for the king had been murdered and it was no longer safe for his nearest of kin to stay in Scotland.

That was when they had fled to Ireland.

Duncan remembered all this, and the warning of his grandfather many years before, as he looked at his uncle and the frightened face of his father; as he, along with Donalbain, followed the king's advisor out of the banquet hall and into the throne room. And he remembered that he was the son of a prince, the nephew of the king and second-in-line to the throne. A very dangerous position to be in at these times. He understood his position only too well.

They waited a long time in the throne room. Time enough for his father to finish three full chalices of wine and Duncan one. When Malcolm eventually came through the large wooden doors, his face was grim and tired.

Both Donalbain and Duncan bowed. Malcolm took his place on the throne.

'Come before me, brother,' Malcolm instructed. 'And, you, my wee nephew.'

Father and son approached the throne. 'What madness is this, Donalbain, that you should think to challenge me in my own court? Do you not know your behaviour is akin to treason?'

'Aye.'

'You and I, it is well-known among the family, hold different views about such things. But, if one day you are to be king, Donalbain, you will need the people's trust – and respect.'

A look flicked over Donalbain's face. It was a look Duncan always recognised before his father launched into one of his rants. This time, however, despite the wine and that he was unsteady on his feet, Donalbain remained silent.

'You are all I have, brother,' the king continued. 'And though you are my subject, you are kin. Let us speak freely to one another for we have suffered much in these past years. But let this honest talk happen away from the ears of spies and the tongues of gossips.'

Donalbain bowed low. 'I beg Your Majesty's pardon.'

Malcolm rose from the throne. 'And I grant you one.' He turned to Duncan. 'Lad, I believe your father is in need of a good night's repose. Will you help him to his sleeping chamber?'

'Certainly, Uncle.'

They watched their king sweep out of the throne room before Donalbain slumped down at the foot of the throne. 'He could have had my head,' Donalbain croaked. 'What a fool! Him and I. Malcolm's soft heart will be the undoing of us all.'

Duncan pretended he did not hear his father's mutterings. Instead, he helped Donalbain to his feet, up the stairs to the upper chambers, assisted his father while he relieved himself and then helped him to bed.

It was at that time Duncan began to feel the true weight of royalty.

Chapter Ten
Glamis Castle

There was a knock on the door. 'Enter,' Duncan called. Firth, Donalbain's manservant, entered with a tray and another servant carried in jugs of wine. At the sight of the lone Duncan, Firth paled. 'It's all right, man. Father has left but I don't think he's wanting food just now. Perhaps if you could have some at the ready.' The servants came further into the chamber and Duncan deliberated over having his meal here alone, in case his father came back, or to go and join the others in the dining hall.

Because he didn't know where his father had gone, nor how long he would be, he decided it prudent to stay put.

As it turned out, it was a wise decision, for not fifteen minutes after the servants had left, Donalbain returned with two of his advisors. Preston had overseen his father's affairs since Duncan was Bree's age; he was a scrawny, bad-tempered man loathed by all the children of the castle. There was always something distasteful about the way he looked at the girls, especially Rachel of late, and the fawning way he addressed Donalbain made Duncan's skin crawl. They did not even enjoy a reprieve when the family fled to Ireland after King Duncan's murder, for Preston had travelled with them.

The other advisor had only joined the castle last spring. His name was Calum and he had a strange way of speaking so that Duncan had difficulty placing where he was from: the Highlands? Lowlands? Further south? That he was educated was obvious and he spoke a number of languages – Latin, French, German and English as well as Gaelic. He didn't say very much, but Donalbain trusted him implicitly.

'Calum,' Donalbain said. 'Duncan here has given some good counsel.' Duncan saw Preston twitch with displeasure, his top lip lifting in a sneer. 'He says to ignore that fool brother of mine and get down to the business of preparations.'

Duncan knew better than to correct his father's loose translation of his advice.

'Indeed, your lordship,' Calum replied, his attentions completely on Donalbain. 'I think Duncan is very wise for his age.'

'Just like his father then,' Preston whined. 'He is a mirror image of you, Sire.'

Donalbain ignored him. 'We need to get the household ready to mourn my brother's imminent death, but we also need to show the people of Scotland that they are to gain a king who has the good of the country and its peoples in his heart.' He spun around to Preston. 'That was good – mark it down!'

And he was off again. For three more hours, Duncan endured his father's exuberance over what would happen in the coming weeks, while Preston fawned over Donalbain and Calum remained the calm amidst the raging storm.

Finally, after the moon was high in the night sky, Donalbain dismissed them and Duncan wearily made his way to his sleeping chamber. When he opened the door, he was surprised to see Rachel sitting on the chair beside his bed, bending her head over some embroidery.

'Rachel?'

She looked up. 'I have been waiting for you, Duncan. I have some things I want to talk to you about.'

He was so tired but it was difficult to refuse Rachel – she rarely asked anything from anyone. He sat down on his bed. 'What things?'

'I'm worried about you.'

This was not what he was expecting. 'You're worried about me?' He frowned. 'Why?'

'You've been pacing these halls for the past months, your face getting grimmer and grimmer. Is it Father that's worrying you? Or Uncle Malcolm?'

Despite his exhaustion, he couldn't help but smile at his sister. 'It's so like you, Rachel, to be concerned about how everybody else is and not see the things likely to bother you.'

'What things?' she asked, echoing his earlier question. 'Nothing is bothering me.'

But he knew that was not true. Rachel, one of the most beautiful creatures in the country, had not long passed her nineteenth summer and as yet no suitor had been found for her. Perhaps if their mother had still been alive, she may have been able to exert some pressure on their father to turn some of his energies towards family matters.

'Well,' Duncan said, trying to deflect the painful unsaid conversations, 'we shall be busy enough with a funeral and a coronation. Father says we are to move to Forres.'

'Why? This castle is much better – it is bigger for one and the lands far richer.'

'Donalbain has his reasons and he does not need to tell us what his plans are. Though, whether they will be best for Scotland is another matter.'

Rachel rested her hands and tilted her head to one side. 'He will be the king, God willing, Duncan. And that means that one day you will be king. There is time enough then for you to be worrying about the state of the nation. Leave matters be and still enjoy your youth before it runs out.'

'Have you been gossiping with Morag?' he smiled. 'She gave me similar advice before supper.'

'Morag is a good, dear soul,' Rachel said standing up, her blue eyes sparkling. 'We do what we have to, to ensure you keep on the straight and narrow.'

Duncan laughed out loud. 'Next, you'll have me spending the rest of my bachelorhood in a monastery.'

'That isn't a foolish idea what with the invitations which come to the castle one atop the other, calling for your company at some lady's banquet.'

He stretched out his length on the bed and rested his arms under his head. 'I have no idea why they persist – I give them no encouragement.'

'That is precisely why they do – you are like forbidden fruit. The more you deny them, the greater the fire of their desire.'

'Ah, that's you and your stories again of princes and princesses. I'm not Bree, you know.'

Rachel clutched the embroidery to her chest as she stood beside him. 'You've always been a sweet boy and now you've grown into a handsome young man. When the time is right, I know you will choose wisely for, in doing so, you will also be choosing the next Scottish queen.'

The idea sent a cold shiver through him. 'Unless, of course, Donalbain finds himself another wife first.'

'How was Father when you left him?'

'Deep in conversation with himself and his wine. I was glad to be dismissed.'

'I'm to bed then and best you not stay up much later. If Father is in one of his states, it will be an unquiet house tomorrow. Good repose, Duncan.'

'And you, Rachel.' He watched her pull the chamber door closed and then turned on his side. He stared, unseeing, at the flickering candle, wishing the fluttering under his ribs would abate. Change was coming and coming rapidly. It was a terrible thing to dread that one's own father would take the crown. Malcolm was ineffectual but Donalbain, with his lust for fortune-telling and his reliance on the three strange women out on the heath, would be unpredictable – possibly even dangerous.

Chapter Eleven
Lochaber District

It was only the shepherd's command of the moment that saved both his wife and Fleance from breaking into pieces.

Agnes had dropped the ladle and fallen back against her husband. 'Him,' she cried. ''Tis him.'

Fleance's stomach lurched. Did she know him? Was she part of the plot? How was it that he had stumbled upon a dwelling where his safety was challenged?

'Madam,' Fleance cried. 'I'm no danger to you.'

'A ghost. A ghost,' she cried. 'Michael, 'tis the master come back.'

'What are you talking about woman?' Michael said, but looking at Fleance with new concern. ''Tis just a lad I found on the road.'

Agnes collapsed onto a stool but did not take her eyes from Fleance. 'You look just like him,' she whispered. 'Just like my wee man.'

Fleance swallowed and cleared his throat. 'Who are you talking of, madam?'

'Banquo, the Thane of Lochaber. General of the king's army. Most brave and honourable soldier.'

His heart froze. She was talking about his father. 'I am not he, I assure you.'

'An' he's no ghost, love. He's flesh and blood. Here,' Michael pulled his wife up and brought her before Fleance. 'Touch the lad – he's as real as you and I.'

The old woman reached out a shaking hand and poked at Fleance which might have been humorous at another time. But at this moment, the cottage was charged with fear and high emotion.

'Michael,' Agnes said, as if Fleance was not in front of her, 'He's the spitting image of wee Banquo. I swear he's him or he's kin.' She clutched her hand to her breasts. 'I need to sit again.'

Fleance was horrified to see tears coursing down her cheeks. 'My poor Banquo. Slain, 'twas said, by his son. My brave master whom I taught to sing and tell stories. My charge that drank in the stories of old that my mam had told me.'

Michael shifted a stool and put his hand on hers which trembled in her lap. 'Agnes, dear. That is long past. You're dreaming now. 'Tis not him.' He stood up. 'I think we should take her to her cot,' he said to Fleance.

Agnes waved him away. 'I'm not stupid, man. My bones may be old but my mind is as sharp as yours.' She looked at Fleance. 'If you're not Banquo then, are you kin to him?'

What to do? Fleance had no memory of this woman in his home. He did know that his father spoke fondly of his nursing maid and the stories she told him. Could this be her? If so, on whose side had she stood – and what about her husband? Were they for the house of Lochaber or against?

Not wanting to be rude and dishonour the offered hospitality, Fleance decided he needed more information. 'Mother, how did the news of Banquo's murder come to you?'

'How?' she squeaked. 'We received posts after the crowning of that most fiendish tyrant Macbeth, our Banquo was murdered and his son, Fleance, escaped – the boy the culprit.' She paused, took in a deep breath. 'I can say that I didn't believe a word of it. Sure, the boy was hot blooded and Banquo spent many an hour schooling his son on keeping his temper, but to murder his father? Never. Though I was past nursing duties and removed to the kitchen, I had seen him with his boy.'

Michael nodded. 'Aye, that is a memory I have as well. The master with his only son spending long days hunting and playing. They shared a most amicable relationship.'

It was clear that the couple had had a connection with his father but, for Fleance, it was not enough to assure him he was safe. 'How stands it with you and the state of Scotland?'

The couple shared a look between them. 'We could ask the same of you,' Michael said.

He was being challenged. Fleance looked at the couple and made a decision. 'I am Fleance. Banquo's son.' Agnes let out a wail and fell against her husband.

After that, it was a tumult of words and cries and exhortations as Fleance and the poor shepherd couple began to piece together their broken world. Even the wee lamb joined in with cries so that Michael was forced to stop attending his wife and see to the feeding of it.

Once Agnes had been comforted and restored, sitting before the hearth, gently stroking the lamb, Fleance told his story. 'For these past ten years, I have been living in England and have no firm thoughts about the state of Scotland save that I know the king is ill and his brother is like to succeed him.'

Agnes cleared her throat. 'So, young man. Why have you come back apart from what you say?'

'Aye,' Michael said as he leant forward. 'Why are you here, lad? This is far from the usual road and only someone with a definite purpose would venture into these hills.'

Fleance looked at both of them. If he told the truth, would it appear he was mad? He sighed deeply. 'I am plagued with dreams and visions and supernatural soliciting. I cannot rest until I fulfil my father's wishes.' It was quiet in the cottage. 'And I have come back to Scotland to avenge my father's murder.'

'So,' asked Agnes, 'your father is nagging at you.'

Fleance smiled ruefully. It had taken him ten years and hundreds of miles, yet here in this humble shepherd's hut, he had finally found someone who understood what he was going through. He replied, 'That is true.'

Michael stirred. 'Well, then, you have a quest. This seems reasonable.' He got up and stirred the stew. 'Perhaps we should eat and we can tell you what happened after your father's murder.'

Agnes laid the plates and spoons on the wooden table. She lifted out a loaf of bread from a pot which sat above the fireplace and put that on the table as well. Michael brought the stew over to the table and she began serving. Once three bowls had been filled and Michael had removed the pot, they sat down.

'Let us give thanks to the Lord for this food,' Michael said, and he and Agnes closed their eyes and bowed their heads. Fleance quickly followed suit. 'Father in heaven,' Michael prayed. 'We give Thee thanks this day for our daily bread and ask that Thou bless this meal to our bodies. In the name of the Father, Son and Holy Ghost, Amen.'

Both Agnes and Fleance murmured, 'Amen.'

'Would you have some bread then, Fleance?' Agnes asked, offering him a thick, dark slice.

'Thank you,' he said and took the bread and dipped it into the stew. There was an explosion of flavours in his mouth. Michael had not been exaggerating. The stew was delicious. 'This is the best stew I've ever tasted,' he exclaimed.

Michael laughed. 'I did warn you. But I'm sure your keen appetite is adding to the quality.' Agnes snorted. 'No offence, my love.'

Fleance smiled. 'It's still the best I've tasted and my adoptive mother is a very fine cook. She would be most displeased, I bargain, to hear me say this about your dish, Agnes.' They ate in silence for a while and then, when he'd finished his first bowl and Agnes got up to fill it again, he asked, 'Could you tell me more about what happened here after my father's murder?'

Michael waited for his own bowl to be refilled and for Agnes to return to her seat before he began. 'It was true, what Agnes said, that word quickly spread you had killed your father, but those of us who knew the family well did not believe for a moment that was the truth.' Agnes shook her head in agreement. 'With you disappeared as well meant we all, at the manor, felt the loss of your family. Father and heir – gone in one swift stroke of the sword.'

'For the next eight months, life was difficult at the fortress with strange soldiers arriving at dawn to herd out the serving staff. Great groups of faithful workers were sent away. It has now been nine winters since Agnes and I were forced to come to this valley to take care of the ragged land and make enough means to give the lord of the manor a satisfied harvest.'

'Once my Banquo was gone,' Agnes said, 'there was no joy left in the place.' Fleance remembered that, although their manor on the Lochaber boundary was a desolated and harsh place, it had been a place filled with laughter, stories and song. This was a memory that would always be with Fleance. 'We were most glad to be rid of the place. Macbeth's legacy still remains despite the king's efforts to bring healing.'

'But,' Fleance said, 'I remember both Macbeth and his wife being so kind.'

'That may be, lad,' Michael said. 'But it seems that what we see does not necessarily show the truth of the situation.'

So, Fleance learnt the facts as the couple understood them. Banquo had been murdered and his son painted as an irredeemable murderer. Because the times were still unsettled, it was good that he had kept well hidden.

'Do you know, lad, if all them fellows sent to destroy your father and you are gone?'

This was the nagging problem. 'No, I don't,' he said. 'I just know, to fix my future, and be free from my father's ever-watchful presence, I need to do what he has commanded of me.'

The couple, again, shared a look. It did not fill Fleance with hope.

'Well then, boy, you've got a great task ahead of you,' Michael said, 'and I don't think we're in a place to offer much more. You will have to go back to Lochaber because, though there is unlikely to be anyone from your time still there, you may happen upon some information that can show you the way forward.'

Michael was a realist. Fleance had to travel back to his home but it was unlikely there would be much joy in finding out what he was supposed to do. But, for his own heart, he desired to go back to at least have one final look at the place of his childhood.

They sat there for a long time discussing things back and forward until the topic moved to more pleasant recollections. Fleance said, 'I do remember Da saying my temper was a beast to master.' He smiled, the late-night air bringing soft remembrances.

Michael chuckled. 'From all accounts, lad, you were not the easiest bairn to raise.'

He got up and stoked the fire which had burned low. One of the candles had gone out in the telling of stories so he replenished them. It was pleasing that the extra light came into the tiny cottage. 'It is late. Tomorrow's dawn brings fresh challenges. I suggest we retire.'

Agnes spread some hay in front of the hearth and laid a blanket on it. 'I hope you will be comfortable here,' she said.

'Thank you again for your most generous hospitality,' Fleance replied. He watched for the old couple to retire behind a curtain before taking off his boots, blowing out the candles and lying down on the makeshift bed. In the darkness he listened to the sounds of the wind buffeting the roof, the whispers of Michael and Agnes and the soft snores of the lamb. Soon, exhaustion, good food and high emotion pulled him into a deep sleep.

Fleance was on the heath with his father. They were practising accuracy with the crossbow. Banquo always, every time, hit the bullseye. Fleance's attempts were more than erratic.

After another misfire, he threw the crossbow to the ground. 'Pox on it,' he shouted. 'The thing's bewitched. I had the sight, and the bolt should have gone true.' He turned to his father. 'I need another weapon – this one is useless.'

Banquo quietly picked up the crossbow and handed it to Fleance. 'Son, this bow was made by the finest craftsman you could find in Scotland. 'Tis not the instrument but the player who is lacking.'

Fleance glared. The shame of failure burned his soul. 'No,' he shouted. ''Tis the bow. I have had better times with it before today.'

Banquo put a hand on Fleance's shoulder. 'True, boy. And that is because you were in a better state of mind than you are now. Tell me,' he said quietly. 'What is bothering you?'

Fleance couldn't help it. Tears sprang from his eyes. 'I miss Ma,' he said. 'One of the boys was laughing about how his ma always does silly tricks and I remembered, Da, I remembered Ma being so good with her stories and tricks.' Now he was sobbing and Banquo pulled him into an embrace.

'Aye, lad, I miss her too. She was a fine woman.' His father held him there for a long time until Fleance's sobs abated. Banquo pushed him in front. 'So, aim to gain a woman as fine but now let's turn back to the stroppy airs of this weapon which has a need of conquering.'

Viciously wiping the wet tears from his young face, Fleance picked up the weapon, loaded it and, with renewed energy, set about getting the target so that, each time, it was a bullseye.

Fleance woke to the sound of movement around the cottage. Agnes struck a flint to some kindling and Fleance watched it flare and give life and light to the lantern. He sat up. Agnes, though elderly, had good hearing and she turned.

'Good morning. I did not mean to disturb you.'

'It is fine. My limbs are still weary but my mind is alert.'

'I'll get this fire going and we'll have breakfast soon.' Agnes set about stoking the fire then she lifted up an iron pot. 'Michael will be in after he has checked the flock. That wee one,' she said, pointing to the lamb, 'will be hungry.' As if to confirm this, the lamb wiggled its tail and gave a plaintive bleat.

Fleance sat up and stretched his arms above his head to get rid of the stiffness in his back. 'Let me do that for you,' he said, pulling on his boots.

'That's very kind of you,' Agnes said and passed him the pot. 'The stream is down the path – you can't miss it.'

He took the pot and went out into the cold morning. The sun was barely up but it made no difference because a thick mist shrouded the countryside. Fleance had to search for the rough path that meandered downhill. He was completely enveloped by the cloud and mist and could barely find his way.

Fleance hesitated. He was surrounded and he had the strongest feeling that the mist was hiding something from him.

Perhaps he should head back because he certainly couldn't hear the stream as Agnes had suggested; perhaps he had taken the wrong path. Perhaps he was in the wrong place. He thought of turning back to the cottage to let Agnes know he was lost but could not bring himself to admit defeat.

Then, no sooner had he thought that, than the bubbling sound of water on rock reached his ears. Thank God.

Within moments of hearing the water, and despite the thick fog which engulfed him, Fleance stumbled upon the small stream which flowed along the path of these rocky outlands.

He filled the pot and turned to face the uphill journey. Getting lost, or at least thinking he might have been and feeling anxious, was a small sacrifice for him compared with what these poor shepherd folk had offered: hearth, hospitality, a haven.

As he trudged up the hill, he went over the events of the night before when Agnes had screamed at the sight of him. He'd learnt so much but he still needed to sift through the details.

Later that morning, as Fleance tacked up Willow, Michael approached. 'Lad,' he said. 'The manor is not as you remember. There be strangers who lord over the castle and the battlements. These are not men who care about your father or the king. Do not declare yourself but, if you keep eyes and ears open more than your mouth, you are certain to find some information without risk to you or to your quest.'

Fleance turned towards the old man. 'Thank you again for your hospitality and kindness. It seems to me that the righting of truth and restoration lies not with single acts but a combination of fellows determined to make the world right.'

Chapter Twelve

Michael's words rang true. It was not as Fleance remembered. Despite three days' trekking, the sight of the castle brought no joy; no relief. Again the mist had sunk low so that Willow was the only reliable means to ensure they headed in the right direction. Some things were familiar, however: the strange outcrop of rock hanging over the road, which Fleance had told his father reminded him of a squatting toad and was thereafter referred to as Toad Rock.

When he did reach the place in the road – which he remembered looked out over a tenement – he could, in fact, see nothing for the swirling sea mist had moved in and surrounded everything. It seemed to Fleance as if he was looking out upon a vast lake with only a few peaks jutting up through the water.

He nudged the horse forward and they began the descent into the valley that held Lochaber, the kingdom's outermost post; the stronghold sited to fend off would-be attackers from the sea. Such was his father's reputation and valour, that King Duncan had given Banquo this thanage – a fierce and faithful warrior who would protect Scotland's weakest flank.

All was quiet. The damp mist swirled away from the horse's movements but muffled all sights and all sounds. Willow stepped deliberately, one careful hoof in front of the other, his large steps jolting Fleance so that the young man rocked from side to side on the saddle. Down. Down. And, with each yard, Fleance's heart beat faster. Though he was chilled, a warmth travelled up his spine and the back of his neck – a heated sense of foreboding

'Halt!' A voice called from within the cloud. 'Name and county.'

Stupidly, Fleance had not reckoned on an encounter such as this. To stall, and to mask, he replied, 'County Fife. The name's . . .' He hesitated. 'The name's Magness. I'm Magness of Fife.'

A lone shadow appeared. Fleance immediately took in the armour, the weaponry. 'Your business, man.'

Stupid, stupid, Fleance thought. Why had he not worked out a story, a plan. 'I lost my way. A shepherd a few days back said I might find rest and food if I kept on.'

The soldier came up to Willow. ''Tis a mighty fine horse you ride.'

'Aye, he was my father's.'

'An' you're from Fife, you say?'

'Aye.'

The soldier pulled off his helmet. He was about Fleance's age. 'That don't explain why you're on this road, coming to this castle.'

'I'm on a pilgrimage,' Fleance said. 'My father oft visited these parts as a lad. I'm looking to honour his memory.'

'He's dead then?'

'Aye.'

The soldier eyed him suspiciously. 'The master does not welcome visitors.'

Fleance sighed wearily. 'Well, man, can I not just water my horse, get some food and have a day's rest? I'll not be any trouble.'

There was a moment's hesitation. 'The master is away at this time. He would not care to know that a stranger had taken advantage of his manor.'

Fleance pressed on. 'Surely, the Master of all masters commands us to open our homes to strangers and the needy.'

He saw the soldier stiffen. 'Aye, but we are not a monastery.'

Still, Fleance could see he was making inroads into this young man's conscience. 'Come on, man. My horse and I are in need of a good night's rest. Surely, your household can accommodate me, just for one night.'

The soldier stood straight in front of Willow. 'I think it would be unwise, sir, for you to proceed.'

'I'm no threat. I'm just looking to feed and rest my horse. For God's sake, please grant me access.'

'What ho, Wallace? Who goes here?' Another shadow came forth.

''Tis a man who says he is on a pilgrimage and just wants rest for himself and his horse.'

Another armed soldier came forward. This man had no face armour and his hair was as white as the mist which surrounded them all. 'Greetings,' he called to Fleance. 'Is what young Wallace says true?'

'Aye, father. I am from Fife.' (The lie stung Fleance.) 'And I know my father, who died in battle for King Duncan, came to these parts. He spoke often about them.'

''Tis his father's horse,' Wallace offered, obviously eager to add to the story.

'And you are wanting, what, from our place?'

'Rest, food and repose, so please you.'

'All because your father came to these parts?' the old soldier asked.

'Aye,' said Fleance.

The old man and the young man looked at each other and moved away from Fleance's hearing. After a long time, they came to him, Wallace speaking. 'Magness of Fife, you are welcomed to Lochaber.'

Fleance bowed his head. 'For this, I am most grateful.'

'But you will surrender your weapons.'

Fleance gave over his crossbow, his father's sword and Magness's dirk. He was uncomfortable entering this place unarmed but he could ask no more of these suspicious people.

'And will I get these back when I leave?'

'Indeed,' the old soldier replied. 'Now, if you would dismount your horse.'

Fleance did as he was told, quietly relieved to use his legs. He lifted the reins over Willow's head and followed the two soldiers down the track.

As they came upon the flat, Fleance's eyes stung. This was so familiar. This was his home. There were the cottages of those who worked the fields. There was the stone wall he'd sat upon and cried when his mother had died. That was the oak tree which he'd climbed to hide from his father the day he'd smashed the first crossbow he'd received.

The old soldier spoke. 'This crop is ripe for harvest and we are well pleased. Many years ago, the previous thane declared it important that each field have a different crop which should be rotated about the seasons to save nutrients and to encourage growth. It was good counsel and the current master has kept the practice.'

Fleance knew this because he had been there when his father had argued with the workers about how they should till the soil and make it produce. Despite the sea mist, Fleance could see a strong stand of barley and he felt pleased. His father's quiet wisdom and patience was still having a positive effect even ten years after his death.

Then they came upon the castle. Fleance's heart lurched and ached. This was his home – and yet it wasn't: his father was not here and his nurse was not here and there were now none who knew him, who were tolerant of his tempers. And he was no longer a boy but a man. Fleance wanted time to mourn for his place in this setting but that would betray him and his purpose.

Instead, he was compliant and went to the stable to bed Willow down. The horse knew his way and made it easier for Fleance. What else could he do to ensure his father's horse was treated to the best?

'I will send someone to you with food and drink,' the young soldier said.

'Many thanks,' Fleance said, 'I will stay with my horse for a while – to settle him in.'

The older soldier nodded towards Willow. 'Seems well settled already. He's got an air about him as if he's the lord of these stables.'

Willow stopped munching on the hay and turned his head around and gave the soldier a look. Then he snorted again and went back to his dinner. The soldier laughed. 'And it seems he can understand us.'

'Aye, he can.' Fleance rubbed Willow's rump. 'He's a faithful beast but we have arguments sometimes.'

'We must return to our post. Supper will be along soon.' The two guards, carrying his weapons still, walked out of the stables and were engulfed by the mist, though Fleance could still hear their tramping feet and the sound of their quiet conversation.

The stable was almost deserted. A small horse stood dozing in an end stall, disinterested in the new arrivals. In his time, it had always been filled with horses and stablehands. Perhaps the new master was away with a group of his men. That would explain the state of the building.

Who was this new master? The soldiers had not named him. Why were they so distrustful and nervous? It would bring some satisfaction at least to learn the name of the one who now resided in his home.

Fleance pushed a pile of dry and dusty straw into one of the empty stalls and laid his cloak over it. A better host would have offered him a warmer bed and perhaps a fire. It looked like he was going to be in for a chilly night.

He looked around the gloomy building – little was different with what he remembered save it seemed more run-down and neglected: long, thick spider webs filled the spaces between the beams and the saddles all looked in need of oiling. Fleance ran his hand down one of the bridles – it was for a small horse, perhaps the one asleep in the stall. Perhaps the master had a child.

There was a cough behind him and Fleance spun around. Standing in the doorway of the stables was a young man, about his age. He carried a tray of food. 'Your supper, sir.'

When the servant lifted his eyes to Fleance's face, he paled. It was a repeat performance of the night at the shepherd's cottage.

'Flea?' the young man gasped. 'Is that you?'

Fleance felt a dreadful clutch of recognition. 'Blair?'

'Aye,' Blair said. ''Tis me, Sire. What are you doing here? I thought you long dead.' Fleance went to him and relieved him of the tray of food. Blair just stared.

Fleance set the tray on the dusty workbench which ran along the side wall of the stable. 'I'm alive and well, Blair.'

'I never thought I'd see you again.' Blair stepped forward and grabbed Fleance's shoulders. 'My but you look like your da.' He grinned widely. 'It's so good to see you again. I have missed you.'

Fleance had forgotten about Blair's tendency to emotion. To hide his embarrassment, he turned to the tray, broke off a chunk of bread and, using the blunt knife (rendered useless as a weapon – he understood the choice of utensil), cut off some cheese. Generously, there was wine in the jug. Perhaps the soldiers meant for him to get drunk.

Blair stood mutely beside him and watched as he devoured the food.

As he chewed, swift memories of the two of them hunting sparrows and playing battle games down by the creek came to Fleance. Fleance had always won these because, if Blair should take the upper hand, Fleance's temper flared and the servant beat a hasty retreat. But Blair had been, despite his low status, Fleance's best friend.

'I missed you,' Blair said quietly. 'And never for one moment did I listen to that gossip that said you killed your da.'

Fleance looked at him sharply. 'I loved my father. He was murdered. We were set upon not far from Forres, the night of Macbeth's coronation.'

Blair looked about nervously and then spied Willow. 'Can it be?' He walked over to the horse. 'Willow?' Willow whinnied and pushed his nose into Blair's stomach. 'Oh, how it pleases my heart to see you.' Blair had been Willow's groom. It had been his sole responsibility to feed and groom the master's horse. Banquo had chosen him because, though he was a young lad, he'd shown a special skill with animals.

'Aye,' said Fleance. 'He's been my constant companion since that dreadful night.' He drank down a tumbler of wine. 'Sometimes he's been the only thing keeping me in my right wits.'

Blair looked over at him. 'Why are you here? This place is not like you will have remembered. Now, we all work looking over our shoulders, shielding our backs for fear that we will be sent packing with nothing more that the clothes on our backs.'

Fleance frowned. 'Who is this master that seems to fill all here with dread?'

'Chattan. He's cousin to the Earl of Ross. Some call him the cat because he goes about his business quietly. Macbeth gave him this castle and the thaneship and King Malcolm does not know for sure if he be for or against him. He cannot remove the master but word is he doesn't trust him either.'

'Where is Chattan now?'

'Abroad but we know not where. Some say Normandy; others Norway; some even say he's carousing with the English.' Blair stroked Willow's nose and pressed his face into the horse. 'Ah,

Willow. 'Tis so good to see you again.' The horse, as if understanding him, quietly whickered. It was not a sound Fleance had heard the horse make since they'd left Lochaber on their fateful journey to Inverness all those years ago.

'Why did you come back, Blair? Could you not find service in another manor?'

'Well,' Blair said. 'This is my home and where I want to be. I'd worked a few farms beyond the Highlands with my father but then Da succumbed to the cough and I had to travel on alone. 'Twas lonely, Flea, and I didn't know where I should I go, but one night I had a dream: your da, he came to me and he said "Go back and be bold". So, that is what I did.'

'Da came to you?'

'Aye. Like flesh and blood he stood in front of me and told me what I must do.'

This was almost too much for Fleance. He believed he was the only one to carry out his father's wishes yet now, in truth, his friend had also been visited by the ghostly Banquo.

Blair wanted more information. 'Why are you here?' he asked again 'What good did you think could come out of it? If they knew who you were, they'd cut your throat as soon as look at you. You're the rightful heir to this place and would be seen as a threat to the master.'

Fleance sighed. 'Truth be told, I've come for information. I need to find out who was responsible for my father's murder. I thought maybe those who had been invested here might have had a connection to that night.'

Blair ran a hand through his curly red hair. It pained Fleance to see the young man so pale, with dark smudges under his eyes. He was thin, too, a far cry from the chunky boy Fleance worked hard to wrestle to the ground. Blair, though, seemed unaware of his physical state and was keen to answer Fleance's question. 'But it was Macbeth who put the master here. Do you think he killed your father?'

Fleance nodded. 'He was at the castle but perhaps one of his supporters saw my father as a threat. I don't know for sure.'

'When I was in Fife, I heard talk about the thane Macduff. That he'd lost all the inhabitants of his castle to the sword. Some fiend, which they think was Macbeth, had ordered their slaughter. They said Macduff, who killed the tyrant, knew the workings of that madman's mind. Perhaps if you travel to Fife, you may seek an audience with him. He may have information that could help you. I think you'll find him a trustworthy soul for I've never heard a bad word against the thane.'

'I remember the name,' Flea replied. 'My father spoke highly of him; but why do you think he could help?'

'Well, the story goes that Macbeth was pacing his castle shouting that none of woman borne could harm him and then Macduff shouts out that he was not of woman borne.'

'How can that be?' Fleance asked, puzzled at the riddle.

'He was cut from his mother's stomach. Macbeth comes onto the balcony and looks down upon Macduff and says, "I have too much blood of yours on my hands".'

'God in heaven,' Flea exclaimed. 'That means he must have murdered Macduff's entire family.'

'Aye, so it seems. Macduff tells him to surrender and give the crown to Malcolm but Macbeth says he would not be like a Roman fool and die on his own sword. So off they went, sword to sword into the bowels of the castle until Macduff appeared with Macbeth's head to lay at Malcolm's feet.' Blair propped himself on a barrel. 'Shouts could be heard but no one could make out what they were saying. Perhaps Macduff can tell you some confession Macbeth made.'

Fleance was amazed. 'You've not lost your art of storytelling, Blair.'

Blair shrugged. ''Tis a pretty powerful story to repeat.'

Fleance thought for a moment. 'This master of yours . . .'

'Blair!'

Both Fleance and Blair jumped. It was Wallace, the young soldier. 'What are you doing? You are missed in the kitchen.' Wallace glared at them. 'I have been sent by cook to find you. A lowly task for a soldier, methinks, and one I don't want to repeat.'

'Sorry. I was just ensuring our guest was well accommodated.'

'That is not your brief. Back to the kitchen.'

Blair gave Fleance an apologetic smile before walking out of the stable. Wallace stood staring at Fleance for some minutes before returning to the mist.

Chapter Thirteen

The night was clear of cloud and the moon was rising, a swollen ball of yellow above the horizon. 'Do you think, Flea, that fate controls our lives or that we have the freedom to choose our own path?'

'I'd like to think I was in charge of my own destiny but,' he hesitated, stroking Rosie's hand, 'often I feel that my life is not my own – that I don't have the freedom you speak of.' He turned to her. 'What do you think?'

She thought for a moment. 'I think that we are not alone.' She stared at the moon. 'There's someone – something – watching over us.'

'You mean God?'

'I suppose but more of a feeling that there are powers guiding us a little like an autumn breeze with a thistledown tossed about. That, if things are meant to be, they will be.' She looked up into his face. 'This same power brought you to me and, no matter what life brings, I know it will keep us together always.'

His heart swelled with deep affection. Her words named his secret hope.

'Do you ever get that feeling that, even when you are by yourself, that someone or something is aware of you?' Rosie asked.

Like a cold finger down his spine, Fleance felt her words chill him for she had spoken out loud his very fear.

It was still dark when Wallace, the young soldier, came into the stable carrying a flaming torch. 'Magness!' he called. 'Magness of Fife. 'Tis time for you to leave.' It took a few moments for Fleance to realise the soldier was speaking to him.

'Aye, I'm awake.' He sat up groggily. The night had been full of dreams and visions and he'd not rested well. He flailed around for his boots and instinctively reached for his dirk. It was not there – of course, they'd taken his weapons. 'Thank you for the timely alarm.' Though, of course, Fleance understood well enough that the soldier had intended to unsettle him.

His kind comments seemed to fluster the young soldier who had obviously tried to be intimidating. 'We will escort you to the place we found you.'

Fleance was on his feet and gathering his things. It was clear it would be too much to expect some food before he set off. Still, at least Willow was well fed and watered. He could top up his water skin and later happen upon some wild fruits until he came to a town.

Willow, alerted by the light and the noise, stamped his feet. Fleance saddled him and put on his bridle, gently speaking kind words to settle the animal. Willow did not like early mornings, a fact which Fleance had learnt many years ago and which, as the horse had aged, had become more obvious.

He led his horse out of the stable and, as they walked into the clearing, looked towards the castle. Lights were blazing from almost every room. Why would this be at such an ungodly time?

As if reading his thoughts, Wallace spoke. 'A messenger has come to say the master's on his way.' It occurred to Fleance then, that this soldier was not trying to intimidate him but to rescue both himself and Fleance. For a stranger to be found on the property when obviously strict instructions had been given to the contrary, would not bode well for the old soldier and Wallace.

Out of the dark, the old soldier appeared, carrying Fleance's weapons.

Fleance spoke. 'I thank you both. I enjoyed good rest and repose as did my horse. I am certain that God in heaven will reward you for your kindness.'

The soldiers said nothing but shared a furtive glance. The three trudged on up the steep incline, the only sound their footfalls and Willow's annoyed snorting. At the ridge where he was met yesterday, they stopped. The old soldier handed him the crossbow, dirk and then sword which Fleance secured in the scabbard. The dirk he put in his belt. He put one foot into a stirrup and gathered the reins. As he swung up onto Willow, he tucked the crossbow into the strap on his back. He turned to the soldiers. 'Again, I thank you. I hope one day to meet you again under less difficult circumstances.'

'Indeed,' replied the old soldier and, flicking Wallace's arm, he turned back and marched stiffly down the road.

It was difficult to see where he was going but coming to Lochaber had not borne the fruit he'd hoped for. Yes, it had been good to see Blair; yes, it had been good to see the castle. But it was not good to know that there were dark lords still in power around the country. It would be several days before he made it to Perth where he hoped to rest and then another few days' travel till he reached Fife. He would stop in at Michael and Agnes's cottage one night as they had suggested; neither he nor Willow would last the distance.

About mid-morning, Fleance dismounted to give the horse a rest and continued walking along the road. His eyes scanned the fields on either side in the hope he would find something to dull the ache of hunger which had been gnawing away for the past three hours.

Being late autumn, there may still be something, Fleance thought. After thirty minutes, the search yielded nothing save a bird-pecked berry hedge. He would have to set up a camp soon and do some hunting. He had seen plenty of rabbits running across the heath and the pock-marked holes in the dusty road told the tale of their workings.

He spied a cluster of trees down in a valley so he led the horse off the road, taking great care to avoid the treacherous rabbit holes. As he expected, there was a small body of water, a swamp which gave life to the crop of trees. He tethered the horse, removed his crossbow and loaded it with a bolt.

'I won't be long,' he said to the horse, patting him fondly on the neck and went out in search of his breakfast, dinner and supper.

Already the mist was coming in so he needed to work quickly. He spied a colony of rabbits across a small valley. Unfortunately, it was too far to attempt a shot so, as quietly as he could, Fleance jogged down the hill and, keeping up wind (not that there was much), he came around to the right of the rabbits, which were grazing. He looked over them and found the fattest. He took aim, squeezed the trigger and instantly the bolt found its target, the force sending the rabbit further up the hill. The rest scattered and Fleance ran up to his kill. It was still struggling so he picked it up by the hind legs and swung it against a nearby rock, shattering its skull and putting it out of its misery.

He removed the bolt and wiped it on the grass. Then, with the rabbit swinging upside down, he jogged back to his camp and Willow.

The water looked unpalatable so he chose not to drink it; however, he used it to clean the rabbit and his weapon after gutting and skinning his kill. With his dirk, he dug a hole in the ground and buried the skin and entrails. Though the skin would have fetched a very good price, this was not the time nor the situation to bother with such enterprise. The waste grieved him.

It took a while for the fire to light as the fog made the twigs and leaves damp. He found a sharp stick, skewered the rabbit and then set it between two upright sticks. It would be some time before the meal was ready so Fleance pulled his cloak tighter and sat, staring into the flames.

As he fed the small fire and turned the rabbit, he remembered the first time he'd felt true hunger.

Nearly a week after his father's murder, Fleance had left the ruins and was almost delirious with hunger. His head ached and his lips were chapped and swollen. He had managed to find water but nothing to eat. He'd left his crossbow back at Macbeth's castle. Though he still had his father's sword, it was too heavy to lift. As Willow plodded on, Fleance sunk into himself. He could not allow himself to sleep – he might fall but worse, he might be set upon.

The sun was beginning to go down and still he had not found shelter or a friendly cottage where he might ask for supper. He came to a rise in the road, clambered off and sank down against the rocks. Willow snatched at the grass, ignoring his young rider.

Suddenly, Fleance was overwhelmed. Tears spilled down his face and great, choking gasps escaped from his mouth. He felt as if his heart was tearing in two. The sound of his father's cries and his murder, the shock at his loss and his burning hunger all caught up with him. He wept for his father. He wept because he had been so afraid and he wept because he did not know what to do.

He was in a foreign part of the country with no friends, no kin and too disturbed to make sense of the last few days. Such was the sound of his sobbing that he did not hear the approach of a cart and horse. It wasn't until Willow alerted him with his whinny that Fleance looked up to see it was almost upon him.

His heart jolted with fear but his body held no strength to flee.

'Whoa, there,' a man's deep voice cried. The man pulled on the cart's brake and jumped down. 'What have we here?'

Fleance struggled to get up but he could not do it on his own. The man held out his hand and Fleance took it, certain that this was to be the end. He would be taken back to Inverness and meet the same fate as his father, of this he was sure.

However, the man pulled him up and studied him intently. 'Miri,' the man called, holding him as Fleance was too weak to stand unaided. 'This wee lad needs some help.' Fleance had been unaware that the cart contained two people – a man and a woman.

Miri climbed off the cart and came around. 'Oh, you poor wee babe – I can see you're starving. Magness, get the boy some bread and wine. I'll help him back on the grass for a bit.'

Her husband spoke gently to him. 'What's your name then, boy?'

Fleance turned to him and in that moment he made a decision: he would keep his identity a secret until he was old enough to understand what had happened.

'Flea,' he said – the nickname Blair had given him from an early age when the boy had a stutter and could not finish pronouncing Fleance's name. 'I am Flea.'

Magness went to the back of the cart and came back with food and drink. 'The name suits you, lad – small and jumpy.'

Miri helped him take a sip of wine. It burned his throat and he coughed and spluttered. 'There, there, lad. Just take it slowly.' In silence the couple watched him eat. After a while, Miri took the food away. 'Looks like you haven't eaten in days. If you eat too much now, you'll bring it all back again and that would be a waste of my cooking.'

Fleance nodded and wiped his mouth. 'Thank you,' he said.

'Where are you going?' Magness asked quietly. Fleance shrugged. 'Where is home, lad?' Again Fleance shrugged. A look passed between the couple. 'Would you like to travel with us for a wee while?' He looked into the eyes of the man and saw kindness and compassion. But also something else: a look of one who had seen much and who had experienced deep sorrow.

'We're going across the border to England,' Miri said, and Fleance was troubled to see her eyes fill with tears.

'I have no kin,' Fleance said. 'I have no one now to take care of me.'

Miri patted his arm. 'Looks like the Lord has seen fit to give you some new kin.' She helped him to his feet. 'You can ride in the cart. I'm sure your horse would appreciate a rest from its rider.'

They tied Willow to the back of the cart and Magness lifted Fleance as easily as if he was a small child and laid him in the wagon. And that was the start of the next part of his life's story.

Chapter Fourteen
Glamis Castle

Duncan awoke to the sounds of his father shouting in the courtyard. 'Up, you lazy fellows. Did you not hear the cock crow? Awake!'

He opened his casement and looked down upon the frantic scurrying of the stablehands. His father was standing in the middle, giving orders at the top of his voice. Preston and Calum were nowhere to be seen. It was quite likely that Donalbain had not gone to bed and had slipped into that feverous state of a man who lacks sleep – nature's balm for disturbed minds.

Duncan dressed quickly and went downstairs. Donalbain's tirade had awoken the whole castle, so that servants were rushing to and fro to their duties in case their master demanded something of them as well at this godforsaken time.

The shouting stopped abruptly, and in the strange quiet there was the sound of a horse galloping out of the castle gates. Duncan suspected his father was heading to the weird sisters and wondered if he would be back later that day for supper, or whether they could enjoy a meal with laughter and light conversation.

It was to be as Duncan had hoped, and he and his sisters enjoyed an intimate and happy supper with Bree telling tales and teasing Duncan and Rachel, scolding them good-heartedly.

Rachel summoned one of the servants. 'Call the nurse to take Bree up.' She turned back to her sister. 'It is well past time for you to be in bed.'

Bree frowned. 'But I'm not tired, Rachel.'

'You never are,' Duncan said. 'You've as much energy as Zeus after he's been lying in the catnip.'

She giggled but stopped when the doors to the dining chamber opened and her nurse came forward. Bree put her hands on her hips. 'I don't want to go to bed,' she howled and stomped her foot. 'It's not fair that you get to stay up late and I have to go to my room.'

'Bree, you are only a child. This is the time for all children to be in bed,' Rachel said calmly.

'But I'm special,' she said.

'And that you are, my dear, and because you are, we must ensure you get enough sleep to grow tall and strong.'

Bree hesitated. 'What happens when you sleep?' she asked.

'The angels come and sprinkle your head with growing dust.' Bree looked from her sister back to her brother, her frown betraying her uncertainty.

'It's true. Why don't we measure you now, and in the morning, I warrant you will have grown,' said Duncan.

Bree walked to the large oak door and stood against it. She was very still and Duncan could see she was holding herself as tall and straight as she could. Solemnly, he marked the spot above her head and then put his hand under her chin. 'It won't happen, Bree, if you don't sleep.'

Bree refused the nurse's hand. 'We shall do this again before breakfast to prove that you are not a liar.'

'You know I am not.'

'Night then, Duncan.'

'Sleep well, chook. I will see you, no doubt, very early in the morning.'

Bree turned to her sister. 'But can I still have your story tonight, Rachel?'

'Of course. We can't leave our hero wandering the moors for too long.'

That seemed to satisfy her and she was surprisingly obedient and followed her nurse through the door.

Duncan signalled for the servants to clear the dishes. When the table was cleared, he stood up. 'Will you join me after the story for a warm drink in the blue room?' The blue room had been called that by the children from the first day they arrived back to the castle. It was a smaller room than most in the castle but their mother had lined the walls with thick tapestry, the most overwhelming colour being blue with pictures of seas and lakes and lochs and all who lived on them and under them. It was a room their father hated for he said it reminded him too much of their mother. Rachel and Duncan adored it.

The fire had been burning for some time so there was a cosy warmth that contrasted with the chilly dining hall. Rachel returned, took her place in her chair and accepted a goblet of warm wine from one of the servants. Duncan did the same and then dismissed them.

It was a relief coming to the end of the day.

'Where did Father go?' Rachel asked.

'I don't know. He was in a right mood this morning. I asked Calum but he was none the wiser either. Seems, though the aides tell Donalbain a lot, he tells them very little.'

Rachel shot him a look. 'Remember what I told you, Duncan; 'tis not your worry.'

'Aye, but I can't just sit about waiting for things to happen.'

'Why not? You're not the king and you're not the head of this house . . .'

'I may not be the king,' he shot back at her. 'And I may not have the title of lord of this manor, but in all my deeds and work, I am.'

Rachel sighed and took a sip of her drink. She stared into the fire for so long, Duncan became concerned he had offended her. 'Rachel?'

She looked at him. 'Sorry, I was just remembering.'

'Oh?'

She flashed him a sad smile. 'The time when neither of us had to be anything other than what we were.'

'That was a long time ago and so much has happened to this family, I fear, that it will never go that way again.' Duncan stood up and put more wood on the fire. 'I just pray Bree can be saved from having to carry the same burdens we have these past ten years.'

Rachel looked at him, her blue eyes made slate grey by the dull light of the room. 'Perhaps it is God's plan that I remain here until all is settled.'

'What do you mean, God's plan?'

'That I . . . that I have not married . . . ' Her voice trailed off.

He stood up. 'Rachel, the reason you have not been married is because *our father* has spurned every suitor who has sought your hand, or interfered with any chance you may have had of love and happiness.'

'Duncan, be not so agitated.'

'Why?' Duncan knelt before her and gathered up her hands. 'You are the most beautiful girl in Scotland.' She shook her head. 'No, it is true. And your beauty is not just in your face but in your heart. Had it not been for you, sweet Rachel, this family would have wasted away to nothing save mad servants and raving cooks.'

'I'll tell Morag you said that,' Rachel said with a smile.

Duncan looked at her and smiled. 'You understand my meaning.'

'Aye, but there's no good in dwelling on what could have been; what might be; what should be.' She now smiled at him but he saw the raw pain even in that.

'He was a worthy suitor, Rachel.'

Tears sprang to her eyes. 'Don't talk of it, Duncan,' she said, harshly.

'Sorry, dear sister. But you have not grieved for him.'

She stood up, angry. 'I will not discuss this with you. God's will has been done and His direction for my life is written. I need only wait.'

'Until what? Until when?'

'Until He brings another. I have faith, Duncan, that there is someone yet to come.'

Duncan laid his hands on her shoulders. ''Tis still permissible to weep for loss.'

'So, does that apply to you as well, dear brother?' she said sharply, her cheeks red. 'You, who constantly pace these halls trying to make all things right; trying to fix all the wrong.' She picked up her goblet and drank deep. 'We are not all so inclined to control the lives of every person.'

'That's not fair, Rachel.'

'So now you talk to me about what is fair. This is fair, Duncan. We live in this godforsaken castle with terrified servants and a mad father. We wait till he is crowned king and fear that day because we both know he is not fit to rule Scotland. Yet, it is God's will and what power do we have to counter that?' Tears streamed down her face but she was oblivious. 'I have faith, like Uncle Malcolm, that our divine Father has plans for each of us and it will all work to our good in the end.' She sniffed and reached for a cloth from the bowl. As she wiped her face she said, 'I, like you, have met with grief and loss but I will not let it cripple me into a place of misery.'

Rachel stood proud and lifted her chin as she looked at him. Duncan was filled with a renewed pride in his sister. This woman could be a queen. ''Tis time for bed,' she said and swept out of the room.

Duncan sat back on his seat, his heart aching – not just for Rachel's grief but for all future worries that would come before them.

Again, he was woken by shouts. 'Long live the king!' came the cry. It was too early. Duncan had stayed late in the blue room and thought about what Rachel had said and also on what could be done to make it better for both his sisters. He'd crawled to bed long after the moon had descended.

Now, to be woken by noise! The knocking was like a mallet on his skull. One of the stablehands was banging on his chamber door. 'Sire,' he called. 'There is a messenger from the king.'

Duncan crawled out of his bed and opened his door. This was not right that a stablehand had access to the castle rooms. But then this castle did not run by normal standards. He pulled open his door. 'What, man?'

'Beg your pardon, Sire, but there's a man here who would speak to the master save the master is not here.'

'Aye. Tell him I will be down shortly.' The stablehand bowed and disappeared down the corridor. Duncan pulled on his clothes and shook his head. If only he could be allowed to take control now, then things would run as they should do.

The messenger, a bright-eyed and keen fellow, smiled at Duncan. 'The king would have me say: his kin is invited to Forres to share a meal.'

Duncan frowned. 'Is he not dying?'

'Aye,' said the page. 'But he wants to leave this world with his dearest close by, having had his last supper with them.'

'Tell the king: Donalbain is from court but the news will get to him and we will be there as soon as the Lord allows.'

The messenger smiled, not aware of the meaning behind Duncan's words. 'That I will.'

He didn't know on what compulsion he did it but he called for his own horse and set out to follow his father. He should have sent the stablehand but this was a duty he alone needed to fulfil.

The day was as gloomy as the mood inside the castle – the wee ones were misbehaving, Bree and Morag's two youngest children; they sensed the tension in the household, Duncan suspected. Even Rachel's songs and stories were not having much effect on their moods. He was glad to be out of it.

He mounted Phoenix and encouraged him down the path his father often rode. Phoenix was reliable. His father was not. Duncan did not know how bad things were. But in his heart he hoped there might be something redeemable for the people of Scotland.

He rode all morning and cursed himself that he had not asked Morag to prepare something for his journey. He had tried the three places he had heard the strange women were known to frequent, but only cold fires and strange symbols splashed on stone were evidence of them being there.

Duncan was about to give up and turn back when, through the mist and fog, he saw his father's horse. Because he was still some distance back, and because of the weather, Duncan was able to approach undetected. Still, he was wary. Who knew what possessed Donalbain's mind on such occasions?

Duncan dismounted and immediately heard a chanting. No, a singing. A humming? A noise from women that did not bear any resemblance to songs he knew. The sound was somewhat enchanting and he was mesmerised.

And just as this thought came to him, he shook his head. He was being bewitched by the songs. He needed to find his father. He needed help to pull him away from such creatures. Duncan leant against some desolate stone ruins and shook his head.

No, he thought. *These agents of darkness are not for me. I must come against them.*

Duncan crept through the remnants of the long forgotten Roman stronghold and came upon a cluster of three women who were singing and chanting. His father sat in the middle of a stone circle, a black blindfold over his eyes, his back against a short wooden stake. One of the witches looked up and saw Duncan but instead of saying anything, she grinned and blew him a kiss.

This was insane. Who were these creatures? They were using their place among the fears and worries of a disenchanted people to work havoc.

Suddenly, out of the cold, misty air, a voice rang out: 'Hail to thee, King of Scotland!'

Then, another voice: 'Beware the son of a murdered father.'

Then another: 'Do not fear, Donalbain, son of Duncan. For no man will harm you.'

'More,' Donalbain roared. 'I have not paid you gold for childish prattle. I need to know more. Who are my enemies?'

The witches were silent but held hands around the seated prince. They began to sway, at first slowly but then became more frenzied.

'What's going on?' Donalbain shouted. 'Take this damn blindfold from me.' That was when Duncan saw his father's hands were tied behind his back.

The three released their hands and danced away from Donalbain. Then the one with a cropped skull knelt down before him and licked his face like a cat. Donalbain, startled, tried to move away. The woman grabbed his shoulder and said, 'Your friends are your enemies and your enemies are your friends.'

'What?' Donalbain began but the woman put a hand to his mouth. 'Shhh!'

The second woman came forward and knelt before him and began stroking his thighs. She moved higher up so that Duncan was appalled to see she was touching his father's manhood. 'Donalbain, Donalbain,' she said in a child-like voice, still caressing him. 'Your greatest strength will be your greatest weakness.'

Duncan swallowed. This was the strangest thing he had ever witnessed. He had always suspected they gave his father foolish counsel but nothing could have prepared him for what was playing out before his eyes.

Finally, the third woman came forward. She, of all the three, looked more like a skinny old man than a woman. She stood behind Donalbain and pulled his head between her thin thighs, her dirty fingers massaging his skull. 'Because of Donalbain, a new Scotland will be born.' She released him and stood back. 'Come, sisters, let us go.'

Singing? Chanting? Offering incantations, the three women came towards Duncan but did not acknowledge him save the second one, who stood before him a moment and then grabbed his crotch. She held him a moment as she looked deep into his eyes and grinned. Though she reeked, Duncan had no power to move away from her. Then she let go. 'A waste,' was all she said and followed the others out.

Duncan fell back against the stones, panting, his head spinning. It was too much to try to understand.

'Come back,' Donalbain called. 'Untie me, you whores.'

Duncan stumbled forward and pulled the blindfold from Donalbain's face. 'What, in the name of hell, are you doing here?' his father snarled.

'We were worried for you, Father. You have been gone a full day and night. A messenger has come from the king. We are to go to Forres at once.' He began unknotting the ties.

'Did you see the three women?'

'Aye.'

'Did you hear what they said, lad? I am going to change Scotland.'

'So they said.' Duncan saw now that his father was in a worse state than he imagined. Had he slept? Had he eaten? Did those strange hags poison him? 'We need to get back to the castle – there is much to be done.'

'And, they said that no man will ever harm me.' Duncan helped him to his feet. His father continued to rant and rave as they picked their way through the ruins to their horses. It was going to be a tedious ride home.

They made it back to the castle in the dark. Duncan was famished and exhausted – Donalbain had talked the whole journey save the last mile. Stablehands came towards them with torches and helped them both dismount. Duncan called for one of the manservants. 'Take the master to his chambers and arrange for food and drink.' The servant nodded and put his shoulder under Donalbain's arm and helped him into the castle.

Rachel came out carrying a torch. 'What has happened?'

'I really don't know. I found him but he's in a strange state. Nothing that a good meal and a night's sleep won't cure, I hope.' He followed her in. 'For me and for him.'

The next morning, Duncan was summoned to Donalbain's bed chamber. His father was running a fever. His face was red, his bedclothes damp.

'You're not well, Father. I will send for Rachel.'

'Aye, my whole self aches. I am in need of some of her medicine.' Duncan went to leave. 'And bring me Calum.'

He met Calum in the hall. 'Donalbain has asked for you. He is ill and still in his bed.' Calum nodded and bowed slightly before heading to his master. Rachel was in Bree's chamber, helping to plait the young girl's hair. Bree was squirming so much, Rachel had to hold her tightly between her knees.

'Bree,' Duncan said. 'If you sit still, it will be done in no time and you may have your breakfast.'

'She's already been told that,' Rachel said. 'But she's a stubborn wee lass.'

Duncan leant against the door frame. 'Father's ill.'

Rachel released Bree and pushed her away. She stood. 'Has he asked for me?'

'Aye and your balm.'

'I will go to him at once,' she said and went out, the sound of her light steps and thick skirts echoing down the hall.

'You,' Duncan said sternly, 'will allow Nurse to finish your hair without fuss or I will have to punish you.'

Bree stared wide-eyed. Her brother rarely growled. She meekly returned to the stool and sat down, all the while staring at him. Duncan saw the faint smile on the nurse's face and turned abruptly lest his little sister see him do the same and have the effect of his manner spoiled.

He went down to the kitchen. It was a warm and welcoming place and he was too hungry to wait until Bree and Rachel had finished with their morning preparations.

'Good morning, Morag.'

'Duncan. I have not seen you forever. How I have missed you and my heart has grieved.'

Duncan laughed. 'I've only been gone a day. You saw me not two days ago.'

'Two days is too long for this old woman to get a look at a handsome young man.' As she spoke she put together his morning meal. 'Are you supping here this morning?'

'Aye. 'Tis a cold place in the dining hall; Rachel is with Father and Bree is up to her usual naughty ways. I have no patience for that.'

'You must be in a fine mood so that you have no patience. You're the most patient body on God's earth.'

A servant appeared. 'Sire, the master has called for you.'

Duncan swallowed his mouthful. 'Tell him I shall be there in a moment.' The servant nodded and bowed before disappearing into the dark corridors of the castle. 'I will need you to prepare food for the family as we have been called to the king's palace. Bree will not accompany us, I think, for it is a long way for a child.'

'As you wish, Sire, and I will ensure your favourite morsels are packed.'

'Thank you, Morag.' He drained his cup. 'And for breakfast. I must go to Father. Have a pleasant day.'

Morag chuckled. 'The best manners in the castle.' As Duncan left he heard her say to one of the kitchen hands, 'An' you could learn well from the young master, you scowling lump of a maid. Hurry up with them vegetables else no one will be eating tonight.'

Duncan grinned. Morag was a force to reckon with and he pitied all who worked in her kitchen if they dared not give their heart and soul and body to her tasks.

Donalbain looked better already though his eyes were too bright and his face still flushed. 'How are you, Father?'

'I am too ill to travel. Calum and Rachel both concur. You will have to go to Malcolm's. Rachel cannot go as I need her here.'

'But it was a command, Father. He will see it as an insult.'

'Damned if I will adhere to my brother's command.' Donalbain glared at his son. 'You will go. He thinks more highly of you.'

'He has called for you specifically.'

Donalbain fell back against his pillows. 'No worries, lad. I will send along a gift so that he understands my affection for him. We can't have the king die and the next in line follow straight after.'

Duncan nodded. 'You are right, of course. I have already asked the kitchen to prepare for the journey. What fellows shall I take with me?'

'Fellows?'

'Will you not allow one or two groomsmen to accompany me?' It was the custom that when they travelled to Forres or to Fife, they had two or three others to attend Donalbain.

'They are not needed. You are strong and will ride swiftly. There is no danger to you. It is only me who must take care.' Duncan knew this was madness but he could not order any of the groomsmen against the wishes of his father.

'As you say. I will make haste. I will be ready to leave within the hour. So please you, send the gift to my chamber.'

Rachel followed him out. 'He's right. He is too ill but he will recover. A journey to Forres would be his undoing.'

He gathered her hands in his. 'I wish you were coming with me. You would have made it a happy journey.'

'I am of better use here. God speed, Duncan,' she said, going on her tiptoes to kiss him on the cheek. 'The castle will be a tedious place until you return. Here,' she added. 'Take the pot with you should either you or the horse be grazed – it has mighty healing agents and will fend off an infection and fever.'

'Thank you. I shall bring you something back, I promise. Some memento or some treasure.'

'And I shall eagerly await such a gift. Now hurry so that you can make the most of the light.'

He leant down and returned the kiss and then went to his rooms to prepare for the trip to Forres, his stomach churning and his heart heavy.

Chapter Fifteen

Phoenix was making good time and Duncan arrived at the town of Perth before sunset. He stabled the horse and paid for a room. The meal was adequate: hot and filling but nothing in comparison with what he'd enjoyed most of his life. He went to bed early and had a dreamless night, waking before the cock crowed to continue his journey.

Though the day began with the sun bright and the sky clear save high clouds rushing by, Duncan noted the pinkness of the dawn – a sign that the weather would turn and he would no doubt need to find shelter before he got caught out. The last thing he wanted was to travel in rain and mud. It would slow him down but worse, it would make him utterly miserable.

Rachel often teased him about his strong dislike of rain. She told Bree one evening about when Duncan was much younger and it had first became apparent he was afraid of rain.

'He was about the age that you are now, Bree,' she had said. 'We had ridden out for the day, but the weather turned bad. Though it was warm, dark clouds gathered over us. There was lightning and the crack of thunder.' Duncan had smiled at his sister's excellent storytelling abilities. He remembered all too well the day in question but even he was captivated by the telling. 'Duncan screamed and Mother could not get him to stop. Then, when the rain came – and mind, Bree, 'twas heavy, heavy rain – Duncan was inconsolable.

'After that, if ever he was playing outside, and it began to rain, he would rush indoors.' Rachel had smiled at him. 'I think it is because you don't like getting your hair wet,' she teased her brother.

Duncan had ignored her and instead addressed his younger sister. 'Let this be a lesson to you, Bree. Every person has at least one thing in their lives which they have a passionate dislike for. Yours is going to bed, mine is getting wet from the weather and Rachel's is—'

'Not any of your business,' she'd butted in. 'No sense in giving the lass silly ideas.'

Atop Phoenix, Duncan smiled at the memory – it was another of the few happy times they had enjoyed at the dining table. It was good to think on pleasant thoughts because the weather was changing rapidly and the clouds were coming thick and fast from the nor'east. Duncan slowed Phoenix to a walk so he could tighten his travelling cloak and then urged him on. He prayed he would find an inn soon.

An hour later, with no sign of civilisation, Duncan began searching in earnest for shelter among the trees. The rain, which had blown in from the north, now fell straight upon them, drenching both man and horse. Through the downpour, he spied a stand of trees and turned Phoenix towards them. As they walked further in, the drenching abated somewhat but the noise was horrendous – a roaring sound as the heavy drops hit the leaves and branches.

Phoenix flicked his ears backwards and forwards. At every thunderclap he startled. It was almost dark although it was not long after midday. Every few minutes, the wood would light up as lightning struck. A few moments later, the booming sound of rolling thunder followed. Duncan spread his cloak around him in an attempt to shield his boots but it did little to ward off the water which ran down the skin.

Suddenly, there was another sound and Phoenix heard it too – wolves. In the next lightning strike the glare illuminated the scene so that he clearly saw three large wolves making their way towards him. Phoenix smelt them now and began to walk backwards, prancing nervously. There was no time – he had to get away from them.

He spun the horse around and dug his heels into the horse's flanks. 'Yeearrggh,' Duncan cried, urging Phoenix on. Behind him, he heard the high-pitched yelps of the wolves – they were fast but Phoenix was faster. It was difficult to see because the heavy rain continued relentlessly. Being in the woods made it more treacherous for the horse.

Soon, though, they broke out into the clear but the wolves were still in pursuit. He would have to push Phoenix on for some time before they gave up the chase. The slippery state of the road slowed all down but Phoenix galloped on. Duncan's heart raced and he leant forward, urging and urging him to go faster.

They galloped on, mud splashing into Duncan's face. Every few moments, he looked back to check but the three wolves were relentless in their hunt. It occurred to him that there had been few battles of late and therefore no corpses for the wolves to gorge upon. These animals were lean and hungry. He dug his hands into the horse's mane and called some more. 'Go, Phoenix! Go, boy!'

Lightning flashed across the sky and instantly there was a piercing crash of thunder. Phoenix squealed but did not falter in his stride. Another flash, and this time the bolt of lightning hit a lone tree off to his left. The noise deafened Duncan and he shook his head to try to clear it. Looking back, the wolves were further off but still following fast. He could hear Phoenix's laboured pants as the horse endeavoured to keep up the swift pace and outrun the predators. Duncan was aware he was putting both of them in danger as he pushed the horse in these conditions. The road was too slippery, the view unclear, his horse nearing exhaustion after a day and a half of travel. He needed to find a cottage, a camp, something to gain refuge from the threat of the creatures behind him.

But there was nothing and Duncan saw they were coming to a fork in the road. He needed to turn right and told Phoenix so. The horse obeyed but the path was uneven and he stumbled. Duncan lost his balance and tried to right himself but there was another bolt of lightning and a crash of thunder. A tree to the left of the path was struck and burst into flames. All of this was too much for Phoenix and he put his head down and bucked so that Duncan, still unsettled on the saddle, was thrown over the horse's head and into the mud.

Phoenix, though brave and sturdy of heart, did not stay. He bolted, stirrups flapping, in the direction they were heading. 'Phoenix,' Duncan cried. 'Come back!' But the horse was gone, leaving Duncan to face the attack of three very hungry wolves.

He scrambled to his feet and desperately looked around. There must be somewhere he could go to get away from this danger. Nothing. The land was desolate and the road empty except for the burning tree. Duncan scouted around for rocks. At least he could ward them off. The trouble was, Duncan had heard the stories about these wolves. So many battles of men with so many dead, that they had feasted upon the bodies of those slain in battle for such a long time they'd grown accustomed to the taste of human flesh.

Just as suddenly, the rain ceased. Thank God. He had one less thing to contend with. Looking around, he saw some stones and stepped forward to collect them but slipped in the mud and fell hard to the ground. The wolves came forward some more and stopped. Their whining and growling reminded him of fawning servants. They were close enough that he could see their tongues lolling and their yellow eyes glaring.

He pulled out his dirk – his only weapon, for Phoenix had carried off his sword. Though his father and his tutors had tried to school him in the art of combat, he was at best only an adequate fighter. Duncan hated warfare and the pain it inflicted upon others. It was bad luck that he had not taken his weapons schooling more seriously for these beasts had chosen him as their next meal and he felt ill-prepared. One by one the wolves lay down on the road. There was no escape.

The first wolf rushed at him but he was ready and the dirk went cleanly into the animal's heart. It was heavy, despite its poor state, and Duncan was thrown to the ground. He had just enough time to throw off the wolf when the other attacked. It bit deep into his arm and the power behind the jaws, even in this terrible moment, impressed Duncan. He grabbed the dirk from his right hand and inverted it before plunging it deep into the wolf's neck. Blood spouted everywhere and Duncan was covered. No mind. The animal was gone and, like the other, he pushed it off his body.

He was badly injured and bleeding and there was one more wolf to contend with. The wound in his arm was serious and he began to feel weak. The third wolf licked its chops and stepped forward steadily.

Duncan had the dirk but not the strength. Phoenix was gone; he was wounded. What would Rachel do if he died? How would Bree fare? And his father. It was impossible to imagine how things would turn out without Duncan's intervention.

Panting, he pulled away from the two animals and faced the one determined to gain victory. He held the dirk in his left hand

and hoped, prayed that perhaps this one would do as the others did and lunge at him.

Not so. It circled so that Duncan had to twist his bruised body around to keep facing the creature. To make matters worse, the weather was not done with him yet and the rain fell again with lightning far off, accompanied by the sounds of thunder. He wanted to shout at the wolf. He wanted to be profane and say the words he'd overheard in the stable. But, remembering Rachel's sweetness and calm demeanour, even during her time of grief, Duncan held back. Damned if he would go so base.

Still the animal circled, howling and whining. Duncan would provide a great meal. And he was weakening. For the first time in his life, he prayed. *'God who loves my sister Rachel, please do not inflict upon her another grief. Save me for her.'*

There was a thwack and the wolf fell dead. Duncan blinked and saw a bolt in the side of the animal. It did not even twitch. Groggy, he looked around. Standing before him was a giant of a horse and a rider atop. The wolf was dead. Duncan fell back with relief.

The rider leapt from the horse and came to Duncan. 'Are you hurt?'

Duncan blinked. 'I am injured,' he offered and held up his bleeding arm. 'I don't know how bad but it is painful.'

'You don't say,' the rider said, and Duncan then saw that he was a young man, around his own age but possessed of an authority which seemed to age him. He leant down to examine Duncan's arm. 'I'll have to wrap it to stop the bleeding.'

Duncan watched as his arm was tidily wrapped and, though it ached, there was no sign of fresh blood. 'I am on my way to Forres but perhaps today was not the day for leaving home.'

The young man in front of him grinned. 'I think so too. So, where is home?' he asked, pulling Duncan to his feet.

'Glamis. If my horse had any sense, he'd have taken himself back there but my sister will now be a-worrying. I saw him gallop on.'

'I think you should ride mine to save your strength,' the man said. 'Let me help you up.'

Duncan put his foot in the stirrup and the rider lifted his other leg so that he was pushed up onto the saddle without using his injured arm.

The horse snorted and rolled its eyes. 'Willow doesn't like the smell of you,' Duncan heard. 'He would rather you walked but I've told him you're hurt.'

Duncan looked down at the young man, dark-haired and fair-eyed. 'Thank you.'

'Well, no thanks needed until I get you safely to a place of rest.' He walked on for a bit then added, 'Did you not think of the wolves?'

Duncan blushed. 'I have to say, no.'

The young man chuckled. 'You're daft then.'

'Aye,' he replied. 'That's the truth.' Duncan felt sick. He'd lost a lot of blood and the day's travelling had taken its toll. 'I have money. I would be thankful if you found us lodging as soon as possible.'

'Don't worry, man, these have been my thoughts exactly. I hear there is an inn not some three miles in front. Once you are well and we find your horse, sir, you can return to your journey.'

'Of course,' said Duncan, remembering now. 'I know the place.'

'And folk call me Flea.'

Duncan regarded the young man who walked tall beside him. 'Thank you for saving my life, Flea. My sisters will be most grateful.'

They arrived at the inn and to Duncan's relief, Phoenix was tethered in front. 'That's my horse, Phoenix,' Duncan said. He remembered, 'My sister has made an ointment which may help with the bite.' Flea helped him down from Willow. 'I will enquire about our lodgings. Would you stay and share a meal with me?'

Flea nodded. 'I will. Thank you.'

Duncan went to Phoenix who, though looking unhappy, had been attended to. This did not surprise Duncan for the horse was well known. This was the same tavern they rested at each time they made the trip to Forres. 'Thanks for leaving me to the wolves,' he muttered as he untied his bags. Phoenix dipped his head. Perhaps he understood.

He and Flea went into the inn. The innkeeper put down the plates he was carrying and bowed slightly. 'Welcome, Sire. We were about to send fellows out to look for you but the horses were too spooked from the weather. Our humblest apologies.'

'No matter, man. This fellow was on hand and saved me. But I am injured and in need of food and rest. Are you able to offer that?'

'Yes, Sire. The master room is available.'

Duncan turned to his new companion who was regarding him strangely. 'Will you order us some food and drink while I tend to this injury?' He addressed the innkeeper, 'Have you a wife or a maid to help me and some dressings?'

The innkeeper nodded. 'Aye, my mam is a midwife.' He caught the eye of a young boy. 'Get your gran and tell her we have the king's nephew and he's hurt.'

There was a sharp intake of breath from Flea. Duncan grinned at him. 'I didn't feel it the time to tell you, under the circumstances, that I was royal kin. My father is brother to the king.'

'Donalbain?'

'Aye. But we will talk more if you like after I am refreshed.' An old woman appeared out of the shadows, arms filled with white cloths and bandages. When she saw Duncan, she bowed. 'Lead on, Mother,' Duncan said wearily.

The room was large and the bed very wide. He sat down, his head pounding. As if reading his thoughts, the old woman gave him a drink. 'This will help with the pain, Sire,' she said quietly. While he drank, she opened his bags and removed some clothes. 'These are damp. I will get them dried but for now, you can wear my son's clothes, if that is acceptable.'

'Completely,' Duncan said, the sweet, warm wine soothing away the thumping in his skull.

Chapter Sixteen

Fleance ordered two meals and two jugs of ale before going back out to the horses. He untied both and led them to the stables. There were a number of stablehands in attendance – evidence that this was a busy tavern and used to much traffic. Already there were four horses chewing on hay, thick horse blankets on their steaming bodies. He was very tired so was grateful to hand over the task of bedding them in. Fleance patted Willow. 'Good job, boy. Da would have been proud of you.' He untied his own belongings and carried them over his shoulder. It had started to rain again; this time, though, it was not the solid downpour of the afternoon but windblown and cold.

He stepped out from the shelter of the stables and, as he made his way towards the warmth of the inn, his eye caught a movement in a field to the left. Fleance turned his head and, through the rain, saw a man standing, staring at him. Fleance's heart skipped a beat – it was the same fellow he had seen, bleeding, in the northern woods of England.

'Are you wanting something from me, sir?' Fleance called out, uncertainty flooding through him. He could not, from this distance, make out the facial features but there was a similarity in the way he stood. Nervously, Fleance looked behind him, back to the stables thinking perhaps he could get one of the hands to accompany him. But, when he turned back, the stranger was gone.

Fleance ran forward, his eyes searching up and down to see if a lone figure was anywhere. But, like last time, there was no sign of him.

With his heart racing, Fleance walked quickly to the inn. It was shadowy indoors but the light from the torches enabled him to see the faces of people crowded at tables. He scanned the room. Not one person resembled the man who had stared from the field.

The innkeeper motioned him to a table where steaming plates of hot food and refreshing cups of drink had been set. A moment later, Duncan appeared in dry clothes, clearly much too large for him. Fleance guessed they belonged to the stout innkeeper.

There were fresh bandages on his arm and the colour had returned to his face.

Duncan sat down. 'Are you ill?'

'Why do you ask?'

'You've gone mighty pale, though it could be the light in this room.'

Fleance shook his head. 'Just tired and hungry. You are looking much more fit to the role of king's nephew.' He tried to smile.

'Yes, well, I am thinking that the title will change too soon.' He began to eat as did Fleance.

After a while, Duncan paused and lay down his spoon. 'Where were you heading when you so fortunately came upon my predicament?'

Fleance finished his mouthful and swallowed. 'Fife.'

'For kin or for business?'

Fleance leant back into his chair and studied the young man in front of him. He was as tall as Fleance though not as solid. His blond hair and blue eyes gave him an air of innocence. But he smiled readily and warmly and Fleance had not detected an awareness of status that he remembered from the royal family when he was a boy.

'I wish to speak with the thane of the county.'

'Macduff?' Duncan asked, a tone of surprise in his voice.

Fleance nodded. 'Aye, him.'

Duncan picked up his spoon. 'Well, it seems our meeting has been most helpful for both of us.'

'Why is that?'

'The thanes have all been called to the king's castle.' He broke off some bread. 'You would have had a wasted journey. It's Forres you need to go to.' He dipped the bread into the hot stew on his plate. 'Seems we are now heading in the same direction.'

This was food for thought and Fleance recommended eating. How was it that he was supposed to follow these signs? Or had what happened been part of the big plan? The stranger he saw in the woods and then just now? The dreams? Blair's dream and his advice to find answers from Macduff? Now this – a change in plan, yet again. He sighed.

Fleance eyed Duncan. 'Perhaps you need me to protect you from the wolves,' he said, smiling.

'It seems I do, Flea.' Duncan shook his head and laughed. 'What a pair we are.'

The young boy came and cleared away their plates and returned with a mug for Duncan. 'Gram says you need to have some more of this – for your injury.'

'Thank you and give thanks to your grandmother.' The boy bowed and scurried away. Fleance was amused at the tenderness with which the young royal spoke to the servant. Duncan was different from what he remembered about the men and women of court. He was very much like his grandfather as Fleance remembered him.

He stretched. 'My body has had enough of sitting and is calling me to bed.' He stood up. 'Good night, Duncan.'

Duncan looked puzzled. 'Where are you going?'

'To the stables,' Fleance said, gathering up his bag and cloak.

'There's a cot in my room, man. It would be rude of me to allow my saviour to bed down on straw when there's a perfectly comfortable bed available.'

Fleance hesitated. The thought of yet another night in a stable was not so appealing as this offer of Duncan's. But what if the dreams came again? What if he betrayed himself in his sleep. 'I snore,' he offered, as a way to allow Duncan to change his mind.

Duncan laughed. 'So do I, so you may rather sleep with the horses.'

What if the man had been following him? What if he was waiting for him and perhaps meant to do him some harm? He would be much safer in the tavern than exposed in the stables. He made a decision. 'Thank you, Duncan, I will accept your hospitality.' He sat down again, still with his bag and cloak in his arms.

Duncan finished his drink and stood up slowly. 'I feel like I've aged twenty years,' he said, rubbing his back. 'I think I'll be stiff and sore in the morning.' He moved off towards his room and Fleance followed.

His father was angry. Fleance had never seen him like this before. He couldn't hear what he was saying but Banquo was shouting at him, fists clenched, then fists shaking in his face. What had he done wrong? Why was his father so furious? 'What, Da?' he called out. 'What's the matter?' But Banquo just paced backwards and forwards. It was awful and Fleance felt like he was a boy again, caught being unkind to Blair. 'I didn't do it, Da. Promise. It wasn't me.' Still his father raged against him. If only he could hear what he was saying Fleance might understand what the transgression was. 'Please, just tell me what I've done.' Banquo grabbed him and began shaking him. Then the dream worsened for blood began flowing from his father's mouth. Banquo seemed unaware and continued to shake him so that the front of Fleance's coat and hands were covered in blood.

Fleance awoke with a start, panting. It took him a moment to remember where he was. He felt sick. The dream was so real and he searched his mind for a memory that would match what he'd just seen. But his father had never lost his temper with him even though Fleance would often disobey him or do the wrong thing. Banquo was ever patient and gentle. Quite the opposite of his son. Fleance had often heard the older servants say that the temper had jumped from his grandfather on his deathbed and into the swollen belly of his mother.

He turned the dream over and over. What was meant by the blood? Mentally, he shook himself. It was just a dream. He was tired. The past few weeks had been very difficult. Perhaps his mind was playing tricks on him and he was thinking about the men he'd killed.

It made for a disturbed night. Instead of accompanying the king's nephew, he would rather have another day and night of sleep. But at the cock's crow, Fleance understood this was not to be. There were other forces in place which seemed to be dictating his actions.

He sat up, his head pounding. Whether it was from the poor night or the ale, he didn't know. He looked over to where Duncan slept but the bed was empty, the covers thrown back. A small worm of concern moved inside his stomach and Fleance tried to ignore it. It was likely Duncan was relieving himself.

The door opened and Duncan appeared. He smiled at Fleance. 'You didn't snore but you do talk in your sleep.'

Fleance froze. 'What did I say?'

'I couldn't understand a word of it but I guessed you weren't dreaming of a lass unless you've grieved one and she's come back to give you a tongue lashing.' He sat on his bed and began to unwrap the bandage. 'When you've got a wife, you better warn her about it as she may find it less tolerable than snoring.'

Though he offered them light jest, Duncan had no idea how his words pained Fleance for he immediately thought again of his Rosie. He climbed out of bed and pulled on his boots trying to ignore the ache in his heart. 'I will go see to the horses and order a meal.' He indicated Duncan's arm. 'Do you need help with that?'

Duncan shook his head. 'My sister is skilled in healing and I've seen her do this often enough.' He took the final wrap and held up his arm. ''Tis clean and no sign of rot, thank goodness.' He picked up the pot of cream and began to apply a thick coat to the bite marks. 'I'll tell my wee Bree that she better pray the wolf had no werewolf in him else her brother is likely to turn at the full moon.'

Fleance put on his cloak. Duncan sitting there chatting reminded him how different the two of them were. Unlike himself, Duncan had few worries or burdens and had lived a privileged life. A life that would have been very much his had his father not been murdered.

To mask his sudden bitterness, he went out.

The morning was wet and the sky fragile. The air was still cold from the north but the worst of the storm was over. Light mist floated above the fields and it swirled and curled around the legs of the cattle as they grazed. Fleance strode over to the stables, keeping a wary eye on the surrounding lands in case he saw the stranger again. They were deserted.

In contrast to the quiet outside, the stable was noisy and full of activity. The horses had already been fed and one hand was grooming Willow, who was swishing his tail and stamping his feet bad-temperedly. 'He's not a morning horse,' Fleance said to the stablehand.

'Aye, I can tell.' He picked up Willow's hoof and began clearing it out. Fleance got to his horse just in time as Willow was about to nip the man's rear end.

'That will do, Willow,' he said, pulling the horse's large head around. 'Mind your manners.' He lifted the bridle from the hook and began tacking up his horse. He looked over to Duncan's horse and saw that it was dozing in its stall as the hands prepared him for the day. Mild-mannered, like his owner, Fleance thought.

When he had tied up his bags and everything was ready, he led Willow to the front of the inn and tethered him. He went inside to have his breakfast. Duncan was already at the table eating, a clean bandage visible underneath the cuff of his shirt.

Duncan smiled at him as he sat down. 'How are the horses?'

'I think they had a more restful night than we did,' Fleance said. He bit into the hot sausage from his plate. 'How far is it, to this place we're going to?'

'Forres is still some distance. Will take us two days to reach it.'

'Providing we don't encounter any wolves,' Fleance quipped. 'Two-legged or four.'

'Indeed,' Duncan said. 'I have a feeling, with your wit and words, the journey will not be as tedious as I had expected.'

They finished their breakfast and accepted a gift of food for the road and went out into the cold morning.

Phoenix and Willow stood waiting; Willow impatiently, a mood shared by his rider. The sooner he could get this over and done with, the sooner he could return to England and his Rosie – if she would forgive him and have him back.

Rosie
England

It was as if there was no future: nothing to look forward to; not spring, summer, not any festivals. In the past, always, there was the anticipation of the next time she would see Flea. Now, the future was empty. Rosie drifted around the cottage in mourning. She hardly ate and no longer sang or smiled. The heaviness of grief sat on her shoulders.

'What shall I do?' Rebecca asked Dougal, finding him splitting wood in the workshop.

He put down his tools. 'Nothing. 'Tis a broken heart and only time – and another beau – will fix it.'

Rebecca swallowed and took a deep breath. 'Perhaps if you hadn't made him choose . . .'

'I did the right thing by her,' Dougal growled. 'Which is more than I can say for that boy.'

Rosie, from her position at the kitchen table, could hear her parents arguing. She agreed with her mother: Da pushed Flea's hand, but then Flea was at fault too – he'd kept things from her, important things – whereas she had opened her heart and life to him. It was not fair. She had done nothing wrong so why was she being punished this way? Why had he been brought into her life only to be taken?

If he had been killed, it would have been better than it was now. Now, she felt the sting of his rejection. He was still a living, breathing, speaking being and she could not be with him. This was hell.

As she thought these things and as the quarrel between her parents washed over her, a shift occurred. She would not be the victim of foolish men whose idea of honour mattered more than the welfare of others. She, an only child, adored by her father, and strengthened by what she had heard, made a decision.

She loved Flea and would love him forever. But she could not stay in this cottage a virgin widow. *He might come back*, one part of her whispered. *He said he would come back. He said he loved me.*

But, argued the other side of her mind, *he left you.* Without warning, as was often the case these past weeks, the tears began to fall again.

She sighed deeply and stood up, wiping them away. Her parents were still arguing but the heat had gone out of their exchange. Rosie took a jug and went outside to fill it with water then carried it into her father's shed. Rebecca and Dougal fell silent.

'I thought you might be thirsty, Da,' she said and poured him some water.

'Thank you, Rosie, my dear.' He took the tankard from her hand.

'I have been thinking,' she began. 'I know you and Ma desire the best for me and, even though none of us spoke the words aloud, we believed Flea to be the best match.' Dougal went to answer her but she stopped him. 'We were right. He is a good man and I know he loves me as I love him.' She lowered her voice. What she was about to say could enrage her father and she did not want to make matters worse. *I will have to tread carefully*, she thought. 'Da, I think you were somewhat misguided in your love for me to challenge him. He was not ready.'

Dougal spluttered and coughed, water from his mouth and nose going over his workmanship. 'You what?'

'I want to go to Scotland and I want you to take me. I cannot go alone but I need to see him, to face him.' If she could, now after so many weeks, speak to him and find out what his pilgrimage was about, she might be able to understand why he could not marry her.

She watched as her mother laid a hand on her husband's arm. 'Perhaps this would be a good thing.'

Dougal, his face red from coughing and frustration, looked at the two of them. 'You would have me go back on my word?'

Again, Rebecca quietly and calmly chided her husband. 'And you, dear man, would deny your only child the chance of a good husband.' Thank goodness Ma was the foil to Da's emotional decisions. Yet her gentle words only inflamed him.

'Good husband!' he shouted. 'What in the name of Beelzebub is good about a lad who leads a girl on only to abandon her?' He turned away from them.

She understood his frustrations and he was right that Flea should have played things differently. Still, Rosie began to see with a little more clarity what had happened back there in the clearing. 'Da, he said he made a promise and you didn't give him a chance.'

'Remember what Miri told us, Dougal?' Rebecca said. 'Flea has been plagued by ghosts and stories since they found him.' She poured him another tankard of water. 'We all have our demons and he's a good lad. How many times have you said to me that he would make a great addition to your ventures?'

Dougal frowned, his plump face wrinkling. 'That was before . . .' His voice trailed off. He looked at Rebecca. 'Can you so easily forget how heartbroken she was?' he asked, nodding in Rosie's direction. 'It broke my heart to see you so bereft, lass,' he told her, his eyes glistening so that she thought he too might cry. 'A father's duty is to protect his family and I could do nothing to protect you from the pain he caused you.'

'I know, Da,' she said quietly. 'You and Ma have given me a good life.' Though she now only had vague memories of that time, Rosie remembered other children in the cottage; older children but, by the time she was truly conscious of things, her memories consisted of only herself, Ma and her father. And, for a time in those early years, a sense that loss and grief were a permanent fixture in their home.

Later, she learnt that her two older sisters and one older brother died when the family came to England. Rosie had been five or six at the time and it was before the troubles in Scotland which affected so many of the people. They had been well out of it for Dougal believed greater riches were to be had in England. However, a strange and vicious sickness swept through the village where they lived. All children in the family save Rosie perished.

There was much history between her parents and, even though her own heart's desire was so strong, Rosie knew she must tread carefully. 'I have enjoyed a happy and contented life thanks to you, Da. But,' she added, standing tall, 'I know there is unfinished business here and I cannot rest until I see him again.' Rosie looked at her father. 'I need to go soon.'

Dougal sat heavily on one of his barrels. 'We can't leave here just yet – look at all the work I have.'

Rosie leant forward, her eyes shining. 'How many times have Ma and I listened to you saying how much you want to go back to Scotland?' Rosie said, catching her mother's eye. Rebecca nodded. 'Here's your chance, Da. We could go together. I will take care of you and you will take care of me.'

Her father shook his head. 'I do not want to leave your mother,' he said.

'If you won't take me, I shall go myself.' She knew she was being difficult but such was her desire to shake up the world and find Flea at the bottom ready to take her, she risked her father's temper.

Dougal stood up. 'You can't do that. 'Tis not safe. Not with the reivers, the skirmishes. What will happen to you?' He shook his head. 'I forbid it. Find yourself another man who will love you as much.'

Rosie's temper flared. 'I *don't* want another man. I want Flea, and you – alone – are what is standing in the way of my happiness.' Her eyes were teary but she would not acknowledge them.

'Tell her,' Rebecca said quietly.

Dougal sighed wearily and looked at Rosie. She sensed his heart ached for her pain and that he himself seemed powerless to make it all better. He coughed and wiped his hand across his mouth. 'Well, 'tis true that I have been thinking of travelling back to Scotland.' Rosie rolled her eyes and went to speak but he held up his hand to silence her. 'A winemaker I met last week said that there was a tavern for sale in Perth. With my trade, I would make a tidy profit.' He looked nervously at his wife. 'I did nae want to broach this for fear of upsetting you further. But now, it seems, it is time to discuss such ideas.' He came towards her and put his chubby hand on her cheek. 'If we did this, how would the news greet you?'

Scotland. Where Flea was. There she could find him. Rosie looked to her father, that kernel of resolve growing. 'I think that would be a fine thing to do, Da. With Ma's cooking and help, we could do well.'

Dougal, clearly relieved, nodded. 'That we could, lass. It would be a good change. We've given England service enough these past years.'

'But, about Flea,' she began, but stopped when Dougal's face clouded over.

'Aye?' he said, his lips tight.

'If our paths do cross, what will be your behaviour towards him?'

Dougal scratched his belly and pursed his lips. 'Well, first I'd want to knock his block off and then I'd challenge him to see if he had come to his senses.'

Relief flooded through Rosie and for the first time in a long while, she smiled. 'I have a feeling I would do the same,' she said and she returned to the cottage with a measure of hope in her heart and something now tangible on her horizon. Being in a tavern was the perfect place to learn about the comings and goings of people. She could get word out that she was looking for him.

Of this she was certain: she would see him again and it would be soon.

Chapter Seventeen
Forres Castle, Scotland

'Tis quite a small castle,' Fleance remarked. 'I would have thought the king to have chosen a bigger one.' They had reined in their horses and now stood atop a rise which gave a magnificent view of the lands below and the castle before them.

'Uncle Malcolm had fond memories of this place. When he was a child, he used to go hunting with his father.' Duncan loosened the reins and Phoenix walked on. 'When we all came back from exile, this is where he chose to live. His English wife liked the sea better than the mountains.'

Fleance listened as Duncan talked of his family, of his childhood, just as he had for the whole of their journey – sharing little of his own history in return, save that he was an orphan and an explanation as to his riding and weaponry skills. Duncan, with true courtesy, did not press him.

They rode the horses through the open gates of Forres, Fleance following Duncan. As Duncan dismounted, grooms rushed up and took their horses. A tall, white-haired man approached and bowed. 'Sire. Your father is not with you?'

Duncan straightened his cloak. Fleance thought his new friend looked uncomfortable with the question. He watched as Duncan drew himself taller and spoke with a formal tone. 'My father is very ill and my sister is tending him. I have come as a representative of the family. This man here,' he said, nodding to Fleance, 'is my companion, Flea. I trust you will accommodate him.'

The old man turned his eyes to Fleance and regarded him for a moment before he bowed to him as well, 'You are welcome.'

'How is the king?' Duncan asked as he followed the servant into the castle.

'He is in good spirits though his body is weakening daily. He will be most pleased to see you.' They walked through the cavernous halls of the castle. Though small in comparison to some he'd seen, Fleance was still impressed with the grandeur and beauty of the place. The old man walked tall and straight backed. 'Would you prefer some refreshments before I bring you to the king?' he asked.

'Perhaps while I am visiting Uncle Malcolm, you could show Flea to accommodation and see to his needs.'

The old servant bowed his head and paused at a door. 'I shall announce your arrival. Please wait here.' He opened the door and went inside.

Fleance looked up at the tapestries. 'These are beautiful,' he said.

'Aye, the queen was gifted them from Normandy many years ago. Some she brought with her from England.' Duncan reached out and stroked the fabric. 'This one tells the story of King Kenneth, my great-great-great-grandfather when he insulted Edgar, the king of England. They say that Edgar was puny of stature and form, yet God and nature had blessed him with an amazing strength. He often challenged those whom he knew to be presumptuous to combat with the intention of putting them in their place. This,' he said, pointing to woven detail of men at a feast, 'shows when Kenneth made a jest about how strange it was that so many provinces of England were subject to such an insignificant being – meaning Edgar. The court's jester took up his insult and from then on retold

Kenneth's comments and even had a likeness of Edgar's face cast so that he wore it during subsequent feasts.' Fleance noted the distorted face of one of the figures, prancing in front of the table.

'Then,' Duncan continued, 'there came a summons from Edgar to Kenneth as if to consult with him about a great secret. King Edgar took Kenneth into the woods and gave him one of the two swords he carried with him. "And now," said Edgar, "you may try your strength since we are alone."

'Foolish Kenneth knew immediately what was happening, that he was being challenged to a duel, but he could do nothing, knowing that his skill did not match Edgar's.' Fleance looked to the far left of the tapestry and saw two men detailed – one large but downcast; the other small but a look of triumph on his face. 'Seems being presumptuous was not always blessed with brute strength and Edgar saw the measure of my great-great-great-grandfather to take him down a peg or two.'

'What did he do?' Fleance asked, intrigued for, in his history and the telling of his family's story, there was a Kenneth, King of Scotland. Duncan was talking also of *his* kin.

'Nothing yet because Edgar hadn't finished chastising him. See here,' he pointed to a place in the lower middle section. 'This is where he puts Kenneth in his place for being so quick to judge and criticise.' The tall king of Scotland was on his knees in front of Edgar.

'What happened?' Fleance was fascinated.

'Edgar told him that there was no one around to witness their combat so he hoped Kenneth was on guard for it was dishonourable to be ready and witty at a feast but unready in conflict. In other words, he'd caught Kenneth off guard which just showed who was greater. Kenneth, as it shows here,' he pointed to the last cluster of illustrations, 'threw down his sword and fell at Edgar's feet begging for mercy – which he got.'

'What a fool,' said Fleance. ''Tis always a bad thing to publicly and negatively comment on another.'

'Indeed,' agreed Duncan. 'But all of us make errors of judgement. Let us hope that when we do, we have humility enough to admit our wrongs and strength enough to forgive those who wrong us.' He turned away from the tapestry and continued walking the halls. 'I suppose this is why those who are skilled with this talent make such things. They see the error of men's ways and seek to warn the future people. To help them avoid the same mistakes.'

Fleance shook his head. 'I have seen little evidence thus far of men learning from those who have gone before. Again and again, we make the same mistakes, whether it is love, war, family or politics.'

'A wise pronouncement, my friend.' Duncan dropped his head and breathed deeply for a few moments. When he raised his head, his face was flushed and his eyes bright. 'Much is expected of me, Flea, and to that end, I know what I must do to fulfil those expectations.'

He said it without bitterness or pride. It was just as it had to be. What might it mean to have in your future the certainty of your place in society as Duncan had? Would he have been similarly placed if his father had lived? He wondered if it was a worry for Duncan, this burden of the state of Scotland. 'Do you think much about what is going to happen?'

Duncan looked at him and smiled sadly. 'Too many times, if Rachel is to be believed. There is nothing I can do to change what will happen. I can only ensure that whatever I do, it is right and honourable and for the best for those in my care.'

'That is a heavy pronouncement for a young man.'

He nodded. 'Though you have not said so in words, I sense in you as much a weighted story as mine.'

Just then King Malcolm's servant came back, another servant with him. 'The king is ready to receive you, Sire. This man will take you to him.' He stood aside to let them pass.

'I will find you anon, my friend,' Duncan said as he squeezed his shoulder.

The old man waited until Duncan was gone and the door to the chambers was closed. 'I will take you, myself, to the guest quarters, if it pleases you.'

'Thank you,' Fleance said, suddenly aware of how tired he was of travelling. 'I would be most grateful.' As they walked further into the castle, he thought about Duncan's last words to him: *my friend.* Apart from Blair, Fleance had never had anyone he could call friend. Rosie was not his friend – she was his soulmate. How strange that Duncan gave of his heart so readily to him. Was it because he felt an obligation as Fleance had saved him? True, the days together had not been unpleasant and, if he was honest with himself, he would say that Duncan's stories were as well told and entertaining as Rosie's and had helped to keep his mind from the sorrow and the fear which was with him always.

Fleance undressed and used the water provided to wash. It was good to scrub clean the grime collected over many days' travelling and, though his collection of garments was small, he'd kept a set clean and free for such a time as this. The dirty pile which sat on the floor could be seen to by the servants.

It took much courage to go into the hallway and summon assistance because this was the first time in ten years he'd stepped foot in a royal house and, with so many people about, he was feeling overwhelmed. Too many years in seclusion had robbed him a little of his manners in company. 'My clothes,' he said. 'They are in need of laundering.'

The servant bowed. 'Certainly, Sire,' and he went in, picked up the pile and left. A memory stirred. A memory of a time when he would ask such a thing without another thought. Though his father had always insisted he treat their servants well, it had not come naturally to Fleance who saw himself as far better than those whose job it was to wash and clean and carry and cook. But that had been a long time ago. Now, after years living a basic life filled with hard work, Fleance had become accustomed to fending for himself.

He looked in the mirror. His face was a dark mass of coarse hair. It made him feel dirty and unkempt so he went out into the hallway again. 'A blade, if you will, to shave,' he said to the servant who, within moments, was back with warm water, lather and a blade.

'Would you permit me, Sire, to shave you?' the servant asked.

This made Fleance pause. No other man had ever shaved him. When he had the need a few years back, Magness had set him down with mirror, water and blade and, like the weaponry lessons, proceeded to teach the young Fleance how to shave. Perhaps it would be a very good learning moment to surrender his face and throat to another. Perhaps it would develop his sense of trust and faith – something Magness often said was lacking in him.

'I am tired. I would be grateful,' Fleance said.

''Tis a pleasure, Sire, to dress such a fine-looking young man as yourself.'

Fleance sat down on the chair in front of a small table where the servant had placed the water and blade. He wrapped a dry cloth around Fleance's shoulders and put his hands into the warm water. Then he brought them to Fleance's face and proceeded to wet all the stubble. He took a small bristle wand and rubbed it vigorously into the block of soap. The feeling of the bristles against his stiff facial hair was a relief.

He closed his eyes and allowed the experienced manservant to do his work. Many a time, as a boy, he'd stood by while his father was treated to such a thing. Banquo's beloved aide would, with swift movement and skill, lather his father's face and then, with the sharpest of blades, slide it over the contours of his face and neck. In the beginning, Fleance thought it was the soap which somehow dissolved his father's bristles and that the blades were simply like the paddles he saw the stablehands use to scrape down the horses. It was only when he'd snuck into his father's personal chamber, stolen away with the blade and presented it to Blair out on the moor, that he understood the hazard such an implement could pose.

He'd got Blair to lie down while he lathered his face. Then, he had proceeded to scrape the blade across his friend's face. Instantly, blood had sprang forth and Blair had yelped, pulling away and holding his cheek. 'You're trying to kill me,' he'd said but Fleance took no notice. He was staring at the instrument in his hand. He'd pulled a strand of wheat from the ground and gently pressed it against the blade. It had sliced the straw in two.

Fleance looked up. 'This is really sharp,' he had said.

Blair was crying. 'I'm cut, Flea. You need to take me to the manor.' He'd held his hand to his face so that Fleance did not at first understand the gravity of the situation. When Blair pulled his hand away, blood flowed easily down his face.

That was the first time Fleance understood one of the rhythms of man. Blood flows freely and to stop this, one must press down on the wound and hold fast which would break the flow. That would save a man's life.

He had picked up his father's personal grooming tools and lifted poor Blair to his feet. 'I'm sorry, Blair. I did not know. Press your hand against the cut. Nurse will know what to do.'

As it turned out, it was not nurse but Banquo who was able to stem the bleeding and allow Blair to live another day.

Later, in his chambers, he was not so pleasant to Fleance. 'What were you thinking? To take a dangerous blade as if it was a play thing? You are a bright boy but this was stupidity.'

Fleance had hung his head in shame. He did not want to tell his father that he had not understood the workings of the instruments. Instead he put up what he thought was a reasonable response. 'Blair was afraid, Father, and would not stay still. He moved just at the wrong time and I cut him. It is good that I knew to hold a firm pressure on the wound otherwise he would have bled out.'

But Banquo understood his son, his temper and his rashness. He had ignored the excuse and instead, putting his hands on Fleance's shoulders and looking him in the eye, said, ''Tis a poor craftsman who blames his tools – or another. Fleance, you could have killed Blair. Do you not see how serious this is?'

That was the moment when he understood so much: that he could no longer excuse his outbursts or his irrational behaviour; that often things were not as they seemed.

Not long after this, they had travelled to Inverness and learnt, in the hardest way, the truth of all his father had told him.

'Sire? Sire?' Fleance awoke. He'd fallen asleep as the servant had shaved him. 'I have finished. Is there anything else you need?'

Fleance blinked and rubbed his hand over his face. It was as smooth and soft as . . . as . . . he immediately thought of Rosie but had to push her from his mind. 'I thank you. Yes, I would like to eat now.'

The servant bowed deeply. 'Sorry, Sire. My apologies. It will be here in a moment.'

He gathered up his tools and hurried out of the chambers. Fleance stood, stretched and yawned. All he wanted to do was to crawl into the huge bed, which sat centre place in the room, and sleep.

Instead, he went to the window and looked out over the castle grounds. In the distance, he could see the spray of the distant ocean, a white mist from the waves stretching out along the horizon. Below him, in the courtyard, horses and riders came and went – it was almost as busy as a village on market day.

There was a knock on his door and the servant entered carrying a tray of food. "Tis just a small taste, Sire, for the banquet will be ready in less than two hours.' He placed the tray on a large wooden chest at the foot of the bed and left immediately.

Despite being exhausted, Fleance discovered he was hungry indeed and finished all the cold meats and cheese quickly. It revived him so, rather than having a sleep, he left his chambers and explored the halls of the castle. As he walked, he thought about how many times his father had walked the same path, for often he would stay a night or two at Forres either in the company of the king or after a long journey.

Banquo was gone from their manor often and for long periods of time. After his mother died, the gap left by his father's constant absences became more apparent so that Fleance found himself more often in the company of young Blair and his plump and hearty mother. However, Fleance did not like her much; he found her harsh voice and loud ways too much of a contrast to his own mother. Mothers should be steady and calm and gentle and beautiful, he'd thought. Not fat and rude and loud and smelly. Still, Blair's mother fed Fleance and took care of his needs when Banquo was absent but, over time, he had learnt to keep to himself unless his father was near.

Fleance didn't know much about the king, Malcolm, as he had only met him that once, on the day they rode to Inverness. Then, Malcolm had been a quiet man and more interested in the birds of the air and his horse than he was in the conversations which had swirled around him.

Now, if the gossips were true and the polite references made by Duncan accurate, he seemed a man well gone from this world already. Not unkind or cruel but less than effective. Fleance remembered the angry exchange between Dougal and Magness about the rule of Scotland and her fate once the crown was placed on Donalbain's head.

What might happen if an unfavourable king ruled Scotland? Would there be unrest and revolt? Or, would another swoop in to help the weak king keep Scotland afloat?

Perhaps it was ill mannered to be thinking such things, for the ruling monarch was still breathing. It was strange, though, despite it being clear to all that the king was dying, there was no sign of mourning. Instead, the castle was alive with bustling and busyness. Servants passed him, hurrying from one task to another, always carrying something. It made Fleance feel somewhat invisible as none took any notice of him.

Now that he was alert and more of himself, the familiar emptiness returned. The first time the feeling arrived was the night he stayed in the ruins just after his father's murder and the emptiness had not strayed far from him since. Only distractions such as hunting or working or time with Rosie had chased the unwelcome companion some distance. And the travels with Duncan, likewise, kept his loneliness at arm's length. Fleance found himself wishing for Duncan's company. To spend time with someone who was able to pull him out of himself.

No sooner had he thought this but he spied him standing at a window looking out. 'Duncan,' he called. 'Is all well with you?'

Duncan turned and gave a nod. 'Aye. But not so well for the king who is sure to go soon.' He walked over to Fleance. 'He is ready to meet his Maker and that brings him and Margaret peace. We did not talk of father but he gave me much advice as to Scotland's relationship with other countries. Advice which I think is sound.' Duncan kept walking. Fleance followed. 'By the by, Flea. You look very presentable.'

Fleance shook his head. 'Perhaps you should be a royal of the Norman house.'

'Why?'

'You are so attune to the sensitivities of the court.'

Duncan laughed. "'Tis because I have grown up with sisters.' He stared at Fleance. 'I am still a man and like the women, so don't be thinking otherwise.'

Fleance, for the first time in a long time, roared with laughter. 'Man, did you think I was questioning your manhood?'

'By hell, you were!'

Fleance shook his head as Duncan had done. 'I just think you notice things most men don't – how someone is feeling, how they are dressed. You have an eye for detail.'

'Aye, and it's a skill that keeps me in with fellows high and low. To understand how a man's mind is put together, what he is thinking and feeling even if his face belies the thought, is something I have learnt to be a valuable skill.'

The seriousness of his words was not lost on either of them. Fleance chewed on his lip. 'I think that would be a handy skill to have. Especially in these uncertain times.'

They entered a magnificent hall with tables set around the perimeter. Down the far end, a number of guests were already seated and servants were ferrying wine and plates of food. 'Hope you're hungry,' Duncan said as he headed to the busy tables.

Nervously, Fleance looked around, scanning the faces to see if there was anyone he recognised – or anyone who would recognise him. He saw that Duncan had moved to the high table and scouted around for a place at one of the lower tables. 'Here, man,' Duncan called. 'There's a seat here for you.' Fleance took a deep breath and followed him.

'Where?' he asked for he could not see a spare place. 'The table's full.'

Duncan smiled. 'Beside me, you fool.' He gestured to a place where someone was already seated. Fleance shook his head. 'There's no room, Duncan,' he said.

'Yes,' Duncan said. 'Here.' Again he pointed to the chair where a man sat, his back to Fleance. Then, the man shifted in his seat and

Fleance froze. It was him. The stranger who had followed him and now dared to sit at the table of the royal. Fleance swallowed thickly, prickles of sweat beading his neck and forehead. The clothes were identical. This was he. At last Fleance could challenge this man who had plagued him for weeks.

'Sire?' he said to the man's back. 'Why do you follow me?'

The man turned and Fleance started. The face which had twice eluded him was instantly recognisable. It was Banquo. He wore the same clothes he'd worn on the night of the attack and Fleance was eleven again and seeing his father's richly woven shirt and enviable cloak. He looked exactly the same as the last time Fleance saw him alive. It was no wonder there was something in the way the strange man had dressed that was familiar to Fleance.

He swallowed the thick lump in his throat and tried to speak. His father sat, as solid and as palpable as the roast chicken on the table. He stared at Fleance. 'Da?' Fleance reached out a hand and repeated himself. 'Da?' Why hadn't his father spoken to Fleance before this? Why had he left him to mourn him alone all these long years?

But Duncan's voice brought him back to the present. 'Flea? Are you all right?'

Fleance continued to stare at his father who now stood. As he did, blood began to gush from wounds in his father's neck and chest. 'Oh my God,' Fleance cried. 'You are hurt.' He rushed forward but when he got to the chair it was empty.

He spun around only to see Banquo walking down the hall towards the doors. 'Da,' he called. 'It's me.' The pain in his chest was terrible.

Duncan grabbed his arm. 'Was the journey too arduous?' He clicked his fingers to a serving man. 'Bring wine.' But Fleance, only vaguely aware of the commotion he was creating, shrugged off Duncan's hand and ran after Banquo. His father was now through the doors and into the corridor before Fleance had a chance to catch him.

When he fell into the hallway, it was empty save for two serving boys who stood wearily outside the doors of the banquet hall. 'Saw you an injured man?' he asked them. The young boys roused themselves, looking shamefaced at being caught lounging against the walls. They shook their heads, faces full of fear that they had been less than attentive at such an important feast.

Fleance looked left and right but there was no one. How could this be? How could he be seeing this? Banquo was dead. He knew that. So, it was a vision then. A ghost. Did this mean the stranger who had appeared in England and in the field opposite the tavern was the ghost of his father? Miri often spoke of such things but Fleance had not given it much weight. His own bad dreams were so regular, he had come to expect them. He believed that if someone said they had seen a ghost, it was because their mind was not right.

Could such things be? If so, then the terrible thing was that, even after all this time, Fleance knew when his father was unhappy. This sight could not be for real but even then, Fleance could make out the manner in which his father walked. It was a manner he long ago learnt to dread. It didn't happen very often and it was rarely directed at him but such was the strength of Banquo's displeasure it made the young Fleance extra careful with his manners and behaviour.

Fleance could sense that the ghost of his father was angry but for the life of him he could not work out why. Had he not abandoned love and happiness to discover what it was he was meant to do to avenge his father's murder? Fleance was working hard and yet this apparition, the sight from his worried brain, told him that he was doing wrong. He could hear Duncan saying something to the guests and there was a roar of laughter and they resumed their feasting.

Fleance was not ready to go back to the banquet so wandered around the castle. Perhaps he would come across the ghost again and find out what it was he was supposed to be doing. He soon found himself beside a lovely fountain which quietly burbled away beneath the main staircase. Was he losing his mind? Had the nights of painful dreams and the grief of losing Rosie taken its toll?

Not long after, Duncan found him. 'Flea? What is wrong? You looked like you had been injured and then you began to shout out bizarre things. Are you ill?'

Fleance closed his eyes and leant back against the wall. 'I don't know. I see things, Duncan, and I know they are why I am here but I do not understand them.'

'What things?'

He opened his eyes and looked at this kind and honourable young man. 'You will think me mad if I say.'

Duncan scratched his chin. 'Well, I already think that.' He grinned.

Fleance managed a small smile in return. 'And I know you're a lass on the inside. All soft and sweet.'

Duncan stared. 'You have got to be jesting me! Me, a girl, and you and your bloody horse and your dreams and visions and your secrets: Flea, you win hands down as to who is the more sensitive. Actually,' he added, 'I think the better word is "evasive".'

Fleance leant forward onto his knees and grasped his hands. 'Duncan, I don't know. You can make fun but all these things don't make sense to me yet. I need to find out more.'

'Well, that may be but *we need* to return to the hall or we will miss out on our meal and offend the queen.' Duncan stood and offered his hand. 'I will protect you from beastly sights.'

Fleance grabbed his hand and was surprised at the strength he found there. 'As I protected you from the wolves?'

Duncan gave him a friendly thump on the arm. 'You're not going to let me forget that, are you?'

'Not so long as you joke about my ghosts.'

As they walked back up the stairs, Duncan patted him on the back. 'I would not make fun of something that is clearly so important to you, my friend.'

Fleance stopped at the top and turned to him. 'Thank you.'

They walked back into the banquet hall which was now more occupied and noisy, the flustered pages and servants rushing from table to table to replenish the food and drink. Duncan went back to the high table and Fleance followed, relieved to see the seat Duncan had reserved for him was empty.

Just then a booming voice called out. 'Young Duncan, you're getting more like your grandfather every time I see you.' The owner of the voice stepped forward and here was yet another surprise for Fleance – it was William.

'Greetings, cousin,' Duncan said, unaware of Fleance's shock.

William spied Fleance. 'An' you, lad. We meet again. I hoped we would.'

Duncan frowned. 'So you have met Macduff already?'

Fleance was puzzled and shook his head 'No. But William and I had some adventures a while back.'

'Flea, this *is* Macduff, my cousin, the Thane of Fife.'

Fleance looked towards the older man. 'You, sir, are the Thane of Fife?'

'Aye,' said Macduff. 'William Macduff, Thane of Fife and Earl to the county.'

Duncan had said the man would be here but Fleance was unprepared for this. He finished his wine and looked at the solid man in front of him. 'William, I would talk with you as I have questions which you may be able to answer. But later, for now it is time to honour the king and queen.'

163

Macduff lifted his chalice. 'Well said, young Flea.' He smiled and took his place among the royals with Fleance unsure of where all things stood for the state of Scotland or in his own whirling mind.

Chapter Eighteen

Queen Margaret arrived midway through the meal. All stood and she made her way around the tables greeting the guests. She was small but not frail and though her clothes were not ostentatious, they had been made by skilled and careful hands. When she came to where Duncan and Fleance sat, she smiled more warmly at her nephew. 'You are looking well, Duncan.'

Duncan bowed his head. 'As are you, Your Majesty.'

'The king is very pleased you came. You know he adores you like his very own.'

'And I hold him in the same way as my duty demands.'

Margaret turned her attentions to Fleance. 'You are Flea, I understand. A much mis-assigned description.'

It was Fleance's turn to bow. 'Aye, madam. It is a nickname I have worn since I was a lad.'

'It is said you have come from England, but your accent tells me you are from the Highlands.'

Fleance felt his face flush warm and a spasm of fear went through him. He was aware of Duncan staring, a bemused expression on his face. Fleance swallowed. 'That is true, Your Majesty. I was born in the Highlands but was orphaned when my father was killed. A couple adopted me and took me to England where I have lived these past ten years.'

She picked up her skirts, preparing to move on. 'You are welcomed back home, Flea.' When she was before her own seat in the middle of the high table, beside the vacant throne of her husband, she raised her goblet. 'I drink to the joy of the whole table and to our king, long may he live.'

The guests raised their glasses and responded. 'Long live the king.'

As everyone sat down. 'Well, she's a clever one, then,' Duncan said, now trying a fruit tart which had appeared before them. 'She got more information out of you in one brief conversation than I have in being with you all these days.'

Fleance stared at his plate: he had not touched the food which was before him – his stomach was still twisted into knots. 'You have to know, Duncan, I have been running from danger and keeping safe these past ten years. 'Tis not an easy thing to reveal oneself when men would cut your throat as quick as wink if they thought it would bring them advantage.'

Beside him, he heard Duncan sigh. 'If I'd had an inclination to do that to you, I would have done so while you slept. Still, when you wouldn't shut up your mumbling, 'twas mighty tempting.' Fleance looked at him sharply. 'I am jesting,' he added with a grin. 'Relax, Flea. Enjoy the meal. Here,' he said, handing him a plate of roasted grouse. 'This is good.'

Fleance picked up the small bird and put it on his plate along with the other untouched food. It had been so long since he'd been to a royal banquet he'd forgotten the variety on offer. And the drink. It was only at feasts such as these that he had ever seen his father drinking.

Across from him, he saw William Macduff in deep conversation with another thane and he wondered what they were discussing.

The other man was frowning but nodded. His eyes widened and he looked over in Fleance's direction but it was Duncan he was interested in.

The queen rose from her chair. There was a loud scraping of stools as the guests followed suit. 'On behalf of the king,' she said, 'I invite you to continue with your feasting. As for me, I shall retire to spend time in prayer and thanksgiving.'

There were murmurs of 'good night' and 'long live the king' as she walked down the length of the dining hall and out the opened doors, followed by her attendants.

A moment later, William and three companions excused themselves and went out. Fleance had a strong desire to follow them but was uncertain of the protocol. He nudged Duncan. 'Where do you think they are going?' he nodded in the direction of the thanes.

Duncan looked over Fleance's head. 'Oh, no doubt to the ante-room of the great hall.'

'Why?'

''Tis quite a cosy place and where men usually go to tell stories and discuss politics.' He stood up. 'Shall we join them? Macduff is a good storyteller.'

This was exactly what Fleance wanted. 'Certainly, I have missed much of what has happened in Scotland since I've been away.'

'Well then, time for some history lessons,' Duncan said, giving a ready smile.

They followed the booming voices of the older men and came upon them as they were making preparations for a long night of talking and carousing.

'Welcome, lads,' William cried. 'Lennox, Ross. This here is Flea. Came across him in the woods of England and he was kind enough to share his meal and campsite with me.' Fleance waited for him to tell about what else had happened but nothing more was said about it.

The two older men nodded towards him but their stares made Fleance uncomfortable. Like William, there was something vaguely familiar about them although he could not find the reason for it in his memory.

'We have much to catch up on,' Lennox said, addressing Macduff. 'Firstly, you can talk of what business took you to England.' Duncan and Fleance sat on some large cushions and accepted the goblets offered by the servants.

The men talked on, though very little domestic or personal accounts were discussed.

In a lull in the conversation, Lennox addressed Duncan. 'How is that fine sister of yours, Duncan? Has she found herself a husband?'

'Not yet, cousin. Suitable prospects are thin on the ground.'

'You should send her down my way, lad. There are plenty of good men to choose from,' the thane replied, smiling. 'I'm sure even my own young boy would be very pleased to meet her.'

Ross made a growling sound. 'Aye, if it's a nanny he's wanting. I don't believe young Rachel, though good with the bairns, would consider a ten-year-old more suitable than the men she's turned down already.'

'Our Rachel is too busy with household things to worry about a match.' There was something in Duncan's tone that made Fleance wonder as to the meaning behind his words.

Just then, another servant came upon them. 'The king has requested an audience with Duncan.'

Duncan scrambled to his feet. 'I will come immediately,' he said.

'Thank you, Sire,' the servant said. 'I will tell him.' And he hurried away.

Duncan addressed the group. 'Entertain my friend here for he carries too much of a worried load – enough for a grown man to drown in.' Then he was gone.

Ross snorted. 'That was deep, even for dear wee Duncan.' He raised his drink to Fleance. 'What have you said or done to him, lad, that makes him say such words?'

Fleance stirred. 'I think it is because I talk in my sleep but do not spill my life's story.'

Macduff cleared his throat. 'Which, I think, is a good habit. Still, we here are fond of Duncan for he reminds us all of his dear grandfather.' There was a murmur of agreement. 'So like he is to old King Duncan that we forget our times and what is before us.'

Lennox roused himself and chucked another log on the hearth. 'We here may not see another time where the current king will reign long and prosperous without threat of war and unrest. However, that boy will one day be king and Scotland will be the better for it.'

There was general noise of approval. Clearly his new friend was highly regarded – though it did not surprise Fleance.

'Even then, if we do not learn from our past mistakes how can we ensure that they are not repeated?' Ross said. 'Try as we might to live our lives according to God's ordinances, there are men among us who spurn the natural order of the world and seek, for their own ambitions, power and prosperity through whatever means necessary.'

A quiet fell upon the group. Fleance studied the men who had gathered in this small ante-room. Almost all were older than Magness. Many had marks and scars on their faces and arms – clear badges of past battles. All were greying – some more than others. Yet, there was a dignity about them. Fleance could feel the strength and determination radiating from each man. As he looked at them, he understood that, behind their jokes and teasing, they shared a common history – a history which held much pain and heartache.

Lennox roused himself. 'I think the answer to that, Ross, is to keep reminding ourselves of those past mistakes; to keep telling the stories to our children in the hope that there are enough people to carry on the lessons we have learnt.'

'Here is your cue, Macduff, to tell us your story again,' a wizened man said. 'I have heard it once but I'm sure many of our company have not.'

Macduff, Thane of Fife, stood. ''Tis a sorry story for it shames me to think there are fellows, as Ross has said, who pretend honour but whose bodies house black hearts.' He drank deeply. 'I was called forth to this place, Forres, for the king had seen great victory over Norway and the traitor, Cawdor.' There was a muffled grumble from a few. 'I know but that is not this story. So, Macbeth, with his valiant sergeant Banquo, led the defence against the Norwegian king. 'Twas that very night Malcolm was named as successor to the throne and King Duncan made it his pleasure to travel to Inverness to celebrate.'

Fleance relived the story through his own memory as he had travelled with his father in this company. He looked hard at Macduff and now realised why he and some of the others were familiar to him – they had been with the king and his attendants that day also. Did they also see some recognition in him? Miri often said how changed he was compared with the skinny, pale-faced wee boy they'd scooped off the side of the road. But, like Agnes, did they see a resemblance to his father? He would need to be ever watchful.

Macduff continued. 'It was a great feast but damned be the souls of those two fiends who all the while were plotting murder.'

Lennox cleared his throat. 'He deceived us all, man.'

Macduff glared. 'Aye, but wounded me more than any man here,' he growled.

Lennox looked away. 'Aye.'

'Lennox and I bedded down in one of the castle's outer dwellings for the king had especially asked that I wake him early the next day. Had I stayed in the castle, I may have taken too much wine.'

'It was a rough night,' Lennox added. 'Storms. Wind. Chaos. 'Twas not a restful sleep.'

'We arrived a little over the time we'd planned – perhaps if we had, we may have stopped the whole sorry mess.'

'You are not to blame, Macduff,' Ross said. 'Men choose the course of their own destiny. Perhaps if the king had not been so trusting . . .'

Macduff shook his head. 'A king should be safe in the home of his cousin and his subject.'

Fleance wanted him to continue with the story, not digress into philosophy. 'What happened next?' he asked quietly.

Macduff looked at him in surprise. 'I'd forgot you were there, lad. Well, 'tis not a nice thing to remember. We greeted Macbeth who had on the face of the innocent and he showed me to the king's chamber. What I saw there has been burned into my brain.' All in the room were quiet. 'The innocent and most gracious king scourged by gashes from his neck to his toes. Blood. There was so much blood – walls, floor, bedclothes. Most hideous. I hardly remember what I did next.'

Fleance did. He remembered the tolling bell and a man shouting out names and people everywhere before his father collected him and they headed back to Lochaber.

'Strange to think we believed it was Malcolm and Donalbain who had done the deed.' Macduff sighed and then took another drink. 'With Malcolm gone to England and Donalbain fled to Ireland, we were left to arrange for the king to be buried on Iona.'

'In all my remembrances,' Ross said, 'I do not know of a more terrible time. While the tyrant lived, men died. And innocents,' he added, looking at Macduff.

'Aye,' Macduff agreed, standing up. 'Well, this night has given me enough of remembrances. I have lost the pleasure of the story-telling. I'm to bed.' He put his goblet on the tray a servant held and walked away.

'Poor Macduff,' Lennox said quietly. 'His still mourns them after all this time.'

'Who?' Fleance asked.

'Macbeth put his whole household to the sword – his beloved wife, all his children, even the infants, the servants and their children, livestock – all gone save two – a man and a wife who were away from the castle that day.'

So Blair was right, Fleance thought. Macbeth had indeed murdered Macduff's family.

'Where was Macduff when that happened?' he asked.

'He'd gone to England to convince Malcolm to return. He saved Scotland but lost his family,' Ross said. Fleance thought for a time about the charming older man and the sorrow he so clearly carried. Another one scarred by the events of that time.

'He could not have suspected how evil Macbeth was – that he murdered his best friend and tried to lay the blame on the son, a wee sprat of a lad. No, once he started in his way of blood, there was no going back.'

Fleance's mouth went dry. 'Who, who . . .' he stammered. 'Who was Macbeth's best friend?' But even before Lennox said the name, he knew.

'Banquo, Thane of Lochaber. The most noble gentleman that ever walked the Highlands.' Fleance's head was spinning. Finally, the truth. He knew, now, who it was that had killed his father and who had tried to kill him. Lennox continued. 'They found Banquo's body in a stream, his throat cut. His son, they never found. He was probably attacked by wolves. Another family, like Macduff's, wiped out on a single night.'

'For what reason did he do that?' Fleance could barely get the question out.

'Who can know the mind of a mad man?' Ross replied.

Fleance stood up. 'If you will excuse me, it has been a long day. Good night to you all.' He did not know how he made it back to his room. He was reliving the night of his father's murder yet again but this time the fear and grief were mingled with some element of joy and relief. At last he had some answers. Finally he knew who had tried to destroy him. Macbeth was his father's murderer and Macbeth was no more. He could stop looking over his shoulder as he had done all these past years. His life was no longer in danger.

But why was he still being plagued by dreams and visions? If the one who was to be avenged against, Macbeth, was killed years ago, what more could he do? *What revenge can I take?* he thought. Perhaps his father meant something different. Banquo would not have known his murderer's fate.

Sighing, he removed his boots and coat. He might not be in danger but he still had to put his energies into working out what it was he was meant to do to stop the nightmares and return home to Rosie.

He crawled into bed and waited for yet another night of troubled sleep.

Chapter Nineteen

Someone shoved Fleance and he woke instantly. The sun was streaming in through the casement and Duncan stood beside him, grinning. 'Are you up for some adventure, Flea?' Duncan asked.

'What did you have in mind?'

'I have to go to Inverness.'

'What or who is at Inverness?' Fleance asked, sitting up and scratching his head.

'A haunted castle, if you would believe the servants.'

'You're mad.'

'But it will make for a great story to take back to the wee one: attacked by wolves, rescued by a handsome stranger.' Fleance rolled his eyes and pushed Duncan out of the way as he got out of bed. 'A deserted castle famous for its most foul murder of the king of Scotland.'

'Are you serious?' Fleance could not work out whether his friend was teasing him or not.

'No, not about that but I do have to go to Inverness. Word has come from my father that I am to go there and find a treasure.'

'Treasure?'

'Aye, he doesn't know what it is exactly. It seems the prophets say that hidden deep within Macbeth's castle is something that will strengthen Scotland.'

Fleance stopped lacing his boots and looked up. 'Macbeth's castle?'

'Aye. One and the same. I hear it is deserted so we won't be trespassing.'

Fleance thought for a moment. The castle where King Duncan was murdered. The castle where it had all begun for him and his father and their fates. Could it be that the ghost of Banquo was somehow directing his path? Helping him to gain information that would eventually fulfil his promise and lead him onto the hope of his future – Rosie?

He frowned at Duncan. 'It's a bit vague, don't you think?' he asked. 'It could be anything.'

Duncan chewed his bottom lip. 'Well, such is the thinking of my father and the weight he puts in the words of three hags who prowl around our county.' By the look on his face, Fleance could tell Duncan was not impressed with this.

Three hags? Could it be they were the same who had accosted him on the road north? 'What are these hags like?' he asked.

Duncan looked at him sternly. 'You should take no mind of them, Flea, for they are evil and poison men's minds. A more disgusting trio of females – though they look less human and more beast – I have never seen. They are trouble.'

Fleance put up his hands. 'You will get no argument from me there, my friend. My father often warned me against such creatures.'

While Duncan waited, Fleance wrapped the last of the leather straps around the top of his boots and stood. 'Fine. I will go with you – who knows what predicament you will get yourself into without me to help.'

Duncan smiled broadly though Fleance caught a flash of anxiety in his eyes. 'It will be a merry distraction from our concerns.

Father may or may not get his treasure but you and I will make the most of our assignment.' He stood by the open door. 'I will meet you at the stables,' he said and dashed out of the room. Fleance shook his head. The optimism, energy and enthusiasm startled him. It was as if, by being here, a load had been taken from Duncan's shoulders. He had no idea what things the king had told him yesterday but whatever it was, it had lightened the young prince's mood despite the clearly frustrating command from his father.

The castle of Inverness was surprisingly as he remembered it except that it was now deserted. On the night he had arrived with his father and King Duncan, there had been much activity and a lot of effort had gone into ensuring the castle was decorated and adorned worthy of a royal presence. Fleance remembered how the pretty Lady Macbeth had blushed when the king presented her with a diamond, right on these very steps where he now stood.

Fleance looked about the courtyard. Nothing living remained. All the occupants had either been killed or had fled during the tyrant's reign. Livestock had gone, so only broken and worthless carts or urns or barrels littered the messy yard. There were signs of many years of disuse and the weather had done its damage. Still, there was something about the height of the castle and the architecture which was defiant. High, solid walls stood silently, their narrow casements like dark eyes looking down at them, wary.

'Come along,' Duncan said. 'Let's explore. I've always wanted to pay tribute to my grandfather at the place where he was murdered — to honour him and say to his spirit he is not forgotten. When I told Uncle Malcolm of our plans, he asked if we would light a candle in remembrance of the souls taken by Macbeth.'

Inside the castle was as messy as the courtyard for there were large holes in the roof and no one to repair them. Bird droppings bleached stripes down the rough-hewn walls, and straw and rubbish cluttered the stairwell. They came to the first level and it was smaller than he remembered. Still, then he had been a boy and now he was a man. A balcony ran around the entire first floor so that one could look down into the yard from any vantage point.

Silently, they made their way along this and then Duncan ducked through an archway which led straight to an interior hall – it ran parallel to the balcony. Off this were doors. Duncan opened the first one they came to. It opened easily enough at first but then came up against something behind the door.

'Help me push this, would you?'

Both of them put their shoulders to the splintered wood and pushed. There was a queer scraping sound and the door inched open. Duncan was the first to squeeze through the gap. 'That will explain that,' Duncan's muffled voice came behind the door. 'What a stench.'

Fleance squeezed himself through as well and closed the door. What they had struggled against was the carcass of a wolf. 'How did that get in here?' Fleance asked, putting his arm over his nose and mouth.

Duncan pointed to the claw marks on the inside of the door. 'It no doubt came wandering in looking for food or shelter, perhaps in bad weather, and the door closed shut.' He looked about the room. 'It looks like he's tried other ways to escape. Poor creature.'

'This must have been a sleeping chamber – the remains of a bed.' Fleance pointed to a far wall. 'It's clear the place has been looted many times.'

'Well, let's leave this wolf's grave and continue on.' Duncan opened the door and passed through. Fleance followed. As they went along the corridor, they saw some doors had been smashed off their hinges altogether or were hanging drunkenly. All the rooms in this part seemed to be sleeping chambers. The last one at the end, though, had an antechamber before the large main room.

There was an area where presumably servants or chamberlains slept or guards stood. The inner room, which was clear of all furniture or furnishings, was bathed in bright light for the roof had almost completely gone. Duncan stood in the middle of the room. 'I think this was the room,' he said. 'Uncle Malcolm described coming in from the second chamber so this must be the first for it is the largest.' He took a deep breath. 'This is where it all began.'

'Will you light the candle here?' Fleance asked. 'It might go some way to restoration for the suffering started over ten years ago. Though,' he added, clearing a space in the dirt and rubbish for Duncan to set down the candle, 'I wager betrayal and murder have been part of our history since the beginning.'

Duncan gave him a wry smile as he set the candle down and struck the flint to the wick. 'You are right. What I meant was, this is the beginning of where things changed for my family.' He scuffed his foot on the dusty floor around the burning flame. 'I sometimes wonder how different my life would have been if my grandfather had not been murdered that night.'

Fleance nodded. 'Aye, so many things would have been different had one man made a different choice.' He went to the doorway. 'Come on, let's keep exploring.'

On the opposite side of the castle from where the sleeping chambers were, sat the great hall. Like the balcony, it was smaller than he remembered. Back then, the smell of roasting pork, a roaring fire and the sounds of booming laughter and music had made the room seem such a festive and welcoming place. There, the king had sat next to his sons; there, his father had sat, deep in discussion with a lord. And there, Fleance had stood, right in the centre, where he had sung a folk song much to the king's delight.

From that time on, however, he had not sung again, even with Rosie's insistence he join her in a song that evening of the carnival. It all looked rather pathetic now. In his dreams and memories, this palace was a place of fear, of danger. But it was not that at all. It had no power. It was just an empty shell where tragic events had occurred.

It was a disappointing end to their adventure. 'Let's look in the dungeon. Perhaps we'll find some skeletons to scare your sisters,' he laughed.

Past the great hall was a landing with stairs leading into the belly of the castle. They followed it down, stepping carefully over fallen debris. When they came to the ground floor, it opened out into another centre space with numerous doorways leading off in all directions.

'Shall we make a game out of this? For I'm sorry to say, apart from the wolf, this has not been much of an adventure.'

'What do you propose?' Fleance asked raising his eyebrows.

'I propose,' Duncan began, 'that we go separate ways and the first to find anything of significance, anything that might be this treasure Father asks for, is the winner.'

'And the prize?' Fleance asked.

'Satisfaction.'

Fleance laughed and looked around him. 'I can not see what either of us may find which would fit with your father's request. Yet, your proposal will add an edge to our search.'

Duncan returned the smile. 'True. So are you up to the challenge?'

He nodded. 'When shall we meet again?'

Duncan thought for a bit. 'When you feel the sun at her highest, let us wait for each other outside the walls of the castle.' He lit two small torches and handed one to Fleance.

'Thank you,' Fleance said. 'Good fortune, then.'

They went their separate ways but Fleance was really only humouring Duncan. What he most wanted was to be gone from this place for it held nothing of significance and the time here was wasted. What a disappointment. Was he putting too much store in signs? Was he reading too much into events which may or may not have a connection to his quest? It was too hard to tell.

On the one hand, he considered himself a man above superstition and dependence on the supernatural. On the other hand, he was seeing ghosts; he had met the three witches who told him things that no earthly creature would know. A part of him wanted to believe that Fate was playing out a predestined hand and, held within that hand, was release from his bond to his father and a secured and contented life with Rosie.

Lost in his thoughts and not really caring where he was going, Fleance wandered into the kitchen.

Again, like the other rooms, there was nothing there but rubbish – no sign of cooking utensils or any evidence that a meal had been prepared here in a long while. There were still large storage cupboards which had not been worth removing by the scavengers.

He opened and closed them absentmindedly. As he closed the third one, a gush of air hit his face. He stopped and reopened the doors. It was a large cupboard, probably for the storage of huge pots of grain, flour and meal. Fleance put his head in and saw that part of the back of the cupboard had fallen away. Beyond was a black void.

Another gust of air hit him and the flame of his torch stuttered. He was intrigued. What was behind? Fleance put the torch in a holder on the wall, lifted out the three shelves and stepped up into the cupboard. He gingerly pushed the wood which backed the cupboard and it swung away easily. It was a door!

Before him was fresh air but also darkness so he climbed back out of the cupboard and retrieved the torch. Climbing in again, he gingerly put one foot forward. He felt a solid step. Then another. Fleance shook his head. Of course there would be a secret passage in a castle. All good stories told of them. These allowed families under siege to escape.

He couldn't see much beyond what light came from the torch so he made his way slowly down the steps into pitch blackness. Only the fresh breeze made him feel better; made him continue.

The last step was not on stone but on dirt and there were no others. He was at the end of the staircase but where was he? Fleance waved the torch around and found another protruding from a sconce attached to the wall. He touched it with the flame of his own small torch and it flared instantly. Holding his own above his head he saw, in the shadows, a dirt-floored room. A cabinet leant against one wall and he went to it, holding up the flame to see more clearly.

The contents of the cabinet were a strange mix – a garment which looked like that used for an infant; a strangely decorated bowl; and though smothered by dust, he made out a large silver ring and a thick book. Fleance put his torch into another holder secured to the wall and carefully lifted the book from its place. He blew off the dust and, with his hand, wiped away the residual grime.

He opened the leather cover and peered at the intricate drawings and elaborate swirls of the letters. It was in Latin, a language he did not know. Perhaps it was *The Bible*. Or, given the nature of the owners, a list of spells.

He shut the book and placed it back on the shelf. Then he turned his attention to a carved wooden treasure box which was beside it. Carefully, he lifted it down and, looking around, he spied a stool which he brought close to the light and sat upon.

The box was carved with obscure images which he could not discern except he saw horse, raven, owl, boar and other animals of vicious intent. He opened the lid and inside found three parchments. These he brought forward and laid on his lap. The first was a letter. It was addressed to Lady Macbeth and was signed Macbeth.

They met me on the day of success in battle and I have since learnt by incredible evidence which I will tell you about, that they have more power and insight in them than we could know. To my friend Banquo, who declared he neither begged, nor feared their favours nor their hate, they turned and hailed him as not so happy but happier, not so great but greater, not to be king but to father kings.

Fleance started and then re-read the last line. What did it mean? How could Banquo father kings if he were dead? To father kings? The only child Banquo had fathered was himself, Fleance. It was mad talk and nonsense. How could a grown man take such words seriously?

He continued reading:

When I burned in desire to question them further, they made themselves air, into which they vanished. While I stood rapt in the wonder of it, there came messengers from the king, who all hailed me 'Thane of Cawdor', by which title, before, these weird sisters saluted me, and referred to me, as if making a promise for the future, with 'Hail, king that shalt be!'

This have I thought good to deliver you, my dearest partner of greatness, that you might celebrate with me these great honours and also know what other greatness is promised you. Lay it to your heart, tell no one and farewell.

What did this mean? He looked it over quickly again. Banquo had been caught up in this as well. The victorious battle Macbeth spoke of must have been the one against Norway and the rebels. So, Macbeth, with Banquo, had met some prophets? Witches? They promised him rank beyond his dreams. Was this reason enough for murder? Murder of kin?

The other parchment was another letter from Macbeth to his wife: it was addressed to her as Queen and this time in a madly scrawled hand.

I must explain to you what has presently been shown so that you can make urgent preparations for the coming time. I sought further counsel from the secret and midnight hags; not from their mouths but their masters', for a king is in need of higher power than these. The first apparition, an armed head, held a warning: 'Macbeth, beware Macduff. Beware the Thane of Fife.' The second, a bloody child, gave better hope telling me to be bloody, bold and resolute; scorn the power of man for none born of woman shall harm Macbeth.

Be of good cheer, my love. Your husband and king shall not be easily overthrown. But the third, though also a promise, brings me to my instruction. The third apparition was another child, crowned, holding a tree in his hand. He exhorted me to be lion-mettled, proud, and take no care of rebels or treasonous advance because Macbeth will never be vanished until Great Birnam Wood comes against high Dunsinane Hill.

I sought more from them though they warned against it. I desired to know whether Banquo's seed would ever reign in this kingdom. What I saw grieved my heart for there came sight after sight of crowned men so like the spirit of Banquo, eight in all with the last one holding a mirror which showed me many more. Finally, the bloody ghost of Banquo appeared again and smiled at me with triumph on his face.

So, though there are promises that I am safe, Fleance lives and while he does, I hold a barren sceptre in my hand, keeping warm the throne until the son seeks to overthrow my fruitless crown. We must away from Inverness for how can trees pull up their roots and march like soldiers? To ensure the certainty of our fate, we must be doubly safe.

Therefore, my dearest Queen, make hasty arrangements to move all to Dunsinane castle. Take all fellows who would come and leave behind all that is not needed – servants, letters, trinkets – for, when this is all over, we can return to Inverness.

I will go before you.

All speed, my dearest chuck.

There was just one more parchment. A recorded list of bizarre statements which were in a different hand. Was a servant or his wife recording the mad ravings of a tyrant? The list was most interesting: names, his father's, Banquo, at the top and second his own, Fleance. Next, added to as time went on were others: Macduff; Angus; Caithness; Ross; Lennox.

Macbeth had decided to murder all who might challenge him to the throne.

Fleance fell back against the stone wall. So, here it was, exactly as Lennox had described – Macbeth killed his father because he was afraid that Banquo would usurp him. This was why his father had been murdered and his own life challenged. He took in a deep breath and tears came to his eyes. Finally some answers to what and when and why things had been so bad.

He swallowed and angrily folded the letters before putting them inside his coat. He held onto the list. He remembered his own encounter with witches. They had said some things which sounded fair. Perhaps . . . ? Fleance shook his head again. How foolish to think one was above the natural order of things. *If a man lives by honour, then he is in need of nothing else save food, clothes, a roof over his head and, if fortunate, the love of a family.* His father had told him this many times and the proverb was ingrained into his thinking.

Come what may, whether the prophecies had any kernel of truth or not, he would do nothing but what he had to do. According to these letters, the witches had given Banquo prophecies just as they had Macbeth, yet he did not use these pronouncements as an excuse to act dishonourably. His father had made the decision to continue on the right path, the one ordained for his life – whether by the hand of Fate or God. Macbeth, though believing in what the witches had said, still took action to make doubly sure the prophecies came true. With bloody consequences for many.

Fleance remembered now after the banquet in this castle's great hall, coming down the stairs and encountering Macbeth.

It was very late and he hardly managed to keep his eyes open. They stopped so that Banquo could put his cloak on, for the weather had turned foul. 'I cannot understand why it is so dark,' he said. 'Here, take this torch for a moment as well.'

Fleance stood on the steps, leaning against the wall, holding his father's heavy sword and then the torch. Banquo, despite laughing a lot, looked pale and tired. 'Are you fine, Da?' he'd asked.

Banquo secured the cloak and rubbed a hand over his eyes. 'I haven't been sleeping so well, son. Bad dreams.'

'Perhaps you should take some of Ma's remedy,' Fleance suggested. Their eyes met. 'There is none left,' Banquo said quietly. They hardly mentioned her of late. Just then Macbeth appeared. 'Are you still awake, my friend? I'm to bed. But it was a good feast and the king was in particularly good spirits.' Banquo reclaimed the sword and torch from Fleance. 'You've been blessed by his generosity tonight.'

Macbeth smiled. 'I do feel his gestures were extravagant because we had barely time to prepare for his royal attendance and so many guests.'

'As always, Macbeth, you and your lady outdo yourselves. 'Tis always a pleasure to be hosted by you.' They began walking down the stairs and Banquo lowered his voice. 'May I speak plainly to you?'

A startled expression flicked over Macbeth's face before he composed his features. 'Aye.'

'I keep having dreams about the weird sisters. To you, some of what they have said has come true.' He lowered his voice further. 'Are you bothered too?'

Macbeth patted Banquo's arm. 'I have not given them another thought. But, listen, after all this is over, perhaps we can meet and talk over what happened. Try to make sense of it.'

Banquo nodded. 'That would help, I think.'

This time Macbeth lowered his voice. 'If you follow my advice and do what I say, I think you too shall see the fruits of those mad women's rantings.'

Banquo nodded again. 'So long as the action is honourable and my conscience remains clear, I am your servant.'

'You and the boy sleep well,' Macbeth said, ruffling Fleance's hair.

'And you, Macbeth.' Then they walked across the courtyard, up another flight of steps to the first level and went into their chamber.

How innocent and benign that conversation had seemed. It was difficult readjusting his boyhood interpretation of that time. Up until a few days ago, he had not even sensed the horror which was to come at the hands of the man who had so kindly and graciously welcomed them. How was it that one man chose one path and another the opposite? Why hadn't Macbeth done as his father said? If God wanted it to be, then it would be.

He pulled out the first parchment again and studied it, looking for answers to his questions. It made less sense than the other two but he placed it also inside his coat. He stood up. He would win Duncan's challenge but no eyes other than his and Duncan's would see these for now. They contained too much potency at this unsettled time.

Fleance made his way back up the stone steps to the kitchen and the cupboard. He walked through the kitchen and into the outer room before stumbling upon the open courtyard. The corpse of another animal lay just outside the door. Pig or wild boar, he could not tell but it did not carry the stench of the recently dead wolf.

Taking a deep breath, he looked around the castle walls. All was silent. Nothing stirred. He'd had enough of adventure and in his pocket were treasures. Time to leave this cursed place and find his friend.

Willow was chomping on grass and, by the way he struggled against Fleance, the horse was most put out that his rider had arrived so quickly. 'Hey, Willow,' Fleance said. 'So you've been resting?' The horse gave him a guarded look. 'I was occupied, all right? We can't always be saviours of every moment.'

The horse stamped his hoofs and turned so that Fleance got a well-deserved view of his backside and tail and returned to the grass. Fleance laughed. 'You, my dear steed, are overreacting. You need to trust me more.' Willow continued to pull roughly at the grass, ignoring his rider, perhaps to make sure Fleance understood his disapproval.

Duncan turned up a few minutes later with a sword. 'Look at this,' he said. 'I can't believe the scavengers missed it. Surely it was Macbeth's?' His eyes sparked with excitement.

'I found something as well,' Fleance said. He pulled the letters from his pocket and gave them to Duncan.

Duncan lay the sword on the ground and began reading, his lips moving silently. Every few moments he looked at Fleance, a shocked expression on his face and then went back to the letter.

After a few minutes, he quietly folded the letters and handed them back to Fleance.

They stared at each other. Fleance waited for Duncan to say what needed to be said.

Duncan swallowed. 'Father must never see these,' he said.

'Duncan,' Fleance started. 'I need to tell you some things.'

'I know,' Duncan said. 'I know who you are, Flea. You are Banquo's son, Fleance, are you not?'

'Aye.'

Duncan sat down on a rock. 'Macduff hinted something to me last night and this letter,' he tapped it on his knee, 'names a Fleance.' He looked up. 'What are your thoughts? Do you think you can speak freely with me?'

187

'Duncan, I'm sorry for keeping it a secret, but I have been hiding for so long and didn't know who my enemies were. Those,' he said pointing to the letters still in Duncan's hands, 'tell me why my father was murdered. But, as Macbeth is dead, I am free to be myself.'

Duncan stood up and handed the letters back to Fleance. 'I think these best not be seen by anyone else.'

Fleance nodded. 'Agreed.'

'Did you find anything else?'

'Just carcasses of dead animals,' Fleance replied. He mounted Willow and was awarded with an impatient shudder. Duncan, after retrieving the sword, also mounted and Fleance noted that he did not favour his arm any more. 'Your wound has healed quickly,' he said.

'Aye,' Duncan said, holding up his arm. 'I have Rachel's balm to thank. Father thinks it has some magic potion in it but I have watched her make it and it is a simple natural remedy.'

'Perhaps she secretly whispers a spell when you're not looking.'

Duncan laughed out loud. 'If you met my sister, you would know there is not a speck of darkness on her soul. She is very devout, much like Queen Margaret.'

They moved off at a good pace for it was at least three hours back to Forres and, though neither said so, they both felt it desirable to be at the castle before the light left the day. They trotted on for a while and then Duncan slowed his horse to a walk; Fleance followed suit. 'I was thinking about what you said back then,' Duncan said.

'What?'

'About the dead animals.'

'Aye, what about them?'

'Almost every room I went into there was either a large dead bird or animal. We saw the wolf, and there was the boar, in the courtyard outside the entrance to the gallery. I also came across a couple of badgers – even a deer. Most strange.'

Fleance thought on this, trying to think of a reason why a deserted castle with no food to scavenge had attracted such creatures only for them to die. 'Maybe the well was poisoned,' he offered. 'Sometime when they arrived they drank and the water killed them.'

'That is very likely,' said Duncan. 'When I told the stablehands where we were going today, one of them was most upset. He told me the castle is cursed and no living creature who enters leaves alive.'

'We're alive,' Fleance said. 'But I did not drink anything there. What about you?'

Duncan shook his head. 'No, but the burn on the west side of the castle – did not the horses drink from there?'

'They did but it was safe – Willow has a sensitive nose.' At the sound of his name, the horse's ears twitched. 'He wouldn't touch something to make him sick – of this I can be sure for he has many times saved me from bellyache by refusing a stream.'

'Do you take mind of such things, Fleance?'

'Willow? Aye, I'm best to if I know what is good for me.'

Duncan smiled. 'No, I mean, curses and signs and things?'

Fleance stared ahead, constructing a reply. 'I think there are more things in both heaven and earth than we could ever hope to fully understand. There are things no one can explain and only God knows their origin. Others are the result of obsession or madness.' He patted Willow's thick neck. 'Why do you ask me this?'

It was Duncan's turn to stare ahead. 'My father, Donalbain, he . . .' He took a deep breath. 'I saw him with the three strange women I spoke of before. They bound his hands and put a blindfold on him.'

'Some men, I'm told, do enjoy such adventure.'

'No, it wasn't like that. They are considered by many to be witches. They certainly have bewitched my father and his brain

189

becomes wrought with the incantations they sing. They tell him things he wants to hear and he believes them to have power more than nature intended any human.'

Fleance was remembering again his encounter on the road past Glasgow. Instead, he offered Duncan what he thought he might like to hear. 'I do not put any store in such gabbling nonsense. Do you?'

'No. I think it is foolishness and dangerous. The king is right to try to rid the country of such creatures.'

They walked on in silence and Fleance thought about what Duncan had said earlier about the parchments. He was right that they should not show others what he had found. It would only confirm what Duncan said about the power of influence over those who choose to trade and traffic with the devil. It would be another secret to keep but it was more than that. It was something tangible for Fleance to use to put together the fragments of his past and maybe even discover the task his father still demanded of him.

Chapter Twenty

For the first time in a very long while, Duncan felt great delight. He'd spent a number of days with Fleance and then a few in consultation with the king. Just being away from the heaviness of responsibility for those in Glamis castle made his heart lighter. Having a companion who was both entertaining and intriguing made for a pleasant week. Finding Macbeth's sword (for Macduff had confirmed it was so) was an excellent trophy. It was a perverse motive, he knew, that made him so pleased. He had the very weapon of the man who had caused such heartache in his family. The one he had perhaps used against Macduff and failed, and these facts meant some measure of triumph for Duncan. The letters were another matter — their contents would only serve to aggravate his father's temper. Had Donalbain learnt the contents he would treat his new friend as a threat rather than welcome him as a lost member of the extended family.

This morning he had been summoned yet again to the king's chamber. Malcolm, though in his bed, was rosy faced and happy. 'Your father will be king,' he said. 'But it is thought by many who are wise that he is not ready to take the role of sovereign. It will be up to you, Duncan, to try to guide him in the right direction – you and the Lord.'

Duncan studied his uncle's face. Malcolm had aged rapidly this past year. His long hair, formerly a burnt red colour, was almost white and now fanned out against the pillows. Under his eyes were bruised smudges and his body, previously lithe and strong, was bloated and yellow.

Still, his eyes were clear and his smile ready. 'I have faith, Duncan, that you, like your grandfather before, have the honour, grace, wisdom and strength to see that the right thing is done for the people of Scotland.'

'Uncle,' Duncan said. 'Am I not free from the demands of the kingdom just at this time?'

Malcolm shook his head. 'No, but you and your father will bring Scotland into strength.' He coughed violently for a few moments. 'Water,' he asked and Margaret put the chalice to his lips. He took a drink, wiped away the drops and looked at Duncan. 'You will be the one who changes and secures the royal house. Your father, my dear brother, I know has ambitions, but I do not believe they rest well with the time. He has always been a formidable presence and often I have locked horns with him over matters.'

'Still,' Malcolm continued, 'he is for Scotland as I know you are and that is the thing.' The queen dipped a cloth into the basin beside the large bed and dabbed the king's forehead and mouth. 'We are not alone and we must look to the east where our good Lord was born for there lies not only our guidance through Rome but the possibilities of prosperity for our nation.' A coughing fit came again and Duncan wondered whether to leave his uncle to his illness but a look from the queen told him to stay. Malcolm took a wheezy breath before he continued. 'As it stands, do not be so quick to trust the King of England despite how they have helped us in the past. Scotland has better friends at this time. But you will need to find these alliances yourself because I do not think my brother understands how things are.'

'I have heard rumours of displaced men who did not come back at my welcome but are now looking to usurp the throne.' Malcolm's hand sought Duncan's. 'Be careful, lad, for there are daggers in men's smiles.'

Margaret took up the lecture. 'It is not an easy role to be royal, Duncan, which is why God appoints and anoints for His good purpose. Many a time, a king has had to make difficult decisions to save the greater good.'

'My grandfather, Edmund Ironside, was once the King of England but, when he died, the people chose Cnut to be their king. My father and his twin brother, both infants, were sent to King Stephen in Hungary for their protection for it was believed Cnut was afraid of them. Sadly my father's brother died but my father, Edward, went on to marry and have a happy life – producing myself and my brother and sister. At the time, it felt a terrible thing to live in exile but it was all for the best. Though we have had our share of struggles, God has always been our guiding hand. For that I am ever thankful for He brought me to Malcolm.' She leant over and gave her husband a gentle kiss on the cheek.

'Margaret is right,' Malcolm said. 'I look back over my life and see that even after tragedy, good comes from it in the end. That's God's way.'

Malcolm had honoured his brother though; through the numerous conversations Duncan had had with his uncle, he knew he had chosen poorly but, he thought, morally. Donalbain was the next in line to the throne and from Duncan's line, so it had to be. 'I trust in God's holy plan. We have to do it this way, Duncan. Whatever may come, He will make it right in the end,' Malcolm said.

Duncan nodded though he did not have the faith of his uncle. He believed enough that if a man acted faithfully and true, the world would be as it should. Still, he did feel a bit uncomfortable with this conversation. Not that this type of conversation was new to him for Rachel too held such firm beliefs. He just didn't agree with the idea of surrendering oneself over to an unseen power – it smelt of reneging one's responsibility as a person. Though the laws of the church were good for guiding moral living, a man also needed to seek strength within himself to help those around him.

'Thank you for your wise advice,' he told them both and they smiled at him. 'I give you my word that I will do all in my power – and in God's power,' he added to please them, 'to keep Scotland at peace, as a country of honour and justice.'

The thing was, he *did* want to make it right. He wanted to be in charge because he saw that his father was no good for Scotland but neither was Uncle Malcolm. Both men, wounded by the murder of their father, had chosen paths which may have helped heal their hearts but were not good for the country and therefore not good for its peoples.

'When I go to my heavenly rest, know that Macduff, a kind and trusting man, has much wisdom in him for he has the remembrance of times past. You can go to him for good counsel. He feels deeply for things but is not swayed by events. Trust him above all others, save the Lord.' Malcolm closed his eyes and the queen pulled the cover up over his chest.

'If it pleases you, Your Majesty, I shall give you time to rest.'

'Thank you, Duncan. I will call if he wishes to talk some more.' The queen stood and Duncan took her hand and kissed it. 'A good evening to you,' she said.

Duncan bowed and left the room.

Outside, he breathed deeply. Though he had not been around death very often, he sensed the king had little time left. This would mean going back to Glamis and helping the household prepare for Donalbain's coronation and the move here to Forres. He walked towards his sleeping chamber. There must be some way to convince Father that the move would not serve Scotland well, he thought. Perhaps the fact Forres was so far away from the main trading centres and from England would be enough of a reason.

He tried to recall exactly what it was the three old hags had told his father but the memory was foggy and disjointed. Duncan felt the familiar dread of his family – the responsibilities of and risks for the three children of a father in thrall to creatures who savoured ministrations from those beyond the grave.

The next morning, just one week before the start of the new year, the bells tolled loud and clear and the cry went through the palace: 'The king is dead. King Malcolm is dead. Gone to his Saviour. God bless his soul.'

Duncan threw off his bedclothes and sat up. It was too soon. He was not ready for the weight of this. Only twenty-one summers had he lived and now, though he was not yet to be king, the responsibility of that role would fall on his shoulders. Duncan sighed and got up. He splashed water on his face and stared into the mirror with the bells and the cries of the pages ringing throughout the castle.

There was a discreet knock at his door. 'Come,' he called, still trying to wake fully.

Instead of a page, it was Fleance. 'I'm sorry for your loss . . . Sire.'

Duncan stared. Already it had started. He placed outstretched arms on the table beside his bed, leant forward and took a deep breath. 'I am Duncan. I would be pleased if you treated me no differently to how you did yesterday.'

He was aware of Fleance standing just inside the door. His friend cleared his throat. 'I'm sorry,' he said quietly.

Duncan looked across at him. 'Thank you, and I am sorry for many things which have been and will be.' He straightened. 'Malcolm will be laid to rest at Iona but I must away to Glamis to help my sister ready the castle for the shift in power. My father will leave much for her to do.' He wiped his face clear with a towel. 'I am very sorry that I must abandon you to your quest while I endeavour to work at my own.'

'I *can* accompany you, if you want,' Fleance said.

The offer was generous but Duncan shook his head. 'You have more important business than me. I could not ask it of you.'

Fleance persisted. 'I would be honoured to help you to carry a heavy burden as you say.' He went over to the stool by the casement and sat down. 'I think my qualifications allow me to make such an offer.'

Duncan frowned. 'What is it that you say?'

'Who knows which wolves might be lying in wait for you.'

It took a moment for Fleance's comment to register and then Duncan smiled. 'A joke tires when used too often.'

Fleance stood up. 'Ah, but I don't think it has done its course. There are more of these still to come.'

Duncan sat down on his bed. Maybe what Margaret said was true: that it would all work out. Still, he was now thrust into the responsibility. Even though on the surface his father was to be the new king of Scotland, it was to him, Duncan, that they would all look to for guidance. Did anyone know how difficult it was going to be with Donalbain's obsession with the supernatural? Perhaps enlisting a reasonable fellow was timely and wise.

He turned to Fleance. 'In truth, your company will be most welcome. It is agreed. You will come with me to Glamis. But, be warned, it is not an easy domestic arrangement, although I have no doubt my sweet sister will charm the life out of you.'

Fleance bowed low. 'As you command, my liege.'

But Duncan did not miss the wry smile of his friend's face. 'Please, Fleance, between us let us behave as brothers.'

Fleance nodded in agreement. 'Whatever you say, my friend,' he smiled.

Because Duncan was required back at Glamis, he could only offer a brief goodbye to his uncle the king. Margaret was stoic and when she said goodbye, held him firmly in her hands and extolled him to trust in The Almighty. Then, she'd turned from him to follow the procession of the body to the sea where it would be placed on a boat and sail to Iona, the resting place of Scottish kings.

That afternoon, he met Fleance in the courtyard. 'Are you ready, then, to make this journey back?'

Fleance smiled at him. 'First, can you promise the journey will not beset by wolves and weather?'

'Not at all.'

'And tell me again why I suggested this?'

'For God and country.'

Fleance snorted. 'Yes and . . . ?'

'Our cook is incredible and Rachel is to love,' Duncan quipped.

However, a grim expression came over his friend's face. 'I look forward to the meals,' he said, his face suddenly closed.

Some part of the secretive life of Fleance, Duncan thought as he watched him mount, was now making itself known to him. He knew that look – it came with unrequited love and rejection, something he had felt too keenly himself. No mind. A small part of his heart was excited at introducing Fleance to his sister. That he would fall in love with her immediately was expected, for all the young men did. And she would find him as charming and intriguing as Duncan did. Perhaps at least one of us can have personal happiness and forget the disappointments of the past, he thought ruefully.

Duncan shook such thoughts from his mind. This was not the time to dwell on what had gone on before but to focus on the present for it held enough problems of its own.

While they made their way south, the cries went out across Scotland. Duncan knew that though the people were kind in their comments, and though this was the king who had destroyed the notorious tyrant and his fiendish queen, he had not been able to restore Scotland to its former time of peace and prosperity. A king, it was known, who sent soldiers into Ireland and England to gather crops, in the name of God, and collect livestock to replenish the depleted royal lands. In the quiet rooms of the cottages, the words 'gather' and 'collect' were replaced with 'loot' and 'steal'.

Still, this was not the moment to air such thoughts and Queen Margaret had been a generous and kindly queen. That she had no children survive infancy was a heavy sorrow for those old enough to remember the days before the troubles.

Malcolm had already proclaimed on his deathbed that the sovereignty was to go to his younger brother, Donalbain, so with the announcement of the death, another one followed soon after of Donalbain's coronation to be held at Scone in a week's time. Duncan had to get home as soon as possible to help Rachel. Who knew what state Father would be in?

He and Fleance had gone from tavern to tavern. Under his suggestion, Fleance thought it best Duncan ride anonymously. The news that Donalbain would now rule Scotland would not be to everyone's liking. Not that his life was in danger; on the contrary, many already spoke bravely aloud that they wished Duncan had been named the Prince of Cumberland – the title given to the waiting monarch.

Would it make a difference, though, to his life? Yes, he could ensure those under his care were kept safe and be free to prosper.

But what about his heart? Would he find someone who had captured it as she had?

She. Duncan rarely said her name aloud or in his thoughts for she was forbidden fruit. When Donalbain had first learnt of the attraction between the two, he had hauled Duncan into his study and berated him about wasting his seed on poor soil; that she was not good enough for a prince. She had lived with the family her whole life but, to Donalbain she was merely part of the castle, not the sweet and kind young girl who had been his best friend growing up and his comforter as a man.

Duncan rested against a tree watching Fleance tend the horses. His cloak was wrapped tightly around his shoulders to ward off the chill of the winter day. Though he would not like to face it, he was upset. He took a deep breath which caused Fleance to look at him. 'Is all well with you?'

Frustration flooded him. 'No, Fleance, it is not.' It was hard for him to say it – to speak of the secret love long held close. He knew his father thought the matter closed but Duncan could not so easily discard her.

Fleance patted Willow and came forward. 'Are you ill? Is it your wound?'

'No, man, it's my heart.'

Fleance looked concerned. 'Do you need to sit, Duncan? Water? Food?'

Duncan waved him away. 'Fleance, it is my heart, my soul, my dreams, my . . .' He pulled at the damp grass growing between the knotted roots of the tree. He hissed through his teeth. 'To be truthful, I don't know what to call it.'

Fleance frowned. 'You are making no sense.'

'Aye, and what man does when he is in love but has the burden of his country on his shoulders?'

'You are in love, Duncan?'

He stood up and sighed deeply, trying to control his feelings but the image of Charissa flashed across his thoughts. 'I am in love,' he repeated, 'with a woman who understands my heart and hopes.'

'Then why are you not with her?' Fleance asked calmly.

'Because I am to be king, Fleance, and unlike other men, my bride cannot be chosen for love but rather from duty and what is deemed correct. Such is the responsibility one must accept with the crown.'

Fleance moved to mount and Duncan, throwing the crumpled grass in his hands into the wind, did the same. 'Then we are both cursed by the same blessing,' Fleance said. Once seated on Willow, he turned to Duncan. 'I'm sorry for you and for me. I hear that the way of true love is never a smooth one,' he said.

Duncan nodded. 'But it's a path I'm not yet ready to abandon.' He flicked the reins of Phoenix. 'Let us to Glamis,' he said. *And to an uncertain future*, he thought.

'I hear the food at Glamis is to die for.' Fleance grinned at him.

Duncan looked over at his companion, thankful that he was trying to lift his mood. 'Aye, it is so but it is also a place fraught with other things. You are well advised to be on guard.'

The horses moved on, plodding through the mud and mist which stretched its soft fingers across the land and tickled the legs of the horses.

They travelled five days from Forres to Glamis, saying little, for Duncan felt an ever-increasing sense of doom the closer he got to the castle. The horses were grumpy, which matched his mood. 'Gee up,' he chided.

'They are weary and dispirited,' Fleance offered. ''Tis not our horsemanship but their tempers which make them disobedient.'

'A lot like servants,' he said, thinking about his father's aides and instantly regretted being so free with his quips. 'Well, despite my father's opinion,' he added to impress Fleance, 'a good whipping never was of much use.'

Fleance laughed. 'Aye, and if I tried that with Willow here, he'd have landed me in a nasty patch of thistles.'

The closer they came to Glamis, the more foreboding the weather. When they left Perth, the hills were bathed in yellow light but now a thick cloud was moving down the mountains and into the valley. Though it was only mid-afternoon when they arrived at the castle, they could barely see two horse lengths in front of them as the mist rolled in across the glen.

At first all was quiet as the horses walked into the courtyard. A lone figure emerged out of the thick fog, wearing a long hooded cloak, and seemed to float towards them through the mist. 'Rachel, dear sister, what brings you outdoors in such weather?'

She lifted the hood from her head and smiled warmly, though she looked pale and strained as she did after a difficult night with Bree. 'Duncan,' she said. 'You have been gone so long and I have worried.'

Duncan dismounted. 'I am sorry, sister. It was the king's pleasure that we stayed longer at Forres.' He gestured to his friend. 'Meet Fleance, my companion.'

Rachel stood by while he dismounted and then turned to Fleance.

'Welcome to Glamis, Fleance.' Fleance bowed his head but said nothing, though it pleased Duncan to see his sister's gaze linger on the face of his new friend.

Eventually, she turned back to her brother. 'Father is in a state. We have had a messenger to say Malcolm is dead.'

Just then his father could be heard shouting. Duncan moved past her. 'Aye, he is. So, sweet sister, get the house ready for Father will be king and you and I the tools necessary to run Scotland.' There was anger in his tone which, by the look on their faces, surprised both his sister and Fleance.

Duncan was angry. He had wanted to give his friend a place of rest for all the kindness he had shown these last weeks. He had wanted time, perhaps, for Fleance and Rachel to get to know each other before the madness of the coming months but it was too late for that. All he now wanted to do was bath and rest but he could not. The moment he entered the castle, he was summoned.

Donalbain was in a frenzy. While thinner, it was clear Rachel's ministering had been effective – his face was of a good colour and his eyes clear. He strode about the castle yelling to servants and his advisors alike. When he saw Duncan, he fell upon him. 'Son,' he cried. 'You are welcome home.' Duncan was taken back by the rush of affection his father showered upon him but said nothing. 'Into the meeting hall as I have questions for you. Calum,' he barked. 'Come.' Calum followed them like an obedient dog.

Donalbain almost ran up the stairs and along the corridor to his great hall, talking all the time – to himself, to Duncan, to Calum.

His father poured drinks and gave one to Duncan. 'Well, tell us how my brother died.'

'Peacefully, Father, and in good spirits.'

Donalbain swallowed and nodded, taking another gulp of his drink. 'We are pleased to hear it. He was a kind-hearted man, much like our father.'

Duncan noticed his father now spoke as the uncrowned king – a sign that he had been more than ready to take up the role. 'He wished you good health and a happy reign,' he said.

'We are pleased to have gained his blessing as well as his crown. After our coronation, we will send word to Margaret of our intention to move to Forres.'

'Do you not think, Father,' Duncan said, 'that Glamis is a more suitable position politically, especially with how the English throne is regarded.'

Donalbain looked at him sharply. 'How it is regarded?'

Duncan swallowed, unsure how much information he should divulge to his father. 'Uncle Malcolm warned me that the people of England are somewhat dissatisfied with their monarch but even more suspicious of Scotland.'

His father nodded. 'And so they should be on their guard. For too long, the English have considered us inferior.'

Something about the way his father spoke chilled Duncan. 'But not a threat, surely?'

'No, but they wish to control us and that is not good for our people.'

His father's open acknowledgement of the needs of the country surprised him. Perhaps, though his thoughts were addled by the prophecies of the witches, Donalbain might have enough sense in him to avoid strange judgement and bizarre prophecies. 'I agree, Father. And that is why I think the crown should stay here where we are closer to the people.'

Donalbain looked at Calum. 'What say you, Calum? Is my son correct?'

Calum nodded. 'Duncan is often wise beyond his years and I do agree that at this time, it would be better that we remain here, close to all important posts.' Duncan detected an edge to the advisor's tone but when he looked at Calum, the pale man's face was unreadable.

His father was silent but chewed his nail, caught up in his thoughts. Outside, Duncan could hear bird calls and the noises of the movements of servants and animals. He wondered where Fleance had gone and hoped Rachel would be a gracious hostess.

Suddenly, Donalbain sprang into action. 'I concur. We will travel to Scone to be invested and then hold a great feast to celebrate.'

After supper, Duncan went to find Fleance. He discovered him in the blue room with Rachel and that caused a small jolt of pleasure. It would be good for them to have time to get to know each other. 'Excuse me,' he said. 'Fleance, I wish to introduce you to Father.'

He saw Rachel nod. 'I think he will be well pleased to learn that his cousin's only son survived.'

Duncan looked sharply at Fleance. 'I have told her my story,' Fleance said. 'Well, most of it.'

He nodded. 'Good. Dear sister, if we could leave you to your needles for a moment. Father was in a good state when I left him.' Rachel's face showed understanding of what that statement implied and she smiled.

'Go quickly then before the mood changes,' she said and went back to her embroidery.

The two young men left the comfort of the room and entered the chill of the castle halls.

'I have been thinking, Duncan,' Fleance said. 'From what you say about your father.' He hesitated and Duncan saw that his ears had gone quite pink.

Duncan put a hand on Fleance's arm and they stopped. 'What is it?'

Fleance rubbed his hand over his chin. 'It's just that . . . well . . . maybe Donalbain won't be pleased to see me alive?'

'Whatever do you mean?' Duncan could not fathom his friend's logic.

'My father, as you know, had a claim to the throne once your father and Malcolm had fled.' He shook his head. 'I don't really know what I'm saying but I get this strong feeling we should just keep my lineage between the three of us – for now.'

Duncan studied him. So many secrets were not good but then, Fleance was right. Sometimes giving someone too much information could be dangerous. 'All right. As you wish.'

They moved off towards Donalbain's chambers but suddenly found themselves confronted by him as he strode around the corner. He seemed not to see them.

'Father,' Duncan called. 'A word?'

Donalbain spun around. 'Eh?'

Duncan was dismayed to see that his father was intoxicated. No mind. He would still introduce Fleance. 'This is my friend, Fleance. We met on my way to Forres.'

Donalbain peered at Fleance and frowned. 'Fleance,' he said, his voice slurry. 'Thassa strange name. Haven't heard that one fer a while.' Duncan inhaled. Donalbain wobbled slightly. 'Good. Good,' he said, waving his hands. 'Now, I must find . . . I must go get . . .' and he walked determinedly down the corridor, only occasionally off-balance.

Duncan turned to Fleance. 'I'm sorry about that.'

'No matter but I do wonder if he will remember who I am in the morning,' Fleance answered shrugging. 'Shall we return to your sister and her stories?'

'Yes, please,' Duncan said, relieved that his father had not made a fuss and that Fleance acted unperturbed by the introduction.

Chapter Twenty-One
Glamis Castle

There was an unusual atmosphere of festivity in the castle even though it was only a week since King Malcolm's death. Hogmanay, the much-anticipated annual New Year's Eve celebration, was to be enhanced by a coronation. The new year would not only bring fresh hopes but a new king for Scotland.

Donalbain was in excellent spirits and was often seen to be smiling. He was even pleasant to Morag and she stored his friendly words into her heart. For the journey to Scone, she and Rachel discussed the preparation of everyone's favourite morsel, although, for the young prince's new friend, both of them were at a loss. This Fleance was always agreeable and polite so that poor Morag could not discover if any of what she designed for the palace meals impressed or appalled him.

Still, there was one whole wagon filled with food and drink and strict instructions from her as to when and where and how it should be distributed. Morag stood in the archway of the ante-room to the scullery and saw off her dear children: Duncan, Rachel and Bree. With them was their father whose demeanour had always worried her. Even when she had been a servant girl at King Duncan's castle,

Donalbain, the youngest son, had always tortured her and made her life almost unbearable.

Many years ago now, when Breanna, Donalbain's new wife, needed to choose servants for the house, she chose Morag to be in charge of the kitchen. So the young servant girl, with her natural understanding of food and taste, was thrust into the important role of cook.

Even when the castle was gathered up suddenly to flee to Ireland, it was without question that Morag accompanied the family.

That one year when they were exiled in Ireland was one of the happiest times for all. There, Morag met her soulmate and, shortly after, produced a son. However, she did not skip her duties which enamoured her to Breanna, busy herself with two wee ones, Duncan and Rachel. All too soon, they were called back to Scotland – the moment dear Macduff slew the tyrant and Malcolm was named king.

Morag wiped her hands on her apron as the entourage made its way out of the courtyard. She crossed herself. God would need to take special care of the bairns, for their future, she predicted, would be full of turmoil not seen since their exile. As the second-to-last cart went past, she spotted Duncan's friend sitting between Rachel and her brother. A warmth flooded through her. This fellow made Duncan (and her Rachel if she read the signs right), happy. Morag crossed herself again. For she wanted God to also look after this striking young man.

Fleance was amused. Just weeks ago he was alone with Willow, trudging through the rough roads of northern Scotland unsure as to what in God's name he was doing. Now, he was sitting with the new heir to the throne of Scotland. It was remarkable.

Beside him, Duncan's sister Rachel had their younger sister on her lap. Rachel stroked her sister's hair and stared ahead. Duncan tapped furiously on his knee. So much so that Fleance thought he might say something.

'Duncan?'

'Aye?'

'So, I talk in my sleep but you jiggle about enough to drive a man insane.' Fleance grinned at him.

Duncan spread his hands wide. 'You cannot accuse me of anything when you are so weird yourself.'

Fleance smiled. 'I'm weird, am I? So what does that look like?'

Rachel roused herself. 'It looks like Calum trying to get Father to understand why water is better for him than wine.'

Duncan nodded. 'Or that the sky is green and the land is blue.'

Fleance snorted. 'Who says such rubbish?' He caught a look between the two. 'Sorry, have I said something out of turn?'

Duncan fell back against the seat. 'No, but it's just that we hear a lot of foolish talk and sayings.'

To change the subject, Fleance reached out his hand to the sleeping Bree's head. 'Although she has your height, she doesn't look like either of you.'

'She has our mother's looks,' Rachel said. 'But our father's temper.'

'My adoptive sister is about her age, and is a cheeky wee thing. She's talented though – plays the lute sweeter than any bird I've heard.'

'What's her name?' Rachel asked and Fleance could tell she was genuinely interested. He told her all about his adoptive family and a bit of his life in England. He did not tell her of the difficult times when Magness would return from his secret journeys, and would brood and snarl for days afterwards. Rather, he recounted the many happy times with the family. Ah, how he missed them. But he would not think of Rosie for he wanted to enjoy the occasion and not spoil it with his melancholy thoughts.

Rachel listened intently and Fleance was surprised and pleased with the intelligent and thoughtful questions she asked without prying too much. Then she told him about her own family, her gentle lilting voice that of a skilled storyteller and Fleance found himself caught up in the events that had brought their family to this point.

'Mother was unable to have any more children after me but we enjoyed an idyllic childhood up until our grandfather was murdered. Father came home in a terrible state – that was the first time in my memory I'd seen him not in control.' She looked out over the fields and sighed. 'I did not even say goodbye to Grandfather. Mother had a cousin in Ireland, so we went there. It might have been awful living in exile and hearing the stories of what was happening to Scotland's people – terrible things like what happened at Macduff's castle and so many being killed, but Father was with us more instead of travelling and going to battles and Mother was very happy.

'The first time I heard them quarrel when we were there was when a messenger came to request that Father join forces with Uncle Malcolm and the English army to fight against Macbeth. Father refused to go but Mother had said it was his duty. After that, there were lots of times at supper when they would not speak to each other.'

Duncan had nodded off and his head fell against Fleance's shoulder. Fleance pushed him in the opposite direction so that he snuggled into the side of the wagon.

'When did you come back to Scotland?' Fleance asked, trying to match his own life's timeline to theirs. He had fled Scotland ten years ago.

'We were away a full year. When Uncle Malcolm was crowned king, another messenger came to us to say the king invited us to return. He gave Glamis castle to Father and Mother was pleased for she thought the country beautiful. We have been here for nine years. Father thought it too small and I heard him tell her it was his punishment for refusing to join his brother in battle but the rest of us love it.

'I was about eight or nine, I think, when mother became ill. It was quite a while before we discovered she was with child which made us all very happy but, though Bree here thrived, Mother did not and she took to bed. There was a very good wet nurse who taught me many things about healing so I helped to make Mother more comfortable: teas to lessen the nausea, grass to wrap around the wrists, which foods to avoid and which would help the baby grow.

'Bree came early but she was a bonny wee babe and I helped to bring her into the world. Mother spent one day and one night with her child before she succumbed and died.'

'I'm very sorry,' Fleance said. 'It is a hard thing to watch a parent die.'

Rachel smiled sadly. 'Aye, but we did not really have time to mourn because this one,' she said, nodding towards the sleeping child, 'demanded our time – night and day. Unfortunately, Father was consumed by grief and could not help us in ours so we leant upon each other, Duncan and I, with the help of our cook, Morag, who is really more than a cook to us.' She frowned slightly and Fleance was surprised to see that it actually made her look even more beautiful. 'Father does not hold Morag in much esteem. However, I suspect that they each share part of a dark history together for she was a servant to King Duncan's house.'

'You have carried a large burden for a long time, it seems and yet, I sense no bitterness in you.'

Rachel smiled, the simple action bringing light to her face.

'What need have I to be bitter – God deals the hand He does but gives us the faith and strength to bear the load.' Bree yawned then, and stretched, her legs pushing quite painfully into Fleance's thighs. Rachel laughed. 'Looks like our quiet time is now over.'

She kissed Bree on the cheeks. 'Hello, young Bree. That was a nice long sleep.'

Bree rubbed her nose vigorously. 'I'm hungry,' she said, which made Fleance laugh loudly so that Bree give him a dirty look.

'Well, that's all good for I see Father has pulled up his wagon, so we must be stopping for a rest.'

Duncan and Fleance sat under an oak tree eating the food Morag had prepared – it was very good and the nagging loneliness was kept at some distance by the unusually fine weather and the good company. A pretty maid came over with another basket of food, this time moist fruit cakes, but it was the look between the maid and Duncan which was of interest to Fleance. Could this be the girl Duncan had spoken of? The maid curtsied and went over to Duncan's sisters.

He nudged Duncan with his foot. 'Who is the maid?'

Duncan's face blushed slightly. 'That is Charissa. She is Morag's niece.'

'And?' Fleance pressed. 'Who is she to you?'

Duncan looked startled. 'What do you mean?'

Fleance leant over to him slightly and spoke in a low voice. 'You have the look of a man in love, Duncan, and it came upon you when she brought us these.' He held up the small cakes.

'Well, that may be but if I cannot wed her, I honour her too deeply to bed her,' Duncan said, his voice tight.

Fleance watched Bree poke leaves and twigs into Rachel's thick tresses. The young woman has the patience of a saint, he thought. 'Why hasn't your sister married?'

Duncan sighed deeply. 'A long story with an abrupt ending, I'm afraid. There was a man about two years ago who had Rachel's heart but Father asked him to take on a dangerous journey – he never returned and we received word he had been killed by the border reivers.' He threw his crusts to some hopeful sparrows. 'Rachel was devastated but she's stoic. And ever the optimist. I believe she is truly a saint.'

Fleance looked again at the two girls and saw the similarities between brother and sister – both had a genuine heart for people and a gentleness which seemed to stay firm in the face of trying circumstances. Rachel looked over at them, caught his eye and smiled warmly. Something stirred within him. Pity? Attraction? He knew not what but for the rest of the journey he was acutely aware of her sitting beside him, her breathing, her singing and her delightfully entertaining stories to keep the fidgeting child settled.

They arrived at Scone in the late afternoon and, despite himself, Fleance began to be affected by the excitement and carnival-like atmosphere. Servants and workers had arrived the day before to set up a large tent and to decorate the coronation seat with dried flowers and coloured ribbons. It was strange yet quite fitting for such an occasion to see gold and white ribbons tied to trees and the brown fields seem to shimmer as the yellow sun began its steady descent into the west.

Fleance watched Macduff, Lennox, Duncan and Calum, who had been chosen to carry the new king in the procession, disappear into the abbey. He stood among the peasants, farm workers, villagers and many from the town who had made the journey to Scone to witness the crowning of this man who many had thought too strange, too unlikely, to be an effective king. He listened to their talk and wondered at the openness of their opinions at such a time. He recalled it had only been in the quiet of the night that Magness spoke so freely and then only to Miri; not knowing Fleance was awake too, terrified of falling asleep.

Soon the stone bearers came from the church; between them they carried a red-coloured oblong stone and placed it in front of Donalbain. He wore white flowing robes with a blue and gold sash around his hips. His hair and beard had been freshly washed and oiled with sweet-smelling perfume. He did not look at all like a mad man but a pleasant and reasonable ruler. Perhaps Magness and Dougal were misguided in their fears about Donalbain becoming king.

The monks from the abbey, led by the bishop, came towards the guests, swinging incense and chanting. Fleance could feel a quiver of excitement move through the spectators. Oh, if only Rosie was here with him to see all this. She would think it wonderful.

'How beautiful they look,' Rosie whispered as they watched the parade of actors and performers moving out into the field. She held his arm tightly. 'Wouldn't it be grand, Flea, to pull on such robes and take on the disguise so that you could be anyone you wanted to be?'

Fleance delighted in her excitement and found his own heart seeing through Rosie's eyes the possibility of simple joy. 'Aye,' he whispered into her hair. 'That would be grand.'

The monks formed a guard in front of Donalbain while the bishop went forth and spoke prayers at the same time as he splashed holy water over Donalbain's shoulders and head. Then he dipped his hand in oil and anointed the new king's forehead before offering up more prayers. Macduff handed the crown to the bishop who placed it on Donalbain's head. Lennox thrust a sceptre in front of Donalbain who took it with his hand. The new king placed his bare feet, one after the other, on the stone.

Using the thick iron rings, the men lifted Donalbain to shoulder height. Macduff shouted out, 'Long live the king!' Fleance watched as the stone and new king swayed slightly, sending a concerned murmur throughout the crowd. However, Donalbain was able to right himself by using the sceptre to aid in balancing.

A roar of agreement came from the assembly as Macduff repeated his cry: 'Long live the king. Donalbain the First!' All gathered echoed his cry.

As the bearers moved towards where Fleance was standing, he studied Donalbain's face. The king looked very pleased with himself.

It was a look of satisfaction; when one has finally gained one's heart's desire. He had not gained the crown through foul means so why shouldn't he be pleased, Fleance thought. Weird fascinations aside, he was the rightful king of Scotland and should be honoured as such.

The cries from the watching crowd continued. Even Fleance could not resist calling out as Duncan walked passed. The young prince looked at him and grinned. Yes, it was good to enjoy this moment and he saw Duncan appreciated his support.

Fleance watched the procession as they moved off and his eyes skipped over the crowd. Many were following the procession but he began walking away from the church so that he could have some quiet space before the small banquet which had been arranged for the evening.

He made his way to a low stone wall and stood under one of the decorated trees. A ribbon had come loose and now was making a jerky dance across the road. Fleance stooped down to pick it up and when he stood up he saw his father standing in the barren field on the other side of the wall. Fear flooded him and he swallowed quickly. But this time, Fleance decided, he would not chase him. He would wait and see if this vision would justify why it continued to plague him.

The mass of people had all but dispersed but Fleance stood quietly as did Banquo. Instead of anger, this time he saw sadness in his father's face. And something else. Concern? Worry? Their eyes were locked and though his brain was reminding him that what he was seeing could not possibly be real, Fleance was at the same time utterly certain as to what his eyes were telling him. Banquo was standing here at Scone where they had stood together some ten years earlier – the same look on his face now as Fleance remembered him having then.

'Are you not well, Da?' *Fleance had asked as they watched Macbeth being carried towards the church.*

*Banquo looked down at him. 'Aye, son. It has been a long day.' But
he did not take his eyes from the retreating king.*

*'Da, I heard some lords talk about King Duncan's sons – that it was
not the chamberlains but them that killed their father.'*

Banquo nodded. 'Aye, that is the story I've heard as well.'

'Do you not think it true?' Fleance asked.

*His father gave him a sharp look. 'These are times, Fleance, to keep
a body alive, that what a man thinks should not always align with
what he says. I suggest, son, you do not discuss these things so openly.'*

*Fleance's face burned hot with shame. It was not often his father
chastised him but this was as close to a public reprimand as the occasion
would allow. 'Sorry, Da.'*

Banquo pulled him to his side. 'The less said, boy, the best mended.'

'Fleance?' A hand touched his arm and he jumped. It was
Rachel. She was staring up at him and frowning. 'Are you not
coming in?'

Fleance looked back to where his father had stood but the area
was empty. He felt a loneliness again. 'Sorry, I was away with my
thoughts. 'Tis said, I'm often doing that.' He tried to smile.

'Are you inclined to share them?'

'Eh?'

'Your thoughts. Sometimes, when one is burdened, it can ease
the load to share half of it with another,' she said smiling.

'It is nothing. Let us go in and celebrate your father's day.'
He offered her his arm, which she took and they walked together
towards the gathering as she recounted Bree's insistence that she
also be carried on the stone until a growl from the king had sent her
scuttling to hide behind Rachel.

Later they partook of communion. The smoke from the burning incense stung his eyes and when Fleance accepted the bread, he
almost choked so dry was his mouth. Duncan slapped him on the
back and the coughing stopped.

'Sorry,' he whispered. 'It's not something I'm used to doing.'

'You're in good company then,' Duncan whispered back, grinning. He pointed to a line of noblemen who were fumbling with the wine and the bread. 'You would think they would have the skill for such an event.'

'It has been a while,' Fleance whispered back. 'Nine years since the last coronation?'

'Aye,' Duncan began but a loud hiss behind them from Rachel made him silent. Duncan pulled a face at Fleance and it was all he could do to avoid laughing and thus encounter Rachel's wrath.

Later they went on to the meal and Fleance once more found himself in Rachel's company. 'Princess,' he bowed. 'I offer my humblest apologies for my behaviour.'

'Is attendance at church not a thing you are accustomed to, Fleance?' she asked, but without any sense of judgement.

'Apart from Shrove Tuesdays and Ash Wednesdays, we rarely cross the threshold of a sanctuary,' he said, remembering Magness's grumbles about having to attend such ceremonies even if they only happened once a year. Fleance could quite clearly hear Magness's voice when they had entered the local church: *Mark this, lad. The church is only a tool used by the throne to control its people and keep them oppressed.*

'God's presence and forgiveness is not contained in a building but it is good that you were given the opportunity to seek His forgiveness,' Rachel said kindly.

'And do I have yours, Rachel?' Fleance asked.

She touched his arm. 'I have no judgement over you, Fleance. I do expect more from my brother who is well acquainted with such ceremonies. I anticipate he will also seek my forgiveness which I am obliged and happy to dispense – though I may make him squirm a bit before I do,' she smiled cheekily, a happy sparkle in her eyes.

Fleance grinned. That would be entertaining to see. He watched Rachel make her way over to Duncan and he followed a short distance behind, thinking about their conversation.

When all the dishes had been carried off, Fleance suddenly realised that Rachel had not left his side all evening. He didn't mind. She was delightful in her quiet way and, although his heart still ached for Rosie, Rachel's easy laughter and gentle manner removed the edge from his loneliness.

Duncan had lost some of his edginess as well and teased him mercilessly. Their gentle ribbing amounted to a wrestle in the clearing, cheered on by the earls, Rachel and a number of the monks.

Fleance was far stronger and swifter than his friend but felt it inappropriate to let the young prince lose face. He made a good show of trying to beat Duncan but did not hold him as firmly as he could, did not apply his strength. Rather, he allowed himself to be conquered by Duncan much to the delight of the watching crowd.

They stood up and shook hands. Bree brought her brother a drink and Rachel brought Fleance his. 'I saw,' she said quietly. 'You could have taken him anytime.'

Fleance drank and then wiped his mouth. 'I don't know what you mean, Princess,' he said. She looked at him with a smile and raised her right eyebrow. Suddenly he was back in the forests of England; back with Rosie who had caught him out with some story. He remembered the lift of the eyebrow and her sweet smile.

He turned away from Rachel quickly and went to the tent where he was to sleep with Macduff, Lennox and the enigmatic Calum.

That night the dreams came again. Kissing Rosie who turned into Rachel who turned back into Rosie and then back into Rachel. Even in his dreams, he knew it was wrong to think of anyone save Rosie. But there was something about Rachel that was comforting. There was none of the passion he always felt with Rosie but, if he was truly honest, it wasn't too terrible being with Rachel on this trip.

When they travelled back to Glamis, however, Fleance made sure he sat as far away from Rachel as he could. He would not be distracted from finishing his quest and then finding Rosie again.

Rosie
Perth

Da had been in Scotland some weeks when he returned to take them both back to the inn at Perth. However, Rosie knew Ma's painful joints would make the trip unbearable. They agreed, when Dougal arrived, they would tell him of their plan that Rebecca would move in with Miri and help her especially as Magness regularly spent many days away now.

But Dougal would have none of that. 'I will not be separated unnecessarily from my wife,' he cried. So it was, then, that they boarded a ship at Newcastle and sailed around the coast of Scotland, up the Firth of Tay then north up the river to Perth. It had been a difficult journey. Ma suffered from seasickness and Rosie had spent a good deal of time below deck helping to nurse her through the worst of it.

Despite her uncomfortable task with her mother, being busy and preoccupied helped keep her heart above fatal drowning. Rosie was relieved to be active and distracted.

But, despite this, it wearied a body to be so long out of the light and swaying beneath decks. By the time they docked, at the river village, she was glad to be on firm land again.

Dougal was cheerfully arranging the transportation of their belongings while Rosie helped Rebecca off the ship and into the waiting cart. Her mother looked too white and her lips were of a bluish hue. Still, she smiled at Rosie as her daughter tucked a travel blanket around her legs.

They left father and husband behind and made the short trip to the tavern. It was a pleasant-looking building with bright-red flower boxes outside the windows. To the left was a large stable. Dougal would be pleased for he judged an inn by the quality of its stables. 'Any self-respecting innkeeper,' he told them on the journey over, 'must have more than adequate housing for the horses as well as good ale from which to make a profit.' Their driver pulled up and Rosie, happy to see her mother was making a recovery, helped her down from the cart. The driver took their bags and followed them as they entered the building.

It was huge. This was the first thought she had. Why had she imagined her father had signed up for some poky little downcast hovel when, in fact, this was a major establishment? Her heart raced. This would be wonderful. This would give them opportunity for much trade and traffic.

The young man behind the counter grinned at Rosie. 'I am mighty pleased to see you, Miss.' He bowed to Rebecca. 'And you, Mam. We lost cook four weeks ago and trade is down. We understand you have the touch and will bring in business.' He pulled up two tankards. 'Here, you'll be wanting these after your long journey.'

Rosie held up her hand. 'Just water, thank you, sir.'

The barman nodded and went out the back. Soon he was back with cool, refreshing water. 'The inn sits beside a natural spring,' he explained. 'And the name's Jethro. I worked here for the previous owners but Dougal was happy to keep me on.'

He was trying to impress. She nodded politely at him and helped her mother with the water. 'Thank you . . . Jethro. You are very kind and we look forward to working with you to make this establishment the best in Perth.'

'No, my lady,' he replied. 'The best in Scotland.'

No wonder Da loved this place, Rosie thought. An ambitious young worker; wine coming from the best place, for grapes prefer ground-fed water. The fates were smiling. The only thing left now for her was to find Flea.

Chapter Twenty-Two
Glamis Castle

When he peered into the mirror that morning, Fleance was shocked to see how unwell he looked from too many nights of vivid and violent dreams. His face was pale and his eyes bloodshot. And tonight there was to be a feast. Donalbain, not content with the meal at Scone, had decided that a large banquet in honour of his coronation was needed.

The day after they had returned from Scone, while at supper, Donalbain had made the announcement that the thanes and earls would be called to the palace and that Rachel was to organise a feast that would be the rival of any other that had gone before: the best food, drink and entertainment.

He decided to call for a bath in preparation for the evening ahead. Perhaps a long soak in a hot tub would ease the exhaustion which plagued him continuously.

Duncan had discreetly arranged for Fleance to be given a fresh set of clothes and it was nice to pull on a soft, clean shirt and a change of breeks. His newly appointed page had set a plate of fruit, bread, cheese and sausage on the table beside his bed and Fleance picked away at these while he dressed. He pulled from his dusty cloak the parchments he'd found at Inverness and put them inside his new shirt. It would not be good if anyone got their hands on these. Though few in the royal court could read, there were enough who could and it would be dangerous, what with Donalbain's obsession with signs and prophecy, to let this information come into the court.

As befitted a celebration, the sun was out but there was still a threat of rain as the sky was watery. A cool breeze came in from the north but it was refreshing nonetheless. He would go see about Willow, who would be grumpy at being neglected, and then find Duncan.

The cacophony of sounds which greeted Fleance as he stepped into the yard almost sent him back to his chambers. Chickens, sheep, pigs, goats, a cow – all were clamouring for attention, crying and squawking and complaining. Hands and servants hurried to and fro, arms filled with fresh straw, baskets of vegetables or piles of fresh linen.

As he strode over towards the stable, a long cart and horse rattled into the courtyard. Fleance barely noticed it until a loud voice bellowed out, 'Drink for the feast – where do you want it?' It was unmistakably familiar – Dougal. Fleance turned on his heel and his heart leapt. Rosie sat beside her father.

'Rosie,' he called and she turned towards his voice. When she spotted him, her eyes widened. He ran up to the wagon. 'Rosie. You're here.'

Her face, which a moment before was radiant with delight, suddenly lost all expression. She politely cleared her throat. 'I would have thought that was *obvious*, Flea. As are you.' She turned to her father who was glaring at him. 'I see you are embraced by this court.'

'No matter,' he said, joy bubbling forth. 'I have news, Rosie. I can explain now. The new king's son . . . he took kindly upon me and—' Fleance gestured to his attire '—dressed me. But it is still me.' Fleance reached up to her. 'It's all right now, Rosie. I can

222

explain it all. I'm sorry but I couldn't before because I didn't know but now I understand.' He was gabbling, but he so desperately wanted to hold her and tell her everything and ask for forgiveness.

'You're making no sense, lad,' Dougal growled. 'Typical.'

Fleance swallowed. 'Dougal, may I have a word with Rosie – I have some explaining to do.'

'You got that bit right,' Dougal grumbled. 'Well, it's really up to wee Rosie here whether she has a mind to listen to your excuses.'

Rosie looked at him for a long moment, then picked up her skirts. 'I won't be long, Da. Will you be right with them barrels?'

'Aye, lass. Looks to be plenty of fellows to give me a hand. Off you go but don't be long.' He pointed at Fleance. 'You should wipe that silly grin off your face – you look like the fool you are.'

Barely able to contain the giddy joy he felt, he ignored Dougal's comments and helped Rosie down from the cart. He held her longer than necessary and felt her stiffen under his hands.

'Let's go to the stable. Willow's been neglected and we can talk openly there.' He led her to the stables but kept turning to look at her. She was not her usual bubbly self and there was a distinct calmness about her. No matter, he thought. Once he told her everything, she would surely understand.

Willow was eating and completely ignored him. To Rosie, however, he nudged her hand and allowed her to stroke his neck. Fleance watched her, his heart too full. He had missed her terribly but seeing her now, the full force of his love hit him solidly. 'You're more beautiful . . .' he started but she shot him a pained look.

'What are you doing here, Flea?' She pointed to his clothes. 'You're dressed like a royal.'

He stepped towards her. 'I can explain everything, Rosie my love, if you will hear me out.' He waited, holding his breath and when she gave a quick nod, he began his story. 'My full name is Fleance of Lochaber. My father was Banquo, Thane of Lochaber.'

She gasped, her eyes wide again. 'Yes. But only Duncan and his sister,' he gestured towards the castle, 'know this yet. My father was a loyal general in the king's army until his untimely murder by Macbeth, Thane of Glamis and Cawdor. Once Macbeth was crowned king, he arranged for my father's murder – and mine.

'He succeeded with Banquo but I managed to escape.' He told her his story. He reached out to her and she did not pull away. 'The last words he said to me, Rosie, were to fly that I may avenge his murder.' He studied her face, trying to see if his words were getting through to her. 'You see, Rosie, I was just a lad of eleven when that happened and, until now, I have lived these last ten years with the fear that whoever killed my father was still hunting me.'

Rosie found her voice. 'But why?' she whispered. 'Why did Macbeth want to kill your father and you?'

Fleance pulled the parchments from his shirt. 'I found these when I went to Inverness. They are letters from Macbeth to his wife. They explain everything.' He read her the contents of the first letter and was inwardly pleased at her surprised intakes of breath.

When he finished it she said, 'So, he murdered your father because he had been there when Macbeth received the prophecies. But why, Flea? Why did he want your life?'

'Here,' he said, opening the second letter. 'He went to the witches again.' He read her the second letter.

'He was insane,' Rosie said when he had finished. 'How can a king put the guidance of his kingdom into the hands of such evil?'

'Aye, the man was mad, that is certain. And this madness drove him to betray even his best friend. It is strange, though, that he believed the witches' prophecies yet thought it necessary to act to ensure they were fulfilled. Rosie, I never heard Da talk of being anything more than what had been bestowed upon him.'

'Flea?' she began her voice trembling. 'The prophecies say Banquo will be the father of kings.'

'Pay no heed to them. 'Tis just silly prattle, Rosie, but there are men here who still believe such things which is why we must not say anything. Only one other knows the contents of these letters and I trust him with my life.' He stroked Willow's rump. 'Likewise, why would I even think of having an ambition that set me as a target for men's envy?'

Rosie frowned as she flicked her long hair over her shoulder in annoyance. 'And yet, this does not explain why you left me.'

'But it does,' he said. 'Can't you see? I have been plagued by the history of this injustice.'

She frowned deeper. 'You make no sense.'

'Rosie. Listen. My father, he has been visiting me. Both in my dreams and when I am awake.'

'You see him?'

'Aye, and he looks mighty fierce.'

'But that doesn't explain why you're here, in this place, with these clothes,' she said pointing to his shirt.

Fleance took in a deep breath. ''Tis a bit of a long story. If you have the time while Dougal is busy I will share it with you.' Rosie nodded and he told her the story of saving Duncan; going to Forres; the death of King Malcolm; of coming here, to Glamis. He touched her cheek gently. 'I am certain my father is directing my course.'

Her eyes filled with tears. 'You are unbelievable.'

Fleance frowned. 'What do you mean?'

'I thought I knew you, Flea. I thought I understood you but this,' she pointed to the letters, 'this still doesn't explain why you left me.'

Fleance nodded. 'I have felt my father's presence with me most powerfully. And though I don't know how I am to avenge his murder, I sense that the answer is not too far from my grasp.'

'No,' she cried. 'What is unbelievable is that you are standing here in front of me as if nothing has changed between us. That you went off so willingly to amend a wrong done ten years ago, to fix something that has plagued you in dreams and visions. And yet I,' she cried, her face dissolving into anger and despair, 'I, who have been in front of you these past months, real, flesh and blood—' she pinched her arm '—was not regarded enough by you in your plans. What does that say about your feelings towards me, Flea? I thought you loved me. I opened my whole life to you and now I learn you gave me nothing but your scraps.'

Her angry words frustrated him. 'You are being unfair, Rosie,' he said, feeling his temper rise.

'*Me* unfair,' she cried. 'While you've been living the high life, I've been trying to mend my heart, broken by you.'

'Do you not think I have been grieving too?' he stormed. She looked away. 'It has been no high life I've lived. Every night, nightmares – horrible, bloody visions so that I spend daylight feeling like I've been in battle. To forever have the memory of watching my father brutally murdered replaying in my mind is not living the high life.' He was almost shouting now but he needed to get through to her. 'All that time in England, Rosie, I was afraid. Afraid. Can you imagine what that must be like? Can you?' She had begun to cry, quiet tears falling down her cheeks but he was not finished.

'And,' he lowered his voice, 'and now to learn that I am in line to the throne, not simply a distant relative of the royal family.' Rosie looked up at him, tears still spilling down her face though she was silent. He took a deep breath to calm himself, though his heart was still beating furiously, and leant his body against the wall.

The two of them stood in Willow's stall, saying nothing. Eventually he straightened up and went to her. 'Rosie, I'm sorry but I had always believed my life to be in danger and if I told anyone, anyone, then, not only would that risk my life, but those whom I love. You,' he added quietly.

Rosie shook her head and then looked into his eyes. 'I'm sorry, Flea. You are right to be cross. My words were mean.' She tried to wipe away the tears but more followed.

'Shhh, love,' he said and pulled her to him. For a moment she went rigid, but he continued to hold her until she relaxed against him.

'Oh, Flea. I have missed you so much – it was unbearable.' She pressed her face into his chest.

'Aye, likewise, but I hoped you would wait for me.'

'I can do nothing else because you are the only one I want.' She was quiet for a bit. 'But you're not finished, are you?' She lifted her head to look at his face. In hers he saw confusion and doubt. 'How much longer do I have to wait? Flea, do you not see your position now? You are part of the royal family. This will make it hard for us.'

He kissed her forehead. 'It will be fine, I promise. Do you understand now, though, why I had to leave?'

'Was it Da, also?' she asked, her lips quivering. 'Was it that he forced your hand?'

'I think that may have just been the prod I needed – I had been putting it off for too long and then when I met you I just couldn't bear the thought of leaving you.' He drank in her beauty, his heart thumping. Then he bent down and kissed her, gently at first and, when she began to respond, more intensely so that for a long while they clung to each other, their mouths seeking a deeper connection. He felt as if he wanted all of her and the touch and taste of her lips sent his mind into another world.

There was a discreet cough and they jumped apart. It was the new king's advisor, Calum. 'Sire,' he said to Fleance, while staring hard at Rosie, 'the prince is looking for you. What would you have me tell him?'

'I will be with him shortly,' Fleance replied and, when Calum did not move, he added, 'That will be all, thank you.'

A dark look washed over the advisor's face and then he bowed and left abruptly.

Rosie giggled. 'You suit the part, I must say, Flea.'

He pulled her to him again. 'Say you have forgiven me.'

She reached up a hand and stroked his cheek. 'There is a peace in my heart now, for I understand your story. I'm still angry with you for putting me through such pain, but I shall think up some revenge to make you suffer,' she said kissing him and biting his lip.

'Ow,' he said pulling back but then planted a firm kiss on those lips and whispered into her mouth. 'I shall look forward to it.' Grabbing her hand, he led her out of the darkened stables and into the bright morning. 'I cannot tell you, Rosie, what a weight has gone from my shoulders. All these years I believed there was someone whose instruction it was to track me down and destroy me and all I love.' He squeezed her hand. 'I am no longer afraid for my life.'

They found Dougal talking with Morag, a tankard in his hand, a bunch of carrots in hers. Dougal put his tankard on a barrel. 'Well, lass? Has he given you a sound explanation and come to his senses?'

'Aye, Da.'

'Just as well or else I'd have to knock it into him some more,' Dougal growled, giving Fleance a hard look. 'You can tell me about it on the journey home.'

A jolt hit Fleance. 'You're going back to England?'

'No, we have bought a tavern in Perth. That's home for us now,' Rosie said. 'Da here has combined his trade with the profitable use of his goods. Ma and me run it between us.'

This pleased Fleance immensely. 'Shall I ride to see you tomorrow?'

Rosie blushed. 'If you wish and Da approves.' Her father grunted but Fleance took that as consent.

'I have the king's banquet tonight but I will leave first thing in the morning.' Boldly, for his heart was too joyous to care, he kissed her on the cheek before helping her up on the wagon. 'I will see you tomorrow, my love. Before tomorrow's darkness falls, you will have me again.'

Dougal lifted up the reins. 'Mind you keep your promise, Flea, or I shall find you and kick your arse.'

Despite this warning, Fleance grinned. 'Nothing, save death, will keep me from her, Dougal – I give you my word.' Dougal flicked the reins at the horse and the wagon moved off. Rosie turned around and blew him a kiss.

He stood there until he could no longer see them then, with a glad and giddy heart, went in to find Duncan. As he began to climb the steps to the castle, a movement above him caught his eye – someone was standing on the balcony but moved back into the shadows. Though the hairs on the back of his neck prickled, he shook off any dark thoughts. Today was a day of celebration – for him as well as the new king.

Fleance was infected by the joy of seeing Rosie and was in high spirits as the guests took their places at the banquet. At the high table, Duncan and Rachel sat either side of their father and Bree, next to her sister.

Beside him, Macduff was eating enthusiastically and, between mouthfuls, telling Fleance about his latest foray into England. 'Harold's a mad old bugger,' he said. 'But he's mighty powerful. The king, Edward, has stirred up a right old mess between himself and the earls.' Fleance found it hard to concentrate with Macduff's account of English politics. That Harold, the English king's brother-in-law, was agitating held little interest for him, but Macduff continued.

'It's Edward's Norman sympathies which are making the people nervous. Seems the similarities between the Scottish house and the English house are adding to the worries.'

'What do you mean?' Fleance asked politely.

'Poor Malcolm couldn't produce an heir and neither can Edward. Harold's ambitious and he's working hard to hold onto his share of the power. The king has to mind him or there will be trouble.'

Fleance thought of Magness and Miri. 'You mean civil war?'

Macduff shook his head. 'I don't think the English peasants will come up against their king because they love him; but Harold has a mighty few followers.' He sighed and took a long drink. 'You can't say it's a peaceful life holding responsibility for your country.' Fleance saw him look over at Donalbain who was talking rapidly to the pale-haired Calum.

Something about the king's demeanour had shifted and Fleance saw him look angrily his way. Donalbain stood up quickly and followed Calum to the back of the great hall. Was it intuition, second sight, that informed him that the king's action had something to do with Fleance?

Suddenly, the king was back in his seat. He picked up his goblet and drank deeply. Then he banged it down with a crash on the table. The room went silent. 'We have a traitor among us,' he bellowed, his words slurring slightly. The guests murmured in response, looking around the room. 'You, man,' he shouted, pointing a finger at Fleance, 'wheedle your way into our house holding poisonous secrets and evil plans.'

Swallowing nervously, Fleance stood up, his hands shaking.

'Father,' he heard Duncan whisper loudly. 'Father, you must sit.' He stood and addressed the guests. 'The king is not well – it has been a difficult time. Please forgive him for he mistakes my friend as an enemy.'

Donalbain shrugged off his son's arm. 'Name yourself boy and tell us what you told that wee lass in the stables this morning.' Fleance looked at Calum who stared back at him with a smirk on his face. 'And tell me the meaning behind these?' The king held up the parchments.

His mouth went dry.

'Guards!' Donalbain cried. 'Take him to the dungeon.'

'Stop!' Duncan shouted. 'This is madness.' He turned to Fleance. 'Fleance, would you not speak to explain yourself?'

Fleance cleared his throat and took a deep breath. 'Your Majesty, I am no traitor. It is true that I withheld some information from you for I thought my life in danger. But in recent weeks I have discovered the true story of what happened to my father.' He looked at Duncan, who nodded. 'I am Fleance, son of Banquo; Banquo who was Thane of Lochaber and most treacherously murdered by that monster Macbeth. My own murder was to follow his but whether through good luck or divine intervention, I escaped on my father's horse.'

There was an excited murmur from the guests and Macduff put a fatherly hand on his arm. 'I knew it all along,' he muttered.

'Yes,' sneered the king. 'We know who you are and we know that you have come back to Scotland to avenge your father's murder by murdering me and my house so that you can become king.' He waved the parchments in the air. 'It says so here.'

Macduff stood up. 'Your Majesty. I believe the lad here is an honourable one. If he came to avenge Banquo's murder then he knows now that I have already done that for him.' He bowed his head. 'I believe you are quite safe – as is your family.'

Calum came forward and spoke into Donalbain's ear. The king nodded and said, 'Until we can consider this matter further with counsel, you will be confined to your chamber.' He nodded to the guards who came towards Fleance.

Macduff patted him on the back. 'Don't worry, son. The king will come to his senses.'

Fleance was marched to his room, the silent guards looking ahead and unspeaking. His stomach was churning and his hands were sweaty. Donalbain had never learnt to read, Duncan had told him this, so what had Calum said was in the letters? Nothing in them incriminated Fleance so why did the king think that his life was in danger?

He poured water into the basin and splashed it on his face. When he looked up into the mirror he saw a man standing behind him. He spun around but the room was empty. He heart was thrashing inside his chest and his knees felt weak. He turned back to the mirror but only his frightened face stared back.

Fleance went over to his bed, sat down and put his head in his hands. He was losing his mind.

There was a bang on the door and it opened. It was Duncan. Fleance stared at him a moment and then shook his head. 'I'm sorry.'

'For what? Were you planning to murder us all in our sleep?'

'No,' he cried. 'For being the cause of all of that,' he said, waving a hand in the direction of the great hall. 'I should have destroyed the letters.'

Duncan frowned. 'Perhaps, but we did not expect them to end up in Father's hands. You know my father takes any words of prophecy very seriously?' Fleance nodded. 'He will think that you wish to do what Macbeth did to *his* father.'

'I am not a murderer,' Fleance said, his heart still racing.

'I figured that,' Duncan said dryly, 'else you would have slit *my* throat before now.'

Fleance looked up, now worried that Duncan thought ill of him.

His thoughts must have shown on his face for Duncan smiled. 'I was jesting, Fleance. When will you let go and trust that I am for you and not against you?'

'What will happen to me?' Fleance asked

'Rachel has put Father to bed. He is very drunk. He may not remember tomorrow. Or, if he does, I will speak to him.' Duncan went to the door. 'The guards will be here until he gives the orders otherwise.' He hesitated. 'Who was the lass Father was speaking of?'

'That's Rosie,' Fleance said and then he groaned in frustration. 'I told her I would see her tomorrow. If your father won't let me out . . .'

Duncan chewed his top lip. 'Who is she to you, Fleance?' he asked quietly.

'She's whom I love,' Fleance sighed. But even the thought of her did not remove the bitter twisting in his stomach. If he did not get to her, she would think he had betrayed her again and she might be lost to him for good. 'Do you think you could send word to the inn at Perth that I am delayed?'

His friend stared at him for a moment. 'I will do my best, Fleance. Now, if you can, I suggest you sleep for I fear tomorrow will be a difficult day – for all of us.'

Duncan left the chamber and Fleance fell back against the pillows. How could a man go from euphoria to despair in less than a day?

Chapter Twenty-Three

It was with a heavy heart that Duncan returned to the great hall. The guests were dispersing, though Calum was still there speaking with Macduff. 'Calum, a word, if you please,' Duncan said and turned on his heel to go to his father's meeting room, the sound of Calum's soft footfalls behind.

When he got there Duncan was grateful that the fire in the hearth had been lit and there was warmth in the room. 'Sire?' Calum said.

Angrily, Duncan turned to his father's advisor. 'What did you tell him?'

Calum coughed politely. 'I am not certain, Your Highness, that even the king's son is to be privy to the conversation between king and advisor.'

'As the king is incapacitated and as I am the heir to the throne, I think you can take it as understood I shall be privy to whatever you say.' Calum's smugness was infuriating.

The young advisor bowed his head slightly. 'As you wish. His Majesty had asked me to check with the stable manager that his new horse would be at the castle by the end of the week as he wishes to hunt. Your friend,' Calum said this with a slight sneer, 'was in the

stable with the daughter of the tavern keeper. As I feel it my duty
to be aware of all the activities of the castle, I stayed to listen, for
he was acting suspiciously. He told the young girl who he was and
that his father had told him to avenge his murder and then he read
her the letters, the contents of which make for disturbing reading.'

'How did you come by them?'

'I took them from his room for I believed the king needed to
see what they contained.'

'As you and I both know, my father cannot read. So, what matters is what *you* told him they said.'

Calum raised his eyebrows. 'Sire, I told him they contained
disturbing prophecies which affected the safety of the crown.'

Duncan shook his head. 'Fleance is no threat.'

'I'm not so sure,' Calum replied. He went to the table where a
jug of ale and goblets sat and poured a drink. 'A young man who has
lost everything: his father, his title, his home and lands,' he handed
the drink to Duncan, 'learns the king is ill and to die. Comes to
Scotland and conveniently meets you.'

'He saved my life,' Duncan said through gritted teeth.

Calum nodded. 'Quite and what better way to win your trust.'

'Not all men are deceitful, Calum. Contrary to what you perhaps tell my father, there are many honourable men among us and
Fleance is one of them.'

'What honour is there in lying?'

'He didn't lie – he withheld information for he feared for his
life. He's been on the run since he was eleven years old.'

Calum sighed. 'And I think he means to take the throne by foul
means.'

'You do not know him like I do. I trust him completely.'

'And that, perhaps, is your Achilles heel, Duncan. Terrible
things have happened to those who have placed their trust in men
who have evil intentions.'

Duncan looked at him. An idea moved through his thoughts. Was it perhaps irony that he felt the same way towards Calum as the advisor seemed to feel towards Fleance. 'You are wrong.'

He moved to leave when Calum called after him. 'I think it best to advise you, Duncan, your father will take the words of the witches above any mortal.'

Once out in the chilled hallway, Duncan began to shake. Calum was wrong about Fleance. He needed to find Rachel. The banquet had started well and Donalbain had been in a mellow temper. He had not taken any drink before the meals arrived so it was a shock to see him become so agitated so quickly. Once the feast had started, his father's goblet was never empty, fuelled either by a page or Calum.

And why had Calum chosen tonight to talk to his father about Fleance? Had he not known Donalbain would create a scene and embarrass himself in front of everyone? It was not a good start to the reign. He found Rachel talking with Lennox.

'Your father is asleep,' Lennox said. 'He didn't put up much of a fight.'

'Thank you, Lennox. He was not himself tonight. I believe the week's events have caught up with him.'

'Aye, well, we are no longer young and have not the stamina we had in our youth – except Macduff. He's as strong as he was ten summers ago.' He bowed his head. 'Good night to you both.'

'And to you,' Rachel said. Duncan glanced at his sister who looked pale and drawn.

'How are you?' he asked taking her arm.

Rachel sighed wearily. 'He was worse tonight than I've seen him.' She looked at her brother. 'I was watching how much he drank and it was not as much as his usual.'

Duncan agreed. 'Maybe he is unwell.' They walked towards the blue room, though it was late. 'Let us put these things to one side, dear sister, while we think how to fix the disaster which occurred this night.' He poured her some water. 'Drink. You will feel better.' Rachel took a tumbler of water and sat on her favourite chair. Duncan joined her and they talked long into the evening about their family, their father and what solutions they could find to heal their wounded hearts.

The next morning, a messenger was sent to fetch Duncan. His Majesty desired an immediate audience with his son. Duncan hurried to his father's chamber and was alarmed to see him still in bed. 'Are you ill, Father?' he asked.

'I let the drink get to me last night,' Donalbain said. 'Water!' he barked at Calum. 'We would have a word with our son.'

'Yes, Your Majesty,' Calum replied.

'Alone,' Donalbain snapped. Calum bowed and made a hasty retreat. The king motioned for Duncan to sit on the bed, something he had not done since he was a wee lad and his mother was alive. 'I need to discuss the contents of Macbeth's letters.'

'Would you like me to read them to you?' Duncan asked.

'Aye,' Donalbain said and reached under his pillows. His hand trembled as he handed them over.

Duncan read them all as his father lay back and stared at the ceiling. When he'd finished, it was clear the news was distressing. 'They warned me,' Donalbain said. 'They said to beware the son of a murdered father. Was not Banquo murdered? And is not Fleance Banquo's son? And, now, here he is, under our very roof.'

'I tell you again Father, Fleance is no threat. I have journeyed with him these past weeks and always he looks out for me – he saved my life!'

'That was before he knew who you were.'

'Do you trust me? Did you not say just some days ago that you found me wise?'

'Aye.'

'Fleance is my friend and I know him to be honourable. I think that there are other folk who perhaps are twisting things for their own ambitions.' Duncan lowered his voice. 'I will caution you to be careful of Calum . . .'

'Calum has my complete trust!' Donalbain spluttered. 'It is because of his wise counsel that I am able to look to see the progressive future of Scotland. We can easily extend Scotland's borders into England.' The outburst exhausted him because he lay there panting.

'He is my friend, father,' Duncan repeated. 'And I am your son. Think about it: he would be a perfect match for Rachel.' Donalbain scowled. 'I can see already she has some affection for him and now that we know he comes from the royal line, it would be appropriate.'

'I need her, still,' Donalbain grumbled. 'She is the only one who can heal these terrible headaches which plague me constantly.'

This gave Duncan some hope. 'But in marrying Fleance, she would stay here to help manage the castle. Fleance has no land and no title, unless you bestow one on him. And, I believe he will make her happy.'

His father looked sharply at him. 'She is unhappy?'

'Aye, Father, she is ever since Ewan's death. She pretends otherwise but she carries her grief gently and is so keen to comfort others. These past weeks, I have seen her laugh and smile more than in the two years since.'

'Well, Ewan was suitable. It was a tragedy he was not a skilled enough soldier.'

The king was softening. 'Trust me, Father. Fleance is a good man; an honourable man. He would be a valuable member of the family. He is a masterful and fearless fighter and seems to read people well.' He waited but his father just stared. 'He would be useful should we need to defend ourselves.'

Donalbain's eyes widened. 'Why would we need to do that? What have you heard? Calum has told me nothing!'

Duncan stood up. 'There are rumours coming through that a rebel force is preparing to attack the Scottish throne.'

'What? Who? Who would want to do that?'

'The word is that a number of groups have banded together, unhappy with Scotland's place and wanting English rule.'

Donalbain sat up. 'English rule? That is mad. Edward has already alienated his people; why would ours want the same? There is sure to be war in England.' He tried to get out of bed but became tangled in his bedclothes. 'Help me, son. I must go to Preston and Calum. They will tell me what to do.'

Duncan helped his father dress, unwell and sweaty as he was. Donalbain leant heavily on his arm as he prepared to leave his chamber, all the time muttering. As they were about to leave, Duncan stopped his father. 'Fleance. What is your ruling?'

Donalbain's eyes were almost unseeing. 'Eh?' He frowned and then waved a pale hand. 'He is of no consequence. Me, I must to the sisters, for they can show me which way the fortunes of Scotland and England lie.'

They were out of his room and into the antechamber. Donalbain signalled to one of the servants. 'The king sends word that Fleance is free to go.'

'Thank you, Father.'

'You have made much sense and your suggestion shows how much you love your father and sister.' Donalbain turned to the servant. 'Go at once and tell him.' The servant bowed low, opened the doors for king and son and then hurried in the opposite direction.

They did not have to wait long for the two advisors. Donalbain began bombarding them with questions about England and news of a Scottish uprising, to which neither had much to say. Eventually, Calum interrupted the king's ranting. 'Your Majesty, it is true there have been rumours of groups talking of joining together against the crown but we have seen no clear evidence of this. We suspect it is just empty noise from those who wish to unsettle Your Majesty.' He gave Duncan a meaningful look. 'As to England, that is of no concern to us.'

'Of course it is,' Donalbain exploded. 'We wish to expand our trade into England and we cannot do this with civil unrest.'

'No, Sire,' Preston said. 'But there is nothing we can do at this time.'

The king turned on him. 'Yes, we know that, Preston, but it is a wise king who is forewarned before needing to be forearmed.' He coughed and Calum brought him a drink of water. Donalbain took a gulp and then spat it out. 'Get wine, not water, fool!'

Duncan signalled to a servant who scurried away.

'Have a seat, Father,' Duncan said, guiding the king towards a chair.

Calum stepped forward. 'What shall we do about that traitor, Fleance?' Duncan glared at him.

Donalbain waved his hand. 'Nothing. Duncan has assured us he is harmless.'

'But—' Calum interrupted.

The king lurched forward. 'There are more important issues now at hand. We must go to the sisters to get more reliable guidance,' he cried and Duncan was amused to see that Calum looked like he had been slapped.

'Yes, Your Majesty.'

Donalbain rubbed his neck. 'Besides, we have other plans for him.' Then he waved Duncan to his side. 'The king feels unwell.'

'Yes,' Duncan whispered. 'Shall I declare a time for your repose?'

The king wobbled his head towards him and nodded. Duncan stood strong. 'His Majesty is unwell. He is recovering from the illness which attended him last night. Preston,' Duncan looked pointedly at the old man, 'and Calum,' he worked harder to avoid the sneer, 'my father is in need of quiet. There will be no more consultations.'

He helped the king towards his chambers after dismissing the advisors and servants. As he grabbed a hold of his father's arm, he was aware of the fragility of royalty.

Sometime later, he went to find Rachel. She was in the blue room as was her custom at this time of the evening. Duncan poured himself some water and drank it down in one long gulp. When he put the cup on the table, hand shaking, it caused Rachel to look up.

'Duncan?'

'Fleance is no longer under house arrest,' he said.

The look of relief on her face confirmed what he suspected. His sister was obviously growing very fond of Fleance. 'That is good news.'

'Aye, but he is now free to go back to his maid.'

Rachel tilted her head. 'So, what is it that actually bothers you, Duncan?'

Duncan sighed and taking up the cup again filled it with more water, this time sipping more leisurely while he sat closer to the fire. 'I had hoped . . .' he hesitated and raised his eyes to Rachel once more.

She smiled.

'I know what you have hoped for, brother. And I know you have deliberately set about pushing us together.' She regarded him for a few moments. 'I enjoy his company and we do share a common bond – we both love and honour you.'

Duncan snorted. 'Honour is all well and good but I want my sister to find a good match – and be happy,' he added.

'A good match?' she asked, her voice strained. 'Duncan, Fleance has already given up much to fulfil his father's entreaties. I think it unwise to ask him to give up more.' She left her own seat and sat by him, taking his hand. 'You know Fleance would do anything you ask of him. Would you have him spend the rest of his life looking at me and knowing it was only through duty that he lost his true love? That would indeed be a bitter cup to drink – for me as well as him. I don't want another woman's cast-offs, nor do I want a man marrying me out of some misguided sense of what is honourable. The husband I choose must choose me first above all others.'

'But you and Fleance are so well suited,' Duncan whispered. 'I know he holds you in high esteem and I have seen how he looks at you . . .'

Rachel shook her head. 'You of all people, Duncan, should understand the power of a first love. Fleance still loves his maid with all his heart. What may or may not happen is God's will. Just leave it at that.' She stood up. 'It has been a long day and night. I am to bed and I counsel that is where you should go as well.' At the door she turned back to him. 'Do not think too much on how things should be.'

She left the room, her head high. But, just as Rachel could read him, Duncan, too, sensed his sister was hiding disappointment at the turn of events. Despite her stoic attitude, he guessed her heart had been captured by Fleance.

Chapter Twenty-Four

It was Duncan who accompanied Fleance from his room to the stables early the next morning. After the business and noise of the day and evening before, the whole castle was subdued.

Fleance felt a deep sadness that things had turned out this way – the angry outburst of the king, being put under house arrest and the small measure of shame he felt towards Duncan for being the cause of such a scene. However, he was looking forward to seeing Rosie again. Duncan stood by silently as he saddled Willow and then walked beside him as he led the horse out of the stables.

Morag hurried out, a bundle in her hands. 'Master Fleance,' she said puffing. 'I have put together some sweetmeats for your journey.' She bobbed an awkward curtsey.

Fleance inclined his head and smiled. 'You are very kind.' He took the food and put it inside his bag.

'I must get back to the kitchen,' she said nervously and curtsied again.

'Go well, Morag,' he called as she scurried away.

Duncan cleared his throat. 'I am sorry that my father reacted so. And I am sorry you are leaving for I have much enjoyed your company – as has Rachel.' He handed Fleance a small money bag. 'You may find this of use until you are bringing in your own.'

Fleance took the bag and held it in his hand. 'This is kindness,' he said. 'Thank you.' He tucked it into a pocket. 'I have found more than I deserve in friendship and conversation – with both of you. I wish you happiness.'

Duncan looked at him for a moment. 'If you ever have need of anything, Fleance, if things do not go to plan with your . . . Rosie, then you have only to ask – send word. Despite Father's behaviour, Rachel and I will always welcome you.'

Fleance put his hand on his friend's arm. 'You have been kind and generous with your companionship and your hospitality. And I hope you will forgive me for not being so open.'

'You have told me why but I have seen men go insane from the secrets they store up in their hearts. To find real friendship, each person must completely give over their heart, mind and soul, for it is in this place of surrender that love, trust and loyalty flourish.' He clasped both hands around Fleance's arms. 'Go well, my friend. I pray to see you again under better circumstances.'

Fleance mounted and looked down at the fair-headed prince. 'One last thing I would have from you, Duncan.'

'Aye?'

'Would you tell me, from your knowledge, the fastest way a man and horse can make it to Perth?'

Duncan laughed. 'I thought you were going to ask me something that was a matter of life and death.'

Fleance grinned. 'Getting to Rosie as quickly as I can is just as important for me, man.'

Duncan put his hands up. 'Fine. Fine. If you take the highway, you will be there after supper, but if, when you come to the woods, you turn right, you can take many hours from your journey and will be there before sunset.'

'I thank you,' Fleance said graciously. 'I wish you well.' He turned Willow's head and gave him a gentle kick. 'Come on, Willow. We have our Rosie waiting for us.' Once he was out of the castle gates, he urged the horse into a canter and they set out to Perth.

After twenty minutes, he came to the forest and turned right, slowing so that Willow could pick his way through the thick woods. Fleance thought about Duncan's words about keeping secrets and knew that they contained wisdom. Rosie had always been completely honest with him. Each time they had met she had filled him in what had happened in her life since the last time they'd been together. He, on the other hand, had always held back. Though he loved her, he had never really felt able to give himself to her completely – until now.

'Well,' he said aloud. 'That is about to change. Rosie can have all of me.' Willow's ears twitched backwards and forwards. Then, for the first time since he was a boy and because his heart was so full, Fleance began to sing.

He did not hear the man who appeared suddenly beside him. It all happened so fast. A figure in dark clothes lunged at Fleance and Willow shied sideways. The horse, in fright, bucked and then galloped off. In a tangle of arms and legs both men fell to the ground. Fleance was crushed beneath the weight of his assailant.

Instinctively, Fleance rolled rapidly three or four times away but it was not enough. The man pounced on him before he'd even had a chance to pull out his dirk. It was to be a fight relying on brute strength.

For perhaps the first time in his adult life, Fleance found himself wrestling with a man more powerful than himself. He feared for his life. This man didn't speak but his actions were clear – he was out to kill. Once, twice the man smashed his fist into Fleance's face. He felt his mouth fill with blood and spat it out angrily. With the man atop him, he could do nothing so, with an almighty roar and with all his bound-up strength, he thrust the man back and was able to get free.

Willow was gone with sword and crossbow but he still had his dirk and he pulled this from his belt. Fleance was in a worse state than his adversary. But he was angry. He did not deserve this. He had done his best to make things right with the world and all it had brought him was sorrow and pain. Hot rage flooded him.

'Forget your orders, man,' he said. 'I am no match for you.'

'Aye,' came the reply. 'You're not and that is why you're easy money.'

This enraged Fleance further. He stood, five paces way from the assassin. His dirk held aloft. 'You do not know who you are sent to kill for I am well armed.'

The man laughed. 'Right, so your horse has taken off; you're on your own and you just have your dirk. I think maybe, young man, you regard yourself more highly than you should.'

He leapt towards Fleance, but neither blade was of use. This was a fight of hand-to-hand combat. Though both held their daggers to harm, they could not. Fleance bit the man's hand so hard that he let go of his weapon. But his would-be murderer pressed down on his arm – the weight of him extraordinary so that Fleance was powerless to do any injury.

The man again punched his fist into Fleance's face and once again he saw stars. The pain; the fight; the need to stay alive. They gave him power. He could not, would not go down at this absurd place: a tranquil wood. Though bleeding and sore, he fought on. And, again, he was able to push the man away so that they stood some paces apart, both breathing heavily.

'Well, lad, you've put up a mighty fight which makes the game so much more interesting.' He rolled his r's thickly and Fleance recognised him as a Highlander – and dangerous.

Suddenly, the assailant swung a great log around so that it collided with Fleance. He fell. He thought that he was done for, but then he thought of Rosie waiting for him at Perth and he knew he must not give up. The wood was silent but Fleance still had his dirk and was still alive. His chest was crushed; he was bleeding but he was conscious.

The man came towards him, an unpleasant sneer on his face, a dagger held steady. Fleance pretended he was gone but, as the man lifted up his blade to end Fleance's life, Banquo's son plunged his dirk into the foot of his enemy.

The man screamed and in that moment, Fleance whipped the dirk out and thrust it up into the belly of his attacker, slicing the blade around to the right. The man's face contorted with agony and despair. Blood poured forth and covered Fleance. He twisted the dirk further so it made a crunching noise – enough to sicken any man's stomach. Fleance gave another push and felt the man's warm blood on his hand. Fleance looked into the man's eyes and watched him slowly die.

The man fell onto him, the last of his hot blood seeping into Fleance's vest. He pushed him off.

Fleance was panting heavily. He heaved, his hand hanging down, red with blood. Fleance had ended yet another's life – the third since he had embarked on his quest. When would the bloodshed end? He stood there for a moment and looked up at the trees. Minutes ago, he was singing and happy and looking forward to seeing Rosie. Now, he had killed another man.

But, what was worse, Rosie was waiting and he had no way to reach her on time.

There were more problems: a corpse which, very soon, would smell high and invite the wolves; he was hurt and bleeding; a man without a horse – a most unenviable position to be in.

Fleance would have to bury the man before he could go on, otherwise he would attract further danger.

He looked around for some softer ground where he could bury the body and found a large gap between two trees. Using his dirk, he stabbed at the soil and then, using his hands, scooped away the loosened dirt. By the time he'd made a shallow grave, sweat was pouring down his back and face, stinging his eyes.

Fleance was thirsty but he could not go looking for water until he had finished his gruesome task. Standing up stiffly, he hobbled over to the body. He went through the man's garments looking for clues as to who had sent him. He found a money bag but, when he opened it, there were only three small coins. He also found a water skin, almost full, but nothing else; nothing to identify him or who had employed him for such a task.

His eyes were still open so Fleance found a couple of small stones which he would lay on the lids before covering the body with soil. He sat the man up and put his arms around his chest then dragged the heavy weight of the body to the grave. It was too small but Fleance had no more strength to dig. Instead, he arranged the body so that it appeared the man was simply curled up and sleeping. Fleance turned the head so that he could close the eyelids and place the stones on them.

He removed the water bag, pouch and knife from the body – it had no need of these now and it could make the difference between life and death for Fleance.

Carefully, he covered the body with the soil. It was not enough. He must find rocks or heavy branches so that no animal would disturb the site.

It took another hour and the sun was very low in the sky before Fleance felt satisfied with the job. It would be dark soon and he needed water and rest – and a safe place to hide.

At the edge of the wood, he found a small burn and lay down on his stomach pushing his face into the cold water, leaving the skin for another time. His lips and cuts stung but there was also relief.

He drank deeply and then pulled off his shirts and soaked them in the water. He washed his hands and rubbed away the last traces of the would-be assassin's blood from his body and clothes.

Watercress grew abundantly along the banks. Fleance picked handfuls and stuffed them into his mouth, refreshed by the tart and tangy flavour of the plants. The light had all but disappeared from the sky. It was time for shelter. He had seen an old oak with large upsweeping branches which looked like the palm of a man's hand. Fleance found it quickly for it stood quite alone from the other trees.

Wincing with pain, he slowly climbed the tree and was pleased to see the centre was like a small platform covered in old leaves. He hung his damp shirt over one branch and pulled his cloak over his bare chest, wrapping himself in it like a swaddled baby against the cold of the winter night.

Fleance rolled over, the leaves at once cushioning him. It meant he could sleep and, despite the pain, he quickly sank into oblivion.

Rosie
Perth

Rosie tidied the small cottage attached to the tavern and readied a room for Flea. She washed her hair and poured lavender oil into the curls at the end. She had repaired one of her best dresses and, just before the evening meal, when they all expected Flea to arrive, she arranged her hair just as it had been when they had first met at the tavern – gathered up in a thick bundle on her head with curls falling around her face.

The table was set with an extra place and Ma and she had cooked a lamb roast with carrots and fresh bread. All was ready and her excitement painted a permanent smile on her face.

Each time there was the sound of a horse, Rosie flew to the tavern door; each time the rider was not Flea. By the time the sun had set and the roast had dried, Rosie began to feel anxious.

Dougal said what she was feeling. 'I heard him myself. He said he would be here before nightfall and look, night fell two hours ago.'

'Maybe he was delayed, Da,' Rosie said, trying to will the gathering knots in her stomach to stay still. 'I am sure he will come.'

Dougal grunted. 'Well, let's not waste this meal though I feel the meat is only good for the dogs now.'

They ate in silence and Rosie tried very hard not to give in to the tears which threatened to spill forth. She would be strong. He was coming; she felt it. He would not disappoint her again.

By the time the meal was finished, the customers either sent on their way or lodged for the night, the dishes washed and the kitchen cleaned, it was midnight and still no word of Flea.

Rosie went to her room and quietly closed the door. She took off the necklace and removed the bracelets. She pulled the clips from her hair and, as the curls fell around her shoulders, she caught a whiff of the lavender. As steadily as her shaking hands would allow, she unbuttoned her dress, slipped off her shoes and climbed into bed in her underclothes.

She lay there, the candle burning down low, staring at the ceiling, reliving yesterday; reliving the look of intense joy on his face. The way he held her, kissed her. The excitement which radiated from him as he told her his story. The way he looked. The way he smelt. And the way her heart filled to overflowing with passion and love. When she was with him, all other things faded into insignificance. The sound of his voice and the touch of his hand and the way he looked into her eyes told her, without any doubt, that he loved her as she loved him.

Rosie sat up and put out the stuttering candle. As she settled back down into the bed, she tried to think of why he had not kept his promise: perhaps Willow was lame? But surely he would have sent word or used another horse?

Perhaps she and Da had misheard and he was coming tomorrow? But she recounted his words as he held her hand *I will see you tomorrow, my love; before darkness falls, you will have me again.* And then the promise he made to Da: *Nothing, save death, will keep me from her, Dougal – I give you my word.* So, then, where was he? Had he been injured? Had he been attacked?

A jolt of fear swept through her. That was it. She sat up and lit the stub of candle. It fizzed into life and she got out of bed and threw a shawl around her shoulders. She took up the candle and went to her parents' room. There was light coming from under the door so she knocked.

'Come,' Dougal called. When she opened the door, both he and Ma were sitting up in bed – they had probably been discussing the events of the evening. 'What is it, child?'

'I think Flea has been hurt. We should send some fellows to go look for him,' Rosie said. 'Perhaps send a messenger to Glamis castle.' Her parents looked at each other. 'Please, Da. I know him and I know that he is a man of honour. He promised me and you. I'm certain that if he could, he would be here now.'

Dougal sighed. 'All right, Rosie. In the morning, we will send someone to the castle to find out where he is. And some fellows to check along the way in case he is hurt.'

Rosie let out an unsteady sigh. 'Thank you, Father,' she said with formality. 'I know you are cross with him still but now that you know his story, you can understand why he had to leave.' Dougal grunted and Rebecca put a hand on his arm. 'He loves me and I him. We are meant for each other just as you and Ma are – I've heard you say so many times when you thought I was asleep.'

Ma smiled at her. 'Yes, my dear sweet daughter. He is to you as your father was to me when I was your age. And it wasn't easy for us then either.'

'Rebecca, no,' Dougal said quietly.

'She's old enough to know,' Rebecca said. Dougal frowned but even then Rosie could tell his father had relented. Her mother patted the bed beside her. 'Come, sit, dear. And let me tell you my story.' She held up her hands, twisted and swollen. 'This began when I was just a child – no more that twelve or thirteen. Your father here, he was known well by my parents and though a number of years my senior, had shown a particular fondness for me and my difficulties.' Rosie looked at her mother's hands and understood – she had suffered all her life with pain and found it a struggle to do even simple tasks easily.

'When it came time for me to marry, Dougal asked my father for my hand which was freely and happily given. Unfortunately, he was suddenly called up by the king to help quell an uprising along the border. He did not have time to send me word and, on the day arranged for the wedding, he did not show.' Rosie gasped and looked at her father who looked away.

'Do not judge your father, Rosie, for he was under King Duncan's command. My parents believed he had reneged on his promise but I knew better. I knew my Dougal.' She pulled his calloused hand into her lap. 'And I knew he loved me as I love him. Whatever was keeping him from me was beyond even his strength.' With her other hand, she picked up Rosie's. 'My dear girl, if you know in your heart that Flea is the one, then he is. Nothing can and will ever stop this from being true. But know this also, sometimes we have to wait for what we are destined for, longer than we think we can bear.'

Rebecca let go the hands of her husband and daughter and took up a drink of water. 'Some feel they have not the strength nor the patience to wait for such love and decide that good enough is good enough. Me, I waited five long years for your father and because of that, I have spent the last twenty years in joy and happiness.'

Dougal shifted in the bed. 'Do you think, woman, it is wise to give your child such offerings?'

'Yes, man. Don't think to know how hard it was for me to wait for you but I did. And I am pleased to have done so. Flea is a good young man and more than enough for what I should hope for our girl.'

Dougal held up his hands. 'All right! All right! We will send forth men to find Flea for the good of my daughter's heart and my marriage bed! So please you, woman, that you don't use my youth's adventures against me – it is too much to bear.'

Rebecca turned herself towards her husband. 'But worth it, my sweet.' She kissed him lovingly on the cheek and Rosie was bemused to see her father blush. Rebecca faced her daughter. 'Your father will send out many men to find him. If he is out there as you say he is, then he is striving to be here with you.'

Tears filled her eyes. 'Thank you, Ma. Da. Thank you,' she choked and turned away quickly before they saw her tears.

Dear God, she prayed as she hurried back to her room. *Let him be alive. Please, let him be alive.*

———

The next day, Rosie was up before even the rooster had begun his ritual crowing. She dressed quickly and set about lighting candles and torches throughout the tavern. She made breakfast and woke her father.

Grumbling and rubbing the sleep from his eyes, he accepted the breakfast and hot mead. 'Shall I go wake the lads?' she asked him, anxious that they got started.

'No, lass, I will do it. Just let me finish my meal first. The boys will keenly do my bidding but much better if they are not woken at so ungodly an hour.'

Eventually, though, much to Rosie's relief, Dougal sent out two of his regular stablehands – one to go immediately to the castle and learn word of Flea; the other to search among the roadsides and adjoining ways in case he had met misfortune and was lying ill in a ditch.

Another day and no Flea and no word from the messengers. Rosie was forced to go on working for Da, pouring ale, making beds and providing nourishment for those who were travelling.

Early the next day, the first messenger galloped into the yard. He and his horse were breathing hard. 'The king's advisor, himself, a strange pale fellow, sent word. He said that the traitor Fleance was seen leaving the castle gates on Tuesday morning and that he had told the hands he was heading south on the road to England.'

'England?' Rosie cried, disbelieving. She turned to Dougal. 'Did we not tell him we are in Perth?'

'Aye.'

'Maybe the king's advisor was mistaken, for the same road leads to England as it does for Perth,' Rosie said hopefully.

In the evening, the other young fellow came back and said he saw, along the road and the byways, no sign of anything.

Dougal stood behind the counter and glared. 'The evidence is clear. He set out from the castle but did not come this way.' He banged his fist down. 'The coward has fled!'

'No,' Rosie cried. 'It's not so. He's out there.'

Dougal turned to her. 'Get over yourself, maid. He's a nobleman and you are a commoner. He cannot and will not be for you. He has made his choice. Don't wait for him, for he will not come. Not now; not ever.'

The words were daggers to her heart. It all seemed reasonable but not logical. Flea loved her and she loved him. But where was he? He had said he would be here but he was not and there was no trace of him.

It had been four nights and three days since she had last seen him. He was not coming. There had been no word from anyone though she questioned the travellers who came through the doors of the tavern whether they had seen a young man on a large dark horse. Each answer was the same. No.

Though she had waited and argued with her father, it was clear that Flea would not turn up and they would not be reunited.

Rosie would not sit around waiting for what might be; she loved Flea but he was not here and, yet again, she didn't know where he was. Father needed help with the business so Rosie continued getting up early, lighting the fires and helping the cook organise the meals. She made the beds and washed the linen and served the customers, alert always for the sound of Flea's arrival.

Dougal came out to the yard where she was throwing grain at the chickens. 'Rosie, love,' he called, his usual gruff tone taking on a softness. 'I need you to do an errand for me.'

Rosie stopped flicking and put the bowl on top of a post. 'What would you have me do?'

'There is a supplier of good oak planks just south of Alnwick, back in England. I hear he has the best quality. I would go myself but there is much to do here and my absence would sorely affect business. Take your mother with you and I'll send along a good strong lad. It would assist me mightily.'

She knew what he was doing. He was offering her a way out – somewhere to go so that she would not be constantly reminded of her disappointment.

'You're a fine negotiator, Rosie, and I can think of no better person save myself who would complete the task.' Da smiled at her and she was suddenly filled with love for his devotion to her.

She flew into his arms. 'I will do it, Da.' She kissed him on the cheek. 'And I will do it well.'

On the evening of the fourth day, Rosie stood angrily in front of her open window, tears in her eyes.

She was weary. Everyone expected so much of her and she tried so hard to help her mother and Da and be kind and patient but all she wanted to do was crawl away and cry for her place in life. Her bottom lip twitched. *God, all I want to do is to go to bed and pull the covers over my head and never arise. No mother with painful joints; no angry father with ambition; no troubled Scotland and no,* she sobbed, *no lover who has disappeared.*

She gave herself a shake. *Stop behaving like a spoilt child,* she chided herself. There are people worse off. She breathed steadily. She would wait for him until she heard word and she would not tell Dougal of her plans. For now, she would swallow down any sorrow and get busy so that she had little time to think.

Come the morning, she would plan her trip back to England with Ma and, when she returned, she would go find Flea herself.

Chapter Twenty-Five

He was lost. The wood was so thick that he could not get his bearings. For three days now he had wandered through the sunless undergrowth hoping to glimpse light which would tell him the forest was coming to an end. He had been unable to find the path that led to Perth and, with Willow gone, he had no way of catching easily something to eat. He was hungry and he was angry.

Who had sent the assassin to kill him? He was no danger to anyone: he was landless and powerless – what possible threat could he be? Surely no one could take the rambling prophecies of three weird women seriously? Who in their right mind would ever look to him as king? Yet again, something beyond his control had intervened to thwart his attempts to reach the one thing he wanted most – to be with Rosie.

She would be furious with him. He imagined her silently cursing him, her face frowning in the sweet way it did. And Dougal, sure, when he finally got out of this blasted forest and explained, then Rosie's father might understand but right now he'd probably be making plans to hang, draw and quarter him.

Get in line, Fleance thought wryly.

In the distance, he saw light and his hopes rose. He picked up his pace but when he broke through into the sunlight, his heart sank. It was just another small clearing. Fleance stood in the middle and looked around – there was nothing save the trees to give him a landmark. He needed to find a stream and follow it – that was going to be his only hope of getting out.

The one he'd crossed yesterday morning was just a trickle and it was not worth going back although he doubted he would be able to find it anyway. Fleance looked to the sky. The sun was low which meant that direction was west and the way he needed to travel. He turned and went in that direction, crossed over the small clearing and disappeared into the thick forest once more.

By the time the birds started flocking back to the trees, he realised he would be spending yet another evening up in the branches. He had not been able to find another resting place like the first night and resorted to tying himself onto the trunk so that he would not fall out. As he settled himself in for the night, the birds calling and singing around him, he sent a quiet message to Rosie. *I'm coming, sweet. Wait for me.*

Fleance was woken before daybreak by the happy sounds of the birds. Their cheerful and optimistic chirruping grated. From his vantage point, he watched a fox and her young scamper past heading in the direction of the way he'd come, the mother with an egg in her mouth.

An egg. It was a chicken's egg. There must be a cottage or farm somewhere close. Fleance untied himself and climbed down. He drank some water – there was little left – and walked the path from where the fox had come.

It must have been an hour later when he noticed the trees thinning and more sunlight shining down on the floor of the forest. He stopped for a drink and to catch his breath. In the distance he heard a sheep bleating. Yes, he thought. I'm getting closer. He was too sore and weak from hunger to move faster but he now knew he would get free of this dreaded wood.

It wasn't long after this, he smelt the tang of smoke and then, coming out of the forest suddenly, he was in a clearing and in this clearing was a small cottage.

Fleance went to the door and knocked. A stout woman answered, about the age of Miri. 'Good morning, madam,' Fleance said. 'I have been lost in the woods these past three days and I would be most grateful for a bite to eat and something to drink.'

The woman nodded, 'Aye, and some patching up as well by the look of you. Come in, lad.'

Once inside the cottage, Fleance smelt something good and then saw that the family was gathered around their table eating. He nodded to them. 'My name is Flea and I was on my way to Perth when I was attacked.'

The children, there were four, stared at him wide-eyed while their mother dished him a large bowl of porridge. 'Get this in you,' she said roughly but not unkindly.

Her husband stood up. He was as stout as his wife but shorter. 'You are welcome though we don't have much. Damn foxes keep getting at the chickens and worrying the sheep.'

The porridge was hot and tasteless but his stomach was thankful for it nonetheless. Fleance nodded to the man. 'I saw a fox and her young come past with an egg in her mouth. She was what got me the idea to head this way.'

The man shook his head. 'I'd love to catch the wee minx and wring her neck.'

'If I had my horse, I'd be able to hunt her with my crossbow, but the dang mule left me to fight my attacker alone.' Fleance caught a glance between husband and wife. 'You haven't seen him by any chance? Large, dark brute?'

'Well, you see, the thing is,' the man looked nervously at his wife. 'I found a horse much like your description. I did go out to look for its rider but found nothing so thought him probably dead with a broken neck. I took the horse to the village and sold him to a traveller.' The shock and despair must have shown on Fleance's face. 'I'm sorry, lad, and I'd give you the money but I used it to buy me a milking cow.'

Fleance was lost for words. Somewhere in the back of his mind, he had just expected he would find Willow in a clearing, enjoying unlimited feed and they would be reunited. Now, not only had his horse gone for good, but the saddle, sword and his crossbow – everything left in the world which connected him to his father – and were also gone.

The woman went outside and came back with something wrapped in sacking. 'We kept these because we thought one day we will teach the children how to use them.' She unwrapped the cloth and there was his sword and bow. 'I'm sorry for your trouble.'

Fleance stood up and accepted back his weapons. 'Thank you.' At least it was something. 'Maybe I could find that fellow and buy back my horse,' he said hopefully. 'Can you show me the way to the village and tell me how far it is to Perth?'

The man took him outside and, in the dirt, drew a crude map explaining to Fleance the direction he should take. 'The fellow might still be there, lad, for it was just yesterday I did the trade. It's half a day's walk to the place and then another half day's walk to Perth.'

His wife came out with some bread and cheese. 'For your journey.'

With mixed feelings of frustration and relief, Fleance said his goodbyes with both man and woman apologising profusely. Fleance forgave them. How could they have known?

Fleance eventually came upon the village just as the farmer had said. It had taken much longer than the promised time for his aching body hindered him from moving as fast as he would normally go. The sun was making its way down when he located the busy tavern and went in to enquire after Willow. 'I fell from my horse,' Fleance explained. 'I came upon a couple who say they found him and sold him here yesterday. I would very much like to be able to buy him back.'

The innkeeper nodded. 'Aye, there was a fellow came and asked if anyone was interested in the horse outside. The man who bought your horse is still abed after a somewhat late night carousing. I don't want no trouble.'

'If you would be so kind as to wake him and tell him I would like to meet.'

The innkeeper hurried off, throwing his cleaning cloth to one of the maids and disappeared out the back. Fleance bought a drink and sat at a table, his head throbbing and his cut lip still stinging.

He had drained the tankard by the time the innkeeper returned with a grey-faced man who looked decidedly the worse for wear. Fleance stood and motioned to the man to sit and for the innkeeper to bring him some ale.

'I understand,' the man began, 'you have some business with me regarding that damn fool horse I bought yesterday?'

Fleance suppressed a smile. Willow was bad tempered at the best of times. He would not take too kindly to a stranger trying to ride him. 'Aye. The cottager who sold him thought his rider dead. I am that rider and, as you can see, very much alive. I will pay you what you paid for him if you would return him to me.'

The man eyed him balefully. 'What's he to you? I can't saddle him; he's tetchy and ill tempered. And he's old. I think the ale I drank yesterday made him appear much better than he is.'

'He is my father's horse and the only thing left of him for he was killed ten years ago.'

'You'd waste your gold on nostalgia?'

'Yes, but I am in need of a horse as well.'

The man downed his drink and stood. 'Right then, it seems God has forgiven me my foolishness and given me a way out of it. Let's go see this beast of yours.'

Fleance paid for the drinks and followed the man, who still walked unsteadily, towards the stables. There was Willow, his tail swishing. Fleance checked him over. There was a long cut down one leg and grazes along his back.

'Hey, Willow,' Fleance called and the horse turned to him. For the first time since he could remember, Willow appeared was pleased to see him. 'Where is the saddle?'

'It's no good,' the man said. 'It's busted. He must have rolled on it.' He told Fleance what he paid for Willow and what he wanted. They briefly haggled over the price so that finally it was an amount Fleance could afford.

He retrieved the last three coins in his bag and handed them over. 'We are even,' he said and shook the man's sweaty hand.

At least Willow had not torn the reins, and after strapping his sword and bow to his back, he climbed up on the horse and set out towards Perth.

Both man and horse were not in the best of spirits as they plodded along the road. Fleance had no more gold left and the only things he had of value were his father's sword and his crossbow but he did not want to spend another wretched night in the open. After days of sunny weather, the sky was dark with clouds and it was sure to rain soon.

'We will have to find ourselves some shelter, Willow.' Fleance scanned the fields to his left and right, searching for some type of building but there was nothing. He did not want to stop until he found some sort of safe place. The light had all but gone from the sky and the moon was obscured by the cloud, its intermittent light throwing up strange shapes and shadows.

Just then, he spotted a light in the distance. Maybe he could ask to sleep in their stables. He urged Willow on and as they approached the building it took on shape. It was a beacon in the darkness and Fleance breathed a sigh of relief – it was a church. In fact, it was the very abbey where the new king had enjoyed communion. Scone.

Fleance slipped off Willow's back and banged on the church door. He waited a good while but then heard muffled footsteps. The door swung open and light flooded out.

'Father,' Fleance said. 'I would ask for a night's repose for me and my horse. I am down on my luck but give thanks for this providential abbey.'

The door swung wider. 'Come in, my son,' the softly spoken friar said. 'I will send someone to tend your horse. We have just enjoyed vespers and you are welcome to sit with us for supper.'

'Thank you,' Fleance said and he followed the friar through the church and to the inner rooms.

The monks attended his cuts and bruises and filled him with roasted lamb and cooked vegetables. It was on a full stomach and a weary body he crawled into the small cot and, despite the loud snores bouncing around the room, he was soon fast asleep.

That night he slept soundly and without dreams.

The next morning, the monks gave him a large breakfast and a long prayer for his safety and he was on his way. They said he would come across Perth before mid-morning. For this he was thankful because rain had started up early and persisted the whole way. It was not enough, however, to dampen his hopes because very shortly he knew he would see Rosie and it was these thoughts of her which sustained him despite the battered state of his body.

Before he knew it, he was at the top of a small incline and the village of Perth was below. Fleance spied the tavern and happily coaxed his weary horse down the hill. With his heart beating fast, he slid off Willow, tied him up and went into the tavern. Dougal was behind the bar and looked up as he came in.

Suddenly and with a roar, Rosie's father rushed him, knocking him out of the tavern and onto his backside. 'You've got a nerve,' he cried. 'I don't know what your excuse is this time but you'll never see her again while I live.'

Fleance was stunned. Painfully, he stood up. 'I was set upon, Dougal. Look at me. See my wounds.'

Dougal hesitated and took in Fleance's injuries. With a sigh he mopped his face and sat heavily on the railing outside the tavern. 'Ah, Flea,' he sighed wearily. 'I can see you've come to some kind of trouble, but lad, she waited and waited for you. Now, I've sent her away. She's not here and you will not find her.'

'What? But I came for her as I promised.'

'Actions speak louder than any pretty promises. She's better off without you, especially now with your new position.'

'No, you're wrong,' Fleance cried. 'You should know that makes no difference to me.'

'Fer God's sake man, stop being so dense. You need to face the truth of the matter. There's always been something canny about you – not the same as us. Now my suspicions are proven right.' He put his hands on his hips. 'Now, away with you, Flea. Go back to your castle. Forget about her as I have told her to forget about you. Go find yourself another because you have lost Rosie for good.' Then he stomped back into the tavern and slammed the door shut, leaving Fleance outside in the rain, his heart breaking, no food, no gold, nowhere to go – but worse than all of this, no Rosie.

Chapter Twenty-Six

After filling up his water skin from the well, Fleance led Willow to the outskirts of the town, hopped up on an overturned barrel and climbed onto the horse's back. For a moment, he just sat there, staring. He wanted to weep, such was the depth of his despair. She had been the one thing which kept him going. Why hadn't she waited for him? Why had she agreed to go away?

He remembered the look of hesitation which crossed her face when they were in the stables at Glamis – perhaps she no longer loved him. Had his desertion wounded her so much that it took away her feelings for him?

Fleance shook the thought from his mind. It could not be; not the way she kissed him.

Where to now? He could go back to Magness and Miri but the thought of that place without Rosie filled him with dread. Willow stamped his hoof impatiently. Fleance flicked the reins. 'Well, then, Willow. What do you suggest? We have no home, no food and no friends.' He stopped. Yes, he did have a friend. Duncan. *If you ever have need of anything, Fleance, if things do not go to plan send word . . . Rachel and I will always welcome you.* That is what he had said. And now he needed a place to sleep and a place to recover while he thought over what to do next.

'Right, horse. We are going back to Glamis. Take the highway and get me there without incident.'

Glamis castle was situated in the middle of a wide lowland valley surrounded by a large open space and, beyond that, many fields and large crops of dense woods. Willow splashed through the stream which hurried over the road marking the boundary of the castle grounds. Fleance was sore, stiff and very hungry. Apart from the few times he had dismounted to give himself and Willow a rest, they had headed determinedly towards their destination.

The rain had not eased, making their journey harder on the wet and slippery road. Fleance was soaked through and cold but to stop would be to invite a slow but sure death. He had to get to the castle.

He was startled out of his stupor by a shout from above. 'Halt. Who goes there?' A soldier called down from a lookout. Fleance lifted his head and saw that the gates were closed.

'I am Fleance, son of Banquo,' he shouted up into the rain.

'What is your business this late in the evening, Sire?'

'If you would send word to Duncan that I am here and have urgent need to speak with him.' Another soldier appeared and they spoke quietly to each other though, because of the incessant hiss of rain, Fleance could not make out what was said. He dropped his head again. His hands and legs were numb with cold. He was so tired. If only he could sleep.

He barely registered the gate being opened and two figures rushing out towards him. Nor did he notice when he fell from Willow. In the distance, he could hear someone calling his name but all he wanted to do was sleep. He felt himself weightless and thought he must be floating down a river for water was splashing over his face. A women's soft voice. Rosie? Fleance turned his head and then all was darkness.

There was a soft rumbling sound coming from somewhere near his feet and the feeling that someone was systematically massaging his legs. Fleance opened one eye and peered down the bed. A large grey creature was kneading the blankets at his feet, a look of utter ecstasy on its face. Fleance lay back down on his pillow and closed his eye. It was just a cat.

Suddenly a body swooped in and scooped the cat from the bed. 'Off you go, Zeus. This is not your bed.' A cool hand pressed lightly on his forehead. 'Fleance? Can you open your eyes?' The voice belonged to Rachel.

He felt like his eyes were stuck together and the light made his head spin. He tried once, twice, three times and was eventually able to focus and saw Rachel's pretty smile. 'What happened?' he asked, his voice leaving his throat unwillingly.

'You took a cold and a gash, it seems, became infected. You have been feverish for three days now.'

He went to sit up but it felt like his body was made of stone. 'I am so weak,' he said.

'I'm not surprised. You've been terribly ill, Fleance,' she said, straightening his blankets.

'Really?'

'Aye. When we found you, you were barely conscious and fearfully chilled. That cut on your hand had festered and you've been battling a fever.' She put her hand to his cheek this time and smiled. 'It seems to have broken.' She straightened. 'I'll call for some broth and tell Duncan you are awake.'

Fleance nodded, almost too tired to speak. Despite his nagging sadness, it was wonderful to feel warm again and be lying between clean sheets and he drifted off.

The door opened and Duncan walked in. 'I'm pleased to hear from Rachel you are much better, my friend.' He sat on the edge of the bed. 'We were very worried for you.'

'I didn't think I was that bad – tired and hungry, that's all.'

'And cold and wet and hurt. Not things to be taken lightly in Scotland.' Duncan smiled. 'I'm pleased to see you. Did you not find your maid?'

Fleance sighed deeply. He shook his head and told Duncan the whole story starting from the moment he was attacked.

'Are you sure it wasn't just a thief taking his chance?' he asked.

'No, he told me that he was being paid. Who would want to do that to me, Duncan? I had nothing save a small handful of gold.' The cat had returned and, subconsciously, Fleance began stroking its soft fur. Zeus was delighted and showed his appreciation by dribbling on the sheets.

'You are safe here. Shall I send out scouts to find her?' Duncan asked.

'No. She made her choice and I have to live with that now. I only wish she knew that it was not through my hand I was delayed.'

Duncan chewed his lip. 'Perhaps,' he began and took in a deep breath. 'Perhaps it is not meant to be, my friend.'

Tears sprang to Fleance's eyes and he turned his head so that Duncan would not see them. Mercifully, Rachel arrived with a maid who carried a tray of delicious-smelling food. 'How is the patient? You're not bothering him, are you, brother?'

Duncan stood and made room for her. While she was busy with the food, Fleance quickly wiped away the tears on his lashes and then rubbed his eyes to conceal his grief.

'I will leave you to my sister's fussing, Fleance. There are worse things in the world,' he grinned and picked up Zeus before leaving. 'Father and his aides are gone from court and I have some castle business to attend. I will come and see you later.'

Rachel came forward. 'Can you try to sit a bit, Fleance?' she asked. When he struggled, she leant forward, put her arms under his and lifted him. He was surprised at her strength. She pulled him up on the cushions and put more behind and on each side as if she feared he would topple over any moment.

All the while he watched her, for the first time really seeing her as someone other than Duncan's sister. How different to Rosie she was. Where Rosie was energy personified, this girl floated on a sea of calm. Where Rosie spoke like loud and happy music, Rachel was the sound of wind in the treetops.

She placed the tray on his knees. 'Would you like me to help you or do you think you can manage the spoon?' His embarrassment must have shown for she stood up briskly. 'I'll leave you to it then. Just small amounts and I'll be back to change your dressing.'

As she turned to leave he called her name. She turned back to him. 'Thank you,' he said.

She smiled. 'My pleasure.' And then she was gone.

He was in bed for a further three days although he was well enough to walk small distances to toilet himself and wash. On the second day since waking, Bree found her way into his chamber and made him tell her stories about his life in England. There were times when she also insisted Rachel share her bedtime stories.

'You're getting spoiled, wee Bree,' Rachel said after one very entertaining account of an incompetent knight and a very grumpy steed. 'Perhaps you should not have your bedtime story tonight.' Bree scowled, and Rachel and Fleance laughed.

It wasn't long before Fleance found himself part of the routine life of the castle: Bree's tantrums, the ever-persistent Zeus, the cat, Duncan's worried face and Rachel's calm among the storm. And it wasn't long before the thought of Rosie was tucked away into a small, secret part of his heart.

It was about two weeks since Fleance's return to Glamis when he heard sounds of galloping horses and shouting. He looked out his window and saw that the king and a number of earls and thanes had arrived. Carefully, he closed the shutters so as not to draw attention to himself.

Though Fleance had spent many a time these last days taking secret walks in the halls of the castle, he sensed the safest place for him at present was to remain in his chambers. At least until Duncan had informed the king of his presence.

After dinner, which Rachel had brought him, Duncan visited, looking pale and worried.

'How goes things, Duncan? Rachel would not tell me what has been happening but it seems there is news which makes her unhappy.'

'Aye, I am not surprised,' Duncan said. 'Things have taken a turn for the worse it seems.'

'How so?'

'The Thane of Lochaber has joined forces with Scottish rebels living in England and has sent word he will march upon Scotland and take the Western Isles and Galloway.' Fleance tried to sit up again but Duncan gently pushed him back. 'Rachel will hound me if I do not take care of her patient. She has said complete bed rest until you are eating normally.'

Fleance didn't argue. It was nice to have a reason to lie in the comfort of the bed but he was concerned with the news his friend had brought. 'Why? What do they want?'

'They don't want Father as King of Scotland and they say they have the support of many of the Highlanders and those to the south.'

'Is the thane thinking of taking the crown?' Fleance asked, knowing that would mean a bloody and violent war. Despite the threats, Donalbain had a huge army.

'No. They want Scotland to join with England and be ruled by her.'

'That's absurd,' Fleance cried. 'It would be like running from a snake into a bear's den.' Then he realised the significance of what he had said and felt his face warm with embarrassment. 'Sorry, I didn't mean . . .'

Duncan held up his hand to silence him. 'You are right, my friend, I know my father's weaknesses well. However, even with a less than effective king, a Scottish king is better than an English one. I had hoped to help Father rule wisely but it seems our hand is getting forced on this.' He stood up. 'Would you like me to open the casement?' Fleance nodded. Duncan threw open the shutters and a watery sky was visible from where Fleance lay. 'I have another matter to discuss with you,' he said his back to Fleance. 'I have asked Father to give you back Lochaber.'

'What?' Fleance was stunned. His home? To be his again?

'Aye. The thane will be caught and tried for treason against the crown. He will lose his title. I have convinced Father that it belongs to you, as it was unfairly taken by Macbeth and given to the present thane.'

'That is very generous of you but I can't see your father agreeing to it. I did not please him.'

'He has other things to occupy his mind but he did say he would consider it – on one condition.'

'Aye?'

'That you would fight alongside me when we face the rebels.'

There was a heavy silence in the room save for the cat's purring. 'It is certain, then, that Scotland will go to war?' Fleance asked.

'Aye,' Duncan sighed.

'Our army will gather at the border come spring. We will to Perth and then by sea to Edinburgh where we will meet them on the heath outside the city limits. It seems when this winter is finished, my friend, we will be at war.'

Chapter Twenty-Seven
Glamis Castle

Fleance agreed to the request that he be a soldier of the king's army. But Donalbain had not left it there. According to Duncan, Calum recommended to the king that Fleance become a general for it was clear Fleance was a skilled fighter and also a leader of men.

How Calum would know anything about Fleance's leadership potential bemused him but Duncan assured him it was a great honour and spoke well of the king's attitude towards him.

'I am pleased to hear the king no longer has concerns that I am here. To any he places under my leadership, I will pass on all that I have learnt from the two men who have guided me.' He grinned, thinking fondly of both his father and Magness. 'The king and his advisor have a strange way of working.'

Duncan returned his smile. 'Father wants what is best and chooses the best. That Calum has signalled you as right for the cause is but honey in the bread.' Fleance frowned at this. 'That's Morag's saying for making sweet or better a dire situation.'

'Duncan,' Fleance confided. 'I am, because of this illness, not as strong as I usually am.'

Duncan shook his head. 'We have time, Fleance. These winter months will allow you to gain strength and to train in readiness for the battle.'

'As you say,' Fleance said, but the idea of going against a vast army was both thrilling and terrifying. He felt so weak and this frustrated him. Never before had he been so hindered by his own body. Never before had it taken him so long to recover from being hurt. The disturbing dreams and nightmares had returned nightly, preventing him from enjoying healing sleep – this surely was hindering his recovery.

So, while Duncan, with the king and other advisors, made preparations for their eventual sojourn to the south of Scotland, Fleance worked hard to build up his strength. He walked a longer distance each day and ate the food Rachel recommended. And yet, every morning, he awoke exhausted. He did not want to let Duncan down so said nothing of his struggles.

One day, however, Rachel cornered him in the garden. 'You are still not well, Fleance,' she said. 'I see you when you've climbed the stairs; when you've gone out with Willow. I have not healed you.'

'I am fine, Rachel. It is taking longer but each day I can feel my body work better than the day before. Leave off worrying.'

Rachel paused and looked out towards the castle walls before continuing.

'Perhaps it is not your body that is still in need of mending,' she said, her voice little more than a whisper. 'Perhaps it is a wound of the heart that grieves you more. My brother spoke of a maid . . .'

'No,' Fleance interrupted. 'It seems her choice has been made with not a backward glance nor hint of regret. Do not worry yourself on my behalf, Rachel. It is simply a burdened memory I have learnt to carry.'

Rachel blushed then turned away. 'If you say so, Fleance. But I know you have to carry a load for my father's army as well. I just want you to be well.'

He looked at her. 'Be assured, I will be. I just need time.'

Rachel shook her head. 'You are a stubborn man, Fleance, and proud with it.' She sighed. 'I will think on what I can do to help you gain back your strength.'

'Thank you, Princess.'

She returned inside. Fleance watched her leave and, for the rest of his walk, found his gaze being drawn back towards the castle.

Later that week, while he was recovering from another training session, a message by way of a farmer delivering vegetables came to the castle.

Morag found him sitting on an upturned barrel catching his breath. 'You have a message, Sire,' she said. 'On the road and coming presently is one who goes by the name of Blair.'

Fleance roused himself and looked up. 'Blair?'

'Aye, the farmer passed him not a mile back walking with a mule.'

Standing up, Fleance stood before her. 'Thank you, Morag. That is happy news. I shall go out and welcome him to Glamis.' Morag went back to the kitchen and he to the stables. In too much of a hurry to saddle Willow, he just bridled him then leapt on the horse's back.

'Come, Willow. We shall meet someone I warrant you will be most pleased to see.' Once out of the gates, he cantered down the road and in no time came up to his childhood friend, walking with a grey mule. 'Scar and all, you are still a beautiful sight, wee Blair,' he said, sliding off Willow's back.

Blair grinned, his freckles seeming to dance across his face. 'You call me wee? I am at least an inch taller than you.'

Fleance embraced him. 'What brings you to Glamis?'

274

'I have come to declare my allegiance to the king.'

'I am glad for that and I am also glad you have come.'

They walked towards the castle leading their animals. 'It's good to see you also, Flea.'

Fleance grinned. 'And you, you corny lad.'

They were soon at the castle gates and Blair stopped. 'The word is that you have outed yourself and are serving in the king's palace. I had hoped I would find you here.'

'I am part of the king's army but I do not feel as ready as I would like. If you would think on it Blair, I would have no other sparring partner to help me prepare.'

Blair rubbed his forehead. 'Well, I've not had much cause for weaponry these last years – I'm no' certain I'd be that much use to you.'

''Tis like riding a horse. You never forget how, though you might feel a bit sore from exposing parts of your body that have almost forgotten they were alive.'

Stablehands came to them, relieving them of their mounts so together they walked into the castle. 'What is your title then, Fleance, that has you in the king's palace?'

'It is a strange position I find myself in. I am friend to the prince; have been made a general in the king's army though he himself is most distrustful of me. I cannot go anywhere but his aides and spies are following.'

Blair looked alarmed. 'What have you done to displease the king?'

Fleance shook his head. 'I have done nothing wrong but Donalbain has received a prophecy, his son Duncan tells me, that I am a threat to him and his family.'

Blair snorted. 'Threat? From what I remember, you have a wicked temper and a soft heart.' They continued to walk the corridors of the castle talking. 'You remember that damn rabbit?'

'Rabbit?'

'I don't believe you,' Blair cried. 'You had a rabbit which your father had found wounded and you'd fixed and nurtured it.'

Like his friend, Fleance frowned. 'Aye?'

'Aye. And the bloody thing was sick and useless and all in the manor wished to put it out of its misery but you cried like a girl and so we, who knew better, stood back so that Banquo could sort through the problem.'

Fleance turned to Blair. 'Really? All I remember is that someone told me the rabbit had to die and I believed that was too harsh a judgement.'

Blair smiled at his friend. 'Which is often the way, my friend. In response to those men whose powerful place in the world holds much strength to determine all outcomes, the rest of us must work hard to accommodate.'

Fleance shook his head. 'Still as deep as the loch, I see. For the love of God, man, speak plain.'

Blair sighed heavily and looked down. Then, taking a deep breath, he faced Fleance. 'You have always been part of the royal family. I am not. I am a servant. You have power. I have not. No one listens to me or my kind. My kind is called to serve yours. Good or bad, that is what we do.'

'No,' Fleance said. 'The wee spawn had no need to die. Do you not think that right?'

Blair laughed aloud. 'Rabbits, horses, dogs, servants. In the end you treated them all the same. Would you still do that?'

'You make it sound like I have sinned against God for doing such things.'

Blair laughed up at the sky. 'No, man. But, looking at you now, I see that things have changed somewhat for your future and, perhaps, Scotland's.'

Fleance stared into the face of the young man, his ally and his friend. But not his equal.

'You *are* my friend,' Fleance said eventually.

Blair nodded low. 'Aye, and you are my commander.'

The next day, Fleance and Blair shivered in the bitingly cold air as they watched over the servants who laid out the weapons and marked the arena where they would practise. Fleance picked up his father's sword and swung it in slow circles above his head, reacquainting himself with the weight of the steel. Though his hands easily held the hilt, Fleance could feel a twinge in his left arm and his shoulders. He remembered the days when Magness made him swing over and over and over until he cried with the pain and frustration. It had worked though and Fleance knew that with more training he would once again possess the strength and stamina needed to brandish a heavy claymore.

Though his precision and deft movement with the crossbow left all others in his wake, Fleance understood that this battle would be won by sword and axe, by might and commitment. And a wit about him to keep himself and those under his command alive and well. Every time he thought on this, Fleance felt a wave of nervousness sweep through him. To be assigned the responsibility of so many lives was both an honour and burden. He felt ambivalent towards the task and only hoped that as the time approached he would be more willing and excited and less afraid.

Blair had been mimicking Fleance's moves and both now felt warm enough to throw off the cloaks which had been hampering their movements. Fleance was surprised to see how much Blair had filled out; under his shirt, thick muscles contorted and bulged as Blair swung the sword out and up to the right before turning and bringing it in and down to the left – over and over, moving forward and spinning around gracefully and almost silently.

Fleance's strength left him long before Blair stopped. A servant brought him over a drink and he swallowed it thirstily. When Blair realised Fleance was not matching his moves, he also stopped.

Fleance waved him on. 'Keep going. My body has yet to fully recover but if you keep up the practice, you'll be as good as any on the field.' He drank some more.

Blair ignored his instruction and came over. 'Shall we rest these a bit, and take up our daggers?'

Fleance was grateful for Blair's suggestion as it would save him losing face before the castle and therefore those in his command. 'Aye. This requires a sure foot and a quick mind.'

The servants took the swords and handed them the dirks with their short blades and sharp edges. For the next hour, they sparred and Fleance was pleased with the natural ability Blair displayed. Fleance showed his partner a number of moves which would enable him to escape from certain death but at the same time end the life of an enemy.

By midday, both were hungry and tired. 'That will be all for today,' Fleance said, wiping the sweat from his face and taking the cloak offered by his servant. 'You have been schooled well.'

'Do you not remember?' Blair asked. 'It was your father who first taught me.'

A vivid image came to Fleance: two young boys holding the dirks and circling each other as Banquo called out instructions and encouragement. Blair was as slippery as an eel and Fleance became more and more enraged because he could not hit the other. Each time, when he thought he had his friend and lunged forward, Blair spun away but not before Blair had hit him with the weapon. After thirty minutes, Fleance threw down the dirk and stormed off out of the stables, fury clouding his mind.

Banquo found him down by the stream, chucking large stones into the chilly water. 'You let yourself down, young man,' his father said, standing beside him on the bank. 'You let anger get control of you.'

'I couldn't get him,' Fleance said, hoisting another rock into the stream. 'He wouldn't let me get him.'

Banquo turned his son to face him. 'That's the point. Blair was in control the whole time. He didn't need to get you because you did the work for him – working up a rage which clouded every sensible thought.'

'He's faster than me,' Fleance grumbled.

'No, you are faster but he is wiser.' Banquo took the rock from the hands of Fleance. 'Son, this will be your great undoing if you do not learn to control your emotions. At the moment, this is your greatest battle.'

Tears spilled down Fleance's face and he felt the humiliation and shame because of the truth of his father's words. More than anything, he wanted to be like Banquo: brave, strong, calm, wise. He would not be beaten by this.

Fleance wiped his face roughly and swallowed back the rest of the tears. 'May we go again, Da?'

Banquo stared at him for a moment and then nodded. 'Aye. But keep in mind that your enemy is your uncontrolled emotion, not your poor wee friend.'

They walked back to the stables in silence and found Blair busily engaged in rubbing down Willow. 'Blair,' Banquo called. 'Do you have time for one more round before supper?'

Blair grinned. 'Aye, if Flea is up to another thrashing.'

Fleance ignored the gibe, picked up the dirk from the bench where someone had placed it, took a deep breath and prepared to spar.

'Aye,' Fleance nodded. 'You whipped my arse almost every time.'

'At the start but once you stopped losing your rag, you were hard to beat.'

'Same time tomorrow?' Fleance suggested.

'Aye,' Blair agreed and took his sword and dirk from the waiting servant and headed to his quarters, one of the wooden cottages which sat huddled at the back of the castle.

Fleance was feeling a burning in his upper arms and back. He was trying to stretch and twist out the knots and pain as he walked towards his chambers. Rachel, Bree in tow, bustled out of the landing which led down to the kitchens, her face flushed and Bree's own face tear-stained. When they saw him, they stopped.

'Are you hurt, Fleance?' Rachel asked, still holding tightly to Bree's arm.

'I think I overdid it today in training. My strength is not as it was before.' Fleance was amused to see Bree glowering at him.

'I have an errand to attend to,' Rachel said, nodding towards her sister. 'But I shall shortly meet you to administer some medicine which I know soothes angry limbs.'

To come to his chambers would no longer be appropriate; nor would being alone to do what he imagined she needed to do. 'I am starved. Could we meet in Morag's kitchen – when you are ready?'

'Aye. I will be there presently.' She gave Bree a wee nudge. 'Come along, Bree. You have need of some quiet time.'

Fleance could not help but suppress a smile. Bree and Rachel both, it seemed. He walked down the cold stone stairs which were used by the family and key servants as access to the main kitchen. Fleance had never gone this way alone, though many a time Duncan had pointed out the door to him: 'Need a quick bite of food or drink – there's your route. Straight to the heart of the castle.'

The smells, noise and heat washed over him before he'd reached the last few steps. When Fleance opened the wooden door, he was unprepared for the sights and sounds which confronted him: colour and steam and movement and music and noise and a wonderful aroma of roasting meat and sweet foods almost sent him back up the staircase. He was already exhausted from his day. To contend with this, might be too much.

'Young Fleance,' a throaty voice called from deep within the chaos. 'Are you here to peel the vegetables?' A woman chuckled. It was Morag.

'Sorry, Morag,' he teased. 'I have no skill with a knife.' Morag roared with laughter, many cooks and maids joining her. 'I've been sent by Rachel to wait. I've hurt my shoulder and she has a remedy.' Fleance caught the looks between the kitchen staff.

Morag came over to him and pulled him over to an alcove off the kitchen. 'Rachel knows what she is doing. Sit here, Sire, and she will come soon, once she's dealt with that tempestuous child.'

Fleance sat on the hard bench and leant against the wall. He observed the busy movements of the staff. Morag, impressively, had it all under control and those who flittered in and out of the kitchen respected her directions. Her niece, Charissa, however, seemed far removed from the frantic nature of her post: she quietly placed vegetables in their cooking pots, took bread from the oven, peeled carrots to place in the boiling pans and still thought enough to fill her aunt's cup with water for it was suffocatingly hot in this place. Yes. He could see why Duncan was enamoured: not only was she extraordinarily pretty, but she was peacefulness personified. Balm for the young prince's soul.

Outside, the snow turned to ice and the water could not be pulled from the well without a fellow descending the walls to break through the ice. Morag, the general of the kitchen, ordered young servants to scale the slippery insides of the castle's inner well to smash the ice so that they had clean drinking water. She had another group go out into the field to bring in snow to be used for the daily needs of the castle.

Fleance watched all the effort that went into ensuring that none of the family knew how much effort was required to keep them all comfortable. Simply they, blessed children of Donalbain, needed comfort at this time. How wonderful, he thought, that there were kind souls such as Morag and Charissa, who went about their daily duties with a generous heart for those they served and loved. To be the benefactor of such care as well made Fleance feel blessed indeed.

He was about to leave, thinking Rachel had forgotten, when she came through the wee wooden door. In her hand was a bowl and over her arm a towel. 'Fleance,' she said. 'I am so sorry you had to wait long. Bree was . . . most uncooperative.' He saw Morag smirk.

'You've a very kind way of saying the bairn's a brat and has tested the patience of every saint in the castle,' Morag said, at the same time pointing out to a kitchen hand to rescue a pot that was spilling over.

Rachel sighed. 'She is hard work, Morag, but you know I don't like to give the child a name lest she grows into it.' She turned to Fleance. 'Now, let's see to these aches.'

'I am grateful for your time, Rachel. I haven't experienced this difficulty nor pain in a very long time.'

She set down her tools and, dispassionately, undid his shirt and pulled it from his shoulders. 'Your limbs have a memory of their ability but they do not acknowledge illness or injury. We need to remind them that, though they can be strong and mighty, it is not without effort.' She rubbed her hands vigorously and then scooped a great wad of wax-like substance from the bowl. Again, she rubbed her hands and then applied them to his shoulders. The heat at once was like a knife but he did not move and then, with her firm manipulations, it began to ease the pain.

Fleance groaned. It was both very sore but such a relief. Rachel continued to press her fingers into the very strips of his muscles. He hung his head. At once he wanted to cry and call out at the pleasure and the pain. Still she massaged his taut limbs and the salve clearly was right for him.

'There's magic in your hands, Rachel,' he said, his throat constricted.

She stopped. 'Do not speak to me about magic,' she scolded in the same tone he'd heard her use with Bree. 'That is foolish talk. 'Tis but a salve – my mother's recipe.'

'Sorry. I did not mean to offend. It was just a figure of speech.' He was annoyed with himself that he had upset her.

'I understand but you know the ways of this castle somewhat and the store some put in foolish words.' She resumed her manipulation of his muscles. He did not want her to stop but after ten minutes, Rachel wiped her hands and stood up. 'The ointment will do its work. You should eat something and then rest.'

Fleance tried to stand up but wavered, so quickly sat back down on the stool, not wanting Rachel to see him so weak.

Morag came to his rescue. 'Wee Rachel. The man has been training most of the day. Let me attend him now. You go. Bless you and, on my part, give wee Bree a smack on the arse.'

He heard Rachel laugh but it was too hot and too much. Groggily, he allowed Morag to lead him up the stairs. She'd already sent a message to Duncan who met them outside Fleance's chamber. 'I'll take him from here,' Duncan said and put his shoulder under Fleance's arm. 'What have you been up to, my friend?' he asked.

Fleance rolled onto his bed and tried to kick off his boots. 'Your sister rubbed some type of balm into my burning muscles. I think I became overwhelmed by its healing.' The damn boots wouldn't pull off.

'Here,' Duncan said, with laughter in his voice. 'They won't come free if you don't unlace them.' He quickly removed the straps and pulled off the boots. 'Are you sure it was only Rachel's cream that overwhelmed you?' Duncan said grinning.

Fleance looked at him. 'What do you mean?'

'Perhaps her kindness and beauty is also working on your heart?'

He threw a cushion at Duncan. 'Go away and leave me to rest.'

Laughing, Duncan did as he was told. But, in the darkness, Fleance could feel Rachel's hands once again on his shoulders and back. He turned over and tried to concentrate on the manoeuvres he would work on tomorrow in his training session, pushing thoughts of Rachel from his mind.

Chapter Twenty-Eight

The next morning, Fleance's head ached. He had not drunk much but yesterday he had pushed himself physically. Though the winter months normally called for hibernation, the men could not rest, for secret armies were planning an offensive against the king.

Macduff had arrived at the castle to work with Fleance and the other leaders within the ranks. 'You need to train your body and mind to move without thinking for there is no time for such things in the heat of battle,' he told them. His thoughts turned back to the times Magness trained him. There had sometimes been a feverish intensity to those workouts. *No, lad! You must not give up. Trust your inner rage at these times for it will save your life. And, maybe, those you love!*

Fleance watched as he showed Blair a routine which had his friend step forward, using a back hand to swing the sword and then bringing the shield in his left hand up to block while the sword finished its arc and came down the other side. If it hadn't been for such a deadly purpose, it would have been considered quite a beautiful dance.

Macduff was patient with Blair and though Fleance shivered in the cold morning, he wondered about the battles Macduff had fought in, the fights he had won and lost, and whether he was plagued by the memories of them.

Soon it was Fleance's turn and he, along with five other fellows, repeated the exercise Macduff had shown them. They trained all morning and, after a meal, into the afternoon unaware that sometime, during that same clear, cold day, Calum mounted his horse, rode out of the castle gates and did not return.

At first, Donalbain was annoyed; then he became concerned and sent soldiers out to scout for the advisor but each one came back empty-handed. It was as if the pale, blond man had disappeared into the snow.

It was a strange thing that Calum had gone from the palace and not returned. Nor had he given word as to where he was going. This, more than anything, distressed Donalbain violently. 'He has been murdered,' Donalbain shouted at supper time when the last post came. 'My good, wise counsellor, struck done by a foul traitor.' He paced wildly in the great hall, his hands and arms flailing around his body. 'I shall find who has done this and, when I do, that day he will draw his last breath.' He stormed out of the room and they could hear him shouting through the castle.

Fleance saw Rachel and Duncan exchange looks, rise from their stools and quickly follow the king.

Blair leant over and whispered, 'Does this happen often?' Fleance gave a quick nod. Blair raised his eyebrows. 'I'd heard the rumours about the king's behaviour but I thought it was exaggeration.' He lifted his fork and pointed in the direction of the retreating siblings. 'What will happen now?'

Fleance exhaled sharply. 'I think it wise, my friend, to ask no questions. The walls have ears and men are not always as safe in their beds as they are led to believe.'

A slow flush of red crawled up Blair's neck. 'Sorry, Sire,' he said quietly and went back to his meal.

Fleance also finished his meal but it sat like a cold stone in his stomach. What had happened to Calum? The man had always made him nervous and it appeared Duncan neither liked nor trusted him. Yet, there must be something powerful about the advisor to hold such sway over Donalbain's thoughts and moods.

He wiped his fingers and mouth with the warm cloth offered by the manservant and stood up. 'Tomorrow, then, Blair. We will practise our sword work and the moves Macduff has shown us.' Blair nodded, his face still slightly red. 'Good. Not too much wine tonight for we have a lot of new strategies to test and learn.'

Fleance stepped away from the table of his men and went in search of Duncan.

His friend was not in his chambers, nor the kitchen nor the courtyard. Eventually, he came across Preston who seemed more aged and worried that ever before. 'Preston,' Fleance called. 'Have you seen the prince?'

'Aye, Sire. He and his sister are in the blue room.'

Fleance hesitated. Though he had been there a few times with Duncan, he had never gone there uninvited. 'Would you send word to him that I wish to speak on a matter of importance.'

Preston gave his strange bow. 'If you could come with me, Sire, I shall announce you for I am certain that the prince and princess would warmly welcome your company.' As he followed the advisor down the halls, Fleance turned the old man's words over and over. Fleance was somewhat uncomfortable with both of the king's advisors, but Preston had been with the family a very long time. Though it had not gone unnoticed that the old man had wandering eyes, especially the way he regarded Rachel, he appeared steadfastly loyal to the family.

They came to the outer door and Preston knocked once. 'Come,' Duncan's voice could be heard deep within the chambers. Preston opened the door, entered and closed it behind him, leaving Fleance to study the jumping shadows of the torches which lined the great corridor. A moment later, Preston returned. 'Prince Duncan welcomes you,' he said and opened the door for Fleance.

The room inside was its normal warm and comforting place. Rachel sat on a low chair beside the fire, rolling strips of bleached material and Duncan stood against the mantle, a drink in his hand. Both looked downcast and exhausted.

'How is the king?' Fleance asked, standing in the middle of the room.

'I have given him something that will help him sleep,' Rachel answered. 'When he gets agitated so, he sleeps little, which only further aggravates his moods.'

'Sit,' Duncan said, motioning to the other low chair beside Rachel. 'Would you have a drink?'

'Aye. But just one. I've told my men they must be ready to train tomorrow and I need them with clear heads. Best I do likewise.' Fleance took the drink and sat down.

'Preston said you wished to talk with us,' Duncan said.

Fleance could feel his face warm at the exposure of his lie. 'Actually, I just wanted an excuse to come join you and I didn't want to say those words to the old man.' Fleance grinned sheepishly.

Duncan stared at him for a moment and then threw his head back as he roared with laughter. Even Rachel grinned at him.

'Have you not yet understood your place here, Fleance? You are as close as kin. You don't need permission to speak with me or Rachel.'

'We welcome your company any time, Fleance,' Rachel said, smiling at him.

Fleance felt himself relaxing. 'Thank you,' he said, leaning back into the chair.

'I am not certain,' Rachel said, continuing a conversation she was having with her brother before Fleance's arrival, 'that Preston is up to task of advising Father on how to manage this war.'

'That may be,' Duncan said. 'But we still have the valued skills and knowledge of the thanes and earls. Lennox, Ross, Angus and Macduff have each pledged men and weaponry when the time comes. Fleance here has our men in hand. 'Tis not like the family is unused to battle.'

'Agreed,' Rachel continued. 'But with Father in the state of mind he is in, who's to say that some of the leaders will pull out if they sense their king would put them at unnecessary risk?'

Fleance listened to the two of them discussing strategies and personalities as if they were appointed heads of state rather than siblings with an unstable father. From Duncan's attention to detail and Rachel's calm but firm enquiries into these details came a clear plan of how and what to do come spring – whether their father was in a right mind or not.

Yet, as they talked, Fleance became mesmerised by Rachel's swift hands as she sorted and rolled the strips of cloth. It took him a moment to realise she was rolling bandages, and it occurred to him that she, too, might be caught up in the fray, attending to the wounded and dying.

A shudder passed through him and she looked up. 'Are you not well, Fleance?' She stood up and came over to him, pressing her soft hand to his forehead. She frowned. 'You don't feel too warm.'

Fleance cleared his throat. Suddenly the cosiness of the room, the drink and close proximity to her was overwhelming. He took her hand from his face and kissed the back of it. Then he stood up. 'Thank you for your concern, Princess,' he said formally and somewhat stiffly. 'Good night.' He hurried to the door.

'Fleance,' Rachel called after him. He turned, heart still pounding. 'Do not push yourself too hard just yet.'

He nodded but grinned at Duncan. 'I will take it slowly for Duncan's sake.'

Duncan snorted. 'I can manage whatever you can.'

Rachel sighed. 'You two are like bucks in the spring.' She finished her roll and picked up another. 'You're on the same side.' She smiled at Fleance. 'Rest well.'

Fleance looked over at Duncan who raised an eyebrow and gave him a knowing grin. Fleance shook his head and disappeared into the coolness of the corridor.

─────

It had been a week since Calum's strange disappearance. The king had rarely been sighted, spending most of his days and nights in his chambers. This morning, after a night of snow, the day had dawned bright. Duncan and Fleance arose early as Macduff was teaching Duncan and Fleance some more moves with the sword. They had not been practising long when Donalbain came running down the steps. The two young men stopped what they were doing.

'What is the matter, Father?' Duncan called. Donalbain seemed not to hear him but headed off in the direction of the stables. 'Father?' he called after him but the king ignored his cries. Fleance reached for his friend's sword. 'Thank you,' Duncan said, his face grim as he hurried after the retreating figure of the king.

Fleance sheathed the weapons and handed them to one of the waiting soldiers. 'The prince and I will resume our practice later, if you are willing,' he told Macduff. He looked over to the stables. Should he go there and lend support to Duncan or would it be best if he stayed out of the king's way? The second option, while preferable, was not one a brave man could take and so, taking a deep breath, he followed Duncan.

Before he got to the stable doors, he heard Donalbain shouting and Duncan's calm voice. When Fleance arrived in the warm dark building, it took a moment for his eyes to adjust to the dim light. The king and his son were standing side by side while nervous stablehands rushed around preparing Donalbain's horse.

Suddenly, Donalbain saw Fleance and gave a strangled cry. 'You,' he pointed. 'You hang around our home like a malignant omen. Ever since you came upon our family, terrible things have happened.'

'Father, no,' Duncan pleaded. 'Fleance is not to blame for the war.'

Still the king glared. 'I shall know for certain after I speak with the sisters.'

'Father,' Duncan said again. 'Do you think it wise to travel with this much snow? Could you not wait a day or two until the weather improves?'

A stablehand led out the king's horse but now stood uncertainly beside it.

'I will go. You need have no fear for my life from any man for that is what they prophesised.' He motioned for the hand to bring his horse outside. Duncan helped his father mount. 'I will be back before nightfall,' he said and then kicked his horse into a canter. Fleance barely got out of the way as horse and rider rushed past.

They watched him go and once again Fleance had to remind himself that what he was witnessing was not some silly child's behaviour but the actions of the King of Scotland. He turned to Duncan. 'Should we send someone with him?'

'Aye. He is a fool to go from the castle alone.' They began walking back. 'Sometimes his passion makes him forget reason.'

'Passion?'

'All my life I've heard him talk about the way Scotland should be ruled. About how he would do it much better than my grandfather and then my Uncle Malcolm. I don't think he ever believed he would one day become king and now, I fear, he is trying to make up for what he sees as decades of poor rule, seeking counsel upon counsel from those hags whom he believes will give him knowledge of the future and therefore power.' They walked up the wet steps. 'He has the drive, Fleance, but not the wisdom which should attend it.' As they walked through the large doors, two servants came forward and took their heavy cloaks. 'He is not a bad man, my father.'

Fleance listened to his friend's concerned tone and wished he could do something to take some of the burden. 'I will send Blair and another to follow his tracks and ensure his safety.'

'Thank you,' Duncan said. 'He is prone to forget the needs of his body when he is distracted by the supernatural.'

Fleance took his cloak again and shrugged it on before heading out into the bright, cold morning. He was uncertain how Donalbain would react when he learnt two of his soldiers had followed him so, as he walked to one of the wooden huts on the palace grounds which housed the soldiers, he mulled over what it was he should tell the young sergeant.

He found the men chucking dice but sought out Blair who was mending a shirt. 'Sergeant,' he called and Blair looked up. 'Choose a good horseman – one who can keep a secret – and meet me at the stables.'

By the time he was halfway to the stables, Blair and a fresh-faced young fellow jogged up behind him.

'The king has gone alone to speak with three strange sisters. You must follow him but do not disturb him. You are to ensure he comes to no harm and see him safely back to the castle.'

Blair nodded grimly. 'Aye, Sire.' The two of them contin-ued to the stables. Fleance hoped neither would have to endure Donalbain's wrath.

With Blair gone and Duncan understandably in no mood for jousting, Fleance decided to practise on his own – he needed to keep building up his strength or else he would be of no use to his men on the day they went to war.

He retrieved his father's sword and a palace shield from the armoury. Back at the courtyard, where the servants had swept away much of the snow, he removed his outer cloak, rested the shield against a water barrel and began, slowly and carefully, to swing the sword in figure-of-eight movements, just as Magness had taught him.

He heard a cough and spun around, panting. Rachel. So lost was he in the mesmerising exercise, he had not seen her approach. He lowered the sword. 'Princess,' he said, bowing his head. 'It's cold out.'

'Aye and it's too hot inside, for my sister has once again tested my patience.' She held out her arm and pulled up her sleeve. There were angry red welts along it.

Fleance went over to her and took her arm, looking closely at the marks. He could quite clearly make out the outline of a bite – not from an animal but a human. 'Did she do this?' he asked, less shocked at Bree's behaviour but more concerned for Rachel's well-being.

'She did and Morag has given her a good spanking. Bree has been sent to her room and I've been sent out here to collect myself. Fleance,' she said, roughly pulling the sleeve down. 'I really wanted to hurt her for doing this to me.' He saw tears in her eyes. 'I can't believe that I would feel that way to my own flesh and blood.'

'I believe she is reacting to your father's temper the only way she knows how,' he smiled. 'She can't punish him for making her afraid but she can punish you because she trusts you will not harm her.'

'If I were a man,' Rachel said, 'I might take my frustrations out with sword and dirk, not weep and wail like I fear I will do shortly.'

This gave Fleance an idea. 'Have you used a sword before, Rachel?' he asked.

'Not really. When we were younger, Father fashioned Duncan and I small swords and sometimes we would go into the fields and play at being duelling knights. We have always been told we come from a long line of fierce warriors.'

Fleance smiled. It was not an image he thought well with Duncan and Rachel. Bree, on the other hand, fitted the picture of fierce warrior perfectly.

'A proposition for you: I have no sparring partner today. If I furnished you with weapons, would you help me?'

Her face lit up. 'That is a perfect idea. Shall we go to the armoury and you choose me a sword?'

'Aye,' Fleance said, sheathing his.

Together they went into the weapons room and Fleance looked along the row of swords, looking for one that would suit. 'We need to find one which you can easily hold; one that is not too heavy.'

'I am stronger than I look,' she replied and, as if to prove her point, she picked up Blair's duelling sword with almost the same ease as its owner did.

Fleance whistled. 'Indeed. Well, since you have chosen your weapon, let us to our training.' On the way out of the room, he selected a shield and carried it as they returned to the courtyard.

Standing in front of her, Fleance showed Rachel how to hold both the shield and sword so that they did not collide. Then, picking up his own weapons, he demonstrated the routine Macduff had shown the men a few weeks earlier.

But Rachel swung the sword in the wrong direction and it arched up and crashed into her shield. 'Oh, dear,' she said laughing. 'It is not as easy as you make it look. Show me again.'

Fleance repeated the movement but again she crashed the sword into her shield.

'I do not think my mind understands left from right,' she said. 'Perhaps I am confused because I am standing opposite to you and what I see is like a mirror and my brain is tricking me.'

'I will stand behind you,' he said. 'And guide your arms the way they should go.'

He put down his weapons and stood close behind her. 'Bring this arm up to your left shoulder,' he said, guiding her right arm with the sword. 'Now, bring it down. No, not that way.' Fleance brought her hand back to her shoulder. He came around to her front. 'You need the downward arc to be led by the back of your hand,' he said, his own hand slowly showing what he meant. 'Do you understand?'

She smiled, her eyes bright with joy. 'This is so much fun,' she said.

Fleance stood behind once more and was pleased that this time her arms did as they were instructed. They walked slowly across the courtyard, Fleance guiding her progress, arms and swords in unison, so close that sometimes her shoulder brushed his chest.

When they came to the other side of the yard, they turned around. 'I believe I will try to do it myself,' Rachel said.

'Wait,' Fleance told her. 'I will get my sword and we will move together.' He ran to where his sword and shield stood and jogged back to Rachel whose warm breath was making steam puffs in the cold air. 'Ready?' he asked and she nodded.

They set off slowly with Fleance calling out the individual moves and in no time were back to the barrel of water on the other side. He put down his sword and looked at her, noting the small beads of perspiration on her forehead and that she was breathing heavily.

'You have done well, Princess,' he said genuinely impressed with how quickly she picked up the skill.

'Thank you, Fleance. It has been a most enjoyable hour. Though I am a healer not a fighter, I would be grateful if you would spare an hour or two in the days ahead, to teach me further.'

He bowed. 'It would be my pleasure.'

'I shall look forward to it,' she replied with a smile. She handed him the sword and shield and went back into the castle. He watched her go.

Putting down the weapons she gave him and picking up his own, he went back to his exercises all the while thinking about the training session with her.

Chapter Twenty-Nine

He was dreaming again – of everything. First, he and Rosie swung Keavy between them, Rosie singing silly nonsense songs so that both he and Keavy were breathless with giggling. But, as they came closer to a copse of trees, the clouds shifted over the sun and it became cold. A wind whipped up and the three of them ran into the trees to shelter but there were already many others huddled there. They kept going, searching for something and then it wasn't just Rosie and Keavy but Magness and Miri. Magness was giving orders, shouting and when Fleance turned around it wasn't Magness but Macduff brandishing Banquo's sword. When Fleance sought to take Rosie's hand, she had disappeared, along with Keavy.

A fear gripped him. He was alone: all had disappeared. The wailing noise from the tree people (for that is how he thought of them) was deafening and he sensed the wood was a dangerous place. In the corner of his eye, he kept seeing a moving blackness but when he turned his head, it was not there – only the people howling and crying under the trees.

Then, in the dream, he was on Willow, trying to find something but he didn't know what. All around him, the feeling of evil and danger. Willow, despite his urging, walked slower and the sense that his life was at risk intensified. He couldn't see it but he could feel something pressing in on him so that a huge weight was crushing his chest and he couldn't breathe . . . .

Fleance opened his eyes to see a figure looming over him. He tried to cry out but something covered his mouth and nose. He was not dreaming – someone was attacking him. He pushed as hard as he could to get his arms free from the iron grip which was holding him down. He moved his head from side to side and was able to dislodge whatever it was that was suffocating him. Then, taking a deep breath, he roared as he gave another powerful push against whoever it was.

The shadow was thrown off and he leapt out of bed, his breath coming in loud, ragged gasps. 'Who's there?' he shouted. 'Who are you?'

Even though the shutters were open, the moon was down so the room was almost completely dark, except for the fire, which had burned low. The sound of his ragged breathing and the blood pulsing in his head made it almost impossible to hear his assailant.

Suddenly, a shift in the air made him spin to his right just as the shadow came upon him again. This time he was ready and fell towards his attacker, grabbing him in a vice-like hold. 'Name?' he demanded through gritted teeth.

The man struggled against him and Fleance felt a punch to this thigh. 'If you don't tell me your name, I will wring your neck,' he roared, a stinging pain now spreading down his leg.

His captive kicked him in the shins and, at the same time, attempted to pull free. His assailant was strong but Fleance was as well.

'You would kill your king?' Immediately, Fleance thrust the man away from him. He heard him stumble and crash into the stool beside the door and topple the washing basin and jug so that it crashed loudly on the stone floor.

Fleance picked up a torch and held it in the embers but kept his eye on the crumpled shape stirring in the shadows. The torch flared and he held it above his head. He went for his dirk but there was a shot of pain in his leg. It was like someone had burned him with a hot poker – such was the feeling in his hip and down his thigh. He stumbled as his leg gave way and looked down. A small dagger stuck out of his thigh. It was his own. He pulled it out and almost passed out with the pain. A shower of blood gushed from the wound. He put his hand on the deep cut and pressed down.

Like a shadow, Donalbain rose up to his full height. Fleance fell back against the bed. The king! He had nearly killed his king. 'Your Majesty. It is I, Banquo's son.'

But Donalbain did not seem to hear. His voice rolled out, filling the four corners of the room. 'You must not live, Fleance. I cannot allow it. For the sake of my son and the throne of Scotland.'

'I am no threat,' Fleance cried. 'I assure you, I am loyal to Scotland and its king.'

'You are a liar,' Donalbain roared. 'I will ensure the words of the prophetesses are fulfilled.' He began to move towards Fleance when suddenly Duncan burst through the door, dishevelled and sleep-filled.

'What is going on?' he demanded, but then saw the stand-off with his father and Fleance. 'Father,' he shouted. 'What are you doing?'

'They repeated the warning,' Donalbain cried. 'You are in danger, my son.' He pointed at Fleance. 'This man will be the death of you.' He went to lunge at Fleance again, but Duncan interceded.

Like two drowning men, they wrestled. The noise of Donalbain swearing and shouting mad things and Duncan's 'Stop! Stop!' filled the chamber. Donalbain, with an almighty heave, sent Duncan tumbling back towards Fleance who caught him before they both went down, the jarring pain in Fleance's thigh making him cry out.

Silence, save for Duncan's breathing.

Both young men looked around the room. Donalbain lay still on the edge of the hearth. His eyes were open but he was not breathing. Duncan rushed to him and Fleance, limping, brought over the torch. A flow of blood seeped out from under the king's head.

'Father?' Duncan cried as he shook him. Donalbain's head wobbled. He lifted his father's shoulders. 'He is dead,' Duncan said his voice strangled and strange. 'My father is dead.'

'He must have fallen back,' Fleance offered, looking about the room. 'See,' he said pointing. 'The rug is pulled up. While I caught you, he tripped.'

'No, no, no,' Duncan whispered. 'This cannot be.' He looked up at Fleance, confusion in his expression. 'Fleance?'

'I will fetch Rachel,' Fleance said quietly and with one hand still pressed against his wound and the other holding the torch he left his chamber.

The torches still burned but they burned low. It was very late. He came to Rachel's chamber and hesitated. It was not seemly for a young man to enter a maiden's bedroom. But then, being attacked by the King of Scotland and having that king now lying dead in one's bedroom was also not seemly.

He knocked loudly, three times, and opened the door. 'Rachel,' he called. 'Wake up. We need your help. There's been an accident.'

In the soft light of the torch he saw her sit up, a look of terror on her face. 'Fleance?' She caught sight of his leg. 'You're hurt,' she said and pushed the bedclothes off her legs and jumped out of bed. She picked up a roll of bandages beside her bed and came over to him.

'Give me the light,' she said and she took it from him holding it close to where his hand pressed against his leg. 'Take your hand away,' she said. Gently, she lifted up his night shirt. Fleance could feel warm blood flow down his leg. 'What happened?' Rachel asked as she applied a thick cloth over the cut and began wrapping tightly the bandage around his thigh.

'Rachel,' Fleance finally said. 'It's not me.'

She gave him a funny look. 'What are you talking about?' As quickly as she had started, the task was finished and she stood up. 'Come. Wash your hands.'

Numbly he followed her to the washstand and, once she had washed his blood from her hands, he allowed her to wash his.

He searched for the courage to tell her. 'Your father,' he croaked. 'Your father has had an accident.'

She inhaled sharply. 'Where is he? What has happened?'

Fleance removed their hands from the bloodied water and picked up a towel. He gave it to Rachel but she was staring at him. He dried her hands and then his. 'Bring your things,' he said. 'He is in my chamber.'

Fleance found Duncan as he had left him: kneeling before the hearth cradling the limp body of the king. His friend was silent, holding Donalbain, staring into nothing. Rachel gave a strangled cry and rushed to his side. Fleance stood in the doorway feeling like an intruder, looking on as Rachel desperately tried to revive her father. Even from this distance he knew it was too late for Donalbain.

Duncan stood up, the front of his shirt soaked with blood, his hands shaking as he pulled Rachel up as well. Both turned to him. 'The king is dead,' Duncan said. 'I will inform Preston.' He walked passed Fleance and out into the corridor.

'But he just fell backwards,' Fleance said to Rachel.

'He fell on the iron spikes,' she said, her chin trembling. 'One pierced his skull at the base. I can do nothing.'

He stood awkwardly, aware of the dull ache in his thigh, but also moved by the pain in her voice. It was then he realised that however much they complained or worried about him, Donalbain was still their father and they still held much affection for him.

Rachel inhaled unevenly. 'We are orphans now. Wee Bree . . .' she broke off and rushed from the chamber. Fleance cursed himself for his inaction and outward lack of compassion. He turned back to the body before the hearth. Just moments ago, this man had tried to take his life and through no other's hands, had himself been killed.

The castle's bells began to toll and, within minutes, Fleance found himself backing onto his bed while Preston, Morag, Rachel, Duncan and a number of servants came into his chamber and collected the king's body. And, as quickly as it began, he was alone again, no sign save the broken pitcher that anything had been amiss. That and the bloodied bandage on his leg.

An hour later, Duncan returned with Preston. 'Fleance,' he said. 'I forgot about you and your injury. Rachel says you were stabbed.'

'Aye,' Fleance answered, unsettled and unsure about what situation he now found himself in. Would they think he was to blame for the king's death?

Duncan pulled up a stool and sat down. 'I have told Preston what I found when I came into your chambers. Could you tell us everything that happened here for we will have to inform the earls and thanes in the morning and we need a clear explanation.'

Fleance recounted the attack but with broken and faltering speech. 'It was the king,' he said in disbelief. 'I don't understand why.' He was horrified. 'I can't believe this has happened.' But the evidence was there. The wound ached.

Duncan sighed. 'Father was in one of his states. I had been waiting up for him. Your sergeant came in just after supper and sent a message that Donalbain had sent them back to the castle. I dismissed them and waited in Father's chambers to speak with him as soon as he came in. I must have fallen asleep because the next thing I remember is hearing him shouting. I followed the noise to here and found him ranting.' He looked at Preston. 'He tried to attack Fleance but I grabbed him to hold him back. As you know, Father is strong and he pushed me off. I fell against Fleance who cushioned my fall. When I looked back, Father was lying there.'

'He must have tripped backwards,' Fleance told Preston. 'Rachel said he caught his head on that iron spike.'

Preston took a torch and held it over the dark iron surrounds which ran about the hearth. He sighed deeply. 'This is most unfortunate.' He straightened. 'Morag and your sister are preparing his body. By now, word will be spreading so we can expect a great number of visitors to the castle. And,' he added, 'there is the matter of who is to rule Scotland.' He came over to Duncan and put his hand on the young man's shoulder. 'I am sorry for your loss but I advise that you take your sorrow and use it as strength to see out these next days for, I believe, by tomorrow's end, you will be king.'

At breakfast the following day, a message came from Duncan to meet him in the blue room. Fleance left his bread and sausage and hurried as quickly as his leg would allow. He found Duncan sitting on a chair, head in hands. 'Duncan,' he said quietly. 'You sent for me?'

Duncan lifted his head. His eyes were bloodshot and his chin shadowed with the beginning of a beard. 'This is a nightmare,' he said. He lowered his head in his hands again and said nothing.

Fleance stood for a moment and then went to his friend, kneeling down in front of him. 'Tell me what I can do,' he said. 'Anything.'

Duncan took his hand and squeezed it. 'I am sorry you are caught up in this.' He exhaled deeply. 'I have been up all night talking with Preston and, though I have never much liked the fellow, a lot of what he has said has the ring of truth to it.'

'Aye?'

'Good Fleance, some might question what brought Father to your chambers and others might suggest that the injury was self-inflicted.'

'But . . .' Fleance began.

Duncan stopped him. 'I was there, too, remember. I can only think that the witches said something to him to enrage his mind and send him after you.' Duncan looked at him for a moment. 'Did you not think, Fleance, he was mighty strong. Stronger than a man should be?'

Fleance thought back to the struggle. Yes, he was almost overwhelmed by the strength of Donalbain's hold. He nodded.

'Me also and though I do not hold store by such things, I think that Father had some supernatural help in his attempt to end your life.'

'I am sorry, Duncan, that this has happened. I was beginning to hope your father would see me for who I really am.'

'I am sorry too. Not just for my personal loss but because this will now throw more peat on the fire. I will need to demonstrate to all that you have my utmost confidence. That I can trust you implicitly.'

Fleance stood up and pushed back his shoulders. 'Duncan, I would die for you. You have my word that I will be faithful always, to you and to the crown of Scotland.' He swallowed thickly for an ache in his throat warned of buried tears.

Duncan stood as well. 'Thank you, Fleance. And for this, I would ask something. Something that will send this message to all that you are favoured by me but, more personally, would gladden my heavy heart.'

'Name it,' Fleance whispered. 'And it is done.'

'I would have you be my stone bearer for the coronation.'

He stared at Duncan a moment, overwhelmed by the simple request. Yet in his heart he understood it was not a light thing

Duncan was asking. To be a weight bearer was an honoured position and one that spoke of the king's absolute trust. For to be carried high on a slab of stone by four men required absolute faith in those below. 'It would be a privilege and honour,' he said eventually.

'Good,' Duncan said, appearing relieved. 'Now we must prepare: first for the funeral and then the coronation.' He put his hand on Fleance's shoulder. 'I am mighty glad of that day the wolves attacked,' he said.

Fleance frowned. 'That's a strange thing to be glad about.'

'I am glad because it brought you into my life. Had I not fallen from Phoenix, our paths would not have crossed. I do not possess the faith of Rachel and I am suspicious of the Fates but, something or someone, dear friend, has a hand in this.'

A chill went down his spine but Fleance shrugged off the feeling. 'Then I am glad too,' he said instead and the two of them left the chamber.

Chapter Thirty

They travelled to Iona to bury Donalbain, the journey made fraught by Bree's tantrums and the impossible cold. The sea voyage was terrible for the waves were high and rough and, despite Rachel's care of everyone, many were violently ill.

Though it did not snow, the intermittent rain was freezing and, when they arrived at the desolate island, even the servants were so affected by the rough journey, little was done in preparation for the burial.

Bree refused to sit where she was told and continued to badger Duncan who was doing his best, Fleance saw, to stay focused.

'Would you have me take the child a while?' Fleance offered.

Duncan sighed wearily. 'Aye, Fleance. That would be most kind. Bree,' he said, calling to his sister. 'Go with Fleance.'

Bree stopped her jiggling and gave Fleance a most hateful glare. Though she was young, the strength of the emotion coming from her made him hesitate. He swallowed and took in a breath, fixing a smile on his face. 'I know where there are some baby seals, Bree, down by the shore. Come along. You will enjoy seeing them.'

The child did not move. Rachel shook her. 'Run along with Fleance,' she chided. 'We are worn out by your behaviour. Go!'

Bree frowned but came towards Fleance, ignoring his out-stretched hand. 'I will hate it,' she declared as she stormed past him.

Fleance and Rachel exchanged a look and then he turned and followed the taciturn youngster.

They climbed down part of the cliff, Bree still refusing any offer of help, and rested on a ledge above the shore. The low clouds and poor light made it difficult to see clearly but Fleance made out a number of sea lions and their cubs dipping in and out of the heavy waves as well as those that rested on the shore.

'I don't see anything,' Bree said, plonking herself down on the wet sand.

'There,' he said, pointing to a crop of boulders. 'Look carefully. See that long rock on the sand?' Bree nodded. 'Watch it for I grant it will move.' Both of them sat still, staring, when suddenly the sea lion rolled over, her large flipper waving in the air.

'I seen it,' Bree squealed. Her enthusiasm delighted him.

'Look a little to the right, nearer the sea.'

'Aye?'

'That's her baby.' A small blue-grey baby seal lay in the sand, every now and then lifting its head to check back on its mother.

'It's beautiful,' Bree said. 'Can we go down and pet it?'

He shook his head. 'They don't look like it, wee Bree, but they can be mighty fierce. When I was a young boy, my father took me to a bay, wild, much like this and we came upon a colony. They look heavy and slow but let me tell you, Da and I only just escaped from being crushed and bitten.'

'Why would they do that?'

'They think we are going to hurt their babies.'

She turned back to study the seals. 'I think they would know I would not hurt them,' she said matter-of-factly.

Inwardly, Fleance smiled. Bree was such a strong force and her self-belief, admirable. 'You are sure to be right but for now, I think, we must go back to the camp. Your father's funeral will start soon.' He reached out his hand and, this time, she took it. They climbed back up the hill.

By the end of the first day on the island, however, Bree's tantrums and Duncan's silence were too much for Rachel.

Fleance found her sheltering in a crypt, sobbing. 'Rachel,' he said, 'I am sorry. Truly sorry.'

She faced him, her eyes flooded with tears. 'It is too much, Fleance. My brother is not ready to take on this responsibility. And I am weary. Bree. Duncan.' She shook her hands at the sky. 'The rain!'

He stepped forward and gave her a kerchief so that she could wipe tears from her face. 'It's a hard thing to lose a father. The weather speaks for us.' He gestured to the barren landscape. 'A place of kings and a place of mourning.'

She gave him a small smile. 'You are mad.'

He smiled back her. 'You were in any doubt about this? It's true, lady,' he added. 'Some see madness in my actions and I was certainly a wayward and fierce-tempered child. But I pride myself in reading a man well and there is much good that I have read in you. I believe you have the strength to get through this.'

Rachel sniffed, wiped her face again, and straightened her skirts. 'Thank you, Fleance. It has been good to talk.' She marched away from the crypt, back to the small crowd who stood forlornly around the freshly constructed grave of the previous king of Scotland.

When they sailed back to the mainland, the waves were calmer as if mindful of the sorrow the passengers carried and they all arrived at Perth without incident. Fleance had the urge to visit Dougal's inn in case Rosie was there but shook the thought from his mind. It was a foolish idea. It had been months since he last saw her – who knew what her situation was. Perhaps she had married? The thought stabbed him so he pushed all feelings of Rosie from his mind. That part of his life had ended and he would not be plagued by thoughts of it any more.

Another exhausting trip back to Glamis saw Duncan, Rachel and even Bree quiet. Fleance was thus left with his thoughts. It had been some time now since he had suffered a nightmare, and he wondered if truly the idea he had seen visions was simply a construction of a heat-oppressed mind. No ghosts, no visions, no nightly exhortations to avenge murder.

This gave him some hope that finally, through whatever means, he had become free of his father's bond.

For the second time in less than a year, Fleance stood with a crowd at Scone ready to help the new king of Scotland be invested. Why was it, he thought, that an occasion such as this was treated as a time of celebration yet, the truth was, it had come about because of some type of tragedy.

Duncan looked dazed and weary and Preston quietly guided his movements. Many, Fleance had heard, were exceedingly pleased with their new king. Duncan was steady and wise and so much like his grandfather before him. That Scotland was facing a war did not diminish the hopes of the peoples.

Macduff, Lennox and Ross had been asked to join Fleance in lifting Duncan on the stone. The new king stood wrapped in the same white robe and sash his father had worn, Rachel standing serenely beside him. The four men went into the abbey. There, below the altar, the stone lay, as quiet and foreboding as the stained windows of the church.

'Take a corner each,' Macduff commanded and they did so. 'We will lift him in one movement to shoulder height. Let us have a practice at that, for to seem as if a deed has come naturally requires much rehearsal.' Fleance went to a corner and stood sideways to the stone as did the other three. 'On my count,' Macduff said. 'One. Two. Lift!'

As one, they bent their knees, grasped the iron rings and pulled the stone high into the air. It was not as heavy as it looked but, with a man atop, it would be a different matter.

'Onward,' Macduff commanded. They marched out of the church with the priests behind.

Carefully, they laid the stone at Duncan's feet and he gave Fleance a strained smile. Poor Duncan, Fleance thought. Not to have any time to properly mourn the loss of a loved one was a hard thing.

Duncan stepped on the stone and lifted his head, staring out at the crowd. The bishop came forward. He flicked water over each of Duncan's shoulders and then poured a small amount over his head. 'Close your eyes,' he said softly and Duncan obeyed. Fleance watched as the bishop dipped his finger then brushed it across Duncan's forehead. *'May the grace of God, the love of our Lord Jesus Christ and the fellowship of the Holy Spirit be with you now and for ever. Amen.'*

'Amen,' Duncan whispered.

'Amen,' Fleance and the thanes said.

Preston came forward with the crown on a blue cushion and the sceptre in his hand. The bishop lifted the crown high in the air and brought it down on Duncan's head. Then he took the sceptre from Preston and offered it to Duncan.

Fleance saw Duncan's back straighten as he reached out and grasped the sceptre.

'Ready?' Macduff muttered. Duncan nodded. 'One, two, lift!' They reached down and hoisted Duncan up. The crowd cheered. With the body of a man atop, the stone was heavy, especially as Duncan shifted his weight to keep balanced. *Please don't let me stumble or drop him,* Fleance prayed as they began to move down the man-made aisle.

'Long live the king!' Macduff shouted and the people echoed his cry so that Fleance's ears were ringing by the time they entered the church and set Duncan down in front of the altar.

After communion, Fleance made his way outside as Rachel had asked him to check that the tables had been set for the celebration meal. He walked across the yard in front of the church where many folk were still gathered and over to where the tables were being laid.

As he suspected, Morag had it all under control. 'She needn't worry, Sire. 'Tis not her burden on this day.'

'Thank you, Morag.'

She gave him some sausage. 'Here, it will be another hour at least until the meal is ready. You look tired.'

Just then, Duncan and Rachel emerged from the church. Fleance nodded in their direction. 'Not as much as they,' he said.

Morag clucked her tongue. 'Poor babes. May God grant them peace for their lives have lacked it.'

Duncan signalled to Fleance. 'I will leave you to your tasks, Morag.' He went to Duncan who pulled him to one side, along with Macduff, Lennox, Ross and Preston.

'A message has come that the rebels have added to their numbers and are joined by a foreign army,' Duncan said, his voice low.

'How long do you think we have until we must go?' Fleance asked.

Macduff pulled on his beard. 'Two weeks at the most.'

Fear curled inside his stomach. Two weeks! It was soon. The men he had been training with all winter were well prepared but Fleance had always hoped in a quiet corner of his mind that Scotland would not have to go to war. Even more so now that Duncan was king.

He looked around the people – all of them were smiling and laughing. They were delighted Duncan was king. Hadn't this been what they had wanted from the start when it was announced Malcolm would die?

Fleance was studying the happy movements of a man and a wife. The husband took his wife's arm and moved off towards the feast. Standing still, grim and silent, was Banquo. Fleance inhaled sharply. His father stared at him, his eyes fierce. Fleance stood his ground. *I will not allow you to control my life,* he said in his head. *There is too much that needs doing here and now that calls my loyalty.*

As if reading his mind, his father's ghost shook his head, turned around and walked away.

The coronation feast was a happy one with songs and speeches. Duncan sat among it all and, hourly, Fleance could see, showed more strength, more determination. The early spring nights were still cold so servants had lit fires in large drums. The bright orange and yellow flames made everyone's faces glow.

Rachel sat next to her brother, her expression fixed as she nodded and responded to those who came to offer condolences and congratulations. Bree, Fleance noted, fussed and argued until her nurse came and took her away to the tent.

It was very late when he joined Duncan and the thanes in the tent. He lay down beside his friend who he saw was staring at the roof. 'How are you?' Fleance asked.

Duncan turned his head. 'I am well and thinking how fortunate I am to be surrounded by good men.' He breathed deeply. 'I had hoped we would not have to go to war, Fleance.'

'Aye. Those have been my thoughts as well,' Fleance said, his voice quiet.

'Are we ready, do you think, Fleance? Do we have enough men?'

'Fellows come to us daily pledging their support. We are ready enough.'

'Well,' Duncan said turning on his side. 'So be it. Sleep well, if you can, my friend.'

'And you,' Fleance said, pulling a rough blanket up around his ears, hoping that the vision today of his father was not a signal that the bad dreams would return.

When they returned to Glamis, Morag was most attentive to them all. It was freezing cold but Fleance was busily occupied arranging the plans for the troops' move to Glasgow. Despite still mourning the death of her father, Rachel threw herself into the responsibility of assisting him. He found her attention to detail remarkable which meant the task was not as arduous as it might have been. Fleance gave to her the job of organising the provisions and employing the surgeons and stretcher bearers while he spent time with the king, earls, thanes and other leaders discussing their battle plans.

Late into the evening, three days after their return from Scone, Duncan summoned him. 'Fleance, I would have word with you.'

Fleance bowed. 'Aye, Your Majesty.'

Duncan frowned. 'Are you so shallow, man, that you would change your manner to suit the times?'

Fleance smiled. 'There is nothing lost in honouring what is honourable.'

Duncan snorted. 'I don't need platitudes from you, Fleance. But,' he said coming forward, 'do give me your allegiance.'

Fleance seized his hand. 'Know this, I am always your servant; and friend.'

'And brother?' Duncan asked.

Fleance's face lifted as he smiled. 'That too. Always.'

'Come, let us go into a warmer place to talk.' They walked silently down the corridor, past the blue room, and into Duncan's private chambers. The king poured two goblets of warm wine and handed one to Fleance. 'I think, my friend, you still mourn for something that you can never have, am I right? This maid, this Rosie – I think, Fleance, she is not the one for you.'

The turn in conversation startled him and he felt anger flare up inside. What business was it of Duncan's? 'What are you saying? She is . . .' But he could not finish saying what Rosie was. How could anyone else understand how much she made him feel so happy and so complete? 'You are mistaken, Duncan. Rosie is special.'

'Aye, I can see that and I can see how you consider her. But, Fleance, she is an innkeeper's daughter and you are . . .' he paused. 'Indeed, after Macduff, you are next in line to the throne. So, think on this: would the people of Scotland accept a commoner as wife of a thane? Do you not think a more strategic union best for all?'

'What care I for the political workings of Scotland?' Fleance said angrily. 'I am here to fulfil my father's command. And to fight this battle at your side. Once that is done, I'm back to England to find Rosie.'

Duncan looked hard at him. Then he sighed. 'My dear friend. Though you have desires for your life, it seems fate has other plans. Let us finish this war and then regroup to consider what is the right path for Scotland.'

Fleance was rattled. At this moment he could not give two oxen for the opinions and gossip of the people of Scotland. What he desired was freedom from his father's ghost and opportunity to be with Rosie for good.

'So,' Duncan began, 'Rachel.'

Fleance frowned. 'What has Rachel to do with this?'

Duncan walked to the window, then turned to look at his friend. 'Fleance, what are your intentions towards my sister?'

Fleance was shocked by the question. 'I have no intentions towards Rachel, Duncan, except those of a loyal servant to the crown. You know of my love for Rosie.'

'Then,' Duncan said, 'you have been misleading her.'

'No!' Fleance cried. 'I have never given Rachel any encouragement. She knows of my feelings for Rosie.' He put his hand to his forehead and then looked back at his king. 'Duncan. Rachel is beautiful. She is kind and sweet and so . . .'

'She would be a good wife to you, Fleance.'

His head was spinning. Why was Duncan pressuring him so? 'How can you say that, Duncan, when I have told you over and over: my heart belongs to Rosie.'

'But this Rosie is gone. You have lost her. You said so yourself.'

'I know!' Fleance said, his voice raised. 'But I will find her.' He shook his fists. 'When the battle is fought and won, I will find her and I will win her too.'

Pressure was building in his head and chest and he struggled against the burning frustration which threatened to overcome him.

Duncan shook his head. He stepped in front of Fleance and put a hand on his shoulder. Lowering his voice, he spoke. 'You are too believing in the faithfulness of mankind, my friend. What woman would endure what you have put her through and still remain true?'

Duncan's words shot through his bruised heart like a hot poker. 'No!'

Fleance cried and shoved Duncan away from him. The king fell, knocking his face against the corner of a chair. Horrified, Fleance fell to his knees. 'I'm sorry. I . . .' he stammered. 'Please forgive me.'

Duncan touched his hand to his mouth, looked at the blood on his fingers and then back at Fleance. 'I didn't see that coming.' Mortified, Fleance stood, waiting to see what Duncan would do next. The new king sighed. 'I've not seen this temper in you before.'

'Duncan,' Fleance began.

Duncan studied him a moment. 'You are as a brother to me, Fleance. I am on your side,' he said quietly. He touched his fingers to his lips again and pressed against the small split. He motioned to a chair. 'Sit,' he commanded.

Fleance dropped into the chair and put his head in his hands. Why had he allowed his feelings to get so out of control? Duncan relied on him. How could he strike the king? He was no better than Bree in a tantrum. 'Why does it have to be so hard to find happiness and contentment?' he said. He looked up at Duncan. 'Why, if I do the right thing and honour God in all my ways, am I not to have the one thing my heart desires above all?'

'You yourself told me that the path of true love is never smooth,' Duncan said as he pulled up a stool and sat in front of Fleance. 'How long has it been since you saw her, Fleance?

He thought for a bit. 'The day of your father's coronation feast.'

'Fleance, that was months ago.' His blue eyes bored into Fleance. 'I think you are making much of a remembered passion.'

Fleance shook his head. 'Listen to me. I understand what it is to love someone and not be able to have them. But, Fleance, after time, the feelings dim and can be replaced with new loves, new hopes.'

Fleance's stomach churned. 'It's just,' he said through a tight jaw, 'that all my happiness is bound up in memories of being with her. No one makes me laugh like her. No one makes me feel like I can do anything like her.' He returned Duncan's gaze. 'It's hard to give that up, Duncan. I have been holding on to her for so long . . .'

Duncan looked down at his hands and his tongue ran over the cut on his lip. 'She is like your father – now a ghost which plagues you. You have to turn away from the past and look to what the future has.'

'I can't,' he cried. 'I need her to understand that it was not my doing that I could not get to her.'

'Fleance, you are a general in my army. You have made a promise to me. I need to believe that I can trust you completely. You must put Rosie aside and focus on our plans.'

Fleance swallowed and breathed deeply. 'I will honour you as I have pledged so long as you permit me to find her after all this is done.'

A look of resignation came over the king's face. 'I would have you happy, my friend.' He stood up. 'I have believed all this time that you have found a measure of happiness and contentment in *our* family.' Duncan stared at him. Fleance sensed there was more to say. Duncan let out his breath, and then spoke. 'I have to tell you that I believe my sister is in love with you.'

'I'm sorry,' Fleance whispered.

'I would be most approving of your union,' Duncan continued as if he hadn't heard Fleance. 'Your king asks you to consider Rachel.'

Fleance nodded. He could do no less. 'As you will, your Majesty.'

Rosie

This was not the journey Rosie had expected to be making. It had been months since she set out for England, expecting to return within a few weeks with the oak for her father. Instead, it was early spring and she was going back to Scotland with Keavy.

She looked down at the girl who was watching the gulls swoop and swirl around the ship's large sails. 'Are you well, Keavy?' Rosie asked.

Keavy smiled up at her. 'This is grand, Rosie. My first boat ride. But,' she said, a sorrowful look passing over her face, 'I do wish Ma could have come.'

Rosie put her arm around the child. 'I know you do but it would have been too much for her.' What she knew in her heart, though, was that Miri did not expect to live much longer, the cough having taken most of her life force. What might have happened, Rosie thought, had I not gone to the Alnwick Inn and heard the news? What might have become of Keavy?

Rosie kept her arm around the bairn. Fate, she mused. The stars took Flea from her and now they were leading her back to him whether she wanted to or not.

It was Lairie at the inn in Alnwick who'd given her the news that Miri was ill of the cough and alone, with Magness off who knew where. A day was all Rosie had needed to arrange her da's business and then she and Rebecca were away to nurse Miri.

Miri was dying. Rosie had seen it at a glance. Even so, she'd dropped to her knees, taken Miri's hand and said, "I'll stay with you till you're well again.'

But Miri, between the coughing spasms that wracked her, had asked something much harder of her. 'You'll have heard about Flea? Important he is now. He'll care for my Keavy. Take her to him, Rosie, at least until Magness returns, and I'll die easy.'

Rebecca and Rosie tried for a month to nurse their old friend back to health. But Miri was right, she was dying.

So here they were, Rebecca returning to Perth and the business of the inn while Keavy and Rosie were on their way to Flea. Flea – friend of the new King Duncan, and a general in his army. She sighed. Little wonder the stars were against their union.

What cruel mischief was it that pushed her to Perth and then on to Glamis to seek out one whom she had loved more than anything else in the world? The one who had broken his word, her trust and her heart.

All Rosie told Keavy was that she must return to Scotland and it would be fun to have Keavy's company. The bairn had been excited the whole trip, her enthusiasm and energy the only thing keeping Rosie from utter despair.

At Perth, they returned to the inn and Da was exceedingly pleased to see her. 'I never thought I'd regret any of my decisions, lass, but seeing your lovely face again shows me I should not have sent you away, especially as you've been so delayed.'

'I'll get wee Keavy here settled for the night and then I must speak with you,' Rosie said after kissing her father on the cheek. 'Come along, bairn. You will like your room.'

The small compartments were freezing and Rosie set about making a fire. 'You can sleep in those clothes for it's too cold. I'll bring you a warming stone from the kitchen.'

She watched as Keavy climbed into the cot and burrowed down among the piles of blankets, only her face poking out. Rosie was back quickly and pleased to feel the room had begun to lose some of its chill. She placed the stone near Keavy's feet. 'Do you want me to leave the light?' Keavy nodded. 'I will come back soon. Try to sleep. It's been a long day for you and tomorrow we have an adventure.'

Keavy's eyes widened. 'Tell me,' she demanded.

Rosie smiled. ''Tis a surprise. And I wager you won't be able to guess.' She tucked Keavy in some more. 'Sweet dreams.' Then she walked back to where her father was wiping down tables after the last of the patrons had gone.

'What news, daughter?' he said, easing his large belly under one of the tables as he sat down.

'Magness has gone. Miri believes he has joined those who will go to battle. Miri is being tended by the village but I fear, Da, she has not long to live. I am to Glamis, in the morning,' she said, staring hard at her father. 'Miri has asked me to take the child to Flea.' She watched her father's face cloud over. 'He has the means to take good care of her and I know he will.'

'What do you really know of him, Rosie?' Dougal growled. 'He's as unreliable as the weather.'

'I'll take my chances for I know he loves her as his sister.'

'It'll end in tears, mark my word. For you and the bairn.' Puffing, he arose. 'But you can take the wagon and two of the hands, for the roads are rough.'

'Thank you,' she said and took herself off to bed, climbing in beside the sleeping child and cuddling into her for warmth.

<hr />

The next morning, Dougal loaded up the wagon with barrels of ale and gave instructions for delivery to two abbeys with the rest for the

319

castle. Though Rosie felt subdued, Keavy chattered excitedly and bombarded her with endless questions making the first part of their journey go quicker. The men unloaded the two barrels at the first abbey and, at the second while the barrels were being taken inside, Rosie and Keavy had a bite to eat.

But by late afternoon, Rosie was cold and exhausted both from Keavy's persistent questions and the fear which began to nag at her. She glanced at Keavy. What if Da were right? What if Flea refused them? What would become of Keavy then?

The cold, post-winter sun was almost down when the wagon came upon the long road to Glamis. Through the trees, they could see the lights of the castle. 'What is that?' Keavy asked breathlessly.

'That, my child, is the king's castle.'

Keavy's eyes widened. 'Really? Are we going to see the king?'

Rosie shrugged. 'I can't say for sure but maybe.'

The child hugged herself. 'Is there a princess in the castle too?'

Rosie smiled. 'Aye, two of them. One is about your age.'

'We can be friends then,' Keavy stated matter-of-factly.

Rosie said nothing but stared ahead, trying hard to ignore the sense of foreboding which pressed all around her.

It was dark by the time the wagon pulled up outside the entrance to the kitchen.

'Stay here and keep well wrapped up,' Rosie told Keavy. She climbed down, straightened her skirts and pulled the hood of her cloak over her head. A soldier stood outside the main door and, with butterflies in her stomach, Rosie approached him.

'I am here to see Flea. Fleance, son of Banquo,' she said her voice shaking.

The soldier opened the door and motioned for her to enter. In the grand entranceway, she was approached by a servant.

'I wish to speak with Fleance,' she said a little more bravely.

'You're in luck, young lady,' he answered, glancing quickly over her humble clothing. 'The royal party are just coming down for dinner. He should be with you shortly.'

At that moment a door opened and noise and laughter quickly filled the entranceway.

Rosie dragged her gaze to the top of the staircase and her heart almost stopped.

There was Flea, looking more handsome than she had dared remember, walking arm in arm with another equally handsome couple. Both were fair, the man tall and with a serious air, the woman about her own age, long blonde hair framing a beautiful face.

But what pierced Rosie's heart was the way Flea was looking at the woman – laughing and open, her beloved Flea sharing something of great amusement with this other woman who was so obviously in love with him.

She couldn't see him now, it had been wrong to come here after so long; foolish, foolish girl that she was to even think he could still love her.

Quickly she turned and made to leave the room but in her haste she stumbled into a side table and a large, ornate vase crashed to the floor.

The party on the landing stopped their talk and looked her way. Flea blanched.

'Rosie,' he cried. 'My God, is that you?'

Rosie swept from the room, even as Flea cried out for her to wait.

He caught her at the doorway and spun her around to face him.

'It is you,' he whispered, 'after all this time. I can't believe it.'

Then his face hardened and he looked like the old Flea on a bad day.

'Why did you not wait for me?'

She lifted her head, clenching her jaw, a buried anger returning.

'You had vanished without a trace,' she said, her voice quiet but hard. 'We sent a messenger to the castle and they told us that you had gone to England.'

Flea shook his head. 'That is a lie! I came as fast as I could but fate intervened, Rosie. First I was attacked and Willow left me; then I was lost in the woods.' He looked at her. 'I was delayed but by five days.'

'You promised—' she began.

'Aye and I kept my promise.' He looked alone, lost, and she wanted to reach out and touch him but pride kept her hands by her sides.

'I believed nothing would separate us,' he sighed.

'It seems,' she said, 'your belief was misplaced.'

'Rosie,' he whispered. 'Nothing has changed.'

'*Everything* is changed, Flea,' she hissed. 'We cannot go back to what we were – foolish young things caught up in ourselves.'

She went to step away from him but he reached for her. 'That may be true for some things but of this I am certain: my love for you, Rosie, has never faltered.'

For a moment she wavered, but then remembered her purpose. Gently, she took his hand from her arm and held it in hers. 'Keavy is with me. I need your help.'

A look of concern flashed across his face. 'Is she hurt?'

'No, but she needs a home. Magness is gone and Miri is . . . dying.' It was hard to say the word. 'She sent me here to you.'

'She sent you? You did not come of your own will?'

She wanted to tell him: yes, I came willingly. I needed to see you. I need to be with you. But none of these words could she utter. She saw him watching her, waiting for her to tell him yes, she came of her own free will. She heard his sigh when she kept silent.

'Where is she?' he asked.

'Outside. In the wagon. I will take you to her.' She picked up her skirts and walked out the door, aware of the sound of his soft breathing as he followed her.

It was colder and Rosie worried that she had been too long in the castle but, when they got to the wagon, Keavy was happily talking with a woman from the kitchen.

'I see she's made friends with our Morag already,' Flea said.

At the sound of their approach, Keavy turned and for a moment sat completely still. Then she let out a squeal of delight and threw herself from the wagon into Flea's arms. 'Flea! Flea!' she cried. 'It's me – Keavy!'

Flea laughed. 'Aye, bairn, I know that.'

'Do you live here?' she asked, her face suddenly serious. 'Are you the king?'

'No. Our king is Duncan.'

Keavy looked over at Rosie, a bit put out. 'Flea is a general in the king's army,' Rosie explained.

'Morag,' Flea said to the woman. 'I'm taking my girls inside. Could you arrange for their sleep and some food?'

The woman curtsied. 'Aye, Sire.'

This formality made Keavy giggle. He put the child down and grabbed her hand. 'Your fellows will find warmth and rest for themselves and the horses at the stables,' he said. 'As for you two, you need warming up.'

The royal family were seated in the dining hall when Flea, Rosie and Keavy returned and Rosie saw they had interrupted a quarrel. A young girl was sitting with her arms crossed and her face red, an expression sour enough as to turn Da's ale. The blonde woman was quietly and urgently speaking with her. The young king was frowning at the two of them.

Flea coughed politely. 'Your Majesty,' he said formally. 'This is my adoptive sister, Keavy, and this,' he put his hand on the small of her back, 'is Rosie.'

The king stood but not before Rosie caught a look between him and his sister. 'Welcome. We have heard much about you. My sisters, Rachel,' Rachel smiled warmly at them, 'and Bree,' who glowered.

'I'm Keavy,' Keavy said to the sulking child at the table. 'Do you want to be friends?'

'Can you tell stories?' Bree asked, the red fading in her face.

'Some, but I'm better with my lute. Rosie tells great stories.'

'So does Rachel,' Bree answered. 'She's the best storyteller in the whole world.'

Keavy grinned. This challenge did not faze her and Rosie glanced at Rachel who was looking kindly at the two children. 'Then we shall have lots of stories tonight,' Keavy said.

Flea put his hand on the bairn's head. 'No, Keavy. Not tonight. You have had a long journey and I can see our Rosie is tired.' Rosie heard his words but her eyes were glued to his hand which played with Keavy's hair.

She shuddered. She must not think back to those times for it would only stir the feelings for him she had pushed deep down away from her heart.

'I have asked Morag to make ready a chamber. I'll take them to her. If you will excuse us?'

Duncan nodded his head and Rosie could feel his eyes boring into her back as she left the great hall.

Once Keavy was settled, Flea took Rosie to a small room down the hall. It was warm and comfortable. He removed her cloak and motioned for her to sit. Then he brought the plate of food Morag had prepared and put it beside her. All the time, they were silent but Rosie felt as if every action, every movement was speaking to her heart.

'Tell me about Miri,' he said.

'I'm sorry, Flea. She has the cough.' She saw the news saddened him.

'She has been like a mother to me, Rosie,' he said.

'I know. I'm sorry,' Rosie repeated.

'Who will make the . . . arrangements then, when she dies?'

'She will be well cared for, Flea. I have seen to it. Do not worry for her. She sends you her love and, if you will have her, Keavy to care for.'

'I'll have to ask Duncan but I'm certain he will be delighted to have Keavy here as would I.' He sat beside her. 'It is such a joy to see you again, Rosie.' He stared at her and she felt her body burn. 'You are more beautiful than when I last saw you,' he said quietly.

Rosie felt her heart race. He took her hand and leant forward but Rosie quickly stepped away from his embrace.

'I'm sorry, Flea,' she sighed. 'I just don't see the point of us continuing this dance. It was wrong of me to come here but I needed to see if there was still some remnant of our love left alive. Your situation has changed and I have been left well behind.'

'I don't understand what you are saying, Rosie. Do you still love me or not?'

Rosie sighed again. 'That is beside the point, Flea. Your situation here has allowed you room for another love, perhaps one more suitable to your current position.'

Flea frowned and he shook his head. 'If it's Rachel you speak of then you are wrong. Yes, she has been kind to me and we do share a special bond. In fact she saved my life on one occasion. I hold her as dear to me as I do her brother whom I have sworn allegiance to. He is my king and I would die for him, and as his sister she deserves an equal loyalty. But we are talking loyalty and duty here and that is a far cry from the love I felt we shared.'

Was he so blind to the changes in their circumstances? 'You have always spoken fine words, Flea, words like honour and loyalty, but in the process you have thrown away love with two hands as easily as a child discards a broken toy. I thought our love would endure but I was wrong – it was wrong of me to come here.'

'Rosie, within the week, I'm to battle,' he sighed and she watched him swallow as if the very mention of the words brought a bitter taste to his mouth.

'I think . . .' He stopped and looked away. 'I think we go to war and I may not return.'

A wave of heat spread over her. 'What are you saying?'

'I'm saying I may not come back and the last memory I have of us should not be one of harsh words and accusations. It seems that everything around us conspires to keep us apart and maybe, in the end, we will both be happier that way. But right now, with the drums of battle almost at our gate, I have to know . . .' here he faltered and Rosie's heart almost broke at the sight of him standing bereft in front of her.

'Know what?' she whispered.

'I have to know whether there is still a chance for us, a chance that despite everything that seems destined to work against us we will get through this. I have to know that while I am fighting for my king and my Scotland, I have you waiting for me. Duncan has promised me I will be Thane of Lochaber – perhaps after this war is over we can start a new life there. I can make you no promises that I haven't already made – the decision is yours whether you choose to still believe them.'

He looked lost again, not the brave soldier but her Flea – tender and kind and quiet. She walked to him and laid her hands on his face.

Flea pulled her into his arms and held her tightly. He smelt so good, so reassuring and she buried her face into his shirt.

'You bewitch me, Rosie. I can never think straight when you are near.'

'Then keep me near, you foolish man,' she said, 'and we can be bewitched together. Perhaps our fate is in the hands of others and both of us will need to learn some patience to see this game through to the end.'

The next morning, Rosie awoke with a peace in her heart she had not felt in a long while. Without a doubt, Flea loved her. This much was as certain as the sun rising and setting. What their futures may hold could not be determined now, but that they had a future she was now sure of.

It was the kind of love Ma had spoken of. She would go home and wait, and pray that the daft lad wouldn't get himself killed in battle.

When Keavy was presented with the news she would stay on at Glamis, the child's only complaint was that her doll still sat with her things in England. When Flea promised to arrange for her belongings to be brought to Scotland, she relaxed and raced off to tell Bree – her new friend.

While arrangements were getting made for the wagon to be prepared, Flea took Rosie's hand and led her to the parapet that looked over the countryside. The soldier in him had returned and he seemed quieter and more thoughtful than the previous evening.

'I will not see you until after the battle is won,' he said.

'Ah, man,' Rosie said. 'I know where you live and I know where you are going.' She reached up and traced her fingers down his face. 'Come back alive. You cannot be lost to a battle as this.'

Flea bent down and kissed her on the forehead. 'I will do my best to return to you.'

Rosie took his face in her hands and kissed him tenderly on the lips. She cared not who could see them, this was her man and she wanted to send him to battle with the memory of her kiss fresh in his mind.

'God speed, my dear Flea,' she said. 'Make sure you come back to me soon,' and she walked down to the wagon, perhaps leaving Flea alone with thoughts other than battle in his mind.

All will be well at the end of things, she thought. *I am beloved of Flea.*

Chapter Thirty-One
Near Kilmarnock, South of Glasgow

D uncan, King of Scotland, paced the dirt floor of his tent. He was both afraid and excited at the same time. The journey to Glasgow and the daily councils with the most seasoned veterans about what to do and when filled Duncan with confidence. True, this was not what he would have chosen to be the first act of his reign. But the choice had not been his to make.

Macduff came into the tent. 'Your Majesty,' he said. 'The scouts report that the rebels have gathered at Kilmarnock. Their trumpets have sounded for the battle to begin.'

Duncan looked at Fleance. 'Are you ready, my friend?'

Fleance bowed. 'Aye.'

The king nodded to Macduff. 'And you, sir, are you sure you will join us in the battle?'

'Aye,' Macduff replied. 'For never was there a more worthy cause to pick up arms once more.'

'Rachel has the surgeons ready though I pray to God we will have little need of them,' Duncan said. 'Let us face our men,' he commanded. 'It is unkind to keep them waiting.' With murmured agreement, all inside trooped out of the tent.

The sound hit them: of horses neighing, of armour and weapons, of men calling to each other, and of feet and hooves. Fleance signalled to the horn blowers to call their men to arms and to assemble.

A resounding chord pierced the air. Men stopped. Horses stopped. And then, in a moment of organised chaos, his soldiers rushed in all directions to get in position for battle.

Duncan put a hand on Fleance's shoulder. 'Stay well, my friend.'

Fleance bowed his head. 'And you, Your Majesty.'

Duncan shook his head. 'Don't give me that. You stay alive or I will whip your arse.'

Fleance laughed. 'It is not often I have heard you be so coarse.'

'Ah, well,' Duncan said. 'Needs must, as Morag says.' He looked around him and then back at his friend. 'You know the plan well?'

'Aye.'

'It is a good plan and one that will bring us swift victory.'

'Aye, there is no doubt in this. Your Majesty, we are in the right and Scotland is not the aggressor. We must do this for your people.'

Duncan looked at his dear friend for a moment and was filled with hope. 'These are fine words and the right ones.'

Fleance put his hand on Duncan's. 'You are my best friend,' he said. 'Whatever happens, know this: you have restored my faith in humankind.' He tightened his grasp on the king's hand. 'You are exceptional. No man in history can replicate your heart's desires and your generosity.'

Duncan laughed. 'I am what I am and no more. Do not make me out to be greater.'

There was a cough. A messenger stood before them. 'Your Majesty – we are called to war.'

The army, 20,000 foot soldiers and 4000 mounted, were gathered on the field and fell silent as the young Duncan rode his horse down the man-made corridor to the front. For a brief moment he felt the weight of his responsibility – so many lives in his hands. Yet he must put aside his own feelings and inspire true confidence in these men who would sacrifice so much.

Duncan turned his steed so that it was side on to the waiting soldiers. 'Loyal friends. We have travelled so far to the middle of Scotland and have only found support for our cause. I bring you the good news that a number of dispossessed in England have ignored the cry to go against us and have pledged allegiance to Scotland. As we speak, we hear word they are gathering together to join us in this most crucial battle so our numbers will be swelled even more.'

The cries of support from the listening soldiers threatened to drown Duncan and he held up his hand for silence.

'The rebel leader, that greedy, selfish man, shamefully has the blood of Scotland in his veins. He now stands not three miles from us with a ragtag group at his back and a foreign power to aid him.

'Who are these foreigners? They are the Norwegians – again.'

A low grumble reverberated through the gathered men. Duncan saw he had hit upon a sensitive nerve. 'Yes, my countrymen. The Norwegians think to take Scottish soil; to take advantage of political unrest between ourselves and England. How many times must our women, children and livelihood be torn from us by these foes from the north? Your king says: No more.'

A roar went up. 'Long live the king. Long live King Duncan!'

Their passion moved him. 'Know this, my kinsmen: from the depths of my soul, I regard your willingness to come forward to defend our place, no small thing. As St Andrew is our guide, so too is he Scotland's. Do not fear life nor death, for both will honour you. We have always trod our paths under God's good guidance and He has given us the power and strength to withhold and endure any advance. Scotland will send a clear message to any other invading army that to do so is fruitless. We will do this so that our peoples of Scotland may forever live in peace.'

'So, in God's name and for Scotland, let us march forward.' Duncan lifted his sword and the soldiers roared back in support. He moved his horse to the side of the mass and watched, his heart racing, as they walked on towards the battlefield, the flag with the silver cross and azure blue proudly flowing above the leading men. The chanting of the name of their patron saint, 'Andrew, Andrew, Andrew', sent shivers down his spine.

Though he did not share his sister's faith, he sent a prayer to God to place courage and strength in every man before him. He looked around. 'Preston. Ride with me up yonder.' Duncan pointed to a rise a hundred yards off to the left.

'Sire, 'tis not safe,' Preston said. 'Lennox was most insistent. You are to stay back from the battle today. We can't put you in the way of any risk. Not yet. Your time will come.'

Duncan turned back to the advancing army. Preston and Lennox were correct. There would be time enough for him to join the fray.

The sound of war sickened him and he wished to be among it but the advisors would not allow him to go just yet. It would be a disaster, they said, if he fell in the first act of battle. Rather he, the king, was needed at this time to give strength and courage to the hearts of their warriors.

'Brother,' Rachel said. 'Can we send back for my women to help bind the wounds? The injured are many and I do not have enough people to help me save them.'

'Aye,' he said, weary and longing for sleep. 'Do you think, Rachel, you can gather enough to help us with this?'

His sister flashed him the smile he had learnt to love. 'Duncan, there will always be people ready and willing to come forth to serve the king. I need only say the word and I will have a troop of girls ready to serve you.'

Duncan paused for a moment. As always, she provided good counsel and good results. He would defer to her suggestions. 'Please, send for your angels, for that is what they are.' Then he retired to the main tent to consider their battle plan and receive reports from the field.

The breeze carried the sounds of his men screaming and dying, fighting and succeeding. Who was victorious? Who was injured? Who had died?

Too soon, the seriously wounded began arriving back at the camp and the surgeons and priests were busily employed to administer comfort to the hurt and dying. Duncan also went among them, offering kind words and encouragement. Rachel, her hair pulled tightly into a braid, worked quickly and skilfully alongside the two doctors who tended to the wounded.

He had to stay strong despite his initial reaction to the extent of the injuries he saw. His army was combating claymore, arrow and axe. He wished he had more surgeons to heal his men.

Many bled out and died.

Was he a failure as king that so many should die trying to protect the Scottish rule? Duncan shook his head. Like Alexander the Great before him, he too was a young ruler sent to battle. He took a deep breath. Perhaps thinking of them would give him more strength.

Duncan stood outside his tent, watching as the men returned. He noted who walked back, who was carried, injured, and who was carried, dead. He went among them to see the tally and was relieved it was not any person he knew or loved.

By nightfall, the camp was flooded again with their soldiers as the day's fighting ended. Lennox, Macduff, Ross and Angus and Fleance met to survey the day's fighting.

'They are not so well prepared, Your Majesty,' Lennox said. 'A group of them have holed up across a burn. They sent arrows our way but few hit their targets.'

'And their casualties?'

The men looked at each other and then at Fleance. 'Your young general here, keen to lead the men by example, shot so many bolts across the stream we had to keep sending for new quivers,' Macduff said. 'And each one hit its mark.'

Duncan's face was grim. 'What news of the leader of these rebels?'

Fleance spoke. 'Not one has named him nor identified him. We have brought back a hundred men as prisoners and they call their leader The Dark Oak.'

Macduff snorted. 'So tomorrow we'll be looking out for a tree in the middle of battle.'

'What manner of man hides behind such a name?' Duncan shook his head.

'One that wears a shamed heart,' Lennox said. 'For to fight against your own kind and kin is a most dishonourable thing. But to lead that fight is unforgiveable.'

'Well said,' Duncan replied. He straightened his back. 'It is time to look after our bodies, for our business is not over yet.'

After supper, it was back to the main tent where he studied the map of the field with Fleance, the earls and Preston who, despite years of making Duncan feel uncomfortable, was turning out to be a most steady and rational commentator. He had sent young scouts out and around to gather information and, as they arrived back with details, he moved painted stones on the canvas.

Just then, a panting messenger came into the tent. 'Sire,' he called to Duncan. 'I have learnt the King of Norway is intent on destroying my lord Fleance.'

Fleance looked up, startled. Duncan shook his head. 'Why would he want anything from Fleance? I understood that Norway's king disappeared five years ago.'

'Aye,' Macduff answered. 'Rumour has it the useless bugger went to Rome and cloistered himself at the Vatican. What kind of king would it be, eh, that hides away under the robes of monks?'

'One that's mad, perhaps,' Duncan replied.

'Indeed. The country is just as mad, refusing to crown any other for their king had not abdicated and was still alive.' Macduff thumped the table, displacing Preston's stones. 'They were content, fools, to be governed by him from afar sending out orders from within the sanctuary of the church.'

Preston cleared his throat. 'What Macduff says is true, Your Majesty. Our spies tell us that his latest order was to prepare to join the rebel forces against Scotland. He said he received a message from God which commanded his army to go forth in the spring.'

Macduff snorted.

Duncan stood tall. 'Did your spies gather details about the motives behind this aggression?'

The old man shook his head. 'As is often the way with words passed from one man to another, the meaning became unclear or lost.'

Duncan breathed deeply. There were more issues to deal with at this time. 'So,' he said. 'We will send a message to this king. Tell him: we have no quarrel with Norway and would seek to end these hostilities without further bloodshed. Scotland is well-armed and a powerful force. We would be willing to discuss any grievances Norway feels it has towards our country. Scotland would prefer to be at peace with Norway. We hope for a positive response.'

The messenger bowed low again and took to his horse, grabbing a white flag from one of the attendees. As he galloped off into the night towards the enemy camp, Duncan whispered a blessing that sanity would prevail – for the young servant and his nation.

'I do not understand why he would have issue with me,' Fleance said.

'Your father,' Lennox said, 'fought against his father many years ago. In that battle, the old King of Norway, Sweno, was killed.'

'What am I to that fight?' Fleance asked.

'Who can fathom the mind of a mad ruler,' Macduff said looking at the other earls. 'Long ago we tried to do just that and came up with no answer.'

Duncan looked across at Fleance and saw his confusion. Fleance had declared his allegiance yet the workings of this battle made things less clear. Before they all retired to bed, he cornered his friend. 'Fleance,' he said. 'How goes it?'

Fleance smiled, albeit wearily. 'I am tired.'

'As am I.' They stood there a moment. 'I hear,' Duncan said, 'you've had difficulties with some of the regiment.'

Fleance frowned. 'Not difficulties, really. Some gossip has been passed onto me but they are foolish rumours.'

'Indeed,' Duncan said. 'Would you tell them to me?'

Fleance inhaled and let out his breath slowly. 'It seems some of our country question my claims.'

'Claims?'

'That Banquo was my father and I am who I say I am.'

Duncan studied Fleance's face. His friend, though exhausted, reflected the quiet determination Duncan often saw in his expression. 'And, I take it, you give no store to such accusations?'

Fleance looked at him and shrugged. 'There is no value in fighting against things which are not true. Macduff knows me; my father's nurse recognised me; my boyhood friend is fighting alongside me. And you,' he added, 'believe me with no other evidence save my word.'

'That is all I need from you, Fleance: your word and your allegiance.'

The next morning, the atmosphere among the troops was subdued. The messenger sent to talk with Norway had not returned. Fleance stood in front of his regiment and listened carefully to Duncan who, once more, encouraged his men.

'You have seen for yourself our strength. You have encountered your enemies' weakness in both heart and body. You, the army of Scotland, are the best of fighters with the swiftest and deadliest weapons known to man. Though our sometimes hostile land can bring challenges, it also breeds warriors such as yourselves, keen and well equipped to deal with any usurper. Over the years, many nations have tried to quench the spirit of the Scottish heart – and have failed.'

There was a low hum of agreement to these words. Fleance looked around the soldiers. They stood tall and proud and he felt honoured to be leading such men who would willingly sacrifice themselves for their king and country.

Duncan continued. 'Our country is peopled by those who live among the vast and cruel and wonderful, and who adore its lochs, its highlands, its lowlands, mountains and ports. We remind you that there come swiftly many keen folk, men and women, who would add their strength to our number. Gird your loins with this knowledge: we will overcome, for our cause is a just one. We defend the weak, the lost and the frightened. We defend our right to follow God's anointed. Go forth, in the name of Scotland and your king.'

The soldiers raised their swords and Fleance felt the vibrations of their combined shouting go through his whole body. He secured his helmet, signalled to the horn blower and marched forward with the continuous blast of the horns echoing around him.

They had been fighting for three hours and only the runners, who came with water and supplies, and their determination to fight to protect Scotland, kept them going. Fleance had trained his mind to see the men before him as difficult branches he had to cut down for Magness. It would undo him to imagine them as flesh and blood.

As Duncan had said, the rebels were not so well armed or trained as they had all been led to believe. Their weapons were inferior and their soldiers poorly equipped. Only anger and strength propelled them forward.

Beside him fought Macduff. The old man talked all the way through his fights with whoever he was up against – sometimes with humour and sometimes with rage. In another life, Fleance thought after one such dialogue, the man would have been a great jester of the court.

Sword and shield moved as if with a life of their own, following the pattern Macduff had taught them. Fleance held up his shield and blocked the crash of his enemy's axe, swinging his sword up and around, driving the blade into the vulnerable gap between the two pieces of armour.

Spinning against the falling body onto the next man. *Block. Swing. Aim for the gap. Hack. Don't think. Don't stop.* On and on.

Many men fell under their onslaught. Fleance was glad to have Macduff by his side as he fought against those who came against him. Some he killed; a number he fought but they, knowing they were outsmarted, quickly ran away.

Such was the case of the last man to try his luck against Banquo's sword. After two attempts to thrust his own into Fleance's side, both times blocked easily, the rebel threw down his sword in defeat and lifted his hands in surrender.

Macduff had dispatched his last enemy and turned to the trembling man who stood before Fleance. 'Away with you, you skanky dog. Take your tail between your legs and tell your leader Macduff says it's a foolish man who tries to conquer Scotland.' The man hesitated a moment and Macduff feigned to charge him. The terrified rebel turned on his heels and sprinted back across the battlefield to his own side. 'The fool,' Macduff growled. 'You were kind to spare his life.'

Fleance shook his head. 'Honour, not kindness. He had surrendered. Had I run him through, it would be murder.'

The field lay before them. Many fellows were down. Sounds of moaning and crying drifted into the cold, spring air. Fleance and Macduff removed their helmets and leant against their swords, breathing heavily.

'You have your father's skill and strength,' Macduff said, looking closely at Fleance.

Fleance shook his head. ''Twas not from Banquo I received this education but from my adoptive father, who spent many long hours teaching me the skills of the sword and crossbow.'

As they rested, catching their breath, Fleance sensed the fight against the rebels was almost won. Many men fled the sight of the Scottish army and, after a gruelling three hours, he could see soldiers from both camps withdrawing, staggering back to their posts into the mist and cold.

Around them, the battlefield was littered with bodies – some alive and some dead. Fleance and Macduff were two of the few left standing. It was a gruesome and sad sight.

Just then, from the direction of the rebels' camp, came a man on a horse. He appeared out of the fog riding towards them. Though he was some distance and the murkiness shrouded his identify, the flag he held told them that he was for the rebels.

Both Fleance and Macduff straightened and lifted their swords. They watched him approach and, some yards away, dismount. He held the flag aloft and walked towards them. Fleance's heart jumped violently.

'Magness,' he cried.

Magness stood before them both. 'Aye. And here you are.'

Macduff paled. 'Magness? You survived?'

Magness turned to Macduff, ignoring his question. 'I received your message from one of my men. It is not foolishness which brings me to lead our army against the king but love of my country.'

'Some love you show Scotland by trying to kill its fellows and its king,' Macduff said.

'Well, it seems, Macduff, you and I have different ways of dealing with politics.'

'Aye, you as a traitor against your own country,' Macduff cried.

'You, Sire,' Magness roared, 'left your own castle defenceless against the tyrant to try to wheedle support from England rather than gather good fellows in Scotland who were more than ready to fight under your direction.'

Fleance watched Macduff pull himself up to his full height. 'You know very well why I had gone – to get the rightful king and an army to overthrow Macbeth.' His eyes blazed.

Magness spat. 'And, in doing so, you allowed Macbeth to rain destruction on your castle.'

Beside him, Fleance sensed Macduff falter. 'It is a sacrifice I live with daily.'

'And I,' Magness said. He turned to Fleance. 'Your friend here left his wife and babes and mine without protection and they were slaughtered.'

Macduff took a deep breath. 'It was the right thing.'

Magness jammed the flag into the soil. 'Man, you have nae idea what is and was the right thing. Your "right thing" saw your wife and babes slaughtered; your right thing meant my five beautiful children were murdered.' He straightened his back. 'Your own wife was forced to tell all that you were a traitor.'

'No,' Macduff cried. 'I was helping Scotland against the madman.'

'And, in doing so, *Sire*,' Magness sneered, 'you and I lost everything. Oftentimes, Miri and I think how much easier it would have been if we had been at the castle that day, joining our babes in heaven rather than suffering in the hell we have these past years.'

Fleance listened, each fact thudding into his mind, making sense of things that for years he had not understood. Magness and Miri had been part of Macduff's household.

'I have made my peace with God and myself. I have no need to justify my actions to you or to any man,' Macduff replied, his defiant tone muted in the thickening mist.

Magness had pulled out his sword and held it aloft.

'What are you doing?' Fleance cried.

Magness turned to him and shook his head. 'Flea, I trained you for just such a moment but never considered you would be on the wrong side.'

'I'm not on the wrong side, Magness. You are. Duncan is a great man; a great king.'

'Aye, but for how long. This family of royals has been so plagued with superstition and indecision; the loyal folk know they need something better.'

Macduff lifted his own sword high. 'This is the talk of fools, you stupid man. Take me on and we shall see whether Scotland needs a man like you or a man like me.'

Magness sprang at him and the crash of sword and shield sounded out over the quiet ground.

In horror, Fleance watched: Magness, whom he loved as a father, and Macduff whom he admired as a wise and wily protector. The clashing of their swords and the sound of their rage filled him with dread. He wanted to intervene but something buried deep within each man was fuelling their fight.

Over and under; jabbing and twisting and moving like dancers at a feast. Macduff pulled out his dirk and was swinging the sword and thrusting the dirk over and over, but only twice did it hit its mark for, each time, Magness deflected the advances, the wound of no consequence. They fought for a long time: a younger man against an older one. Backwards and forwards in the mud and blood and corpses of the fallen soldiers.

To Fleance's eyes, Macduff was the more experienced fighter but Magness's rage seemed to give him inhuman strength and endurance.

'Give over, man,' Macduff cried. 'This is in vain.'

'You would surrender?' Magness challenged.

'Never, for I stand for the king and for Scotland.'

Magness brought his sword down but Macduff held it off. Both were breathing hard through gritted teeth as they pushed against each other. Suddenly Macduff had the upper hand and shoved Magness so that he fell onto his back. He pointed his sword at Magness's throat, breathing hard. 'I would not kill you while you are down, for my hands are charged too much with the blood of your children. Surrender yourself to Scotland and face the consequences of your treachery as a man.'

Magness spat at Macduff. 'I will not surrender and be forced to kiss the ground at young Duncan's feet. You will have to kill me.'

Just then, there was a swift movement from behind Fleance and, with a sickening thud of heavy metal on soft flesh, Macduff was down.

'No!' Fleance cried and turned to see the killer. A rebel soldier was now swinging the weapon that had felled Macduff in his direction: a vicious spiked ball and chain. Without thought, he brought his father's sword up and caught the chain as it came towards him.

The weight and movement knocked them both sideways but the soldier had no other weapon.

Fleance ran his dirk up and under the man's ribs, just as he had done with the assassin all those months ago. Hot blood poured from his attacker and Fleance pushed him to the ground.

'You,' the dying man panted.

Fleance recognised him. Kelvin: the man who had attacked him and Macduff in the woods all those months ago. He lifted up his sword. 'For Macduff,' he shouted and brought it down on Kelvin's neck, ending the man's life as violently as he had lived it.

'I see you still mind my words,' Magness said getting to his feet.

Fleance turned to him, rage drowning out all other thoughts. 'This was a cowardly killing,' he roared, pointing to the pulverised skull of the thane. 'Are you content now?' he screamed, his father's weapon held out before him. 'Does this settle your score?' His head was pounding and he felt hot tears in his eyes. 'Is the blood of your children avenged now, Magness?' Fleance, his chest heaving, the full force of his rage and sorrow threatening to overwhelm him.

'Well, young Flea, here's your chance to make it right. You must fight and kill me. Or you can let me go.'

Fleance, his hands sweaty and shaking, looked down at the slain body of Macduff. His fury over this senseless killing would undo him. He must not be fooled into engaging when grief and anger surged through his body.

He lowered his sword. 'You have been as a father to me,' he cried. 'Keavy would never forgive me if I killed her father.'

Magness looked at him a long time, his face dark and closed. 'Forgiveness is over-valued, Flea. I advise you not to care about such a word, for it makes a man weak.' He wiped his sword and placed it back in its scabbard. 'The times have changed and Scotland needs to look further for its leadership. We would prosper under English rule.'

'The people deserve better,' Fleance shouted. 'Duncan will restore Scotland and bring our people peace and prosperity.'

'You are too young, lad, to understand the foolishness of such hopes.' He whistled to his horse who came trotting up. 'Miri always said you were from a royal household and to be none other than Banquo's son and under our roof,' he bowed. 'It has been an honour.' He mounted. 'You've got a good heart, Flea, but a soft one.' He gathered the reins and looked down on Fleance. 'You will regret that you let me live.' He turned his horse around and cantered into the fog.

Fleance went over to the body of Macduff, dropped to his knees and let his sword fall. He had known in his head that war and fighting meant death. He had killed but he had not known or cared for any who fell under his sword. Macduff was dead and killed by one who thought nothing of fighting dishonourably.

His throat burned and the air seemed not to fill his lungs.

There was a hand on his soldier. 'Sire?'

Fleance looked up. Two young soldiers stood beside him.

'Stand aloft awhile. I must tend to him.' After a moment, Fleance wiped away his tears and turned the old man over. Taking a cloth he removed the mud and soil from Macduff's face and mouth and pulled down the lids over his eyes. 'God rest you, my friend,' he said. Two soldiers came forward. 'The king has sent us to enquire as to your safety,' one said.

Fleance stood up, his legs weak and his head pounding. 'I am well but Macduff is dead,' he said, his voice shaky. He tried to breathe deeply but still his chest felt tight. 'Take him back to the camp and do so with respect and dignity for he was a mighty man and one Scotland will surely miss.'

He watched them wrap Macduff's body in a large cloak and tie a rope around to keep it secure. Between the two of them, they hoisted the body onto their shoulders and grimly marched their sad cargo back to camp.

Fleance turned towards the direction Magness had gone. How could he have not known the extent to which his adoptive father would go to try to change Scotland's fortune? Then he remembered the look of rage on Magness's face when he fought Macduff. It had been a pointless fight, yet it had been fuelled by a desire for revenge and unshed grief. All those years Magness had stored up his resentment, but the death of Macduff had not made anything better. Their children were still dead and with the shedding of more blood came the cry for yet another score to be settled.

How could it be that he felt this way towards Magness, especially after all he and Miri had done for him? He shook his head. Rosie had been right that day in the stables. Things had changed. 'Go, Magness,' he said under his breath. 'But if we should meet again, I will kill you.'

Then he followed the retreating figures of the soldiers, a heavy burden weighing on his soul.

Chapter Thirty-Two

Fleance did not want to return to the encampment; did not want to face the truth that the great Macduff was dead; did not want to answer Duncan's questions. But most of all, he did not want to think on how he was so foolish as to be off guard.

If only he hadn't been so caught up in what Magness was saying, he would have seen the rebel lying in wait. *I could have prevented Macduff's death*, he thought, his heart full of grief, *if I had been a better soldier.*

The sound of Duncan arguing brought Fleance out of his thoughts and drew him into the tent to investigate.

'It is not right that I stay back here while my men are being slaughtered on the field,' Duncan was saying. At the sound of Fleance's entrance, those gathered turned.

'Fleance, what news?' Duncan cried. 'I am told Macduff is down.'

Fleance nodded. 'Killed by a cowardly strike from behind. A man whom Macduff had once spared. I ran the dog through and now he can face his eternal reward for all his evil and treacherous ways.'

'Tomorrow, first light, I will set out with you, Fleance,' Duncan said. 'It is decided.'

Lennox and Preston began to argue. Duncan held up his hand. 'We will not have our people whispering behind their hands that the king was too weak and fearful to face those who came against us.' Duncan fastened his cloak. 'Besides, who better to fight beside than this man,' he said, putting a hand on Fleance's arm. 'You yourself have boasted of his skill.' He dropped his hand and went to the door of tent. 'The light has almost gone from the day and we see our men returning. Go, give them what comfort and aid they need.' He swept out leaving Fleance with the others.

Lennox, Ross and Angus looked downcast. 'I am sorry about Macduff,' Fleance said. 'I have not known him as you have but I respected him greatly.'

Lennox exhaled. 'Our dear Macduff was the most animated among the thanes. We have ridden together and fought alongside each other for many years. Out of all of us, he was the one who suffered the most yet he would not allow his grief to crush him. He took that pain and converted it to righteous anger. It was an honour for him to lay the head of the tyrant at the feet of King Malcolm.'

They were silent, each man thinking of the Thane of Fife, William Macduff, whose cold body lay on a wagon to be taken back to his castle.

Fleance roused himself. 'I will take some time to check on men who have been hurt. Will you join me?' he asked the thanes. Each nodded and followed him out leaving Preston behind studying the battle plan.

Fleance was surprised to see Rachel still on duty. A number of other women were also in the makeshift hospital, carrying bowls of water or piles of bloodied bandages. When the four of them came through the tent flaps, Rachel looked up and smiled. 'A good evening to you, sires,' she said, her voice without a hint of tiredness or despair. 'Your fellows will be heartened to see you.' She returned to her tasks, dressing the head wound of an old soldier, speaking quietly to him.

Once he had been down the rows of cots, he went to Rachel. 'It has been a long day for you, Rachel.'

'Aye, and for you and them. All of us are doing our duty.'

Fleance was amazed at her stamina and her calmness. Few women, especially of royal blood, he thought, would cope as well as she. He bowed his head. 'We and the men are most thankful for your ministrations.'

She put her hand on his arm. 'As are we for your fearless courage.' A man's cry took her attention and she was gone, moving quickly down the tent. Fleance watched her as she calmed down the young soldier. She, like her brother, was a gift to the people of Scotland: pure and kind of heart. Confident and sure of purpose. The sort of people the country needed.

The next morning, Duncan roused him. 'Fleance,' he said. 'I wish to be in front of the men today. You will be by me.'

Their horses were ready and though Fleance missed the large comfort of Willow, he was pleased the old horse was safe back at Glamis. The time for battles was long over for his father's horse. Instead, he rode a young mare, a quiet and strong creature – well suited to the needs of a battlefield.

Scotland had lost at least 8000 men and many of their horses. On the third day of the fight, the rebels began targeting the horses. By midday, Duncan called the cavalry back and commanded that this battle be fought man to man on foot.

However, after much pressure from his advisors, Duncan agreed he would travel into the field on horse but leave his steed with a soldier.

Fleance felt an extra burden with the king in his care. Not only would he be fighting for his own life but he now had to look out for

Duncan. The young king was a competent fighter but had no battle experience. He had never killed a man nor had another's blood on his hands.

They dismounted and handed their reins to the spotty-faced young soldier who, by his expression, appeared very relieved to have this responsibility on this day rather than go into the fray.

Duncan turned to his army who had walked behind them. 'For Scotland!' he shouted, punching his fist into the air.

The men roared back. 'For Scotland!'

They marched forward, spreading out to left and right, the sounds of their weapons and stamping feet sending chills down Fleance's spine. Such was the power of a collective strength.

In the distance, they watched the approach of the enemy and pulled their swords from their scabbards. Suddenly, there was a roar ahead and the rebels charged towards them.

All too soon, the enemy came upon them. Like the day before, Fleance had a companion at his shoulder as he fought. He quickly found a rhythm as he and Duncan made their way against those who came upon them.

Despite keeping an eye on his own foes, Fleance was mindful of Duncan's efforts. Less fluid than many of the experienced soldiers, he still held his own against the enemy. However, he had just downed a man when Fleance cried out, 'Behind you!'

Duncan spun around and brought up his shield just as a heavy sword came crashing into him. Using the shield as leverage, Duncan lifted up the man's arm and thrust his own sword into his stomach. Then he pushed him to the ground.

There was no time to respond for another wave of fighters was upon them. At times they fought side by side; at other times, back to back – protecting and helping each other to gain victory and to stay alive.

About an hour into the battle, there was a lull in the fighting. The rebels retreated and Duncan held up his hand to stop his men from advancing. 'Take our wounded back,' he shouted. 'We will consider our next line of offence.'

Fleance and Duncan walked among the fallen. There were more of Magness's men than Scotland's. In the distance, they heard another horn – different from any they had heard before. It came from the west and, when they looked, were dismayed to see another army advancing.

''Tis the Norwegians,' Duncan said. 'Give the signal,' he cried. 'Regroup and rearm.' He turned to Fleance. 'I fear it is now we will be truly tested.'

They had time to be refreshed with water and some small morsels of food but, by mid-afternoon, the fighting was at its most intense. Fleance was sore and bruised but not injured. He lost count of how many fellows he killed. This army brandished more axes than swords and called for a different type of fighting. Within an hour, his shield was dented and had sustained numerous poundings.

Again, like the morning, he and Duncan found a kind of rhythm in their fighting and, like a slowly turning wheel, they moved around and around, fending off those who came near.

Fleance dispatched two fellows quickly and then three others, their blond hair quickly reddened by the blood of their wounds. Behind him, he heard Duncan engaged in a fierce struggle. Each time there was a lull in his own battle, he looked around to see the young king fighting with a large fellow. But he had no time to aid Duncan for still the Norwegians came upon them.

Behind him, the Scottish horn sounded and Fleance heard the heartening roar of fresh soldiers advancing. There was no time, however, to rejoice. They were in the thick of the fighting. Spurred on by the good news of more men, Fleance found more strength deep within himself. He stood and forced his enemies to come to him. Some charged. Some danced around him. All died by his hand.

Fleance had just killed the last soldier who came to him when, suddenly, there was an anguished cry. Fleance turned around to see that Duncan had fallen, his shield laid bare but his sword held forth towards his attacker. The man put his foot on Duncan's shield and stomped down so that the king cried out in pain and let his own weapon fall.

The Norwegian soldier lifted his sword high to bring it down on his enemy but Fleance threw himself forward and knocked the man sideways. Both rolled over and leapt to their feet. 'You will not take out my king,' Fleance cried angrily.

The man before him uttered words Fleance did not know but he understood their tone – that of hate and anger. Fleance charged forward, the weight of his father's blade propelling him so that he came up against this man's own weapons. They pushed and cut and thrust and swung their swords against each other until Fleance gained an advantage by applying a swift move Macduff had taught him. Fleance kicked hard at his foe's shin and then brought his knee up into the man's groin. The foreigner cried out in pain, doubling over so that Fleance could bring down the sword on his enemy's neck.

Fleance spun around to find Duncan. The king was on his feet but his left hand hung loosely at his side. 'I am injured, Fleance. I can no longer fight.'

Only their men were left standing though, further off in the distance, Fleance saw soldiers still engaged in combat. The field was littered with bodies. 'I will get you back to camp and then return to help finish this fight.'

As Fleance said this, there was another loud blast of a horn from the west. It went on and on and with it, the Norwegians retreated. The Scottish army ran after them but Duncan cried out: 'Enough, men! Scotland is victorious. Send word. We have won this battle.' Duncan's face was pale and sweating.

'We must get you to Rachel,' Fleance said, 'to look to your injury.'

Duncan nodded. 'Aye.' He held up his arm. Fleance saw the blue and black stains already bruising the skin. The arm was surely broken.

'Rachel will mend you.'

'Thank God we are done,' Duncan said. 'Too many dead and wounded.'

'Indeed,' Fleance said. He sheathed his sword and picked up Duncan's. They walked towards the rise where their horses stood. He helped Duncan mount and then swung up on his own mare. Together they looked down upon the vast battlefield.

'This is a sorry sight,' Duncan said and Fleance heard the sadness in his voice. 'May the wounds inflicted upon Scotland these past days heal quickly and without disease.' He patted the neck of his horse. 'We will gather up our dead and set them on the pyre. I will not have the wolves glut themselves on my fallen. Then, let us quickly back home to Glamis.' Duncan looked at Fleance. 'It seems, my friend, that our family will forever be in the debt of yours. First your father, now you. Ask anything of me and it's yours.'

Fleance was suddenly quiet. 'There is one thing I would ask . . .' he hesitated.

'Anything,' Duncan said, 'anything at all.'

'I wish to take up your offer and return to Lochaber as thane . . .' he hesitated again and glanced towards Duncan, '. . . with Rosie as my wife. I have asked much of her and she has always stayed true to me – even when I couldn't fully confide in her. I love her with all my heart, Duncan. As my king I ask for your blessing in this.'

Duncan sighed. 'Fleance, I envy you this.' He grimaced and Fleance wasn't sure if it was from his wound or something deeper. 'To marry someone you love and who loves you, regardless of what duty asks of you – that is something, as king, I can never have. Perhaps if fate had been kinder to me and this crown had not been thrust on me with such haste I too could have found the way to marry the one I love.'

He looked at Fleance once more, then smiled.

'You have my blessing, my friend,' he said. 'Go to Lochaber with your maid and be happy. But be prepared for many visits from your king. I will miss you, my friend, and I have got used to having you by my side these past months – it will be dull of an evening without your company.'

Fleance laughed. 'You are more than welcome, my friend – you and your sisters.'

Though the grim task of removing their dead and injured continued, sounds of laughter and singing swirled around the encampment. Rachel had ordered wagons to shift the injured whose hurts would heal back to their homes and families to be tended by them. The next morning, she and two of her nurses planned to accompany the first group heading north.

She found Fleance and Duncan in the main tent. 'I have come to say my farewells, brother, and to go ahead to prepare for your return.'

Duncan went to her and kissed her on both cheeks. 'I will not be delayed by much. God speed.'

'And you,' she said. 'Fleance, I charge you with ensuring my brother here does no more injury to himself.'

Fleance bowed. 'I will take care of him, I promise, though the task you set me is a difficult one,' he smiled.

Duncan gave him a shove. 'You will worry my sister unnecessarily,' he said grinning. 'Rachel, I am capable of looking after myself.' He took her arm and led her from the tent to the waiting carriages. 'Give Bree a kiss from me.'

'Aye, I will. Goodbye, Duncan. Fleance,' she said as the carriage drove off.

They raised their hands to wave her goodbye and then turned their attentions to the remaining soldiers.

Duncan called his men to assemble and, on top of his horse, his arm in a sling, he addressed them one more time. 'Citizens of Scotland. This day your king gives you thanks. Your bravery and courage, determination and faithfulness will not go unrewarded. Not only will you enjoy the fruits of your labours by the knowledge of victory but we shall reward each man extra gold. And for our brothers whose lives were lost, their families will receive their reward also.'

A cheer went up from the crowd. 'Long live the king! Long live the king!' Duncan allowed the chant to go on but then held up his hand to silence them. 'Though our loss is great, it has been a sacrifice which secured Scotland's victory. We have sent a clear message to any country or rebel cause that Scotland is strong. Scotland is brave. Scotland will never be vanquished!'

Again, the men cheered and this time Duncan did not stop them. Instead, he left them and rode back to his tent.

The next morning, Fleance was restless. Blair had not come back and no one could tell him where he was. He would go back into the field and systematically look at every fallen man to see if it were his friend.

The spring morning heralded again only mist and no sound. Occasionally, Fleance heard a cry way out on the heath and his heart contracted. Maybe, in looking for Blair, he might save others. He dressed swiftly and went into the mess tent for a bite to eat before his gruesome errand. There he found Duncan.

'Why are you up so early, Sire?' he asked. 'Is your wrist hurting?'

Duncan frowned. 'My wrist is fine, thanks to my sister and her disgusting medicines,' he said holding up his bandaged arm. 'But why, after all this time, Fleance, must you address me so formally. Did we not agree we were brothers and friends?'

Fleance tilted his head. 'Why does it bother you so? Duncan, you are the King of Scotland. You are my liege. My lord. My king. And though I love you, yes as brother and friend, nothing changes the fact that I owe my allegiance to you. Why do you find it so hard to see it this way?'

Duncan, as was his habit, chewed his top lip. 'I think because I was never prepared for this, Fleance. In my early years, it was always Uncle Malcolm who would be king. I think that I did not take in the seriousness of events when it was clear he could not produce an heir and then got sick. It all happened so fast.' He spread out his hands. 'And here am I. Not yet seen twenty-two summers and the reigning monarch of Scotland.'

Fleance studied his friend and understood. Duncan had been through so much in his life that he could be forgiven for not thinking forward. Whereas, he, Fleance, had been constantly wondering about his future because of his father's ever disapproving presence. He stepped forward and placed his hand on his friend's shoulder. 'I am grateful for your understanding. Though many have suggested I am not as I appear to be, you have steadfastly seen me as I am.' He removed his hand. 'Duncan, I am not an angel and I am not perfect but I am honest and I am honourable.'

Duncan chuckled. 'Yes, Fleance. You are all of those things and I know you. And, I know what your heart desires.' He paused and drew himself some tea. 'What are your plans today?'

'Blair has not returned and I wish to find him.'

'I will come with you,' Duncan said.

'This is a mundane task for a king. I am in no need of an escort.'

'Aye, but would a friend be of use?'

355

Fleance shook his head. 'No other companion would I wish but you, Duncan.'

'Then, it seems, I am about to go once again into the field.'

Fleance could not argue with the king so the two of them set out onto the battlefield.

It was not a pleasant task and with each body they checked, Fleance could see that his friend was hurt and shaken. A young boy who had just weeks before rode in on his village's horse and enthusiastically declared his desire to fight for his king, lay savagely cut down, his clear young face looking utterly surprised at what had happened. He lay in the mud, eyes and mouth open as if he was about to say *But wait. I have things to finish*.

As they systematically walked through the mist, checking each fallen man, they began to talk.

'Do you think a man is ever ready to take on responsibility?' Duncan asked.

It was a question Fleance had been considering of late. 'Well, I think of the likes of Macduff, Lennox, Ross. They have seen many years of turmoil. Yet, they remain hopeful, by all appearances, and willing to keep going for the good of the country.'

'Ahhh,' Duncan cried. He put his hand to his face. 'How can a body become so disfigured?' Fleance looked at where his king was standing. Some soldier (who knew if it was for or against Scotland) had his face completely sliced off so that only ears and hair remained.

'War is bad, Duncan. We are young but already we know this.'

Duncan shook himself. 'No, my friend. Men are bad. Men are vicious, corrupted animals.'

'Come on. Let's move quicker.' He pulled Duncan forward.

An hour later, both exhausted, Fleance found joy. Blair, his dear friend from old, was sitting in the field talking to one of his men.

'Blair,' Fleance called. 'Are you hurt?'

His face white and drawn, Blair tried to smile. 'You are a sight which gladdens the heart.'

Duncan indicated to the man in Blair's arms. 'Who is this man you hold?'

Blair looked down on the dead face of the soldier. 'This soldier saved my life many times but I could not save him.'

'Sergeant,' Fleance said gently. 'Leave him and go back to camp. Call forth bearers to bring in our dead.'

For a moment, Blair looked unsure but then roused himself. 'Aye, Sire.' He gently rolled the dead soldier from his lap and stood up. 'I will be back anon.'

They watched him walk awkwardly across the heath, tripping over and avoiding bodies. Duncan breathed deeply. 'You have a loyal following.'

Fleance shook his head. 'Maybe, but many of the men have connections to those who have chosen to fight on the rebels' side.'

Duncan stopped walking. Around them were many dead and many who would die. He raised his hands. 'What do I do with this, Fleance?' he cried. 'How do I make this right?'

'You have, Duncan. You have made it right by winning against any who should seek to bring down the royal house of Scotland.'

'At what cost? My father wanted Scotland to be progressive. He saw the potential of our lands and our peoples to make much of this world. Too long have we dealt with superstition and misguided religion to operate effectively.'

'There will always be someone who will seek to destroy you because of their own ghosts. You have not inherited a brand new land but one where many look, licking their lips, to see if they can grab a piece of it.'

'Well,' Duncan conceded. 'We shall see what fate next deals us.'

No sooner had he said this than a shout went out and they were both startled at who confronted them.

Chapter Thirty-Three

Calum, on his horse, stood beside the butchered body of a soldier, a crossbow armed and aimed at Fleance.

'What are you doing, man?' Duncan challenged. 'All these months and you've turned your loyalties?'

Calum ignored him but addressed Fleance. 'You are a fool,' he said, his voice shifting in tone so that, for the first time, a trace of a Nordic accent became more obvious. 'As was Donalbain. The witches were right. He needed to be wary of the son of a murdered father.' Calum sneered. 'He thought it was you. But you are no threat to anyone, Fleance, Banquo's son!'

Fleance could not understand why this man spoke to him with such bitterness and rage. 'You are making no sense, Calum. Put down your weapon for the battle is lost by you and won by Scotland.'

Calum lifted his head to the sky and laughed. 'So naïve, you Scots. You forget too easily. I don't care one iota for this skirmish between our foolish countries. I am here to avenge my father's murder.' Fleance and Duncan exchanged looks. 'For this past year I have served mad Donalbain to ensure that my information is complete. And, how easy it was to ingratiate myself into his,' he gestured to

Duncan, 'father's inner circle. The idiot abided by everything I said except he could not kill you – despite my efforts. I wasted money on that foolish assassin and when I could see no other way to get rid of you, I convinced Donalbain to put you in the front line of the army. I had hoped you would be killed in battle but it seems as if even that is a task I will have to carry out myself.'

'Kill me? But why, Calum? I am nothing to you,' Fleance said, staring at the pointed shaft of the bolt.

'Nothing!' Calum roared. 'You, stupid boy, are everything that stands in the way of my gaining peace from the plague on my house. You are Banquo's son. Banquo who murdered my father.'

Fleance held up his hands. 'Calum, you make no sense. My father was not a murderer. He was an honourable and kindly man. General of the king's army.'

'Yes,' he spat. 'And that general killed my father.'

Duncan put a hand on Fleance's arm. 'I think he's talking about the battle against my grandfather. The one where Macbeth and Banquo dealt with the rebel leaders.'

Duncan called to Calum. 'Was your father Sweno, King of Norway?'

'Yes,' Calum spat. 'A more brave and noble king you could not find.' His face reddened. 'My father was a great man and he, foolishly, thought he might make a difference in the world but, it seems, he joined the wrong side.'

'That is the way of warfare, Calum,' Fleance said.

'No. When he realised what he had taken on, he attempted to negotiate with the Scottish generals. Your father, though having been told *my father's* request, denied it and slaughtered him. Just before he died, he gave a message which was to be sent to me: *Calum, this is not finished. This is betrayal. I know you can avenge.*'

Fleance recognised the same haunting he himself suffered. But within Calum he saw something more: obsession? madness? definitely, determination.

'Can we not change the course of history and forgive the past?' Fleance asked.

'You didn't. You made yourself go across country to fulfil your father's wishes. This is my brief also.' Still he held the crossbow aloft and pointed at Fleance's chest.

What to do? 'We are the next generation,' Fleance said. 'Let us not repeat our fathers' follies.' Fleance put down his sword and started to walk towards him.

Duncan grabbed his arm. 'Don't,' he said. 'He is as crazy as my father. You cannot reason with him.'

'Calum, I believe that I am no threat to you or your kingdom. Let us just walk away with our lives,' Fleance pleaded.

'No,' Calum cried. 'You will die to pay for my father's death. I have saved my last bolt for you.' He raised the crossbow again. 'I will have vengeance,' he said.

It all happened so quickly: Fleance saw Calum squeeze the trigger and tried to move to the left. At that same moment, Duncan stepped forward, just in front of Fleance. 'Here, man, let us discuss . . .'

Too late to do anything, Fleance heard the bolt thud into Duncan's chest.

Calum threw down his weapon, enraged.

'You fool!' Fleance screamed at Calum, picking up his own sword.

Calum turned his horse around and glared down at him. 'I had hoped this to be the end of the matter but it seems fate is destined for us to meet again.' He looked behind Fleance, turned his horse again and galloped away.

361

'Coward!' Fleance cried but it would not change anything. He saw a number of their party running towards them. With his heart beating rapidly he turned his attentions to Duncan who lay on the battlefield, blood leaking from the wound. The bolt had embedded itself just below the collar bone.

'I'm fine,' Duncan said, trying to sit up. 'Just get me to Rachel and all will be good.'

The bolt was a problem. Fleance turned to the soldiers. 'Take His Majesty to the surgeons – quickly.' Between them, they lifted Duncan and, as quickly but as carefully as they could, they carried him to the tents.

Duncan said little but Fleance could see that he was in pain. Sometimes he closed his eyes tightly as they negotiated the field. A messenger ran ahead of them to warn the surgeons and to make preparations.

After what seemed like an eternity, they laid Duncan on a long wooden bench and the two doctors began their work. Fleance stood by Duncan's head and tried to keep him distracted. 'I guess we're even then,' he offered.

'Why is that?' Duncan replied, his breathing laboured.

'You saved my life.'

Duncan closed his eyes and smiled. 'You're daft keeping score. I hope that we will have years together to continue to look out for each other.'

Fleance's stomach chilled and he swallowed. 'Aye.'

One of the doctors came forward with a drink. 'Take this, Your Majesty, it will help with the pain.' He held his head as Duncan sipped the foul-smelling liquid. In sympathy, Fleance screwed up his face.

Lennox rushed in. 'Your Majesty,' he cried.

'I'm all right. 'Tis not much of a wound. Many have had far worse and survived to tell their tale.'

Lennox took a deep breath and helped them to remove Duncan's armour and coat, cutting around the bolt, then stood back. Duncan's chest now lay exposed, pale and vulnerable. The bolt stood firmly, half of it buried in his chest. A deep bruising was already spreading across the chest and, around the shaft of the bolt, the skin had begun to swell.

The other doctor came over with a small stick. 'Your Majesty, we are going to remove the bolt. You will need to bite down on this because it will be very painful.'

'Perhaps you should leave it in, then. I could treat it like an adornment,' Duncan quipped but there was fear and pain in his eyes.

He put his hand on Duncan's shoulder. 'It doesn't suit you.' He gave a gentle squeeze. 'It will be over quickly.'

Duncan nodded and took the piece of wood from the doctor's hand and placed it between his teeth. He breathed deeply, coughed and then closed his eyes.

'Hold his shoulders,' the first doctor said and Fleance did as he was instructed. 'You,' he added, pointing to Blair, 'hold down his hips.' Blair pressed his weight down on Duncan's hips.

One doctor stood to the side with a large bandage at the ready and a bottle of spirits, while the other placed one hand on Duncan's chest and the other he curled around the shaft. 'On the count of three,' he said to Duncan. Duncan nodded, his eyes still tightly closed, his pulse beating rapidly in a small vein in his neck. 'One. Two.' He yanked hard and the deadly weapon was pulled free.

Duncan screamed between his teeth but the doctors ignored that while they poured some warm wine on the hole which was bleeding profusely and then pressed large wads of bandage against the injury to stem the flow.

Fleance took a cloth and wiped away the thick veil of sweat that had broken out on Duncan's face.

Duncan removed the wood from between his teeth and opened his eyes. 'You can't count,' he said to the doctor.

'The bolt came out cleanly, Your Majesty.' He looked at Fleance. 'If we keep the wound pure, all will be well.' They wrapped his chest tightly and brought him a clean shirt.

Duncan signalled for Lennox and Fleance. 'You and Angus stay behind until every last man is brought in. We will go on ahead with the remaining injured and the Thane of Ross.'

Fleance shook his head. 'I would travel with you, Sire. I promised your fair sister that I would return you safely to her.'

'Aye,' said Lennox. 'There is but a day's work left and it would be best if Your Majesty were quickly back to Glamis for rest and the healing hands of your sister.'

Duncan looked first at Lennox and then Fleance. 'It shall be done then. Come, Fleance, you will ride beside me.' Two soldiers came forward and helped Duncan into the wagon which had been prepared with a soft bed.

Once he was settled, Fleance called for his horse. He mounted the mare and looked down at Duncan. 'Are you comfortable?'

'Enough. I will be better under Rachel's skilled care.'

'To Glamis it is then,' Fleance cried and the party moved off.

They sailed from Edinburgh and made good time. Fleance was worried, however. The wound was bleeding little but Duncan was in pain. By the time they arrived at Perth the following day, the king was breathing rapidly and with difficulty. They placed him on another cart and this time Fleance sat with him, the mare trotting behind.

And, as was Scotland's custom, it began to rain.

All the covered carts had gone earlier with Rachel so Duncan and Fleance had to endure a quiet but persistent soaking. Fleance removed his cloak and held it above Duncan's head and chest in a vain attempt to keep out the rain.

'I have always hated the rain,' Duncan told him. 'I dislike feeling wet and cold.'

Fleance laughed. 'A bit tough for a Scot.'

They were quiet for a while and Duncan slept. Though he looked at ease, Fleance had a nagging feeling of fear at the back of his mind.

Sometime later, Duncan roused. 'I do not feel so well, my friend,' he said, breathing hard between words. 'My heart is racing and I feel faint.'

Fleance grabbed his hand. 'It has been a hard journey back, Duncan. We are not half a day from Glamis.' Duncan's hand was sweaty and it trembled.

'Witness,' Duncan whispered. 'Get another.'

Fleance frowned. He was unsure what Duncan was asking. 'You want someone else?' There was an almost imperceptible nod. 'Stop the wagon,' Fleance called. 'The king asks for a witness.' Blair and Ross came running back. Fleance looked back to Duncan. 'Blair and the Thane of Ross are here as your witnesses.'

Duncan's eyes were closed and his chest moved up and down with dramatic movement. Each word was spoken slowly and laboriously, a breathy pause between almost every word. 'I. Duncan. The Second. King. Of Scotland. Name. Fleance.' He stopped. They waited and watched as beads of sweat formed on his forehead and above his top lip. 'Son of Banquo. Great. Grandson of. Kenneth. The Third.' Again, another wait while he caught his breath. 'To be my. Successor.' Fleance and Blair looked at each other. 'I have. No heir. He is. Next. In line.'

Fleance was stunned. 'Don't ask this of me, Duncan,' he begged. 'You know what taking that office will mean to me . . . what I will have to give up. Besides you will go on to live a long life and have many bonny bairns . . .'

Duncan turned to him and Fleance now noticed how blue his lips were.

'Please,' he whispered.

Fleance wiped Duncan's face. 'My friend, we have no need of this proclamation for once we get you to Glamis and in the tender care of Rachel, you shall be laughing with me in years to come about your generous offer.'

Duncan turned to him and Fleance despaired. What was wrong? They said the bolt came out cleanly. There had been little blood loss. Why was he so ill?

Duncan was panting. 'Rachel. Bree. Now yours.' He stared hard at Fleance who was more afraid than at any other remembered time.

Then Duncan smiled weakly. 'This rain. It is not so bad. A bit like Bree's wet kisses.'

Suddenly, his body gave a violent lurch, his eyes widened and the life went from his eyes.

A cold sweat swept up Fleance's back. 'Duncan?' He shook the king. 'Duncan? Wake up.' But Duncan's pale blue eyes continued to stare sightlessly. Fleance got up on his knees and shook the young man by the shoulders. Duncan's head wobbled uselessly. A painful ball of grief had lodged itself in Fleance's chest. This could not be happening. He pulled his friend into his arms and wept, only dimly aware of the crowd of soldiers around the wagon.

Sometime later, he was roused by Blair. 'We are all very wet, Sire. We must continue to take His Majesty home.' Fleance looked up, dazed, still holding the now cooling body of his friend. 'I will go ahead with the news.' Blair climbed aboard the cart and gently took Duncan and laid him back down on the bed. Then he lifted the blanket and pulled it over Duncan's head.

A few hours later, wet and cold and miserable, they plodded into the courtyard of Glamis castle. This time, it loomed over him and added to his misery.

The main doors to the castle opened and Rachel, Morag and Charissa came rushing down the steps. Fleance leapt off the back of the cart and stood between the women and the body of the dead king.

'Where is he?' Rachel cried. 'Where is he?' she repeated. She rushed to the wagon but Fleance caught her. 'Let me see him,' she said. 'I want to see my brother.'

'Rachel,' Fleance shouted, his own voice choked with sadness. 'I am sorry.'

There was a hysterical cry from beyond. Fleance looked up to see Charissa had collapsed at her aunt's feet, wailing. He watched as Morag knelt down and put her arms around her. Charissa, her face distorted with grief, made such a heart-wrenching sound, it sent chills through Fleance.

He was still holding Rachel. She pulled back from him, her face red and angry. 'You were supposed to protect him,' she yelled. 'You promised me.' She began flailing at him with her fists. Eventually he had to grab her hands and forced her to stop.

Ross stood beside them. 'Madam,' he said, his voice also unsteady. ''Twas Calum, your father's advisor, who did this. The bolt was meant for Fleance but the king stood in the way.'

She gave him a wild look. 'I don't care what happened and why.' She turned to Fleance. 'How could this happen? He was so kind and loving and gentle and . . .' Tears streamed down her face. Her grief more than matched his.

He pulled her into his arms and held her tight. 'I know,' he whispered. 'He was.' His own tears were again free to fall. 'He was,' he repeated as he held her close, his face pressed into her soft hair.

Chapter Thirty-Four
Glamis Castle

Duncan's body was carried from the wagon to his chambers where his manservant and attendants would prepare it for the journey to Iona.

So distraught was Rachel that Fleance lifted her in his arms and carried her to her room, whereupon Morag, after attending to poor Charissa, had brought a sleeping draught. Rachel drank it numbly and Fleance sat with her until she was asleep.

As if in a trance, he went to Duncan's room and stood in the doorway and watched while they prepared the body. On the large bed, he looked so small. His eyes were closed and he looked peacefully asleep.

Fleance asked them all to leave so that he could sit alone beside his friend. How did this happen? One moment they were celebrating victory over the rebels and three days later he was sitting here staring at the body of one of the most special people he had had the privilege of knowing. Tears welled up again. So did his anger.

And just as suddenly, the words of the witches came to him: *Hail to you who will gain the prize amidst bloodshed and sorrow.* Was 'the prize' the crown? If so, then they were right, for the last time he felt such sorrow was when he was an eleven-year-old boy fleeing for his life.

He stood up and then leant forward and kissed Duncan's hand. 'Goodbye, my friend. I promise you I will look after Rachel and Bree as you asked.' He moved to the doorway and looked back. It was a most pitiful sight.

When he walked into the great corridor, Preston was waiting, his face more pale and drawn than usual. 'Sire, a word?' Fleance nodded. 'The thanes and earls have gathered in the great hall and wish you to attend.'

Fleance sighed wearily. 'Tell them I will be along shortly. First I must change into dry clothes.'

Preston bowed low and shuffled away. Fleance went in the opposite direction to his room.

He paced the floor. This was not how it was supposed to be. Though the threat to Scotland had been quelled, it was like a heavy summons lay upon his heart. He had failed to protect his king and his friend and, instead of a celebration feast, the king lay dead in his chambers, his sister overcome with grief and he was now summoned before the thanes and earls to give an account of himself.

He dressed quickly and splashed water on his face. Then he hurried to the meeting hall, an anxious knot in his stomach. A grim silence greeted him. Lennox, Ross, Angus, the bishop from the abbey, Preston, even Blair, plus a number of others whose names he was not certain of but whose faces were familiar. But not Macduff and not Duncan. The sadness threatened to overwhelm him.

The bishop came forward. 'Fleance,' he said, his voice rumbling around the hall. 'Duncan named you as the one to take the sovereignty and Ross and your sergeant here were witness to his command. You, who are Banquo's son and, through him, great-grandson of Kenneth the Third, are the rightful heir. God has selected you, Fleance, to rule Scotland. What is your answer to this?'

Lennox stepped over to him, placing a fatherly hand on his shoulder. 'We here, Fleance, are all in agreement with Duncan's command. You are your father's son but you are more than that. We have seen you fearless and faithful. You are strong, honest and noble. You will rule Scotland wisely – of this we are all certain.' There was a murmur of agreement.

Fleance looked around the hall. What preparation could there possibly be for a moment like this? He needed time to think. To be king? But, if that was to be, what about Rosie? His head was spinning. Magness's story and the intense hatred he had seen in his adoptive father's face; Calum's threats. Was he ready to take on the weight of all that for the people of Scotland? For people like the old shepherd couple, Michael and Agnes? Accepting the crown meant his life would not be his alone to direct.

Ross cleared his throat. 'Fleance, we understand that this is a difficult thing to consider for few men even dream of the possibility that they could one day be king.' Fleance stared at him, struggling to understand the simple words of the thane. Ross continued. 'You will not be alone for all in this room will guide you and support you.'

'As will the Lord,' the bishop added.

'The people will accept you, Fleance,' Lennox said. 'No other man has a rightful claim to the throne. To choose another will pull Scotland back into civil war.'

The sights and sounds and smells of the battle still clung to Fleance and he shuddered. It would be a dreadful thing to go so quickly back to that.

'It is an honour bestowed upon the one the Lord has chosen,' the bishop said. 'And, though it will require personal sacrifice, He will reward you abundantly for your obedience.'

The word 'sacrifice' stung him for he understood what that would mean. Should he be King of Scotland, then his life's course would change completely. After the battle he had intended to return to his home at Lochaber with Rosie beside him and to live out his days rebuilding his life and in service to his king.

Now, the king was dead and a new path was opening out in front of him. He could say no and tread the journey he had planned. He could turn his back on this offer but, even as he thought it, Fleance knew that he could never do that. If, as Lennox said, another was chosen and Scotland went back to bloodshed and death, he would be pulled into the fray and those he loved would be in danger of their lives. It could not be.

Fleance inhaled deeply, straightened his back and lifted his head. 'I will accept the crown,' he said. The bishop nodded and signalled to Preston.

'Again we take the journey to Iona but it is advisable, Sire, that we carry out the ceremony at Scone immediately. Your people need to feel secure after such a time.'

'Aye, but they also need to grieve. Is Duncan to be forgotten so quickly?' Fleance asked.

This time, Ross spoke. 'Like his grandfather, like your father, Duncan will never be forgotten but you must no longer look back. Though we defeated the rebels, this is still an uneasy time. We will send out word to all the land that you are named. Some fellows will go with the king to Iona; others with you to Scone.'

'Aye, but no word until I have spoken with Rachel,' Fleance said.

Ross nodded. 'I will see it is done.'

'Thank you,' Fleance replied and then walked out of the hall, his head spinning.

The next morning, the rain, which had started lightly, began to buffet the castle. Fresh and angry winds from the north stirred up wet leaves and twigs. The weather's mood was matched by those inside.

Fleance found Rachel in Morag's kitchen. Her skin was pasty and there were dark smudges under her eyes. Morag was encouraging her to eat. Across from Rachel, sat Charissa. She was weeping and her nose was red and swollen.

He stood there looking at them, unsure how to find the words to offer comfort or the news he must break to Rachel. He coughed politely. 'Rachel, I must speak with you.'

She looked at him, her eyes bright with unshed tears. She nodded and stood up. 'Thank you, Morag,' she said quietly and then followed Fleance out of the kitchen, up the stairs and into the main corridor.

'Let us go somewhere warm,' she said and led him to the blue room.

When they were inside, they both instinctively looked to the empty chair where Duncan used to sit. They remained standing.

'What is it you wish to speak to me about?' Rachel asked and Fleance noticed her formal tone.

He moved his jaw to speak but could not find the words. He cleared his throat and studied the rich blue rug at their feet. 'I am sorry,' he started.

'So am I,' she replied. 'I should not have said those things to you.' Tears began to slide down her face. 'Morag has told me the men have spoken of your bravery and how many times you saved him.'

'But I didn't in the end, Rachel,' he cried. 'I could not save him and the bolt was meant for me.'

She frowned. 'I don't understand.'

'All this time it was Calum trying to destroy me.'

'Calum?'

'Aye, these past years he has been a spy in this household. He wormed his way into your father's head and whispered unwise plans into his ears.'

Rachel frowned and sat down on her chair. She looked up at him. 'Why would he do that?'

'Do you remember your father one night yelling about being in danger from the son of a murdered father?' She nodded. 'Donalbain thought it was me but those evil hags were talking about Calum. His father was killed in the battle against your grandfather. Killed by my father.' His head ached from lack of sleep and too much emotion. He went to the side table and was pleased to see a jug of water. He poured a drink and drank it thirstily. 'Calum is the King of Norway,' he said. 'He aimed to kill me to avenge his father. He spent his time in this household determined to exact revenge on your family as well.'

Rachel put a hand to her forehead. 'All these secrets; all these foolish men wanting vengeance and power and gain.' She looked up at him. 'Why can't men live in peace, Fleance? Why does there always have to be war and bloodshed?'

'Because in the secret chambers of men's hearts there is always ambition. And ambition without honour or restraint leads to ruthless and violent action.' He put down the empty goblet and went to her. 'There is something else I need to tell you, Rachel.' He knelt before her and took her hands in his. She looked at him, her eyes searching his face. Fleance took a deep breath. 'I am to be king.'

Her eyes widened and she pulled away. 'King?' she whispered. He watched as confusion made her frown and shake. 'But, Duncan.' She stopped, eyes searching the room as if trying to find the clues to make sense of all he was telling her.

'Aye. I have already been named. The thanes are sending word out this morning. You will journey with Duncan to Iona and I will go to Scone.'

Rachel stood and pushed back her shoulders. She moistened her lips and swallowed. 'God has chosen wisely,' she said. 'I must tell Bree of our brother's death.'

She went to leave but he reached out and held her arm. 'Rachel, I made a promise to Duncan before he died, to take care of you and Bree. I make this promise to you also. You, Bree and Keavy are my family.'

Rachel stared at him for a moment. 'Is that how you see me, Fleance. As a sister?'

The question came from nowhere and he was unprepared.

The unspoken was now before them.

Fleance released her arm and turned to look out the window.

Behind him he sensed Rachel standing, waiting for an answer.

'Rachel,' he sighed. 'I have made no secret of the fact that my heart belongs to another. In truth, if all had gone well and Duncan still ruled, I would be on my way to Perth right now to ask Rosie to marry me.'

He turned and took her hands in his once more.

'However, it seems Fate and God have other plans for me and I must now choose honour and duty over love. It seems whichever way I turn with this I will be causing someone pain.'

Surprisingly, Rachel smiled although her eyes had filled with tears.

'Fleance, remember I too have felt the pain of a lost love. It's true I had hoped you would help me forget this pain and perhaps I have read too much into the small crumbs of kindness you have shown me.'

She sighed once more and moved to sit in her usual chair before looking up at Fleance once more. 'Perhaps we can help each other here. I can't take the place of Rosie in your heart nor can you be Ewan in mine . . .' Here she swallowed quickly and Fleance recognised the emotion was still raw and tender.

'However,' she continued more forcefully, 'I feel we can achieve something as strong and enduring as the love we have both experienced, something to aid us both through the pain of Duncan's death and the demands ruling this country will bring. Remember, I told you once before I am a descendent of a warrior clan. I am not a shrinking flower that will snap at the first sign of hardship. You must do what is right for you, Fleance, but remember, you will not be alone in this. Think on this when you ponder what needs to be done.' She rose and laid a hand gently on his arm for a moment.

'Now I must tend to the children,' and she was gone.

Fleance was left alone, his mind reeling.

I am to be king, he thought. It felt as if his world had been turned onto its head. He needed air and he needed space. Fleance went out of the castle and into the stables. He found Willow snoozing contentedly in his stall.

'Hey, old man,' he said. Willow's head bobbed up and he gave Fleance a hostile look. Fleance ignored him and set about brushing him down and then tacking him up. He led the horse outside and mounted. Just then he spotted Lennox and Ross coming through the castle gates and rode over to them.

'I have given the news to Rachel. You can send the posts out. I am in need of a ride to clear my thoughts. Please inform Preston I will be back by midday.'

The men bowed their heads and went on.

He pushed Willow into a fast canter and was soon comforted by the rhythmical pounding of hooves and the rise and fall of the horse's body. The cold rain bit at his face and stung his eyes but he didn't care. It was as if wild weather were urging him on. At the boundary of the palace grounds he slowed Willow and they walked on.

All his life, he had been guided by the voice of his father telling him to live with honour and loyalty; to be faithful and honest. And he had done his best to live out the example he'd seen in Banquo. Now he was being called upon to live his life publicly and to continue to uphold the same values he held dear. In the past, he was responsible only for those immediately in his care; now it was the whole of Scotland who would look to him for leadership.

The power frightened him. Without Duncan he felt uncertain, for his friend had always known the right thing to do.

You must do what is right, Fleance, but you will not be alone. Remember that. Rachel's words came back to him. He may have lost Duncan but there was still his sister: wise, gentle, unflappable. A calm presence to walk beside him.

But how could he choose?

If he was to be king, he could not consider his own heart and desires. To choose Rosie was to choose for himself and his passion. Fleance turned Willow back towards the castle. What was best for him? he thought. What was best for Scotland?

He looked up at the miserable sky. Perhaps the answer would come to him soon enough.

Chapter Thirty-Five

Two days later, Queen Margaret, now called the queen dowager, arrived at the castle. Fleance watched from his chambers as Preston helped her down from her carriage. She was dressed in white and though she gave the advisor a smile, grief was etched deeply into her face. Fleance looked down at his hands and sighed. Rachel had sent for the dowager but a message had come before her arrival that the old queen wished for an audience with him as soon as possible.

Every time a message came that someone wished to speak with him, Fleance's stomach chilled. Apart from Rachel's outburst a few days ago, not one person had pointed the finger of blame at him. They did not need to for Fleance held the full weight of blame in his arms. He was to blame for Duncan's death. Had he not gone looking for Blair, nor agreed to Duncan's company, then instead of a funeral meal, they would all be celebrating a victory feast. Instead of facing a future he had not dreamed of, he would be making happy plans for the rest of his life.

There was a knock at his door and Fleance turned from the window. 'Come,' he called. The door opened and Preston entered. 'The queen dowager wishes to know if you are ready to see her.'

Fleance nodded quickly. 'Aye. Where is she?'

'Waiting in the blue room,' he said, holding the door wide for Fleance. He wished it was another room for that one held so many good memories and he could not go there without thinking of Duncan.

The old queen was sitting on Rachel's usual stool, hands tucked under a soft, woven scarf. She stood as he entered the room. 'Fleance,' she said, her voice soft and warm. 'My dear boy, what a terrible time you have had.'

Her graciousness and sympathy threatened to undo him. 'For us all, Madam.'

The queen dowager patted the seat beside her. 'Sit next to me,' she said. 'I have some counsel for you if you would be so kind to hear me out.'

Fleance wondered what she could say that might help him remove the rocks of sadness embedded in his chest. 'I would be glad for it,' he said.

'I am informed that you have made a pledge to a young maid in Perth.'

Fleance started. This was the last thing he imagined she would speak of. He swallowed. 'Yes. Rosie.'

She looked at him kindly for a few moments. 'I can see that you hold her in very high regard. She is no doubt a wonderful young woman.' Fleance could only nod. 'You understand your situation now, Fleance, don't you? You cannot wed her if you are to be king.'

'I have thought on this already.'

Margaret patted his hand. 'Yet, you will need a queen to help you and bear you heirs.' She paused, considering her words. 'It would be a very good match indeed if you chose Rachel as your wife.' Fleance got to his feet and went to the hearth.

She continued. 'Do you not think, lad, that for a moment you could lay aside your feelings for this Rosie and allow Rachel the centre stage of your heart?' Fleance stared into the flames. 'She is very fond of you and, I think, a bit in love with you as well.'

Sorrow pressed into him. Why could he not, for at least a bit of time, have a chance to grieve the death of his dear friend? Why couldn't he just take a moment to gather his thoughts about the decision he must make?

The needs of the country said *there is no time.*

Fleance bowed his head to the old queen. 'What you say is wisdom, and though my heart strains against your words, I want to do the right thing.'

She joined him by the fire. 'Fleance, there are three kinds of love a person may experience in a lifetime: the first is passionate love. It is the most powerful love a young person will experience. It is potent and the colour, though it will fade with time, remains as a warm shadow on your heart; the second is love that bears children, God willing. It is the kind of love a man feels towards the one who is the mother of his children; the third is loving companionship and lasts until death.' She was silent for a while. 'If you are fortunate, as I was, all three can be experienced with the same person.'

Fleance nodded though he could not imagine anything other than what he felt for Rosie. The queen continued. 'Both you and Rachel have enjoyed the happiness and pain of a first love. Neither of you will forget how it changed you. Nothing and no other person can replicate that love. But bigger events now turn both your heads in a different direction to what you had planned.

'Know this also, Fleance, that holy men at their death have good inspirations. Duncan's naming of you as king and his desire for you to wed Rachel is inspired by God. Do not think on his wishes lightly.'

Fleance looked at her. 'I cannot ask Rachel when my heart is still owned by another.'

'Neither would she take you unless she knew you were completely committed. You must to your maid and ask that she let you go so that you are free to love Rachel as I know you will.' She smiled up at him. 'I don't doubt that your love is true and honourable but it is a young man's love. I will leave you to your thoughts and go now before our Lord on your behalf.' She gathered up her skirts and went out.

Fleance watched her leave. Her last words flowed over him and began to work their way into his head. Something of what she spoke made sense but she could not know the full extent of his love for Rosie. There had to be a way to make things right.

At first light, Fleance sent for Blair. 'We ride to Perth and meet the others at Scone. I have some business to attend to before I take the crown.' They walked together to the stables and Fleance watched as Blair lovingly saddled Willow before tending to his own horse. Then, without a word, they mounted, rode out of the stables and through the castle gates.

When they passed the road which took a shortcut through the woods, Fleance spoke up. 'We will stay on the highway,' he said. Then he recounted his misadventures. What he did not tell Blair was that he wanted to ensure that, this time, nothing would stop him from speaking to Rosie.

The air was still and cold, the clouds low and heavy. Blair must have sensed Fleance's mood for the companion joined him in his silence. Fleance's mind was reliving times with Rosie, relishing all the happiness.

They were about halfway into their journey when Fleance heard a familiar humming – the same sound he had heard many, many months back just after he and Macduff had parted ways. Looking ahead, he saw three figures shuffling towards them.

'What are they?' Blair asked, startled.

Willow flicked up his head and snorted. Fleance steadied his horse. 'They are the hags I have told you of. Witches.'

Blair paled and he reached for the cross around his neck. 'Are we safe?' he asked.

'Aye. So long as you pay no heed to their poisonous lies.' Even as he said this, anger began to well up inside. He kicked Willow. 'Onward, horse. They are not to be feared.' Prancing, Willow jumped forward and then stopped dead in front of the three women. 'Stand aside!' he shouted.

The women looked at each other and then up at him. 'Hail to thee, Fleance, King of Scotland!'

'Enough!' Fleance shouted. 'No more of your meddling. We will hear nothing of your venomous riddles.'

As if he had not spoken, the first witch cried up into the sky, 'Happy and unhappy.'

The second witch continued, 'Fruitful and barren.'

'No!' Fleance said, dropping his reins and putting his hands over his ears. 'You will not confuse my mind!'

The final witch turned her back on him and spoke to a shrub which was beside the road. 'Maker and destroyer of kings.'

Fleance squeezed his eyes shut to try to stop the words getting into his head. He would not think on them; remember them; consider them. He would live his life by his own hands and without the interference of the supernatural.

When he opened his eyes again, he was surprised to see the three women cowering to the side of Blair and his horse, hissing and crying. Blair looked terrified and was rooted to the spot. Fleance reached over and took his horse's bridle, at the same time urging Willow forward. 'Blair,' Fleance cried. 'You are safe.'

Blair shook himself and looked nervously over his shoulder. The women were wailing and hissing at the sight of him. Fleance turned Willow around to face them. 'This is a command I give you: no more will you trade and traffic with evil and smear your blight on the good people of Scotland.' His anger intensified. They were the root cause of much grief in his family and Duncan's. 'If I learn of any meddling of the supernatural kind, you will be executed,' Fleance roared. 'Now, be gone!'

The three pitiful women hurried away, whimpering.

'Are you all right, Blair?' Fleance asked, shaken by the force of his temper.

Blair nodded. 'To think I have seen battle and not been as afraid as I was just now.'

'Aye, but you are not facing flesh and blood but beings which dabble in the spirit world – a place no man in his right mind should wish to go.'

'They were terrified of me,' Blair said.

'It was your cross, man. That and your good heart.' Fleance gathered up his reins. 'Come, let us get to Perth for I have a meeting which will be, I fear, a more distressing one than this we have encountered.'

It was raining lightly when they descended the small rise towards the village. The river was dark grey and moved sluggishly towards the sea. Despite it being close to supper time, the streets were busy with fishermen pushing barrows or children rushing home, wet, muddy and happy. They stopped outside Rosie's inn and dismounted. Fleance threw Willow's reins at Blair. 'Take the horses and wait for me. I wager this meeting will not be a lengthy one.'

Blair hesitated a moment and regarded Fleance. 'Do you need my help inside, Sire?' he asked.

Fleance shook his head. 'Only I can do this task, but thank you for your kind offer.'

He turned towards the door, took a deep breath and pushed it open.

It was overly warm, filled with smells – of damp clothes, ale and hot food. Fleance spied Dougal behind the counter, lining up full tankards while Rebecca was talking with some customers. And there was Rosie, delivering plates to a table across the room.

Suddenly, everyone went silent and all turned their eyes towards him. Some removed their hats, some stood and then bowed. Others just stared.

Rosie straightened and looked in his direction. Their eyes met and her face filled with joy. His heart skipped a beat and his lips went dry. She came over to him and pulled him into the nearest empty table and chair.

'You made it back,' she said, her eyes moist with tears.

'Yes,' he whispered, a pain stabbing him in the chest. 'Rosie, I must speak with you.'

Immediately, the light left her face and she stood up. 'Aye, you must.'

Fleance looked around the room. 'Is there somewhere private we can go?'

Rosie shook her head. 'All the rooms are full. We can walk a bit if you don't mind the rain.'

'It's not so bad.'

'I'll get my cloak and meet you outside,' she said just a bit too brightly.

Fleance looked across to the bar, at Dougal glaring. Fleance nodded his head and went out.

The rain, thankfully, had stopped though the road was awash with puddles. In a moment, Rosie was beside him. She took his arm and led him towards the bank of the river.

They stood alongside it staring for some time. Eventually, Fleance cleared his throat and said, 'I am to be king.'

For a brief time she did not answer, and he wondered if he had spoken too quietly. He was about to repeat himself when she turned to him, tears down her cheeks. 'I have heard. And, I understand.'

'Understand?'

'Flea, you cannot choose me if you choose to be King of Scotland,' she said, her chin trembling.

Fleance winced as if she had struck him. To hear such things from Duncan or Queen Margaret held little power compared with the strength of hearing them from her mouth. 'Rosie, I said after the battle I would return to you . . .' His voice trailed off. 'I never imagined things would turn out this way when I made that pledge to you.' He took her arm. 'You are my first love, Rosie.'

'And you, mine,' she cried, tears welling up.

'I'm sorry. For everything. For leaving you. Missing you. Making you wait for me.'

'You did not *make me* wait for you. I could never think of another while you were free . . .' She gave a kind of choked laugh, smiling through her tears. 'Never has someone made me so happy, so angry and so sad.' She swallowed and dabbed her nose with a kerchief. 'Da will be wondering where I have got to,' she said, her voice unsteady.

Fleance reached for her hand and lifted it to his lips. 'I love you, I always have and always will. My duty is but one part of the life I must live but my love for you is constant . . . never forget that.'

He stopped and turned quickly away from her, trying to mask the tears that threatened to flow. Outside the tavern Blair stood holding Willow with one hand, the royal pennant flying from the standard he held in the other.

Rosie wiped the tears which spilled down her face. 'I wish I was more stout of heart,' she said, trying to smile. 'I love you, Flea, and I always will.'

As if on cue it started raining again.

Then she reached up and tenderly stroked his cheek.

'My liege,' she said, barely audible above the rain that was now falling relentlessly.

Then she spun on her heel and ran to the tavern, the door closing firmly behind her.

Flea strode across the yard and took Willow from Blair. He mounted in one swift movement and left Perth without a backward glance, riding towards Scone, towards his future.

Acknowledgements

To the babes: Danielle Browne, Penelope Couper, Imogen Davis, Dannielle Hall, Katarina Konings, Laura Schep, Annie Welvaert, Flavia Wilson – how can I tell you the deep appreciation I feel from your faith in me and your incredibly diligent editing. Your passion and interest in this story buoyed me.

To Lynn Wainwright and her husband Chris: it wasn't the easiest time for you but, without your knowledge and expertise, this book would be a fake. Lynn – I miss you.

My brother-in-law, John Roxborogh, who is a paragon of wisdom and knowledge of church history in Scotland. You're easier to deal with than Wikipedia (though, yay to Wikipedia for its enormous help in key moments when I needed to know about soap in the 11th century). The books, the talks, the quick phone calls and the sermons – all food for the broth.

Fleur Beale – again, you stand beside me and behind me cheering me on. The hours on the phone, persistent questions, the exhortation to 'Be mean! Be mean!' are why this book is better than it might have been without you. Your generosity and hospitality are boundless. Your reward should be at least ONE trip to England, don't you think?

Vicki Marsdon, who never fobbed me off. What can I say but your belief in me was staggering and for this I am eternally grateful. If every writer had the privilege of working with such a talented and passionate publisher, we would fill the world with brilliant stories. Short thanks because words are not enough to tell you how much I appreciate everything you have done for Flea.

To Dr Veron Smith from Maniototo Medical Central for helping kill one of the sweetest characters.

To Josh Getzler, 'Agent Man' – thanks for your astute tweaking and for keeping faith in the worth of this story.

Thanks also to God who I believe gifted me with this story and the supporters to go with it. Thanks for keeping me in good health and heart.

Husband, Phillip and daughters, Mackenna (who helped write the first Rosie extract) and Brianna. Nothing new, eh. Another summer where you lose wife and mother to the computer.

About the Author

T.K. Roxborogh lives in Dunedin, New Zealand, and has been an English and Drama teacher since 1989. She is the author of many published works across a range of genres: novels, plays for the classroom, Shakespearean texts, English grammar books and adult non-fiction. She teaches English at a secondary school, writes and reads at every opportunity and, with her husband, runs around after her family – both the two- and four-legged kind. Roxborogh loves watching movies and TV shows, and staying in her pyjamas for as long as possible.